Carefully Gleia untied the knots in the rag and touched the Ranga Eye. The warmth spread up through her body and once again she saw the fliers. The male spun in ecstatic spirals and the others danced their jubilation. She could feel them drawing her out of her body. She wanted to let go. She wanted desperately to let go, to fly on glorious wings, free and joyous. So easy, it would be so easy just to go sailing away from all the pain and misery of her life here. Why not? Why not just go, let them take her to fly in joy under a butter-yellow sun. . . .

A BAIT
OF
DREAMS

—a five-summer quest—

JO CLAYTON

DAW BOOKS, INC.
DONALD A. WOLLHEIM, PUBLISHER

1633 Broadway, New York, NY 10019

DAW Collectors' Book No. 613

Some sections of this book were published in
Isaac Asimov's Science Fiction Magazine, including in slightly different versions those
parts entitled *A Bait of Dreams, A Thirst
for Broken Water, Southwind My Mother,* and
Companioning. These are copyright © 1979 and
1980 by Davis Publications, Inc.

First Printing, February 1985

1 2 3 4 5 6 7 8 9

PRINTED IN U.S.A.

A BAIT
OF
DREAMS

A Bait of Dreams

As Gleia hurried along the uneven planks of the walkway, pattering around the bodies of sleeping drunks, slipping past workmen and market women, Horli's red rim bathed the street in blood-red light, painting a film of charm over the façades of the sagging buildings.

She glanced up repeatedly, fearing to see the blue light of the second sun Hesh creeping into the sky. Late. Her breath came raggedly as she tried to move faster. She knocked against people in the crowded street, drawing curses after her.

Late. Nothing had gone right this morning. When Horli's light had crept through the holes in her torn shade and touched her face, one look at the clock sent her into a panic, kicking the covers frantically aside, tearing her nightgown over her head. No time to eat. No time to discipline her wild hair. She dragged a comb through the worst of the tangles as she splashed water into a basin. No time to straighten the mess in the room. She slapped water on her face, gasping at the icy sting.

Rush. Grab up the rent money. Snatch open the wardrobe door and pull out the first cafta that came to hand. Slip feet into sandals. A strap breaks. With half-swallowed curse, dig out the old sandals with soles worn to paper thinness. Rush. Drop the key chain around her neck. Hip strikes a chair, knocking it over. Ah! No time to pick it up. Plunge from the room, pausing only to make sure the lock catches. Even in her feverish hurry she could feel nausea at the thought of old Miggela's fat greasy fingers prodding through her things again.

Clatter down the stairs. Down the creaking groaning spiral, fourth floor to ground floor. Nod the obligatory greeting to the blunt-snouted landlady who came out from her nest where she sat in ambush day and night.

The sharp salty breeze whipped through the dingy side street, surrounding her with its burden of fish, tar, exotic spices, and the sour stench from the scavengers' piles of scrap and garbage. The smells slid by unnoticed as she ran down the wooden walk, her footsteps playing a nervous tattoo on the planks. As she turned onto the larger main street, she glanced up again. Hesh still hadn't joined Horli in the sky. Thank the Madar. Still a little time left. She could get to the shop before Hesh-rise.

Her foot came down hard on a round object. It rolled backward, throwing her. She staggered. Her arms flung wildly out, then she fell forward onto the planks, her palms tearing as she tried to break her fall, her knees tearing even through the coarse cloth of her cafta.

For a minute she stayed on hands and knees, ignoring the curious eyes of the workers flowing past her. Several stopped to ask if she was hurt. But she shook her head, her dark brown hair hanging about her face, hiding it from them. They shrugged, then went on, leaving her to recover by herself.

Still on her knees, she straightened her body and examined her palms. The skin was broken and abraded. Already she could feel her hands stiffening. She brushed the grit off, wincing at the pain. Then she looked around to find the thing that had brought her down. A crystal pebble was caught in one of the wider cracks between the planks. Shaped like an egg, it was just big enough to fit in the palm of her hand. "A Ranga Eye," she whispered.

Blue Hesh slid over the edge of the roof above her, reflecting in the crystal. Gleia looked cautiously around, then thrust the Eye into her pocket and jumped to her feet, wincing at the pain that stabbed up from her battered knees. Limping, she hurried on toward the center of the city.

"You're late." Habbiba came fluttering through the lines of bent backs, her tiny hands thrusting out of the sleeves of her elegant black velvet cafta like small pale animals. Her dark eyes darted from side to side, scanning the girls as she moved.

Gleia sucked in a breath, then lowered her head submissively. She knew better than to try to excuse herself.

Habbiba stopped in front of her, moving her hands constantly over herself, patting her hair, stroking her throat, touching her mouth with small feathery pats. "Well?"

Gleia stretched out her hands, showing the lacerated palms. "I fell."

Habbiba shuddered. "Go wash." She flicked a hand at the wall clock. "You'll make up the time by working through lunch."

Gleia bit her lip. She could feel the emptiness groaning inside her and a buzzing in her head, a tremble in her knees. She wanted to protest but didn't dare.

"Go. Go." Habbiba fluttered hands at her. "Don't touch the wedding cafta with those filthy hands and don't waste more time."

As Gleia went into the dark noisome washroom, she heard the soft voice lashing first one then another. She made a face and muttered, "Bitch." The falling curtain muted the poisonous tongue.

Hastily Gleia scrubbed at her hands, ignoring the sting of the coarse soap. She dried them on the towel, the only clean thing in the room. Clean because a filthy towel might lead to filthy hands which could damage the fine materials the girls worked on. Not for the workers, nothing ever done for the workers. She felt the crystal bang against her thigh as she turned to move out, felt a brief flare of excitement, but there was no time and she forgot it immediately.

She slid into her place and took up her work, settling the candles so the light fell more strongly on the cloth. White on white, a delicate pattern of fantasy flowers and birds.

Habbiba's shadow fell over the work. "Hands."

Gleia held out her hands. Small thumbs pressed hard on the drying wounds.

"Good. No blood." Habbiba's hand flew to the shimmering white material protected from dust and wear by a sheath of coarse unbleached muslin. "Slow." A finger jabbed at the incomplete sections, flicking over the pricked-out design. "I must have it done by tomorrow. A two-drach fine for each hour you take over that." Her shadow moved off as she darted away to scold one of the girls who was letting her candle gutter.

Gleia caught her breath, a hard frustration squeezing her in the middle. Tomorrow? Sinking her teeth in her lower lip, she blinked back tears. She'd been counting on the money Habbiba had promised her for this work. Twenty-five oboli. Enough to finish off the sum she needed to buy her bond, even to pay the bribes and leave a little over to live on. Now . . . She looked around the cavernous room with the misty small lights flickering over bent heads. She stiffened. Damn her, she thought. I'll finish this on time if it kills me.

Resolutely she banished all distraction and bent over the work, her stiffened fingers slowing her until the exercise warmed them to their usual suppleness.

As the band of embroidery crept along the front panels of the cafta, Gleia felt hungry, her stomach paining almost as if she were poisoned, but that went away after a while.

While she sewed, her mind began to drift though her eyes clung tenaciously to the design. In a painful reverie, she relived brief images of her life, tracking the thread of events that had led her to this place at this moment. . . .

First memories. Pain and fear. Dim images of adult faces. A woman's arms clinging to her, then falling away. A man, face blurred, unrecognizable, shouting angrily, then in pain, then not at all. Then a string of faces that came and went like beads falling from a cheap necklace. Then . . . digging in garbage piles outside kitchen doors, fighting the scavengers—small shaggy creatures with filthy hands and furtive

eyes—for scraps of half-rotten vegetables or
bones with a shred of meat left on them.

Habbiba came back, jerked the work from her
hands and examined it closely. "Sloppy," she
grunted. She held the work so long Gleia clenched
her hands into fists, biting her lip till blood came
to hold back the protest that would spoil all her
chances of finishing the cafta on time.

A smile curled Habbiba's small tight mouth into
a wrinkled curve, then Habbiba thrust the material back at her. "Take more care, bonder, or I'll
have you rip the whole out."

Gleia watched her move on. For a minute she
couldn't unclench her fingers. *She wants me to go
overtime. She wants to make me beg. Damn her
damn her damn. . . .*

After a minute she took up the work again, driving the needle through the fabric with a vicious
energy that abated after a while as the soothing
spell of the work took over. Once again she fell
into the swift loose rhythm that freed her mind to
think of other things.

Begging in the streets, running with packs of
other abandoned children, sleeping in abandoned houses, or old empty warehouses, barely
escaping with her life from a fire that took
twenty other children, wandering the streets,
driven by cold back into the houses where the
only heat was the body heat of the children
sleeping in piles where some on the outside
froze and some on the inside smothered, children dying in terrible numbers in the winter,
only the toughest surviving.

Being beaten and hurt until she grew old
enough to fight, learning to leap immediately

into all-out attack whenever she had to fight, no matter what the cause, until the bigger children let her alone since it wasn't worth expending so much of their own meager energy to defeat her.

Being casually raped by a drunken sailor, then forgotten immediately as he staggered away, leaving her bloody and crying furiously on the cobblestones, not wholly sure of what had happened to her, but recognizing the violation of her person and vowing it would not happen again, screaming she would kill him kill him. . . .

Running in a gang after that, being forced to submit to Abbrah, the leader, bully-stupid but too strong for her, taking a perverse pride in being chosen, never liking it, realizing about that time the vulnerability of male pride and the superiority of male muscle.

Learning to steal, driven to stealing by Abbrah, stealing from a merchant's warehouse, caught, branded, bound into service with Habbiba.

Scrubbed up and forced to learn . . . the lessons, oh the interminable lessons, shadowed impersonal faces bending over her, voices, hushed and insistent, beating at her. . . .

She started. A cowled figure moved soundlessly past, the coarse cloth of his robe slapping against her ankles. She watched the Madarman halt beside Habbiba and begin talking. Habbiba nodded and the two figures moved out of the room, both silent, both trailing huge black shadows that spread depressingly over the sewing girls. What's that about, she wondered. Madarman sucking about. . . .

*   *   *

Cowled figures, voices demanding, learn or
be beaten, memorize and repeat, mechanical
rote learning, paying no attention to what is
learned, cram the songs, the histories, the
Madarchants into the unwilling little heads.
Repeat. Repeat. Work all morning, then, when
her body rebelled, when she yearned for the
freedom of the streets with a passion that
swamped even her continual hunger to know,
set to school by order of the Madarmen to
save her pitiful soul.

History in chant. Jaydugar, the testing ground
of the gods. The Madar's white hands reached
among the stars and plucked their fruit, the
souls that needed testing, catmen and mermen,
caravanner and hunter, scavenger and parsi,
plucked wriggling from their home trees and
dropped naked on the testing ground. Chant of
the Coming. I take you from the nest that
makes you weak and blind. I take from you
your metal slaves. I take from you your far-
seeing eyes. I take from you the wings that sail
you star to star. I purify you. I give you your
hands. I promise you cleverness and time. Out
of nothing you will build new wings.

New wings. Gleia snorted. Several girls turned
to look at her, their faces disapproving, she smiled
blankly at them and they settled back to work.
She could hear the furtive whispers hissing between them but ignored these. Her needle whispered through sheer white material, popping in
and out with smooth skill. She sniffed scornfully
at the other girls' refusal to accept her into their
community.

New wings. She frowned down as she looped the
thread in a six-petalled flower and whipped the

loops in place. It might make an interesting design
... new wings ... the stars ... she drove the needle
through the material in a series of dandelion-bloom
crosses. Did we all come here from other worlds?
How? Her frown deepened. The Madar ... that
was nonsense. Wasn't it?

The Madarman came down the aisle and stopped
beside her. He held out his hand. Reluctantly Gleia
set the needle into the material and gave him her
work, biting her lip as she saw the dark crescents
of dirt under his fingernails. She held her breath
as he brought the cloth up close to rheumy eyes.

"Good," he grunted. He thrust the cloth back at
her and stumped off to rejoin Habbiba. Gleia took
a minute to stretch her cramped limbs and straight-
en her legs as she watched Habbiba usher him out.
Looks like I'm up for a new commission, she
thought. She looked over the line of bent backs,
feeling a fierce superiority to those giggling idiots
raised secure in homes with fathers and mothers
to protect them. Here they are anyway, doing the
same work for a lot less pay than I'm getting. Me.
Gleia. The despised bonder. The marked thief. She
wriggled her fingers to work some of the cramp
out of them, touched the brand on her cheek. Then
she sighed and went back to the design. Her
thoughts drifted back to her life.

Remembering

Being forced to learn rough sewing, then
embroidery, taking a timid pride in a growing
skill, taking a growing pride in making designs that she soon recognized to be superior
to any others created in Habbiba's establish-
ment.

Learning she could buy herself free of the
bond if she could ever find or save enough

money. Fifty oboli for the bond. Fifty oboli for the bribes. More to keep herself while she hunted for work. Joy and despair. And joy again. . . .

Demanding and getting special pay for special projects. Her work brought fancy sums to Habbiba's greedy fingers and more—a reputation for the unique that brought her custom she couldn't have touched before. The old bitch tried to beat her into working, but Gleia had learned too well how to endure. She was stubborn enough to resist punishment and to persist in her demands, sitting resolutely idle through starvings and whippings and threats until she won her point.

Gleia jabbed the needle through the cloth. It glanced off a fingernail, coming close to pricking her finger and drawing blood. She leaned back, breathing fast, trying to calm herself. A drop of blood marring the white was all she needed. Not now. Not so close to winning. She couldn't stand another month of this slavery. She fingered the mark on her cheek and knew they'd throw her into permanent slavery as an incorrigible felon if she tried to run away. If they caught her. Which they would.

Sometime later Habbiba made her last round, inspecting the day's work. She stopped beside Gleia and picked up the cloth, running the unworked length of design through her plump white fingers. "Fah! too slow. And there." She jabbed a forefinger at the last sections of work. "You did finer work when you were learning. Tomorrow you come in one hour early. Abbosine will be told to let you in." She pinched the material between her fingers "Take out that last work to here." She thrust the strip of embroidery into Gleia's face and indicated a spot about two palms' width above the last stitches. "I won't tolerate such miserable cobbling going out under my name."

Gleia closed her eyes. Her hands clenched into fists. She wanted to smash the old woman in the face, to smash—smash—smash that little weasel face into bloody ruin, then wipe the ruin on that damn cafta. But she doubted whether she could stand without tumbling over, so she managed to keep her head down and her mouth shut. When the old woman went off to scold someone else, she sat still, hands fisted in her lap.

Habbiba's scolding voice faded as she left the room. The other girls moved about, chatting cautiously, eyes turning slyly about, watching out for the sudden return of their employer. When they had all trickled out, bunched into laughing clusters of workfriends, Gleia forced herself onto her feet.

The world swung. She grabbed at the sewing stand and held on tight until the room steadied around her. With neat economical movements she folded her work and put it in the box, then she walked through the rows of silent tables, a fragile glass person that the slightest shock would crack into a thousand fragments.

Outside, the darkening twilight threw a veil of red over the crowded streets, blurring covered carts with screeching wheels into horsemen riding past in dark solid groups into single riders gawking at the city sights into throngs of people pushing along the wooden walkways. She hummed the Madar-chant of the peoples. *Chilkaman catman fishman hunter, parsi plainsman desert fox herder, firssi mountainman caravanner hawkster. . . .* In spite of her fatigue she sucked in a deep breath and watched

furtively the fascinating variety of peoples flowing
past her. Chilka catmen from the plains with their
hairy faces, flat noses and double eyelids, the inner transparent one retracted into the damp tissue
folds around their bulging slit-pupiled eyes. Caravanners, small and quick, pale faced. Mountain
hunters, far from their heights with dark gold skin
and brown hair bleached almost white at the tips,
leading horses loaded with fur bales.

A breath of salt air, cool and fresh as the sea
itself, stung her nose. A flash of opaline emerald.
Impression of scaled flesh flowing liquidly past. A
seaborn. Ignoring the irritated protests of the other
pedestrians she turned and stared after the slim
amphibian walking with the characteristic quick
clumsy grace of the sea folk. She didn't recognize
him. Disappointed, she edged to the wall and stumbled tiredly through the crowd thinking about the
only friend she'd ever had, a slim green boy . . . so
long ago . . . so long. . . .

She walked slowly into the dingy front hall of
the boarding house, putting each foot down with
stiff care, wondering how she was going to get up
all those damn creaking stairs.

"Gleyah 'spinah." The hoarse breathy voice
brought her to a careful halt. She inched her head
around, feeling that her burning eyes would roll
from her head if she moved too quickly.

"Rent." Miggela held out a short stubby hand.

Gleia closed her eyes and fumbled in her pocket,
sore fingers groping for the packet of coins she'd
put there earlier. Her fingers closed on the egg-
shaped stone; she frowned, not remembering for a
minute where the thing came from.

The rat-faced landlady scowled and flapped her
pudgy hand up and down. "Rent!"

Gleia slid her hand past the crystal and found

the packet. Silently she drew it out and handed it to the old woman.

Miggela tore clumsily at the paper. Her crusted tongue clamped between crooked yellow teeth, she counted the coins with deliberate slowness, examining each one with suspicious care, peering nearsightedly at the stamping.

Gleia rubbed her hand across her face, too tired to be irritated.

Slipping the coins into a sleeve pocket, Miggela stood staring up into the taller woman's drawn face. "You're late. You missed supper."

"Oh."

"And don't you go trying to cook in your room."

"No." She wasn't hungry anymore but knew she had to have food. Her legs trembled. She wanted more than anything to lie down. But she turned and went out. She walked carefully, slowly, over the uneven planks, heading aimlessly toward the edge of the nightquarter and a familiar cookshop.

Gleia strolled out of the cookshop feeling more like herself with two meat pies and a cup of cha warming her middle, a third pie in her hand. She sank her teeth into the pie, tore off a piece and drifted along the street chewing slowly, savoring the blended flavors, watching the people move past her.

Horli was completely gone in the west with only a stain of red to mark her passing, while the biggest moon Aab was thrusting over the rooflines to the east, her cool pale light cutting through inky shadows. Gleia knew she should get back to her room. There were too many dangers for a woman alone here. Sighing, she began working her way through the noisy crowd toward the slum quarter. She finished the pie, wiped her greasy hands on a bit of paper and dropped the paper in the gutter for the scavengers to pick up in their dawn sweeps through the streets.

The crowd thinned as she left the commercial area and moved into the slum that held a few decrepit stables and row on row of ancient dwellings converted into boarding houses. Some were empty with staring black windows where the glass was gone—stolen or broken by derelicts who could find no other place to sleep. One by one these abandoned houses burned down, leaving behind fields of weeds and piles of broken, blackened boards.

Gleia looked up at the gray, weathered front of Miggela's place. She was tired to the point of giddiness but she felt such a reluctance to go inside that she couldn't force her foot onto the warped lower step; instead she went past the house and turned into the alley winding back from the side street. Moving quickly, eyes flicking warily about, she trotted past the one-room hovels where the small scurrying scavengers lived anonymous lives and desperate bashers hid out, waiting for sailors to come stumbling back to their ships. She went around the end of a warehouse, the last in the line of those circling the working front where the bay was dredged. The water out here was too shallow to accommodate any but the smallest ships.

She saw a small neat oceangoer, a chis-makka, one of the independent gypsy ships that went up and down the coast as the winds and their cargoes dictated. The ship was dark, the crew apparently on liberty in one of the taverns whose lights and noise enlivened the waterfront some distance in toward the center. Out here it was quiet, with ravellings of fog beginning to thicken over the water. As the waves slapped regularly at the piles the evening on-shore breeze made the rigging on board the chis-makka creak and groan.

Gleia edged to the far side of the wharf and kicked off her sandals. Then she ran along the planks, bent over, making no more sound than a shadow. She slid over the end of the wharf and pulled herself onto one of the crossbars nailed from pile to pile under the broad planks. Ignoring the coating of slime and drying seaweed, she sat with her back against a pile, her legs dangling in space, her feet moving back and forth just above the rocking water.

For a long while she sat there, the sickening emotional mix settling away until she felt calm and at peace again. The fog continued to thicken, sounds coming to her over the water with an eerie clarity.

Something pushed against her thigh. She remembered the Ranga Eye that had thrown her so disastrously in the morning. As she reached into her pocket, the water broke in a neat splash and a glinting form came out of it, swooping onto the crossbar beside her. In her surprise she nearly toppled off into the agitated water, but the sea-born caught hold of her and steadied her.

Her face almost nosing into his chest, she saw the water pour from his gill slits and the slits clamp shut. The moonlight struggling through the fog touched his narrow young face and reflected off his pointed mother-of-pearl teeth as he sucked air into his breathing bladder then grinned at her. "T'ought it was you. No ot'er land crawler ever come here."

"Tetaki?" She closed her fingers around his cool hard forearm. "I haven't seen you in years." Shaking her head, she smiled uncertainly at him. "Years."

"Not sin' you was finger high."

"You weren't any bigger." She shook his arm, amusement bubbling inside her. "Brat."

He perched easily on the narrow bar, his short crisp hair already drying and springing into the curls that used to fascinate her with their tight coils and deep blue color. "Good times. We were good friends then." He was silent a moment, watching her. "T'is isn't the firs' year I come back. You never come here."

"I was thinking about you earlier today." She pushed away from the pile and touched his knee. "The only friend I ever had."

His hand closed about hers, cool and metal smooth, his flesh unlike hers but the touch comforting despite that. "I come each time. You never here."

"At first I couldn't," she said, her fatigue and depression coming back like a fog to shroud her, smother her spirit. She sighed. "Later . . . later, I forgot."

"What happened?" His hand tightened on hers. She looked up. The shining unfamiliar planes of his face seemed to banish the fog. Then he smiled. His teeth were a carnivore's fangs, needle sharp and slightly curved. "Forget me? Shame."

She laughed and pulled free. "I turned thief. Abbrah made me. Remember him?"

His teeth glinted again. "I got cause."

Gleia watched her feet swinging back and forth over the dark water, almost black here under the wharf but flickering with tiny silver highlights where the moonlight danced off the tops of wavelets. Remember. . . .

• A delegation of amphibian people had come to negotiate trade rights with the Maleek; Tetaki's father was a minor official. She remembered a slim scaled boy with big light green eyes and tight-coiled blue hair poking through a dingy side street looking eagerly about at the strange sights. Alone. Foolishly alone. Abbrah's gang gathered around him, baiting him, working themselves up to attack him. Something about his refusal to give in to them stirred a spark in Gleia that lit old resentments and she fought her way to his side in that stubborn all-out battle the gang knew too well. So they backed off, shouting obscenities, reasserting their dominance by showing contempt for her and her protégé. She took him back to his father and scolded the startled seaborn for his carelessness.

"You got caught."

"I was a lousy thief. Yes, I got caught. And bonded. See?" She turned her face so he could see the bondmark burned into her cheek. "What about you?"

He chuckled, waved a hand toward the chismakka's shadow. "Ours. This is t'ird summer we come to the fairs."

"Hey." She patted his arm, too weary to enthuse as she should.

He bent closer, staring into her face. "You don' look so good."

She yawned. "Tired." She swallowed another yawn. "That's all."

"Come wit' me. Temokeuu would welcome you. You could live wit' us."

She stroked the mark on her cheek but didn't answer for a minute. He settled back, content to let her answer when she was ready. Finally, she shook her head. "Can't, Tetaki. I'm stuck here till

my bond is cancelled. You going to be here in
Carhenas long?"

"We been having good trading." He frowned.
"Two, t'ree days more I t'ink."

"At least we can talk some. I've missed having
someone to talk to."

"Come see Temokeuu. He like you." Tetaki
grinned at her. "And we show you our ship."

"Sure." She yawned again. "I'd better get back.
I have to be up an hour early tomorrow." She
swung herself up onto the wharf, hung her head
over the edge a minute. "See you."

Her room looked like someone had taken a giant
spoon and given it a quick stir. The sheet, blanket,
and quilt hung over the side of the bed where
she'd kicked them. Her one chair was overturned.
She remembered her hip catching it on the way
out. The wardrobe door hung halfway open. The
sandal with a broken strap sat on its side in the
middle of the floor.

Gleia stretched, feeling the spurt of energy from
the food beginning to trickle away. Yawning repeatedly, she pulled the bed to rights and straightened
the mess a little, then tugged the ties loose and
pulled her cafta over her head. The crystal bumped
against her and she fished it out before she hung
the garment away. Turning to Ranga Eye over and
over in her hands she strolled across the room to
the nightstand. She dropped the Eye in the middle
of the bed and took out her cha pot, setting it next
to the water tin. From the bottom drawer in the
stand she pulled out a tiny sway-bellied brazier,
set it up on the window ledge. Using the candle
and strips of paper, she got the charcoal burning,
then set the tin on the grill. Making sure the window was wedged open, she left the tin to boil and

went back to the nightstand. She dumped a palmful of leaves into the pot and got a cup ready, then let herself collapse on the quilt.

She folded the pillow twice to prop up her head and reached out, prodding the quilt, finally fishing the Eye from under the curve of her back; she began turning it over and over, examining it idly.

A Ranga Eye. She'd heard whispers of them. A frisson of fear shivered down her spine. If they caught her with it . . . if they caught her, she could forget about buying her bond. Or anything else. If I could sell it . . . somehow . . . somehow . . . if I could sell it, Madar! Bonded thief with a Ranga Eye. If I could sell it. . . .

The crystal warmed as she touched it. At first a few tentative sparks licked through the water-clear form. She felt a surge of delight. The tips of her fingers moved in slow caressing circles over the smooth surface. The colors began cycling hypnotically, then the color forms began to shift their nature, impreceptibly altering into images of a place. As she watched, the picture developed rapidly, blurred at first, then sharpening into focus.

Gentle hills rolled into a blue distance, covered with a green velvet carpet, a species of moss dotted with small star-shaped pseudo-flowers. Other flower forms as large as trees were spaced over the slopes, each form at the center of a hexagonal space roughly as wide as the stretch of its four leaf-stems. The leaves were eight-sided and multiple, marching along wiry black stems curving out from the central stalk at a spot halfway up to the bloom, four black arcs springing out at the same height from the ground. At the top of each plant great brilliant petals rayed out from a black center that gathered in the butter-yellow light of a single sun.

Another sun. She stroked the crystal, dreaming of another place, a better place, feeling a growing excitement. The tin on the fire began to whistle softly. Gleia dropped the Eye on the bed, levered herself up, and scuffed across to the brazier. She poured the bubbling water over the cha leaves. While they were steeping, she tilted the rest of the water onto the glowing coals. Head tipped back to avoid the billowing steam, she let the blackened water trickle down the side of the building. Then she knocked out the wedge and pulled the window shut.

With a cup of cha in one hand and the Eye in the other, a clean nightgown on her body and the pillow freshly folded for her head, she lay and watched the play of colors in the crystal. The image began to move through the flower trees, as if she were seeing through the eyes of some creature flying just below the petals of the flower tops. Before she had time to get bored with the lovely but monotonous landscape, she flew out into the open, skimming along brilliant white sand. Blue waves rolled in with white caps breaking cleanly, rhythmically. The sky stretched above, a glowing cloudless blue only slightly lighter than the sea. As she hovered in place she saw other creatures come flitting from the flower forest. A delicate-boned male with huge black eyes danced up to her, spiralling in complex pirouettes.

Huge black eyes soft as soot and as shineless. Thin arms and legs. Hands whose long slender fingers like jointed sticks were half the length of the forearms. Body short and broad, the shoulders muscled hugely. Butterfly wings abstractedly patterned with splotches of shimmering color outlined in black, opening and closing with slow hypnotic sweeps. He rode the air in swoops and glides, wheeled in front of her, small mouth stretched in a wide inviting grin, narrow hands beckoning. . . .

The exhaustion of the day caught up with her and she sank into a heavy sleep, the remnants of the cha spilling on the bed, soaking into the mattress. The crystal rolled out of her loosened fingers.

When the alarm bell woke her in the morning, the cha spot was still damp and the leaves were smeared over her shoulder and back. The crystal had worked along her body and ended up in the hollow between her neck and shoulder. When she picked it up to put in the drawer, it seemed to cling to her fingers, quivering gently against her skin, shedding a pleasant warmth that slid up her arm and made her feel soft and dreamy. She shut off the alarm and stumbled to the wardrobe still half asleep. With the Eye clutched in her hand she fumbled for a cafta. After she wriggled into the garment, she slid the stone into the pocket, not noticing what she was doing, tied the ties, and smoothed the material down over her body.

The cavernous sewing room was dark and silent when Gleia walked in. She wound through the close lines of sewing tables and settled in her usual place. She lit the candles and took out her sewing. Holding the delicate material close to the flame, she examined the last bit of embroidery. It was good enough. Damn if she was going to pick it out.

She threaded her needle with the silk. Tongue clamped between her teeth, she snipped at the loose ends, dropping small bits of thread haphazardly over the floor, over her cafta, around the table, scattering the pieces of thread with a gleeful abandon.

Sometime later, after the room had filled and the other girls were bent over their work, Habbiba came by, her sharp eyes darting over the scattered ends of thread. Her mouth pursed in satisfaction, she sailed past to pounce on an unfortunate girl who chanced to look up and stretch at the wrong time.

Gleia swallowed a smile, feeling a warm, buoyant satisfaction at fooling the woman.

At the end of the long day, she stretched and rubbed her red, tired eyes. She stood motionless beside the sewing table a minute with eyes closed, then she shook out the cafta, ran a quick eye over the lines of embroidery, put the cafta on a hanger, and carried it to Habbiba.

"Finished," she murmured, keeping her head down to hide the triumph that flushed her face.

Habbiba took the cafta and pulled the bands of embroidery close to her eyes as she went over the work, stitch by stitch. When she was finished, she grunted sourly, her small black eyes darting at Gleia, then she sailed off, the cafta a fluttering white banner beside her small black figure. Gleia waited tensely. Twenty-five oboli, she thought. I won't take less. But she knew that she would, that she had to. Habbiba didn't know that. Oy-ay Madar, she couldn't know. I've fought her too often and even won a few times. She has to think I'll fight her on this. Has to think. . . .

Habbiba came back. She stopped in front of Gleia. "Not your best work," she grumbled. Her small plump fingers were closed about a small bag of coins. "Hold out your hand." With painful reluctance she eased the drawstring loose and pulled out an eight-sided gold coin. "Pentobol. One." She pressed the coin into Gleia's palm, her fingers sliding off the metal with a lingering, caressing motion.

Slowly, releasing the coins as if they were drops of her own blood, Habbiba counted out five pento-boli into Gleia's outstretched hand. Holding the bag with the remaining coins pressed tightly against her breast, Habbiba looked at Gleia with distaste. "You be on time in the morning. The Maleeka wants a cafta with embroidered sleeves for the name day of her youngest daughter." She hesitated. "You'll be paid the same," she finished sourly.

Gleia bowed her head farther, rounding her shoulders. Hai, you old bitch, she thought. No wonder you paid me the whole. Blessed Madar the Maleeka. How you must be preening at the thought.

She went out into the street and wandered along, feeling tired but elated. She had the money. No more aching back. No more passive acceptance of abuse. She fingered the mark on her cheek. Closed her fingers on the coins in her pocket. The Eye rolled against her hand but she ignored it, happily planning her visit to the House of Records.

Her feet eventually took her to the boarding house. Looking up at the shadowed façade, she scratched her chin and hesitated. She could smell the awful stew Miggela had cooked up for them, an unappetizing mess with a few shreds of cheap meat, tough vegetables, and thick filling of soggy barley. The rancid smell followed her as she walked away toward the cookshop where the grease was fresher. Foolish as it was to wander about with all that money in her pocket, it was good to walk and feel free for a while, to let the seabreeze riffle through her hair, to sluff along the walkway, winding in and out of the men and women walking purpose-fully homeward, the noisy influx of sailors from the wharves, the streetwalkers who were coming out to start their peculiar workdays. She looked

eagerly around trying to spot another of the seaborn but saw none.

She came out of the shop munching on a pie,
enjoying the taste all the more when she thought
of the stew her fellow roomers, that collection of
losers, were stuffing down their throats at Miggela's
table.

She stopped at the alley leading to the wharf
but shook her head. That would be a bit too stupid.
Sighing, she clumped up the steps and went inside.

Miggela popped out of ambush. "You missed
supper."

"I know." She nodded and moved away to the
spiral staircase with its collection of creaks and
groans.

In her room, she crossed to the window, leaned
out, hid the money in her special place under the
eaves. After lighting her candle she tidied the room
a bit more and heated water for cha. When she
was finally ready for bed, face washed, a clean
sleeping shift pulled on, she was surprised to find
the Eye in her hand. She didn't remember picking
it up. For a moment she was frightened, then
curious. The crystal warmed in her palm as she
walked slowly across the room and stretched out
on the bed.

Sipping at the cha, the quilt pulled in a triangle
over her middle, she held the Eye up, enjoying the
flow of the colors.

Then she was flitting again under the flower
tops. She came out on the beach, farther on this
time. Hovering over the white sand, she looked
curiously around and saw distant buildings perched
on slender poles, a line of graceful points and curves
on the horizon. Then the butterfly man came sailing out of the sun, a black shimmer with gold
edges dancing on the breeze, an ebullient joyful-

ness that made her quiver with delight and feel
the swoop of laughter in her blood. She joined
him, dancing, turning, twisting over the green-
blue of the wrinkled sea. Cool wine air slipped along
her body and her dance became more intense. Others came and they laughed a silent laughter, long
slender feelers clicking in telegraphic wit.

The mug dropped, spilling a last few drops of
cold cha on the bed as she drifted to sleep, fingers
still curled tightly about the Eye. In her dreams
the air dancers whispered: come come come come
　　join us　　come

In the morning she dragged herself out of bed
and dressed with one hand, clutching the crystal
in the other, ignoring the unmade bed and leaving
her sleeping shift on the floor where she'd stepped
out of it.

She listened distantly as Habbiba described the
cafta to be embroidered, took the ruled paper and
went to her table to draw the designs.

Her fingers slipped into her pocket and moved
slowly over the warm sensuous surface of the
crystal.

Habbiba came scolding when she saw nothing
on the paper.

Gleia looked at her vaguely, listened until the
wizened little woman was done with her tirade,
then bent over the paper. She began sketching
flower forms under a single sun and dancing soaring butterfly figures, working the whole into a
rhythm of lightness and joy.

Habbiba watched for a minute then went quietly away, smiling with greedy satisfaction.

Gleia went back to dreaming.

　　　　　*　　　*　　　*

In her room that night she stripped off the cafta, hung it on a hook and forgot it. Forgot to wash. Forgot to make her cha. She picked up the night-gown from the floor and slipped it over her head, ignoring its damp musty smell. She lay on the wrinkled sheet turning the crystal over and over in her hands.

They came swooping around her, taking her through the line of houses perched on slender peeled sticks that raised them high above the flower-dotted moss below. Through open arches pointed at the top—past arches filled with knotted hangings accented with polished seeds—past walls bare and pearly gray, with brilliant hangings as strips of color against that bareness. Over floors upholstered with padded carpets, different colors in different rooms—through room on room on room, separated from one another by cascades of multi-sized arches. Antennas clicking with laughter, the butter-fly people darted about, showing off their homes.

come   come   (they whispered to her) leave your miseries behind and ride the wind with us
    come come

In the morning she dragged herself out of bed, put on the crumpled cafta from yesterday. Dressed with one hand again, not aware that her move-ments were limited by the warm and throbbing crystal clutched in her right hand. She thrust it finally into her pocket and left the room without washing herself or doing anything about the mess she left behind.

At work she sat hunched over the layout paper, running her pencil idly over the sketch from the day before, dreaming as idly of the crystal's world.

Habbiba came by sometime later and looked over her shoulder. When she saw the whole morning had gone by with nothing done, she exploded with rage. "Hai worm!" she shrieked. Her small hand buried itself in Gleia's tangled hair and jerked her head up. "What're you sniffing, bonder?" She peered into Gleia's dull eyes. "By the Madar, I'll teach you to waste my money on that filth. Abbosine!"

The big tongueless watchman came from the small room where he spent his days. He took Gleia's hand, pulling her down the hall into the punish room. He pushed her against the wall and closed a set of cuffs about her wrists, her struggles as futile as fly tickles against his unthinking strength. He looked morosely at Habbiba. When she jerked her head at the door, he shambled out.

The furious little woman slammed her fist into Gleia's back, driving her against the wall. "You never learn," she hissed. "You never learn, bonder. Maybe I can't make you work, fool, but you'll hurt for it." She stepped back and swung a many-tongued whip. The sharkskin tails slashed down, slicing through the worn cloth of the cafta, cutting lines of fire into Gleia's back. She gasped.

Grunting in a fury that showed no sign of abating. Habbiba lashed at Gleia again and again, screaming her rage at Gleia for all the times the girl had successfully defied her. For all the lovely coins the girl had milked from her. Finally, shaking, eyes bloodshot, face flushed, Habbiba dropped the bloody whip and went away.

Gleia hung from her wrists, her legs too weak to support her weight, the crystal dream cleaned out of her system by the pain that turned her body to mush.

Slowly she began to feel stronger; though as the shock passed, the pain bit deeply into her. She pushed against the stone floor with stiff numb feet and took the punishing weight off her wrists. Standing face to the wall, she came to the humbling conclusion that she was a fool. To be trapped by a Ranga Eye when she knew better. To be trapped by dreams like any giggling girl. Dreams!

She felt the crystal press against her leg, sending warmth through the material of her cafta into her flesh. She jerked the leg back, disgusted at herself as she trembled with the memory of the beauty she'd seen in the Eye, longing intensely (at the same time shuddering with revulsion) for the freedom of soaring on the air with the butterfly people of the dream. Though she knew better in her waking time, she couldn't help feeling that they were real and not mere phantoms of a drugged mind. That their world was real. Somewhere. She couldn't comprehend how the crystal could serve as a gateway to that world, but as she shifted to reduce the pain in her legs she felt she could pass through the gate into a gentle world unlike the rough, unfeeling one she'd been born into.

"I'm not going to touch you again," she muttered, resting her forehead against the cold damp stone. "I'll sell you. I will I'll find a way." The crystal bumped hard against her thigh, sending a stab of pain through her already aching body. "We'll see who wins once I get out of this."

Her feet were cramping. She couldn't put her heels flat and the strain of her arches was beginning to be more than she could endure. Her arms ached, stretched without respite over her head. Fatigue and the effort of fighting off the insidious invasion of the crystal brought her close to fainting, the thought that Habbiba intended to leave her there all night in a final attempt to break her spirit made a cold knot in her stomach. She knew that if the old bitch did, the crystal would have her.

She smashed her hip against the wall, letting out a scream of anger and pain when the crystal ground into her muscle, striking hard against nerves. Sweating and breathing raggedly, she hung in the wrist cuffs, tears of pain streaming down her face, struggling to regain a measure of control over her body.

When she could think again, she shook her head. "No good," she muttered. She couldn't shatter it, maybe she could ease it out of her pocket. Pinning the material against the stone, she pressed herself to the wall, counting on the pain to keep the crystal from charming her. Wriggling, contorting her body until she was bathed in a film of sweat, she struggled to work the Eye out of her pocket.

It fought back. Whenever she managed to squeeze it an inch or so from the bottom of the pocket, it wriggled like a thing alive and eeled away from the pressure.

She kept trying until she was exhausted, shaking too hard to control her body any longer.

It was dark in the room when Abbosine shambled back. The huge mute unfastened the cuffs and watched with massive indifference as she crumpled to the floor. Stolidly he wound his thick fingers in her hair and dragged her through the building and out into the alley where he dropped her in a heap beside the workers' entrance.

Gleia pushed herself onto her feet and stood swaying, supporting herself with a hand pressed against the side of the building. Then the anger that simmered under the haze of fatigue gave her the strength to start walking toward the street.

She went to the wharf. Gritting her teeth against the pain she swung down onto the worn crossbar that was her only refuge at so many crises in her

life. Clouds sailed with clumsy grace over the darkening sky, tinged with a last touch of crimson
though Horli had slid behind the horizon some
time ago. Here and there a star glimmered in the
patches of indigo sky visible between the cloud
puffs. On the water the fog blew in thickening
strands, coming up to curl around her feet. The
air had a nip that marked the decline of the
summer. Winter coming, she thought. Three hundred days of winter. I've got to get away. Somehow.
Get south. . . . Her back itched and stung. The
bruise on her thigh was an agony whenever she
moved her legs. But she was free from the Eye and
tomorrow she would be free of Habbiba too. She
leaned tentatively against the pile, closing tired
eyes once she was settled. Tomorrow. After the
House of Records. What?

The water splashed and Tetaki was perched on
the bar beside her. She jumped then winced as her
back protested.

"What's wrong?" His mouth opened, baring the
tips of his shining teeth. His eyes searched her
face, reading the pain there.

"I was stupid."

"Turn." His hand was cool on her arm. "Let me
see."

She pulled back, shook her head.

"Gleia."

"If you must." Holding onto the slanting brace,
she swung around so he could see her back. With
her face hidden, her head resting against the pile,
she spoke too loudly. "I told you. I was stupid! I
knew better than to provoke her. Especially when
she'd just had to pay me a bonus."

His hand touched the lacerated flesh with exquisite gentleness. It still hurt. She sank her teeth
into her lip to keep from crying out.

"Come wit' me."

"What?"

"To the ship. We got med'cine. Your skin's cut. Unless wounds are clean you have trouble wit' them."

"I suppose so." She eased herself around. "Help me up."

He sat back on his heels, an odd look on his face. "Firs' time you ever ask for help."

She hauled herself to her feet and risked a crooked smile. "Give me a boost, friend."

On the ship, he nodded to the watch and took her below to his cabin. "Wait here. I get med'cine."

She sat on the narrow bunk and looked around with appreciation of the neatness, comfort and convenience of the small cabin—a shelf of books running around the top of the wall, locked in place by an ingenious webbing; a desk folded away against the wall; a chair folded and latched flat; two long chests; a shell lantern hanging from the beam bisecting the ceiling. The light coming through the translucent shell touched the room with rosy gold warmth. The oil was perfumed with a pleasant fresh smell that made her think of green growing things.

When Tetaki came back his father Temokeuu came with him. The older seaborn pushed gently on her shoulder, bending her over so he could see her back, easing the cafta down off her body, moistening the places where dried blood glued the material to her skin. "This isn't the first time," he murmured.

"I learn hard."

"What lesson?"

"Submission."

"Hmm." He took the jar Tetaki was holding out. "This will hurt."

The salve was living fire as he smoothed it on her cuts. She gasped, bit her lip till blood came, squeezed her eyes shut until tears came, then suddenly her back was cool and there was no more pain. She straightened and moved her shoulders. In spite of all of her experience in bearing pain and degradation she felt uneasy now, having had little practice with kindness. She reached out and caught hold of his wrist. "Thank you." She stumbled over the words. "Thank you," she repeated, then she eased the tattered cafta back over her shoulders and turned to face him.

Temokeuu touched the brand on her face. "Bonded?"

"Yes." She hesitated, stared in embarrassment at her scuffed and scarred feet in the old ragged sandals. "I was caught stealing."

"How long?"

"Since I was bonded? Six years standard. Two summers ago. A third of my life."

"To go?"

"Until whenever. The term was left open. It always is. Until I buy myself free, that's the sentence."

"Ah." There was heavy contempt in that soft syllable. She looked up at him, startled. "How much is the bond?" he went on.

"Fifty oboli. But you've got to add on the bribes. At least as much more, say a hundred, hundred-twenty oboli."

He looked disconcerted. "So much?" Then he stroked a finger beside his mouth, his eyes on her face. "Never mind. How does one buy a bond?"

She stared at him, astonished at what he offered. For a moment she thought of letting him do this for her, then felt a surging overpowering distaste for putting her life into someone else's hands. "Temokeuu, no. I can't accept that. I've already earned the money. I found I had a talent and the stubbornness to make it good." She caught his hand and held it against her face. "You're very good, you and Tetaki." She held out her other hand to the young seaborn. Then she laughed, the sound surprising her with its joyousness. "I've got the money to buy the bond and pay the bribes, though I wouldn't tell that to anyone else in this place." She stood and shook her hair back over her shoulders, stretched and sighed, laughing again when one hand swung against the roof beam. "You're the only two people in the world I'd tell it to, my friends. It took the skin off my back to get that money but it was worth it. Tomorrow, Tetaki, Temokeuu. Tomorrow, during my halfday I go to buy my bond."

Temokeuu folded his arms across his chest. "I have some small influence."

She frowned. "I don't understand."

"I will stand for you in the court." He smiled suddenly, the shimmering tips of his opaline teeth barely visible behind his wide smooth lips, his dark green eyes glinting with a sardonic amusement. "It is surprising how much alacritous justice becomes in the presence of influence."

She shifted uneasily, abruptly conscious of the smallness of the cabin, the closeness of the two seafolk males. "My debt becomes heavier by the minute. What do I say?"

Temokeuu's mouth twitched as he recognized her growing discomfort. He moved back and opened the door. As he stepped out, he said, "When your bond is cancelled, what then?"

"I don't know. I thought about heading south for the winter." She shrugged. "Or stay on with

Habbiba now that I don't have to lick her feet or watch her humors."

"Come here." He noted her hesitation. "Think about it. I'll leave you to make your decision once we're finished at court but there is a place for you in my house if you choose to take it." He went quickly up the steps of the ladder and swung out onto the deck.

Gleia scrambled up beside him and stood quietly waiting for Tetaki, enjoying the feel of the breeze fingering through her hair. "I'm a thief, remember?"

"I owe you my life. My son's life." He chuckled, a warm affectionate sound. "A small dirty-face wild thing scolding me like my mother for letting my boy walk into danger." He touched her face. "A good spirit in so small a package. That is why I let Tetaki spend so much time with you. You were good for him. Come with us. Be a daughter of my house."

"I want to work my own way." She looked uncertainly at him, looked away.

"What makes you think any of the People are allowed to drift at other's expense?" He laughed. "Go back to your place, young Gleia. Rest. Here." He handed her the jar of ointment. "Put this on what you can reach in the morning. I will wait beside the Hall of Records."

On the wharf again, she found the fog had closed in thickly. She could hardly see the lanterns hanging from the mast. A muscle twitched in her thigh, reminding her of the Ranga Eye. She shuddered. No, she thought, no more chances. I don't need to sell it and it's too dangerous. I can damn well get along without it. She limped to the end of the wharf and pulled the crystal from her pocket. For a moment she hesitated as her fingers involuntarily caressed the smooth seductive surface. Was it so bad after all? Beautiful. . . . The crystal throbbed and warmth began to climb up her hand. "Go charm a fish," she cried and flung the eye out into the water.

The fog was bunchy and treacherous around the scavengers' hovels. She walked with intense wariness, moving silently along the rutted path. The last few meters she ran full-out, forgetting the pain in her leg as shadows came at her out of the dirty yellow-white muck. She slammed the door on the reaching hands and scurried up the stairs, flitting past Miggela's ambush before the ratty figure could come out and stop her.

She stood in the doorway, wrinkling her nose at the unlovely mess waiting for her; cursing the crystal she lit a candle at the guttering tallow dip smelling up the hall, then marched inside, slamming the door behind her. After bringing a measure of order into the chaos, she got out the brazier and the cha fixings, using the candle to light shreds of paper beneath the last of her charcoal sticks. While the water was heating, she yawned and scratched, feeling amazingly good in spite of the miserable day behind her. She pulled the cafta's ties loose and dragged it over her head. Once she had it off, she turned it over to examine the ruined back where the whip tails had sliced through the cloth. There was a weight dragging the pocket down.

She thrust her hand in and her fingers closed on a smooth curved form. Warmth leaped up her arms. Her hand came out. Came up. She couldn't open her fingers. The films of color danced around her, painted the streamers of fog crawling through the open window. I threw it in the bay, she thought. I

heard it splash. I felt it fly out of my fingers. I
heard it splash. . . .

> *come come come come sister lover sister no more
> trouble no more pain we love and laugh and live
> in butter-rich sunlight there is no anger no hate
> no oppression here there is no anguish here there
> is no hurting we live in beauty no hunger no
> want no abandoned children we have as gift
> everything everything we want we need don't
> fight us come all you have to do is will it want it
> come you can come sunlight and beauty sun-
> light and joy come come sister lover (They were
> all around her, glorious wraiths twittering allur-
> ingly, antennas flicking encouragement, affection,
> love, promising all those things her soul longed
> for.) come sister (they whispered) come lover*

The whistle from the boiling water reached her,
the small shrill sound cutting through the spell
the fliers had woven. She swung around, deliberately bashing her fist into the wall, the sudden
pain breaking her loose from the Eye's hold. She
ripped a piece off the ruined cafta and tied the
crystal in it, then hooked the rag over the handle
of the wardrobe door, breathing a sigh of relief as
she walked across to make her cha.

At the House of Records, Gleia watched Temokeuu walk toward the main entrance. He looked
over his shoulder at her, the sharp angles of his
narrow face throwing off glints of red and blue
from the two suns, then he vanished through the
door she had no right to enter. She sighed and
pushed through the bonder's gate.

In the salla, body disciplined to the proper stance

of humble submission, she stopped in front of the clerk's desk and waited for him to notice her.

"What you want, bonder? Be sure you don't waste my time." His fat arrogant face was creased in a frown meant to emphasize his importance. He fiddled impatiently with some papers piled in front of him.

"By Thrim and Orik, the bonder's law," she said meekly. Fishing in her pocket, she pulled out a silver obol, laying it on the desk in front of him. "Thrim and Orik." She placed two more oboli on top of the first. "I come to buy my bond."

He grunted as he swept the coins off the desk. "Straighten up, bonder. Let me see your mark."

She lifted her head.

"Closer. You think I can read the sign across the room?"

She leaned across the desk. He touched the brand. "Thief. That's fifty oboli." His hand slid down her neck and moved inside the cafta, stroking the soft skin there as he moved his pale tongue over dry lips. "And an investigation to see if you've reformed. There's a lot of work in voiding a bond." He took a fold of her flesh between his fingers and pinched. She closed her eyes against the sudden pain. "Unless you can convince me how reformed you are."

Gleia stiffened. She hadn't planned on paying that sort of bribe. If she refused him, he'd set a thousand niggling obstacles in her way until she exhausted her money and her strength and sank beaten back into the slow death of her bondage. For the moment anger paralyzed her, slime trying to make himself big, then she forced the anger and the sickness down. If that was the price, it was no big thing. No big thing, she told herself. Not when set against the very big thing she wanted, the right

to spit in the face of slime like this and walk away.
She thought of Abbrah. No big deal. She leaned
into the fat clerk's hand, smiling at him.

He wobbled his pudgy body around to the gate
and swung it open. "Interrogation room this way."
When she'd moved through the gate, he shoved
her along the hall and pushed her into a small
bare room with a lumpy couch, a soiled chair, a
washstand with a basin and cracked ewer on it.
Gleia pulled off her cafta and lay on the couch
waiting for him.

The Kadiff was sitting behind his high bench
looking bored. He tapped long slim fingers on the
desk top as the clerk led Gleia in. "What's this?"

"Bond buyer, noble Kadiff."

"Umph. Bring her here."

Gleia came to the desk, suppressing her annoyance at the servile behavior expected of her. She
glanced quickly and secretly around as she bent
her body into a low bow. Temokeuu came quickly
from the shadows and stood beside her. The Kadiff
raised his eyebrows and looked a trifle more
interested.

"Noble and honored Kadiff, may I offer a small
evidence of my appreciation for your Honor's con-
descending to disturb your magnificent thoughts
to hear my small and unimportant petition?" She
reached back and touched Temokeuu's arm, inviting him to share her game. His fingers touched
hers, nipped one lightly, letting her know he was
appreciating her performance. Her irritation faded
in the pleasure she felt at this sharing.

The Kadiff inclined his head and she came closer,
feigning a shy timidity, inwardly contemptuous of
the man for swallowing her mockery, he was no
better than that nothing clerk grinding on her body

dreaming himself a rutting male taking his pleasure though what pleasure he could get out of that
business she certainly couldn't see. After a hasty
calculation she placed six gold pentoboli on the
table in front of him and backed away.

He tucked the coins into one of his sleeves. "You
have investigated her reform?" he asked the clerk,
his words perfunctory, making it obvious he was
bored with the whole thing and didn't care what
the man said.

"Yes, noble Kadiff."

The Kadiff sniffed. "No doubt. Have you sent for
the bond holder?"

"Yes, noble Kadiff. The caftamaker Habbiba. The
wardman was sent and should be here momentarily."

"While we're waiting you'd better send for the
brander. If we have to cancel the bond, he should
be here."

"It will be done, noble Kadiff." The clerk scurried out, looking pale at having forgotten this.

The Kadiff tapped the end of his long nose with
a neatly polished nail. "It's unusual to see one of
the seafolk in this place." He looked around disdain-
fully. "Let alone one of your status, ambassador."

Gleia fought to keep her face a mask. A little
influence, he said?

Temokeuu bowed his head with a delicately exaggerated solemnity, that delighted Gleia. "I owe
blood debt to this person, noble sir, and would
stand surety for her."

The Kadiff folded his hands. His attitude altered
subtly. He sat straighter, looked more interested
and considerably more respectful. "Fifty oboli for
the bond. You need ten more for the brander."

"I have it, noble Kadiff." She kept her eyes on
her feet.

"A lot of money. You're fortunate to have a sponsor, young woman."

Temokeuu bowed slightly. "The honor would have been mine, save that my daughter has earned the money to redeem herself."

"I didn't know sewing girls made such pay."

"If you please, illustrious Kadiff, my designs have received some praise and brought much money into the pockets of Habbiba my bond mistress and she has seen fit to share some of the bounty with me," Gleia murmured.

"Share!" Habbiba came storming into the room, the hapless wardman trailing behind. "The creature wouldn't work without extra pay. Why am I dragged out of my house? For this?" She jabbed a shaking finger at Gleia, then her hands went flying, touching her earrings, dabbing at her lips, brushing down over her chest. That and her angry lack of respect provoked the Kadiff into a scowl of petulant displeasure.

"Be quiet, woman." He glared at the wardman who hastily came up behind the angry Habbiba. "You are here," he went on, "as required by law to witness the canceling of a bond."

"What!" Forgetting where she was, Habbiba shrieked and lunged at Gleia, small hands curved into claws. The wardman caught her and got a scratched face for his pains. He wrestled her back, holding her until the Kadiff's astonished roar broke through her rage, putting her on notice that she was in danger of a massive fine. The thought of losing money quieted her fast. "I most humbly beg your pardon, noble Kadiff," she shrilled, falling onto her knees in a position of submission. "It was only my anger at the ingratitude of this girl that made me forget myself. I gave her a home and a trade and paid her well, better than she deserved, and now she wishes to leave me when the Maleeka herself has asked for her to work the cafta her daughter will wear on her nameday."

Gleia saw the Kadiff lean back, his eyes shifting uneasily between them. "May a lowly one have permission to speak, magnificent Kadiff?" she asked.

"Granted." His eyes moved from the fuming Habbiba to the stern face of Temokeuu. Like black bugs they oscillated back and forth as he tried to calculate where his best interest lay.

"The design is completed," Gleia said. She spoke slowly, clearly. "The design is the important thing. There are sewing girls with skills greater than mine to execute the work."

Driven—as far as she could see—by his distaste for Habbiba and his instinct to bow before the power Temokeuu represented, the Kadiff scowled at Habbiba, willing her to confirm what Gleia said. "Is that true?"

Habbiba glared furiously at Gleia but didn't quite dare lie. "It's true," she muttered.

"What?"

"It's true."

The Kadiff sighed with relief. "That answers your objection, woman. And you, bonder, I hereby cancel your bond. The fifty oboli, if you please."

Gleia stood in front of the wardrobe. Deliberately she unhooked the rag bundle and took it to the bed. She sat holding the bundle in her lap. "Well."

The crystal moved inside the cloth like something alive.

Rubbing the skin beside her new brand, Gleia contemplated the bundle. "Looks like I've got several ways I can go from there." She poked at the cloth, rolling the hidden Eye about. "I can stay

here and work for Habbiba. If she gets bitchy I can
quit any time and go with a competitor." She
wrinkled her nose and stared at the window without seeing it. "And I'll know what every day will
be like the rest of my life. Every day." She shivered.
"Or I could head south." She poked at the crystal
some more, scowled at the straggles of thread un-
raveling from the edges. "A bit too hairy, I think.
Look what happened to me in Carhenas and this is
a place I know."

She scratched the end of her nose, feeling warmth
stroking down into her thighs from the stone. "I
know what you want. Mmm. I could go with
Temokeuu and Tetaki. That's a leap in the dark
too, but at least I'd have friends." She smiled. "I
have some influence. Hah! Ambassador. My friend,
oh my friend."

Carefully, moving with slow deliberation, she
untied the knots in the rag and touched the Ranga
Eye. The warmth spread up through her body and
once again she saw the fliers. The male spun in
ecstatic spirals and the others danced their jubilation. She could feel them drawing her out of her
body. She wanted to let go. She wanted desperately to let go, to fly on glorious wings, free and
joyous. So easy, it would be so easy just to go
sailing away from all the pain and misery of her
life here. Why not? Why not just go, let them take
her to fly in joy under a butter-yellow sun.

"No." She jabbed her thumb into the burn on
her face, using the pain to wrench herself from the
Eye's influence. "No. You promise too much," she
muttered. She folded the rag about the Eye, knotting the ends to make a neat bundle of it. Levering
herself onto her feet, she took the bundle to the
wardrobe, opened the door and tossed the rag with
the Ranga Eye into the back corner. "No. You're

too much like a trap. How could I trust you?" She shook her head. "I'm free now. I don't owe anybody anything and I won't stick my head into any trap."

Patting her pocket to make sure her money was safe, she went down the stairs for the last time, nodded pleasantly to Miggela as the squat figure came out of her nest. No reason to bother about the old rat any more. Gleia laughed to herself as she remembered dreams of telling her landlady just what she thought of her. But it wasn't worth the wasted energy.

She stepped into the cruelly bright afternoon, pulling the cafta's hood up over her head. Without hesitation she turned into the alley, leaving behind with few regrets the drab reality of her past and the glittering dreams of the crystal. Temokeuu was waiting, would wait until sundown for her answer. She smiled and began to run past the stinking hovels.

Interlude Among The Shaborn

I n the late spring a mammal came among the seaborn on Cern Myamar, walking quietly behind Temokeuu the Shipmaster. At Midsummer Eve the conches were blown to announce her formal adoption into Temokeuu's clan, though there were some who opposed this. After the horning, Jaydugar swung twice more around the double sun while Gleia lived those 2100 days as Temokeuu's daughter, enduring for Temokeuu's sake the scandal and hostility around her until her quiet ways won a place for her and she found a few friends.

2100 days. The snow came and retreated twice. On the mainland, the tribes drove their armorplated yd'rwe in great loops across the two thousand stadia of grassland of the Great Green and back again to their winter places in valleys heated by scattered hotsprings, fighting their magic wars on both arcs, ceasing only at the tradefair where Caravanners came to buy and sell. And the Caravanners made their spring and summer rounds twice, rumbling along their trade roads and in the mountain valleys where the parsi farming clans twice harvested their crops and three times celebrated Thawsend. As did the other divers members of humankind and otherkind scattered about the world. In little pockets everywhere the descendants of a thousand ships that came crashing down on the shiptrap world struggled with legend and nature back to a nine-tenths-forgotten technology.

2100 days of peace, of study, of swimming and laughing and teasing and testing. Most of all 2100 days of healing. Gleia had two brand scars on her face and far more than that inside. Temokeuu's salve healed the new brand, his affection and care and Tetaki's teasing did more than the passing of the years to heal those old wounds deep inside her.

But as the third thaw came and spring brought warmth and growth to the land, Gleia began to grow restless.

The spring that took the mammal to Myamar brought a ship to circle Jaydugar, brought a man back to a world he'd left behind long ago and thought never to see again and set him on a quest for an ancient evil.

THE FOURTH SUMMER'S TALE

A Thirst For Broken Water

Jevati touched the honor medals dangling over her flat chest. "I think he'll die today."

"I didn't. . . ." The sail began luffing the moment Gleia pulled her eyes off the telltales. Her mouth clamped shut. The breeze was maddeningly unreliable, while her patience seemed to have deserted her with the winter ice. A twitch of the tiller filled the white triangle belly-taut again.

Behind them Horli's giant bulge was a velvet crimson half-circle above the jagged line of Cern Myamar's central ridge. She risked a glance at her friend. Jevati stirred, Horli's light sliding like bloody water over the delicate angles of her face. "Keep on this tack much longer and we'll be in the Dubur's Teeth," she said.

Gleia tightened her fingers on the tiller bar, suppressing her irritation, uncomfortably aware that

she was overreacting to nearly everything these days.
"Watch your head." The boom came sliding across
in a smoothly controlled jibe, skimming just above
the seaborn's tight blue curls. The sail filled again
and the *Dragonfish* began gliding along the port
tack.

"Nice." Jevati straightened. "For a mammal."

"Fish." After a minute, Gleia said. "You look
better."

Jevati tugged at the son-honor. "It was a hard
birth." Her hand fell into her lap, fingers pleating
her fishskin swimtrunks. "It'll be a long time before I go through that again. I'm sorry the old
man's dying, but I don't want another of his
wigglers." She lifted her head and let the breeze
blow drops of water across her face.

Gleia frowned at the fluttering telltales, more
worried than she cared to admit by her friend's
frailty. "You're not much more than a wiggler
yourself. If you don't marry again, what are you
going to do?"

"Wiggler!" Jevati slapped at the rail in disgust,
then shook her head. "I don't know. Depends."
Her fingers moved back and forth along the rail. "I
have to survive the Widowjourney before I make
plans."

The red sun was giving the air a real warmth
even this early in the day. Thaw was over and the
long summer was finally more than a memory
frozen in the ice of deep winter. Jevati let the
silence build between them, comfortable with it—
unlike Gleia who worried at what she'd heard.
Widowjourney? Survive? Ask or let it rest? The breeze
teased tendrils of brown hair from the leather thong
she used as a tieback and whipped them about her
ears. Even after six years-standard with the seaborn she still came upon occasions when she was

uncertain about what she should do. She sighed and surrendered to her curiosity. "Widowjourney?"

"Home to Cern Radnavar." Jevati stretched, delighting in the feel of the wind and spray playing over her body. "Thanks for getting me out of that tomb. I was about ready to escape through the underways."

"Firstwife didn't like my coming around. I thought she was going to snap my head off."

Jevati sniffed. "Firstwife Zdarica never has approved of me." She grinned. "Matter of fact, I don't know what she does approve of." Her mother-of-pearl teeth glinted crimson like small bloody needles as they caught and gave back Horli's light. "Idaguu's woman-ridden. I've always wondered how he got up enough nerve to add another wife to his household. Temokeuu-your-father is a man of sense. Only one soft little mammal to tease him."

"Jevati!"

Jevati stopped giggling and looked wistfully at her webbed fingers. "I'd give this hand to be you."

"Head down." Gleia eased the boat into the final tack that would take them into the mouth of the small bay at Cernsha Shirok, the smaller volcanic island out beyond Radnavar's harbor. "Why did you marry him? Sixth wife. You must have known how that would be."

"My clan owed Idaguu a lot of money. From the time our own Cern blew its top and we had to move to Radnavar. He was a Shipmaster and Councillor then and tighter than a starving suckerfish." She scratched absently at the skin on her knee. "He came to Radnavar to arrange for payment and there I was. He liked what he saw and said he'd take me instead of the pile of oboli that would have beggared the clan." She arched her body, bending her head back until her skull rested against the rail, cushioned by the springy blue hair that wasn't hair at all but a complex sense organ. "It wasn't so bad. He was nice enough to me. But old. And the other wives . . . well, they were all from Myamar clans and I was an outsider." She straightened, smiled at Gleia. "Till you came I was lonely as a schoolless herring. There's not much news from Radnavar." She waved a hand to the south. "It'll be good to see my people again. If I survive the swim."

"Get the sail, will you?" Gleia's voice was sharper than she intended. Jevati's nose wrinkled again, but she uncleated the halyard and let the sail slide down. As the boat rocked gently in the calm waters of the small bay, Gleia examined the seaborn's bland face. "What did you mean by that?"

"What?" Jevati walked her fingers along her thigh muscle, apparently absorbed in the small dents they made in her flesh.

"Idiot! You said it twice. If you survive the swim."

"Oh. Nothing much." She pushed herself onto her knees and looked over the side. "Want me to let Vlevastuu know you're here?"

Gleia pulled the tie from her hair and ran her hands through the curly mass. "Little fish, sometimes. . . ."

Eyes twinkling, Jevati settled back in the bottom of the boat. "Gleia, Gleia, you make it so easy I couldn't resist, I have to tease you."

Gleia wiggled her fingers. "You forget your little weakness. Talk, fish, or I—"

"About what?" Jevati opened her eyes wide in exaggerated innocence then shrieked as Gleia raked fingers across her too-prominent ribs. "Truce," she squealed. She pushed at Gleia's hands and lifted herself on an elbow.

"Truce."

When she caught her breath, Jevati shifted out
of her awkward crouch to a more comfortable position leaning against the side of the boat. "After all,
it's not so funny for me. Widowjourney. Simple.
When Idaguu dies, all his wives must go back to
their birth clans."

"I don't see . . ." Gleia rubbed her hand across
her forehead. "What's the problem?"

"Obiachai. I've got to make it on my own." She
slid her shoulders against the side, her glassy scales
moving with a papery sound over the wood. "The
others, they swim a few body lengths. Me, I head
for Radnavar. If I make it, fine. If not, too bad."

"Obiachai!" Gleia clenched her hands into fists.
"I'm sick of that word. When Temokeuu brought
me here that's all I heard. Obiachai! That's the
way things have to be done because that's the way
they've always been done. It's a matter of clan
honor. Don't disgrace us. You can't do that. Hunh!"

"Yelling doesn't help."

Gleia sucked in a breath and blew it out again.
"You're right, dammit. I really must be dim this
morning."

"You are. Where's Cern Radnavar?"

"Huh?"

Jevati nodded gravely. "I thought so. Listen and
learn, little mammal." She paused then spoke in
an exaggerated singsong chant. "Cern Radnavar
swims six hundred stadia south." She laughed at
the consternation on Gleia's face. "Two weeks, swim
in untamed water. Now do you see?"

"Why can't Temokeuu give you passage on one
of his chis-makkas when they go trading south? He
won't worry about being paid."

"You're not listening. Obiachai binds him as
much as me. He'd be exiled if he tried to help me."

"That's stupid."

"That's the way things are." She took hold of the mast and pulled herself onto her feet. "Vlevastuu obviously doesn't know you're here. Temokeuu won't want to wait for his breakfast melons." She slid over the side and disappeared into the depths of the bay.

Gleia paced restlessly along the edge of the water, her cafta brushing against salt flowers and trailing kankaolis. This room was built out over the harbor and took in a portion of the shoreline. The roof was checkered with panels of translucent kala shell, letting in enough light to keep the plants growing and healthy and was supported by rough beams of twisted sinaubar wood exensively imported from the mainland. This was Temokeuu's study, his particular retreat. No one came here except by invitation and he seldom invited intrusion. Gleia was the single exception to this rule. He watched her prowl about for a while then looked down at the papers in front of him.

"Seems god-Meershah speared another starfish."

Gleia dropped onto a bench. "Translation please."

"A starship came down in the sea by Cern Vrestar. Jaydugar has gathered to herself another branch of man or other kind."

Gleia smiled. "The Madarmen would say the Madar saw man-corrupt and plucked him from his wicked ways as she did my parsi and your seaborn and all the other sorts. Plucked them from their evil paradises and set them here to be men again by the labor of their hands."

Temokeuu leaned back in his chair and smiled affectionately at her. "They didn't make much impression on you."

"They caught me too late. The streets taught me to believe more in my hands and feet." She chuckled. "And teeth." She jumped up and came to stand beside him, one hand on his shoulder. "Those are reports from Tetaki?"

"Mmh. As you see. He says the starfolk are starting to clean out the ashes from the house on Vrestar. Apparently they're land dwellers."

"Mammals?"

"He doesn't say." Temokeuu turned over the top sheet. "They're small, dressed in bulky gray coveralls." His long slender forefinger touched a few lines of writing. "With tails they can use like another hand." He sighed and looked worried. "He says he's going to try talking to them." He picked up a stylus and began twisting it through his fingers.

Gleia felt his muscles tensing and smoothed her hands over his shoulders. "He'll be all right. He's as tough and wily a trader as his father." Temokeuu laughed and patted her hand. She snorted. "I'm not flattering you and you know it." She moved away from him and began prowling about, feeling more restless than ever. "I was talking to Jevati this morning."

"Oh?"

"It's idiotic to send a frail child all that way alone."

"Obiachai, Gleia-my-daughter." Smiling at her grimace of disgust, he went on. "It is sometimes idiotic, I must admit, but it gives us stability and makes us remember our origins when others forget." He set the stylus beside the pile of papers and watched her stalk about, kicking at the hem of her cafta until it belled out around her body. "All this isn't just for Jevati, is it? I've watched you growing more restless as the winter passed."

Gleia threw herself down on the bench. "I don't

know. I have everything anyone could want. I've been happy here."

"Been?"

She ran her hands through her hair until it was a wild tangle. "Everything I tell myself sounds not quite right. I'm not idle; I think I do help you, that it's not play you're making for me. I think I'm spoiled for peace." She looked helplessly at him. "I'd be a fool to leave and I'd miss you terribly, Temokeuu-my-father."

He pressed his hands on the desk top. "Most of the seaborn prefer the quiet order of the Cerns. But some of us have a taste for broken water." Amusement lit his eyes and his mouth twisted into a smile. "I understand you better than you think, Gleia-my-daughter. You're bored. There's no challenge left here."

She sat up, alerted by the look on his face.

He touched the pile of papers in front of him. "I want you to find Tetaki and see what he's doing. These . . ." He tapped his fingers in the center of the pile of reports. "These are several weeks old." He turned grave eyes on her. "This will be your home when you need it again, Gleia-my-daughter, but now you must try the broken water." He fell silent, frowned at the kala shell panels in the side walls. "I'll have the *Dragonfish* provisioned for you. There's no hurry. You might take the long way round, stop at Radnavar before you head out to Vrestar."

She flung her head back, bubbling with excitement. "I told my little fish you were the wisest of men."

His smile flashed again. "Not wise, Gleia-my-daughter, merely old in much foolishness." Then he sobered. "Don't talk about this other thing. As far as anyone will know, you're out to see Tetaki.

Jevati can do what she pleases about joining you. I don't think you'll have to warn her not to discuss her intentions." He walked over to her and smoothed down the wild spikes she'd clawed into her hair. "I enjoy having you about the house. I want you free to come home."

Gleia paced over the sand, looking repeatedly out toward the tall fingers of rock that poked through the seawater at irregular intervals. The barrier pillars. Horli was a bead of fire between two black fingers, turning wisps of fog into crimson smoke. She turned and trudged back up the slope to the beached *Dragonfish*. This was her second day of waiting and she was beginning to worry.

Horli drifted higher and Hesh poked up his deadly blue head. As a few clouds scooted amiably across a sky that already shimmered with heat, Gleia tucked the ends of her headcloth into the binding cord, dug her toes in the sand and hugged her knees against her chest.

The suns crept higher. Wavelets began lapping at the boat's stern. Shading her eyes with her hands, she searched the water until tears streamed down her cheeks and black spots danced like new-hatched teypolei in front of her. She rubbed her eyes. *A whole day late. Damn, it's hot.* Jerking the headcloth off, she dropped it into the boat and waded out to where the water was waist deep. One last time she looked around, then plunged under and came up sputtering but feeling a bit cooler.

"Gleia. Gleia." Behind her, closer to the beach, Jevati crouched on her knees, the shallow water washing around her body. Gleia waded to her and helped her stand. Together they stumbled up the gentle slope to the patch of shade developing at the foot of the cliff. Jevati collapsed, arms dangling limply, resting her head on her drawn up knees. A few drops of blood oozed from a cut on one arm, leaking around a fine membrane that held the torn flesh together. After a few minutes the harsh explosions of breath grew softer. She raised her head and leaned carefully against the shaded rock.

"What happened?" Gleia touched the small webbed hand quivering on the sand. When Jevati shook her head, still sucking in great gulps of warm air, she said, "Take your time, little fish."

They sat quietly in the widening patch of shade, enjoying a companionable silence as Jevati's strength gradually came back. The tide rose until the water's edge was a short distance past the *Dragonfish*. The little boat began to rock in time with the beat of the waves.

Jevati sucked in a deep breath, pushed up onto her knees and scanned the horizon, relaxing only when she saw nothing but the bright expanse of water foaming about the barrier pillars.

Her eyes on Jevati's troubled face, Gleia said, "What's wrong?"

"Can you launch the boat now?"

"It's coming up high heat. Are you strong enough for that?"

"We can't stay here."

As soon as she had the *Dragonfish* running southeast on a broad reach, Gleia settled back and fixed her eyes on Jevati. "How'd you get that cut on your arm?"

Eyes half-closed, stretched out comfortably in the bottom of the boat, Jevati smiled sleepily. "Nag, nag."

Gleia sniffed. "What happened?"

"Well, after they locked the doors against me, I

walked down to the bay and started out." She
looked past Gleia, frowning slightly. "The strang-
est feeling. Like the whole city was empty when I
knew it wasn't. Even the bay was empty." She
yawned suddenly. "Ohhhh, I'm tired. I could sleep a
week."

"Jevati!"

The seaborn stroked her throat slowly. "I was
just passing Cernsha Sharoo, surface swimming
for a change, when a miserable rat-nibbled dhoura
came round the point. I swam right under the bow
and some idiot tried to harpoon me."

"What!"

"You're surprised?" She giggled and shook her
head. "You should have seen me. He creased my
arm and scared me stiff. I mean really stiff. Damn
if he didn't pull in the barb and try again. Missed
me completely that time, but I was bleeding and
sending out signals for every blood-sniffer within a
dozen stadia. I got myself into the island just in
time to avoid being eaten by a cheksa." She looked
down at her arm, touched the film on the wound.
"By the time this was set, the men on the dhoura
had spotted me. I could hear them yelling. I went
deep, found a ledge to rest on. Spent the night
there. As soon as Horli stuck her head up, I was
coming for you fast as I could."

About mid-afternoon Jevati yawned and sat up.
"Where are we?"

"Past Cliffend."

Jevati looked out to sea. There was a dark smudge
low on the eastern horizon. She sighed. "Cern
Vrestar," she said. "The cone is still smoking after
six thaws."

"Temokeuu told me . . ." Jevati's gasp interrupted
her. The seaborn was staring past her. Gleia glanced

back and saw the peak of a triangular sail. As she watched, the sail grew until most of the dhoura was visible. She heard a splash and swung around. Jevati was over the side, gone deep in her panic. Gleia turned *Dragonfish* and raced toward the line of barrier pillars. The water inside was too shallow for the dhoura and the spaces between pillars too narrow to admit the seagoer. Reaching along a course parallel to the pillars, she chewed on her lip and waited to see what would happen.

Jevati came up out of the water and thumped into the boat, dripping slathers of water into the bottom. "Sorry," she said. "That thing scares me."

Gleia laughed. "I'd say you had reason." She watched the sail grow larger as the dhoura came dipping toward them, riding the brisk wind that ruffled the water into lightly foaming peaks. "Think they saw us?"

"Probably."

"Well, better safe than fast. Unless you have a deadline."

"No." Jevati looked wistfully at the smudge darkening the sky in the east. "Maybe we could see Vrestar first once the dhoura's past."

The dhoura came even with them about an hour later then started pulling ahead. In the west Horli's bottom edged behind the inland mountains. Hesh had moved a double fingerwidth across her middle and was sitting close to her left side, still several hours from touching down. Gleia looked at Jevati, raised her eyebrows. "Still want to go?"

Jevati nodded. "Wait a bit longer," she said. "The dhoura's too fast and too close yet."

Five discs came out of the smoke smudge and hovered above the dhoura like large black coins tossed into the air. Gleia glanced at Jevati. "I've never seen anything like that before."

"Me either." Jevati crouched in the bow watching as the discs circled slowly over the ship. "The dhoura's in trouble. Look at the way the sail is jerking."

As they watched, three of the discs sank until they were behind the pillars and out of sight. The fourth continued to hover. The fifth came darting toward them. Jevati gasped and went overside again. Gleia swung the *Dragonfish* around and raced for the shore.

Gleia blinked and sat up. Her head throbbed. She clutched at her temples and groaned.

"Here." A man's voice. She jerked around, then squeezed her eyes shut as the dull pain drilled through her brain. A hand closed around her wrist and pulled her arm down. She felt her fingers close around cool metal. With his hand covering hers, supporting her, she lifted the cup to her lips and gulped down several swallows of the stale water. Then he took the cup away. "Sit still a minute and the pain will lose its bite." She heard him straighten and move away.

After a few minutes she opened her eyes, reluctantly convinced she would live. The pain was still there but it had subsided to a dull ache like that of a rotten tooth. She looked around. They were alone in a small bare cabin. She sat on the floor, her shoulders against a bunk bed built into the wall; when she managed to tilt her head back, she saw a second berth stacked above the one she was leaning on. In the far wall a small square porthole let some light creep through but no fresh air. The man was perched on the end of the lower bunk watching her.

He was thinnish and pale with a tangled thatch of hair so red it was a shriek of fire in the half-light. His eyes were pale, a nearly colorless gray—or maybe green or blue. She couldn't tell which. They changed as she watched. His face was a stubble-shadowed blunt triangle with clean-cut angles as neat and delicate as Jevati's. He sat with long legs pulled up, long narrow hands resting on his knees. His jacket had wide sleeves, the ends cut in square scallops to make a frame for hands and wrists—bright blue-green outside, dark yellow lining; his dark blue leg coverings—thick material that clung to the long muscles of his thighs—disappeared into knee-high boots. His jacket hung open, showing a wedge of pale, well-muscled chest.

Moving cautiously Gleia used the side of the bunk to pull herself up. "How'd I get here?" She swallowed and leaned her forehead against the side of the upper bunk. "Where am I anyway?"

"Thissik brought you." She looked blank. "The disc riders," he went on. "This is Korl's *Cuttlefish*."

"A dhoura?"

He watched her a moment, pale changeable eyes touching her face and fisted hands. He nodded.

"Was I brought in alone?" She waited tensely then relaxed as he nodded once more. *Jevati got away*, she thought. *Madar be blessed*. "Who are you? How did you get here?"

"Shounach. Juggler. A humble passenger." His mouth curled into a sudden broad smile. He cupped his hands, swayed them until she almost saw the bright balls circling above them. Then he dropped his hands on his knees and raised an eyebrow. "You?"

"Gleia." A large shoulder bag made of a shiny green material, sprinkled with red and blue stars sat on her end of the bed. She lifted it, found it surprisingly heavy, set it on the floor—a floor that was rocking in long smooth swells—and settled in its place on the bed. "What's going on?"

"Better just wait to see what happens."

"Not many choices available if you won't talk." She sighed and leaned back. "I gather we're captives."

The sky was dark with black smoke burping out of the cone in scattered lazy puffs. The waters of the bay swallowed the drifting smuts and occasionally spat back surges of gas. Gleia tried to breathe shallowly as she followed the sullen scowling crewmen off the dhoura onto the short pier near the last of the clanhouses, built around the inner arch of the bay. She shivered as she looked around at the tormented earth. *No wonder Vrestar's seaborn abandoned their holding.* The houses were drowned in pale ash that grew deeper as the wings of the arc approached the center, where congealed lava rose in waves around the tormented lumps that marked the council hall and the high market.

Their thissik captors prodded them toward the Endhouse. It was already dug clear of the ash. Farther on, Gleia could see small gangs of men working on the other houses. She glanced over her shoulder at the Juggler and saw him looking sharply around, his changeable eyes moving and moving, his pale face shuttered into inscrutability. He saw her watching and shook his head slightly.

Inside the house the walls had been washed down and the bright colors of the murals glowed like jewels in the light from short tubes that had replaced the oil lamps. The thissik herding them along were small creatures, dressed in gray overalls that concealed most of their bodies except for the long tapering tails held rigidly erect. Each thissik held a strange crooked rod in one hand.

The sailors avoided these, rounding their shoulders and pulling in their arms whenever one of the thissik moved past. *Weapons of some kind*, she thought.

In the Day Court all the benches had been moved out, leaving it desolate except for the gentle rippling pool in the center. At the far end of the room the kala-shell panels were painted over but glow tubes lit that end with bright red light. A thissik sat there at a delicate shell table. The gray fur on his pointed ears faded through silver to white and the short plush on his face was paler than that of their guards. Behind him were banks of machines and several sturdier tables covered with untidy piles of paper. He said something in a high squeal to one of the guards, oscillating rapidly between high and lower notes. At times his mouth moved but no sound came out. The guard answered with a brief burst of the same sort of sound. Then the Elder turned his large round eyes on the captives. "I am Keeper. Who of you iss masster?" He spoke parsi with a strong hissing accent and an occasional hesitation as he searched for a word.

"Me." Captain Korl took a step forward, stopping abruptly when a guard hissed and jabbed at him with the crooked rod. He was big, looked powerful, but his belly strained the seams of his tunic and bulged over his wide leather belt. His elaborately ringletted black hair was streaked with gray as was his bushy beard and moustache. His face was seamed and craggy, a ruin of power.

"I'm my own man." Shounach stepped apart from the sailors, ignoring Korl's malevolent scowl.

"I also. I speak for myself," Gleia said hastily. She moved as far as she could from the sullen crewmen.

The Keeper exchanged a rapid set of questions

and answers with the guard, then turned back. His eyes flitted over the line and stopped on Shounach. "That seemss reassonable. Kneel now. All of you."

Gleia hesitated. Shounach's hand came down hard on her shoulder, pushing her down with him as he knelt. She smoothed out a wrinkle under her knee and waited, wondering what was coming. Without warning, one of the sailors jumped up and ran cursing at the Keeper. A guard flipped up his rod. The other sailors scrambled desperately away from the berserker as a cone of light licked out from the rod. He was silhouetted like a black doll against the crimson light then was gone, wiped away.

"It iss to be hoped the resst of you will not be sstupid." The Keeper picked up a dull gray metal ring. At one side it had two trapezoidal lumps. He let the ring dangle from one small hand. "You are now. . . ." He hesitated, looked down at the ring then back at them. His tail began jerking back and forth, the naked tip moving like a pinkish metronome behind his head. "You are now slaves. The people of shipThelar . . ." His mouth tightened and his face was suddenly bleak. "We are here very much against our will and our desiress, but here we are and here we musst sstay." He spoke slowly, the tips of his ears twitching slightly, the tip of his tail slowing and moving in a small circle. His hissing accent began to diminish until his sibilants were barely noticeable. "We must build our lives here and build them quickly. You will help make these houses liveable for us. The guards will move behind you and place these rings about your necks. Anyone causing trouble will be removed immediately. By removed, I mean what you have just seen. We have neither time nor inclination to tolerate fools."

Two of the guards slipped medallion chains up over their heads and dropped them onto the table; then they put the rings about each neck. The locks snapped home with small sharp clicks. A third guard circled wide around them and stopped about a body-length behind them. The ringers picked up their medallions, put them back on, then stood beside the Keeper.

"You may sstand." The Keeper sounded tired as if he had spent too many days in a battle where even the winners lose. The pale tufts on his ear points twitched as he folded small fine hands on the table in front of him. "For honorss' ssake I sspeak." His large eyes closed for a moment then opened again, sinking back into the loose folds of grayish skin that pleated around them. "We are free traders whose ship was our life. That is over. Yet we still exist, and existing, must adapt. We are under pressure of time and need and must do things . . . things we find abhorrent." His eyes moved slowly along the line of men, stopped at Gleia. He examined her then seemed to shift uneasily in his chair. Then he faced Shounach; his pale tongue touched lightly at thin lips and the tail tip behind his head began to jerk erratically. He looked puzzled, then he straightened his narrow shoulders and turned back to Korl. "The collars you wear limit you three ways." He tapped the table-top with the nail of his forefinger. In the silence the small click seemed disproportionately loud, making several of the captives twitch; Gleia started, scraped a foot across the floor tiles. The Keeper's eyes turned briefly toward her then slid away. "One: You may not approach any thissik closer than one body-length." The nail tapped again, twice. "Two: You may not go farther than one hundred body-lengths from this house. Three: you may not

seek to remove the collars without the key that is
kept on my person."

Once again he paused and moved his eyes down
the line, stopping briefly on each face though he
skipped rapidly over Gleia and paused longer on
Shounach. "It is to be hoped you are less stupid
than that man," he told them. "One: If any of you
seeks to approach a thissik, you will feel pain that
increases as you move closer. A demonstration."
He waved a guard forward.

As the small gray figure came up to them, the
pain was like a minor burn at first but increased
in intensity until it became unbearable. Gleia
backed away then screamed as she passed the limit
of the thissik behind her. She crouched, arms
crossed tight against her breasts, rocking and
moaning.

Then the pain was gone. The guard was back
beside the Keeper who waited until the captives
had recovered then went on. "Two: If you attempt
to go beyond the tether limit, the same thing will
happen. If you endure the pain and press farther,
at one hundred fifty body-lengths the collar will
explode, neatly removing your head."

Gleia glanced sharply at the alien face, thinking
she heard a touch of grim humor behind the even
words. For a second he reminded her of Temokeuu.
She put the idea aside for later consideration and
continued listening.

"Three: If you attempt to remove the collar
whether by torch, saw or lock pick, the collar will
explode." He fitted fingertip to fingertip with neat
precision and contemplated them. "Once the houses
are ready and the contents retrieved from our . . .
from where they are, there will be no more need
for your services. You will then be freed from the
collars."

He didn't look at us, Gleia thought. *He would not mention the word* ship *in connection with freeing us.* She felt a chill. There were a lot of ways to read his last statement, most of them not comforting to think about. She rubbed at her arm as she watched the Keeper lean back, some of the stiffness passing from his small body. *He looks so terribly tired,* she thought.

The guards herded them out of the Endhouse into a red dusk. Horli-set. Overhead, the two moons Aab and Zeb were on the point of kissing, their pale ghosts gradually beginning to glow as the sky darkened. A number of small boats were tied to the pier, dwarfed by the black silhouette of the dhoura. Gleia touched the cold metal at her throat. *Without that. . . .* She sighed and trudged along behind the Captain's broad back.

The new captives were taken into the second house, moved through dusty airless corridors then directed through a wide doorway into the long narrow room with grilled windows marching down one side. A number of men lay about on the floor, bone-weary from a long day's hard labor. Most of them were already asleep. At the base of the unpierced sidewall a long trench was half-full of water. The trench passed under the far wall but a grill had been fitted over the opening so that the men inside could not get out. The heavy door slammed shut behind them. Gleia looked around and shivered, the hairs lifting along her spine. She was the only woman in the room.

"Take this." Shounach's voice was a thread of sound as he pressed a hard object against her back. She reached around and found the hilt of a knife pressed against her palm. She moved a little away from him, then glanced back. His face was a pale mask, cool and indifferent. As he walked away, she turned to watch the Captain.

Korl had appropriated the corner nearest the door, evicting the sleeping men already in possession. He and his crew were standing in a muttering huddle, their eyes repeatedly seeking her out. She shivered once more and looked about a little desperately for the Juggler. He was leaning casually against the wall near one of the last windows. The other men were negligible, most of them not even awake. Korl and Shounach. One at each end of the room. Two poles of power. Gleia moved her fingers along the hilt of the knife now hidden in the folds of her sleeve. *You make your choice*, she thought, *and then you pay the price*. She swallowed, feeling a little sick at losing the integrity of body that six years-standard of peace had given back to her. Keeping the knife hidden she turned her back on Korl and began moving toward Shounach.

A meaty hand came down hard on her shoulder and swung her around. "You goin' the wrong way," Korl said.

"Take your hand off." She kept her voice calm, spoke with cool contempt.

His fingers tightened on her shoulder. Chuckling, he pushed her toward his watching men. "That skinny nothing not for a nice little thief."

Gleia brought the knife up, slashed at his arm and whirled away as he howled with pain and slapped at her head, spraying drops of blood over several startled sleepers. Gleia held the knife ready and danced back, watching his hands.

Korl's eyes narrowed. He looked at the blood still dripping from his arm, then at her as she stood holding the knife in a street-fighter's grip, close in to her body. He grinned and slipped off the leather shipmaster's vest. "Little cat," he said and flicked the end of the vest at her head.

Gleia ducked and twisted past the vest, slashed at his arm, opening a deep cut, and was away before his hand could close on her. He looked down at the cut, amusement replaced by rage; he roared and charged at her, counting on his strength and reach to outmatch her knife. Gleia danced back then dived under his arms, opened a cut on his leg, ran full out away from him, leaped over a watcher and stopped in a small open space. Korl staggered, then jumped forward. He was between her and Shounach, the grin gone from his seamed face. He began moving toward her, far more cautiously now. Gleia retreated step by step, not daring to take her eyes from him. She began to sweat, wondered how close she was getting to the crew. Korl's eyes shone with anticipation.

He stopped suddenly. "Juggler." His voice was hoarse; he was breathing heavily. "Where you stand in this?"

"Nowhere." The deep voice was cool and disinterested.

"Do I watch my back?"

"I'm not moving. Read that how you want."

Korl grunted. He flicked the vest at Gleia's head and came in low when she leaped back. He flicked it again. She stumbled over a watcher and nearly went down, scrambled frantically and managed to tear free when his hand closed on the sleeve of her cafta. She left the sleeve in his hand and glanced over her shoulder to see how much room she had left, forced down panic when she saw how little it was.

The Captain was panting, sweat streaming down his face, and the cut on his leg was bothering him, slowing him down. She tried passing him again but misread the crouch. His hand closed on her ankle. Squealing in her fear and anger, she slashed repeatedly at his hand, wrenched her foot loose and rolled desperately away.

The Captain shook the blood off his hand. He had trouble closing his fingers into a fist.

Gleia got to her feet and pushed at hair plastered by sweat to her face. Eyes on the Captain, she edged along the wall toward the Juggler. She mopped at her face and let her shoulders sag. Before her eyes dropped, she saw Korl's begin to shine again. She stepped clumsily back and bumped into the wall—then darted at him low and fast, slashing at his hamstrings. As he crashed to the floor she was up and running.

Breathing hard, she stopped in front of the Juggler. "Well?"

"Good job," he said calmly. "Companion?"

Briefly she wondered why—and why he'd given her the knife—then she nodded. "Companion." Handing him the knife, she stepped into the corner behind him and sat down, feeling every wrench and bruise now that the excitement of the fight was gone.

Korl was groaning and clutching at his leg. His men watched, then one of them walked quietly over to him—a skeletal gray shadow, an emptiness in the shape of a man. He knelt and examined the hamstrung leg then without a word moved on his knees along the body, touched the Captain's suddenly pale face, then plunged the knife into his neck. With the same lack of emotion he cleaned the knife on the Captain's shoulder, resheathed it, flattened his palm on the dead man's chest and pushed himself back on his feet. Without looking back he walked heavily to the corner and the watching crewmen.

Gleia closed her eyes but still saw the spurt of blood. "Not even hate," she murmured. "Like a butcher."

Shounach eased himself down beside her. "What does it matter once a man is dead how he got that way?"

Gleia looked down at trembling fingers. "It has to matter."

There was a clear space around them. The crew was still huddled together at the other end of the room and the others had drawn away. Shounach was sitting as he had been the first time she'd seen him, knees drawn up, long clever hands resting lightly on his knees. She turned her head away. The glow tubes went out suddenly, plunging the room into darkness filled with the breathing of the man beside her. Through the window just beyond her feet Gleia saw suddenly bright stars in an ill-omened shape—the Crow. She shivered and moved closer to Shounach. "Them Empty Man. What's wrong with him?"

Shounach scratched at his chin, working his fingers through a two-day stubble. "Addict. Ranga Eye. Saw him with it a few days back."

"It ate him?"

"He's lasted longer than most."

She swallowed. "You knew what it was. Have you ever. . . ."

"Once."

She watched the Crow's beak dip out of sight, remembering the egg-shaped crystal that had tripped her up one morning in a street in Carhenas, remembering the images it brought to shimmer around her, butterfly people wheeling and dipping under a golden sun, glorious, enticing images that had nearly sucked the soul out of her body—had

nearly eaten her like the Eye had eaten the Empty
Man. "I found an Eye when I was still bonded,"
she said very softly, stroking the brands on her
face, speaking from a need she couldn't define.

He moved her fingers aside and touched the two
brands. "Dangerous for a bonder."

"I know." She pushed his hands away. "Deadly."

"What happened to it?" He waited but she said
nothing. "Did you sell it to buy your bond?"

"No. Who'd buy such a thing from a branded
thief? I threw it away."

"Why? How?"

"It tried to own me. All my life I've had to fight
to keep a piece of myself for me." The whispered
exchange had a strange soothing quality. She found
it absurdly easy to say things to the dark form
beside her that she'd never spoken of before, even
to Temokeuu. "The beauty—that was the hardest
thing. You know."

He hesitated then said slowly, "Yes. I know."

"Everything around me was so ugly. It would
have been easy to give in, except. . . ."

"It would have eaten you."

She nodded even though she knew he couldn't
see her, looked up at him. "Some things cost too
much. You must know that. *You* broke free."

He was silent a long time. At first she thought he
wasn't going to say anything. She turned back to
the window, feeling better as the Crow's tail inched
down behind the sill. "I've had training to resist
such things," he said finally.

"Shounach?"

"What is it?"

"Do we stay awake all night?"

"How do you feel?"

"Sore. Tired. Otherwise all right."

"Feel up to taking first watch?"

"Yes. Go to sleep. I'll wake you at Zebset."

Shounach shook her awake. She opened her eyes, blinked when she saw how light it was. "It's late."

He pulled her to her feet. She turned slowly, looking around. The room was empty except for two thissik standing by Korl's body. "Where are the others?"

"Sent to work. The thissik on the left speaks some parsi. When they saw the body, he asked what happened. Captain's crew told them."

"I can imagine what they said. What about you?"

"No one was asking me."

"Why didn't you wake me?"

"You were tired. Might as well sleep."

The thissik finished the examination of the body and came to them. "You come." The speaker pointed at the door. "To Keeper."

Thissik went in and out of the Day Court ignoring the two standing by the shell table. When the Keeper finally appeared, he looked wearier than ever. He moved slowly past them and sat behind the table. "A man is dead." He straightened his back. Gleia felt her back ache in sympathy when she saw the effort he put into that small movement. "We were told you killed him."

"No." Shounach smoothed his hand over the side of his bag. "Putting a woman in with two dozen men was idiotic. Bound to cause trouble."

"I don't know your customs." The Keeper's hands twitched and his eyes turned restlessly about the room, avoiding Gleia. With a quiet dignity, he said, "Whatever the cause, a man is dead at your hands, Fox. Yes, I know you."

Gleia was tired of being ignored. Without waiting for Shounach's answer she burst out, "That's wrong. He didn't touch the man. After I cut him up, one of his own crew finished Korl."

"The woman fought the man?" The thissik shifted in his chair, losing the momentary calm he had acquired as she spoke. He still would neither look at her nor speak directly to her. He seemed to have trouble even speaking about her.

"Yes, I fought him," she snapped. "I didn't feel like being mauled about by that ..." Her lips closed over the words she wanted to say. Temokeuu had finished what the Madarmen had started, giving her a certain fastidiousness about the language she used. "I didn't kill him. Why should I? Hamstrung, he was no danger to me. Ask your own men. Two cuts on his arms, deep slashes on the back of one hand, a cut on his leg, the hamstringing. Those are my marks. The neck stab was a present from his crew."

The Keeper's ears twitched. The tip of his tail moved over the tiled floor, scraping slowly at the small bright squares. Once again he straightened his slumping body and spoke to the guards in the squealing whistling thissik tongue. He listened intently to the reply then stared down at the table, a short thin forefinger moving idly over the translucent sections of shell cemented together to make the table top. The tip of his tail tapped rapidly at the floor. At last he sighed and leaned back in the chair. "Do you confirm, Fox?" When Shounach spoke his brief affirmative, he nodded. "To prevent more trouble, the woman will be housed apart."

Gleia laced her fingers through Shounach's. "Let him be lodged with me." She felt a flicker of amusement at the annoyance in the Keeper's weary face. His expressive tail was jerking about like a demented snake. Her voice bubbled with that amusement when she spoke again. "You wouldn't be bothered by me then; he could do the talking."

The Keeper's mouth twitched but he quickly suppressed the smile. "An extraordinarily convincing argument." His tail jerked upright, the tip swaying gently just above the top of his head. After his momentary lapse in courtesy when he responded almost directly to Gleia, he was very much on his dignity. "The woman will cover her face in the presence of the thissik. She will not speak to the thissik. You both will work. The guard will direct. If there is any more difficulty, you will speak, Fox. The woman will not come here again." Without waiting for an answer he put his hands flat on the table and pushed himself erect with some difficulty then marched past them, tail held high.

As they followed the guard out of the Endhouse, Gleia glanced idly toward the pier. She gasped, then broke away and ran down the slope into the arms of one of the seaborn waiting there. "Tetaki-my-brother, what happened? How'd the thissik get you?" Her eyes moved over the startled faces of the seaborn. "Mladuu? Drazeuu? Chikisui? And the rest of you? Can't say I'm glad to see you here, ornamented like me." She tapped her finger against one of the ring weights.

Tetaki hugged her, then grinned. "In the middle of trouble as usual, Gleia-my-sister. I was almost expecting you to show up." He touched the ring around her throat, scowling to hide his distress, then stroked a finger across the thief brand on her cheek. "The thissik weren't in any mood to honor embassies. Before I could open my mouth they had the collars on us." He glanced past her. "Your escort is getting impatient." His arm about her shoulders, he walked her back down the pier. "I saw Jevati last night," he murmured when they were far enough from the others. "When the thissik took you, she went deep and came straight here."

Weak with relief, Gleia stumbled and would have fallen except for his supporting arm. "She must have been worn to a thread." She looked up the slope at the agitated guard. "What are you doing for them?"

"Salvaging material from the starship. They herd us out there in the morning, bring us back just before Horli-set."

She stopped at the end of the pier, turned, put her hand on his arm. "If I can, I'll promote a swim around Horli-set so we can talk."

"Take care." He stepped away from her and strolled back to the others as she returned to Shounach and the guard.

Tail switching back and forth in nervous annoyance, the guard marched along the path kicking up clouds of powder ash. Shounach scowled at her. "That was a damn fool thing to do. You might have been killed."

Gleia smiled at the guard's stiff back and twitching tail. "Would they shoot a woman?"

"Don't press your luck. Who's your fish friend?"

"My brother." She giggled at his grunt of disbelief. "Adopted of course." Her eyes narrowed. She licked her lips, spoke slowly and very clearly, her voice deliberately pitched to reach the guard's ears. "Our father is a very important man among the seaborn. When he hears about this. . . ." She broke off with a little cry of pain as Shounach's fingers closed hard around her neck. "What. . . ."

He looked disgusted. "Stupid," he muttered, "Why not just beg them to burn you?"

"Oh, damn." She rubbed at the bruise on her

neck, feeling as stupid as he'd named her. "I didn't think of that."

The guard waited for them at the tumbled gate-posts of Threehouse. "Stay here," he told Shounach. "I fetch tools."

Shounach watched him trot off, his short legs scissoring rapidly through clouds of pale gray powder ash. "How is your father supposed to learn about your captivity?"

Gleia brushed off one of the gate stones and sat down. She rubbed at the dust on her hands, then sat watching her toes wiggle. After a minute she said, "Why should I tell you?"

"That's up to you." He stroked long fingers over the smooth material of the bag he never left behind and smiled blandly. "The guard just went in Endhouse. I wonder why he did that."

"You win." She stretched and patted a yawn away. "Tetaki told me a friend of mine is out there free. A seaborn. She saw me taken and followed."

"Good friend?"

"Very. Like a sister."

"And she's gone to tell your father what happened?"

"Temokeuu already knows they're here—the thissik, I mean. He sent Tetaki to them. Could be the Council is discussing this right now." She shrugged. "Could be not. Jevati—my friend—is staying around to see if she can find some way to help, I'm sure of that."

His fingers began tapping slowly on the material of the bag. "Has she any weapons?"

"A knife. All seaborn carry knives. Why do you take that bag with you all the time? And why didn't the thissik take it away?"

His mouth curved up. He dipped into the bag and pulled out two shimmering blue spheres. He

popped one into the air then the other. They caught
and threw back sparks of Horli's crimson as he
kept them swinging in an easy rhythm. "The tools
of my trade," he said. "Not that easy to replace."
He kept the spheres going a moment more, then
caught them and slipped them back in the bag.
"Nothing else in the bag; why take it. Our little
friend had just come out of the Endhouse. Not
hurrying now."

"Think I've really wrecked things?"

"Wait and see." He looked across the bay. "Your
friends are in a boat heading out. They seem to be
on a longer tether than the rest of us."

"They have to be. They're bringing up things
from the ship."

"Ah." He moved his fingers thoughtfully along
the gray metal of the ring. "Ingenious things, these.
They let a handful of guards control a much larger
number." He grinned. "To get them off we'd have
to part the Keeper from the key. But we can't get
close enough to take the key from him so we can
get close enough to take the key. If you see my
point." He wheeled suddenly and stared at her.
"Your friend? Jevati!"

Their words crossed and both started laughing.
He pulled her off the stone and swung her around
and around until she was breathless, then he set
her back on her feet and smiled down at her. His
thumb caressed her cheek, moving across and across
the brands. Then he bowed his head and his mouth
moved softly on hers.

Gleia pulled away, rubbed the back of her hand
across her mouth. "Don't. I don't like it." She let
her hand drop. "If it's a problem for you, I pay my
dues. I won't enjoy it, but that's never mattered
much before."

The expression went out of his face. "I'm not that much in need."

The day passed slowly. Gleia worked inside Threehouse, digging at the ash that had drifted through broken windows and shoveling it into sacks constructed from a tough coarse fabric that made her itch whenever it touched her skin. When one was full, she dragged it outside and Shounach carried it away. When he wasn't carting off her bags, he was digging at the ash banked up against the walls. The thissik guard kept after them to work faster. They were permitted a short rest and given a cold lunch at midday then sent back to work under the nervous harassment of a new guard.

At Horli-set Shounach laid down his shovel. "Gleia," he called. "Quitting time."

She tottered out of the building. "I ache all over," she moaned. "And look at my hands." She spread them out. Fluid from two broken blisters cut trails through a layer of grime. "I've got to have a bath."

"Got an idea." He climbed the slope to the ruin where the guard was sitting. About midafternoon the thissik had gotten increasingly shrill and agitated. His tail had gone limp and started sweeping about in the powder ash. Eventually he'd retreated to the shattered building and spent the rest of the time crouched in a corner where the roof was still intact.

Gleia watched as they talked. At first the guard was stiffly unreceptive. Shounach waved his arms about. She couldn't tell what he was saying though the sound of his voice floated down to her. The guard turned his head from side to side; his tail twitched then seemed to sag. Shounach waited. Finally the guard shrilled a few words and turned his back on the Juggler.

Shounach trotted back to her, grinning, jumping

nimbly from rock to rock. He stopped beside her. "Want to go for a swim?"

"Do you need to ask?"

Gleia splashed happily about in the shallow water. Her filthy cafta floated up around her but she ignored that and scrubbed at herself with handfuls of coarse bottom sand, ignoring also the stabs of pain from her blistered hands. She sighed with pleasure and watched Shounach paddling about a little farther out. "This is a marvelous idea."

He slapped idly at the water. "Naturally."

She ran her stiffening hands through her hair, grimacing at the oily feel. "A little soap would be nice though."

"Greedy."

A hand touched her leg. She suppressed her start and looked down. The seaborn's body was a shadow by her feet, barely visible in the deepening twilight. She stretched and yawned. "Shounach, my love, come help me scrub my back."

The Juggler splashed over to her. "What is it?" he muttered, lips barely moving. "Be careful. Sound carries over water." He scooped up a handful of sand and began rubbing at the material pulled tight over her shoulders.

"That feels good." She sighed, moving her back muscles under his hand. "I never asked. You speak seaborn tongue?"

"I speak a lot of languages. Why?"

"Look down."

Keeping their bodies between him and the shore, Tetaki slid his head out of the water. "How you doin'?"

"They work us." She patted his cheek. "Forget parsi, Tetaki-my-brother. The sea-talk's better here. Besides you have trouble setting your mouth around some of our sounds." She switched languages and said. "Any trouble about this morning?"

"The Keeper asked some questions. By the way, he knows sea-talk. So watch it. I said you were my adopted sister. You lost your parents when you were a baby and my family took you in. Thought you ought to know what I told him. Asked me about our father, how he stood among the seafolk. You been bragging?"

She sighed. "Some."

"Stupid."

"I've heard enough of that." She glanced around at Shounach who was rubbing lazily at her back.

"Think next time." Shounach straightened, stretched and took a look at the guard. "Our friend is starting to twitch."

Tetaki grinned. "Telling Gleia to think's a waste of time. Her mouth runs faster than her head."

"Fish!"

Shounach pinched her ear. "Shut up, Gleia. Tetaki, how much is left in the ship?"

"Hard to say. We've been bringing these things up for the past seventeen days. Looks like quite a bit left."

"Mmh. What about weapons?"

"I'd say they got those out themselves. First thing." He wobbled as he changed position slightly. "I'm getting stiff. Anyway, I've got no idea what half that stuff we pulled up is used for. Talking about ideas, if you can figure a way for getting at the Keeper, Jevat's not collared."

Gleia looked at Shounach. His eyes were bright with amusement. "Great idea, Tetaki," he said.

The seaborn looked from one grinning face to the other. "A bit late, I see. You figured out how we can reach him?"

"Sorry. You?"

"Not a glimmer." Tetaki scowled. "He's always surrounded by dozens of thissik."

The guard's shrill hysterical summons brought Gleia to her feet. "Watch yourself, brother, and keep Jevati safe," she whispered.

His dagger teeth gleamed briefly then he slid beneath the water and faded away, a shadow lost amid shadows.

Shounach strolled into the middle of the room and stood looking around. When Gleia started to speak, he shook his head and put a finger to his lips.

She watched, bewildered, as he dug in his bag, pulled out a faceted yellow crystal and began tossing it idly in the air as he moved about the room. In one corner a deep basin was filled with clear salt water from the bay. It was about two meters wide and three long. He stopped beside it. "What's this?"

She crossed to him and looked thoughtfully at the slowly rippling surface of the water. She knelt, pushed up her sleeve and thrust her arm into the water up to the elbow. A gentle current tugged at her arm and she pulled it out, shaking the sleeve back down. "They must have fixed the windpumps." She settled back on her heels and watched his face. "It's a bed."

He raised an eyebrow then walked away, whistling softly, tossing the crystal up and down, watching the play of moonlight on its facets. Gleia sniffed. "Big man."

He laughed and finished his circuit of the room then moved past her to the barred windows in the end wall. He slipped the crystal on the ledge of one of them and came back to her.

"What was that about?" she said.

He dropped beside her. "Checking to see if the thissik planted an ear or an eye on us."

"What?"

"Never mind. Any idea where the Keeper might sleep?"

She shook her head. "These houses are built to shelter a lot of people. Given Jaydugar's winters, it's better to build one big house, not a lot of little ones. At least when the people living there have some kind of ties. The seacoast cities on the mainland don't count. Too many strangers." After a minute's silence, she said, "You seem to know something about the thissik. I saw the Keeper recognized you. That should give you more of an idea where he could be than any knowledge of seaborn architecture."

"Good point." He scratched at his chin and stared thoughtfully past her shoulder. "Trouble is, what I know doesn't fit this . . ."

The door slammed open. Two thissik walked in. One approached Shounach and both carefully did not look at Gleia. "You are required, Fox. Come." He turned and walked out, the other following.

Gleia trailed Shounach to the door. "Luck," she said finally, not knowing what else to say.

He looked amused, his changeable eyes twinkling as he smiled into her anxious face. "Don't worry," he said. He pulled the door shut behind him. She heard the bar chunk home then the staccato clicks of his boots moving crisply down the corridor outside. She scuffed across the room and pressed her face against a windowgrill that let her see a short section of the pathway. After several minutes she saw the two thissik and Shounach heading for the Endhouse. She stayed at the window a while after they passed out of sight, then moved restlessly about the shadowy room, kicking at the hem of the still soggy cafta.

She stripped the cafta off. There were three windows in the back wall; the glass of one was broken and a stream of cooling air was pouring through it. The window grills had a series of stubbs at the top. She hung the cafta over a stub, spreading it out over the broken window so the air coming in would dry it a little faster. Trailing her fingers over the fitted stone, she moved slowly along the wall to the third window. The two moons were still behind the houseridge, but they were beginning to lighten the gloom outside. In the west above the bit of Endhouse roofs she could see a halo of red coming through the kala-shell roofing over the Day Court. She stood watching the steady glow as the Crow slid into view and arced toward the western horizon. She shivered and moved slowly along the wall, stopping at the cafta to squeeze the cloth between thumb and forefinger. It was still wet. She looked about the room. It was filled with shadow, soft dark shadow hanging still and comfortable. In the corner the rippling water surface painted a net of reflected light on wall and ceiling while fragments of moonlight danced across it. She sighed and lowered herself into the water. The lightweb danced wildly on the wall and lines of light rippled in arcs around her body.

She lifted her head as the door opened and Shounach came in. He walked briskly to the center of the room, looked briefly at her. "You're talkative tonight," she said. He shrugged the bag off his shoulder and lowered it to the floor, then dropped the dark bundle under his arm on top of it.

She moved and the water danced. She watched the light-web settle again then said, "What did he want?"

He squatted beside the bundle and began working knots loose. "Clothes for you. A veil. Some blankets." He began tossing things aside. "And someone stole the Ranga Eye from your Empty Man." Thrusting his hand into his mysterious bag, he began pulling out glassy blue spheres and a number of small rods.

"What's that for?"

"Bath's over. Climb out of there."

"Don't want to." She paddled to the side and propped herself up on crossed arms, watching him fit small rods together into a latticed pyramid.

"Shy?" He sounded amused.

Gleia sniffed. "Comfortable," she snapped.

"Too bad. I need you to bang on the door and get the two guards in here."

"Why?"

"You'll see."

"Do it yourself." Then she sighed. "Never mind, I'll do it." She rolled up onto the floor and shook out the thissik dress. Long. Black. Soft. She ran fingers over the material, enjoying the silken feel. "Nice. What is it?"

"Later. Get them in here. I want to try something."

As she slid the dress over her head, she saw him touch the point of the pyramid. When her head came through the neck opening, red and yellow light was cycling upward. The Juggler had settled himself behind the pyramid and was spreading an opaque white paint on his face.

She smoothed the dress down, excitement itching at her. Eyes sparkling, heart banging in her throat, she ran across the tiles and slammed her heel at the door, screaming for the guards. When they stood in the narrow opening, she swept a hand around, pointing at the Juggler. "He wants you."

Red and yellow light rose and fell at the Juggler's feet. Glowing blue balls circled the white mask, their changing blues flickering across the heavy paint.

Two balls
then four
doubling   doubling again   they were a circle of blue glowing   a blue halo   shimmering blue pale bright   dark   up and over   never stopping   never   sometimes many   sometimes melting away to two   always changing
   and the black rings around the Juggler's eyes
   narrowed   widened   and the dark mouth
   curving up
   curving down
a blue ball unfolded
was a shimmering golden dragon swooping the circle
and was gone and   another
was a jewel-bright dancer
and was gone and   another   was   a
and was gone and   another   was
and was gone
and was
and

Gleia blinked. The two thissik were glassy-eyed, rigid. Shounach caught the balls that remained and set them carefully aside.

"Thissik." His voice was gentle, musical. "Put your weapons on the floor."

To Gleia's open-mouthed wonder, the guards bent stiffly and placed their rod-weapons on the floor.

"Pick them up." The whisper came hastily. Gleia saw Shounach frowning as he seemed to struggle against an invisible pull. The thissik opened with the same jerky movements. "Return to your posts and forget what has happened." He waited tensely until the door was shut again, then he started breathing again.

"Why'd you send them away?" Gleia sat on the floor watching him as he began cleaning the white from hands and face.

A corner of his mouth curled up. "Tough little creatures. Hope I got them out in time." He fingered the collar and his smile broadened. "How close would you want to get to them?"

She grimaced. "Point taken. Now tell me what all that was about."

"Information. Possibilities." He yawned. "You want a blanket over you tonight, you'll have to share these." He touched the bundle with his toe. "Since we're supposed to be paired. Trust me?"

Gleia shrugged. "It's that or shiver."

Gleia woke shivering. She had rolled out of the blankets onto the tiled floor. Icy drafts from the broken window circled along the tiles. She jumped up and rubbed hands over her arms trying to warm them a little. Shounach was deeply asleep, traces of white visible along the line of his jaw. She wrinkled her nose at him and began pacing about the room, toes curled, walking on the sides of her feet.

Picking at the dead skin poking up from the broken blisters in her palms, she crossed the room and stood looking out the end window, the one with all its glass. Outside, the night was still and dark. Both moons had set. The Crouching Cat was low in the west, the two brilliant eyestars floating just above the horizon. *Late,* she thought. She pressed her face against the bars and glanced toward the Endhouse. There was a red glow shimmering above the roof.

Trembling with excitement, she ran to Shounach, went down on her knees and began shaking him awake. In one swift surge he was up, awake, frowning. "What is it?"

She sat back on her heels. "There's something I want to show you." Grinning at the expression on his face she jumped up and fled back to the window. The red glow was still there. "Shounach!"

Yawning, wrapping the blanket about his long lean body, he came across to stand beside her. "What is it?" he repeated.

"Look."

He leaned past her. "At what?"

"No. I want to know if it means the same thing to you. Look!" She knew the moment he realized what the glow could mean. He stiffened and his fingers closed around the bars, one hand on each side of her head. "I see."

"Finally." She ducked under his arm and ran across to the blanket still on the floor. Sitting down on it, she rubbed her feet and watched Shounach's back. After a minute his hands came down and turned to face her. "He's always tired," she said. In the faint light from the stars she could see his mouth twitch into a smile. He crossed the tiles with three quick strides and dropped on the blanket beside her.

"You think the Keeper's still working." He unwound the blanket. "Come here before you freeze."

She stretched out beside him, beginning to feel warm again as his body heat reached her through the thissik dress. With the blanket beneath them and one tucked around them, the cold air was a pleasant nip rather than a bone-shaking chill. "I think it's the best chance we've got."

He tugged at a curl. "Well?"

"They've got the windpumps working."

"That doesn't explain much."

"That means they're using the underways. Remember the pool in the Day Court?" His eyes narrowed then he nodded. "There's a conduit that runs from there straight to the bay. A big one."

His eyes darkened; in the dim light she couldn't see color but the change meant he was feeling amused. "Leave me something to do, love, or I'll start feeling useless." His voice was filled with laughter.

She pushed the hair back off her face. "Plenty of problems left for would-be heroes." She yawned. The warmth under the blanket was blending with the aftermath of her surge of excitement to make her sleepy. Her eyelids dropped. She snuggled against Shounach and drifted off to a deep and dreamless sleep.

The next day dragged by. At Horli-set Gleia and Shounach were barely talking to each other. Gleia flounced away and stood at water's edge, ignoring man and thissik until the guard ordered Shounach to fetch her. He wouldn't let them swim, just herded them back to Twohouse. They picked up two food trays and a jug of water, then he marched them to their room and slammed the door on them.

Gleia crossed to the window and pressed her face against the bars. Behind her she could hear Shounach stripping, the small splashes as he slid into the basin and started washing. She closed her eyes. "Juggler."

"What?" She heard a larger splash as he pulled himself out of the water.

Watching smuts and ash drift past the window, she said, "There's a screen in slots at the end of the pool nearest the outside wall. Pull it out."

She heard the soft slither of clothes as Shounach got dressed. Then he padded to his tray and sat down. She heard him pour some water in a cup. "Big man," she sneered and turned around. He was sitting with a plate on his lap, chewing placidly on a mouthful of cold fish. His eyes, icy gray, came up to meet hers then dropped to his plate. He went on eating.

Pushing impatiently at her greasy hair, Gleia stalked over to the basin. She untied her sandals and kicked them away, ripped off the veil and flung it aside, then lowered herself into the water. The gentle current washed the top off her accumulation of grime and sweat, taking a large part of her irritation with them; as her body cooled so did her temper. She bobbed against the outlet, eyes closed, letting the water work the tension out of her muscles. Finally, she turned and began struggling with the screen.

Muttering impatiently Shounach stalked over, jerked the screen out of its slots and tossed it aside. He thrust a hand at her. "Come out of there."

She splashed out and stood dripping on the tiles.

"Drowned rat." The green was back in his eyes.

Gleia plucked at the fine black material that clung with disconcerting fidelity to her body. "Wonder if this shrinks."

She dripped over to the window bars. "How come you know so much about the thissik?" She stripped off the dress and pulled the wrinkled cafta over her head. "Just who are you, Juggler, and why'd the Keeper call you Fox?" She hung the thissik dress over the stubs, then came back to him, pushing at her hair. "I'd kill for a jar of soap."

He was sitting, his back against the wall, his hands resting lightly on his knees, his eyes flickering between green and blue. "I'll remember that."

"Well?"

"I could spin a tale for you." He sounded comfortably drowsy. "Oddly enough I'd rather not."

"Oh." She settled in front of him, arms wrapped around her knees. The light was still good enough to let her see his face. It had a worn look as if time had rubbed away at the flesh until it was like very soft, very thin, very old leather, crossed and recrossed with hundreds of fine wrinkles. He had an unconscious arrogance, a sense of superiority so ingrained he'd never know it was there. Very much a loner. She could recognize one of her own kind. Could recognize a deliberate distancing. Allowing no one to creep inside his shell and touch the places where he was vulnerable.

She sighed and began examining the palms of her hands. The blisters were filming over with tough new skin. She picked at the dead skin until she'd peeled it loose, then pulled her palms several times over her hair to work the oil into her rough, crackling skin. After a while she looked back at Shounach. "I twitch-talked to Tetaki when I went to stand by the water. Told him to get in here tonight if he could."

"Twitch-talk?"

"The seaborn do it." She smiled. "They say a good twitcher can put a year's history in a single wiggle." Shounach raised both brows. "Well, maybe that's a slight exaggeration." She sighed. "Tetaki says I'm worse at it than a one-summer wiggler with a bad case of stutters."

"It's the truth and you know it." Tetaki came

out of the water, the faint light gleaming on nacreous needle teeth when he grinned at them.

Gleia swung around. "How was it?"

"A mess." His thin nose wrinkled with disgust. "Once I thought I'd have to go back. The conduit narrowed to a hole the size of my arm. But the plug was soft enough to dig through."

"What about the outlet?"

"The screen was a little warped but I could move it." His light-green eyes narrowed as he scanned her face. "I know you, Gleia-my-sister. What's this leading up to?"

Gleia started to rise then settled back. While she and Tetaki had been talking, Shounach had crossed the room and was looking out the window. "Is the light on?"

Without answering he walked slowly back and stood looking down at them. "It's on," he said finally. "Too early to tell if he's sitting up to work. What's your situation, Tetaki? Could you get out around Zebset?"

"No problem. The thissik don't bother guarding us. They count on the collars to keep us around. Why?"

Gleia leaned forward. "The Day Court lights were on past Zebset last night. We think the Keeper might be working late."

Tetaki's grin widened until it was no longer a grin but a snarl of rage. "Tonight," he hissed. "I want this off tonight." He pulled at the ring, then his taut body folded in on itself. "They might just leave the lights on all night."

"Well, Tetaki-my-brother, that's why we need you. The Day Court pool is full and it has the scrollwork screen around it. Swim up the conduit and take a look, then let us know what you saw."

The seaborn closed his eyes, his breath grew

harsh and irregular, then the gasps grew quieter
as he worked to calm himself. "Sorry about acting
like a cheksa in a feeding fit," he said. "But I'm
not going to wait till Zebset. I'm going in as soon
as the Crow's down."

"To look."

He laughed. "To look."

Shounach was a shadow in the shadow veils.
Gleia prowled about, rubbing at her arms, more
nervous than cold. She kicked at the ragged cafta
swaying around her with a life of its own as the
tattered cloth answered the strengthening breeze
coming through the broken window. Both sleeves
were gone, one torn off in the fight with Korl, the
other cut away because one sleeve made her feel
like a clown. It was heavy with ground-in dirt and
greasy sweat and torn in a hundred places. The
black thissik dress fluttered at the window. Gleia
wandered over and took it down, looking briefly at
the sky as she did.

The Crow's tail was still visible. *Half an hour at
least before he goes in.* She pulled the cafta off and
dropped it on the floor, then worked head and
arms into the thissik dress, wiggled around searching for the sleeve holes, then smoothed the dress
down over her body. As she pressed the front clo-
sure shut, she said. "This closing they make. I
wish I had it on all my caftas. I get so sick of all
those ties." She ran her hand along her side, enjoying the soft sensuous feel of the material. "No
wrinkles," she said. "What do they make this cloth
out of? Even avrishum needs to hang a while. Not
that I've ever seen much avrishum." She waited.
"Shounach?"

When he still didn't answer, she turned and stood
leaning back against the wall watching him. Aab

was floating over her shoulder now, sending through
the window enough light to transform the sitting
man into a statue of black and silver. Legs crossed,
booted feet tucked up on his thighs. Eyes paled to
a shimmery silver. Face with a soft unfocused look.
The backs of his hands resting on his knees, hands
relaxed, fingers curling upward. As she watched
she began to feel the stillness that spread out from
him to fill the room. She touched the edges of it
and felt herself settling into a quiet peace where
she was one with the earth and the stones around
her. She slid down and sat leaning against the
wall. Stillness washed over her, filled her, expanded
her, without knowing she touched him, began to
merge with him. . . .

He moved and the stillness snapped back inside
her.

"Why did you do that?" Her mouth felt numb,
unused to forming words.

His eyes narrowed as he bent toward her; she
sensed puzzlement and surprise in him. Then he
said quietly, "I needed to consider the consequences
of intervention."

"What?" She shook her head, still feeling strange.

"Gleia," he began then stopped, looked hesitant.
That startled her; it seemed out of character. The
moon was shining on his face, painting silver on
his cheekbones and black in the lines running from
nose to mouth.

"What do you think of the Keeper?"

Gleia rubbed a thumb along her upper lip, then
she shrugged. "He's a slaver, holding us here against
our will. He sends out raiding parties capturing,
even killing, people who've done him no harm."

"That all?"

A lock of hair fell across her face and she shoved
it back impatiently. "No. Of course not. If you look

from the other side, he's a man working under impossible pressures to save his people." She opened her hands and stared into the palm. "Not like Korl."

"Impossible pressures?"

The lock of hair fell down again, brushing at her lips; she slapped it back with a muttered exclamation. "I don't know what they are. How could I? What does that matter, just look at the man!"

Shounach nodded. "A thissik ship has five castes on board," he said slowly. "Engineering. Life support. Navigation. Administration. Trading. Each caste contains a minimum of four extended families but the traders are the only ones that leave the ship. Ever." There was a faint sadness in his voice, a remote compassion on his face. "I'd say there are over a thousand thissik on this Cern."

Gleia shook her head. "That has to be wrong. I've only seen a dozen altogether."

"In the rooms beyond the Day Court I think you'd find row after row of dreaming thissik, waiting in improvised life support for the Keeper to prepare a place for them. A shelter." He laid stress on the last word. "They were born within ship's walls and expected to die there. A thousand-year culture drowned when that ship came down." He brooded a minute, eyes focused beyond her head. "I wonder if they'll make it. They're fortunate in their Keeper."

"The ones we've seen are?"

"Traders, of course. They're better able to handle openness."

"Why the strange attitude toward females?"

He looked down at his hand. Again she sensed a sadness in him. "Rumor says there are fewer thissik born each generation, fewer fertile females. Their women are both adored and enslaved, kept in luxurious idleness."

She shivered. "I'd go crazy with boredom." With a yawn and a groan, she stretched arms and legs. "Talk about impossible pressures. Ugh! Shounach."

"What?"

"We can't kill him. That would be like ... like cutting all their throats."

"Consequences of intervention."

"Fancy words for murder." She wrinkled her nose, then shook her head. "The Keeper's small and tired, but he's no fool. Jevati won't get near him when he's awake. Tetaki will have to use his knife. He's very good at throwing it."

"Would he insist on that?"

She rubbed her forehead, then smoothed her hand back over her hair. "Tetaki's no killer." She laughed. "Except when he's trading."

"Mmmh. Would he trade with the thissik if he had a chance?"

Gleia grinned. "Yes."

"That's all? Just yes with no qualifications?"

She giggled. "Wave a few market in front of Tetaki and watch him salivate." She hugged her arms across her breasts. "His mouth must be watering already over the things he's bringing up from the ship. Probably has a few little tidbits stashed away hoping to collect them if he gets away. Can you get the Keeper to listen?"

"I can try."

"He's going to kill us when the clean-up's finished, isn't he."

He looked sharply at her. "So you caught that."

"So am I stupid?" She sniffed. "Shounach the Juggler. Juggling lives." She yawned and closed her eyes. "This night is crawling along. Where are you going after you get loose?"

"Here and there."

"Off world?"

"You say that with remarkable equanimity for a young woman in a low-level technology."

She chuckled drowsily. "Big words, big words. Some of the seaborn have forgotten less about their origins than the other sorts here. Temokeuu says it's because of long lives and a very stable culture."

"Your father?"

"You say that with remarkable equanimity," she murmured. "Some people consider my relationship with him sick and shameful—mammal consorting with fish—and the other way around depending on who's talking."

"Affection transcends form," he said gravely.

"Affectation obscures sense." She snorted and opened her eyes. "Did you crash here too? Temokeuu told me about the . . ." she hesitated, trying to remember just what he'd said, "the way things are around our world and our suns. Like marshland trapped with quicksand, some places safe enough and others that twist and tear the starships until they are destroyed or tumble down on us." She pulled her knees up and wrapped her arms around them. "Temokeuu says there are hundreds of different worlds out there. Is it like going from Cern to Cern? He says the distances the ships travel are so great I can't even begin to imagine them. Have you seen many worlds? Are they anything like Jaydugar? Tell me. . . ."

"Slow down." He was laughing so hard he swallowed the words. "Later, Gleia," he managed. "Plenty of time later."

The bar chunked back and the door swung open. Tetaki looked in. "Come on," he said. "The only guard is half-asleep by the front gate."

He led them swiftly through a maze of corridors then ducked into a room. A section of the wall had been knocked to powder by a stone spat out during the eruption. Tetaki wriggled through and helped Gleia out. Shounach had more trouble, being both longer and wider than either of the other two, but he got out, leaving some skin on the wall stone.

Tetaki strolled down the slope and waited for them on the path. "The keeper's in there all right, but he's not alone for very long," he said. "Thissik go in and out all the time. I spent almost half an hour there. He's sitting at a worktable, writing when he's not talking with the other thissik." He shook his head. "We'll have to kill him fast, let Jevati get the key and get out of there like a triseal with a cheksa on its tail."

"No! Tetaki, we can't kill him."

"How the hell else is Jevati going to get the key?"

"I'll take care of that," Shounach said quietly. "If you can get me in there."

Tetaki ran his eyes over Shounach's length. "How good are you underwater?"

"Good enough. If you'll provide a tow."

Tetaki nodded. "That'd do it. You're right." He grinned suddenly "What the hell. Rather not kill him. I cooled off a while back, started thinking about getting loose."

Night-black water slapped softly at the pier's stone pillars, throwing back flickers of moonlight. Aab was directly overhead, swimming in and out of thickening clouds, while Zeb hovered low in the western sky. The wind tugged persistently at Gleia's hair, lifting the heavy oily mass from her neck. She put her hand on Jevati's shoulder, shocked by her painful fragility. "You sure you want to do this?" She shook her head. "You look terrible."

Jevati grinned. "I could say the same." She wrinkled her nose. "You stink."

With a low laugh, Gleia pushed at her hair. "I know what you mean. When there's no breeze I even offend myself." She looked up at the dark almost invisible bulk of Endhouse. "Did Tetaki tell you?"

Jevati nodded.

A seaborn jumped down from the pier with a coil of rope in one hand. As Gleia and Jevati watched, the rope was cut in two pieces, and loops worked in both ends of each piece. Shounach slipped his arms in the loops on one piece and began wading out from the shore.

"Come here, Gleia," Tetaki flipped the rope about, slapping it against his thigh. "Time to put you in harness." He slipped the loops over her arms and pulled them up to her shoulders. Then he tugged at the rope. "That hurt?"

"No. The sleeves keep it away from my skin." She moved her arms tentatively. "Feels peculiar."

Tetaki laughed softly. "You can stand that." He sobered. "You'll go in on your back. There's quite a current coming out. You'll have Vanni and Uvoi towing you. Don't try to help. Just relax. When you feel two jerks like this—" he tugged on the rope—"that means you're about under one of the standpipes. Pull yourself up. Breathe. When you're ready, tug three times, then three more." He looked past her. Gleia turned.

Shounach floated on his back. He was smiling and his eyes were darker than usual. *He's enjoying this*, she thought. He breathed deeply several times then took a normal breath and tugged on the rope. His body went smoothly under the water.

Gleia closed her eyes. She was terrified of shut-in places. She'd never told anyone, not even Temokeuu. The thought of going so far in the dark unable to breathe brought her close to panic. When she opened her eyes Tetaki, Jevati and the others were gone. Vanni and Uvoi stood quietly at her side waiting for her. She looked up at the moon, knowing she could wait here without shame. Tetaki would bring the key to her. But she couldn't do it. In spite of her terror, curiosity drove her to go. She had to SEE. She waded out, lay on her back. When she was ready, she tugged on the rope and they took her down.

The glimmer of moonlight vanished too quickly and she was gliding through a blackness colder than death. She felt a tiny touch on her arm, then another, then hundreds more were tickling at her face and hands. She almost panicked before she realized the touches had to be weeds growing on the walls. Her lungs began to hurt; blood pounded in her ears. She almost missed the double tug. It came again and she struggled up, feeling at the weedy circle and pulling her head up until she was gasping and spitting out water in the narrow circumference of the standpipe. She stayed there until she felt cleansed, then breathed deep, breathed light, held her breath and signaled them to take her on. They pulled her back into the wet dark and the weeds fluttered about her again. Like fingers laughing. Mocking her.

The signal. More air. A precious faint light high above. And darkness. Black water. Weed. The chafing pull of the rope. A ghost of light. Flashes around her like tiny fish. Not fish. Reflections of red light on the twisting weed. Red light. Like swimming in blood. Brighter and brighter. She was arching upwards, hands about her, helping her. Her head broke the surface gently like a leaf drifting up instead of down. Hands covered her mouth. Breathe in ... out ... through the nose. Quiet. Then she was clinging to the edge of the pool. They were all there, Shounach, Tetaki and the other seaborn.

They waited. The thissik came in and out. The Keeper was seldom alone for more than five minutes. Finally the intervals between visits grew longer and longer. Still they waited. The glow tubes blinked out around the court leaving three still lighted by the worktable. The Keeper was reading a paper and marking on it with a stylus, stopping every few minutes to sip at a cup sending up thin wavers of steam.

Shounach was up and over the screen in a quick smooth movement. Then he strolled toward the Keeper.

The thissik looked up at the small sound of the splashing water. His hand darted toward a small dark cube then drew back as he recognized his visitor. "Juggler." He smiled. "I've been expecting you, Starfox."

Shounach reached into his bag and pulled out two glowspheres. Smiling slightly, he began putting them into the air. One two, up and over, more into the circle, up and over. After several revolutions another object circled with the spheres, a clear egg-shaped crystal that began sending out veils of soft color as it warmed to his touch.

Gleia began to shudder until she barely had the strength to cling to the poolside. The Ranga Eye. *He stole it,* she thought. *He wanted the Eye. Shounach.* She felt sick.

"You wanted this," the Juggler said. The Eye left the circle and flew in a lazy arc toward the Keeper. His hands seemed to move of their own volition, reaching out, catching the Eye. He looked down at what he held and could not look away.

Shounach slipped the glowspheres back in the bag. "Jevati," he said quietly.

Tetaki boosted her out of the pool and followed after her. The other seaborn surged out behind him, but Gleia didn't attempt to move.

"The key. What does it look like?" Jevati spoke in a hushed murmur.

"Small black rod. On a chain around his neck."

Jevati nodded. As she sped across the tiles toward the rigid Keeper, Shounach bent over the screen and took Gleia's hand. "Push," he said.

She stumbled over the screen and nearly fell. He caught her, then stood looking down at her. "Almost over."

"Will there be a happy ending in our tale?"

"Ending?"

"Hunh! I'm not in the mood for ponderous platitudes."

His eyes burned blue and he nearly choked on stifled laughter.

Jevati came back with the key. When all the collars were off, Shounach dropped them into the pool. Then he crossed to the table where Tetaki was indulging his curiosity by poking through the papers and picking up and putting down the bits of instrumentation scattered among them.

"Want to leave? Or see if you can do a deal with the Keeper?"

Tetaki grinned. "You need to ask? What about him? He wasn't anxious to listen the last time. I've had all the collaring I want."

"He'll listen."

Tetaki rubbed at his chin. "Worth a try. Can you wake him up a bit?"

Shounach leaned over the table and plucked the

Eye from the Keeper's hands. The thissik screamed, then collapsed. Dipping his hand into the bag, Shounach brought out a black disc. He reached across the table and pressed it against the thissick's neck, held it there a few seconds, then pulled it away and stood watching.

The Keeper sighed, then sat up. He moved his eyes over the collarless seaborn, then looked at Shounach. "What now?"

"Up to you. Do we leave or talk a bit?"

"What did you give me?"

"Inaltaree. It'll wear off in about two hours, that dose. And you'll crash for twenty."

The Keeper groaned. "I. . . ." He touched the papers in front of him. "I don't have twenty hours to spare."

Shounach's wide mouth curled into a slow smile. "Tetaki, here's a man you should understand. Proud as a seaborn. Won't take help."

Tetaki rubbed his thumb across his fingertips. "Might buy himself some if he works it right."

The Keeper straightened, a glow brightening in his eyes. His tail had been moving listlessly across the floor. It came up to a carefully non-committal angle. He touched fingertip to fingertip and let out a long slow breath. "Offer," he said crisply.

Gleia lowered herself onto the screen. "I think it's going to work," she murmured as she watched the animated exchanged between the Keeper and Tetaki. The other seaborn threw in a word now and then, skillfully backing their leader. Shounach watched with a sardonic smile on his pale face, thoroughly enjoying the scene. Gleia touched her tongue to her upper lip then dropped her eyes to her hands. "How do you feel, little fish?"

"A little tired, that's all. Fuss, fuss, worse than a

mother." She sounded amused. "I'll rest when I get to Radnavar."

"You still have to make that journey?"

"Nothing has changed."

Gleia pushed at her filthy hair. When she glanced back at Shounach, he seemed to feel her eyes and smiled at her, then he went back to watching the lively bargainers. The argument was picking up momentum and gathering noise as it moved along. Gleia closed her eyes. Worlds on worlds opened up for her with Shounach, but there was no way Jevati could finish alone, her frailty now after this brief interlude was evidence enough of that. "What happened to the *Dragonfish*?"

"As soon as they took off with you, I put the anchor over and bagged the sail. Unless the cable broke or some stickyfinger came along, it might even be there still. If not, plenty of boats at the pier."

"We'll need one anyway. I can't swim that far and you shouldn't." She pushed herself onto her feet. "With the current behind me I won't need towing. You go first."

Jevati's cool smooth fingertips touched Gleia's cheek in a brief caress. Then she was gone, tipped over back into the water. Gleia looked a last time at Shounach, then eased her body into the water. She sucked in a breath and dived into the darkness.

FIFTH SUMMER'S TALE
(PART ONE)

Southwind My Mother

Spring came finally to Cern Radnaver and Gleia grew restless again. When the ice melted in the harbor, the soft wind that blew in from the south whispered to her of things she'd never seen. While the double sun Horli-Hesh pushed up over the cern behind her, she climbed a rock nesting in the noisy water near the harbor's entrance, displacing as she did this a few dozen birds and more small scurrying things she didn't bother trying to identify. Legs crossed, hood pulled well forward to shield her head from the blue sun's bite, she perched on the rock and stared out toward the open water.

"Southwind," she murmured. "I was a beggar, then a thief, then a slave in all but name in Carhenas. And I left Carhenas at my own pleasure. I was daughter to Temokeuu-my-father, adopted

into the seaborn, comfortable and warmed by
affection. And I left him. Southwind, I live in comfort and affection here with my seaborn sister Jevati,
as much almost from her family, especially the
little wigglers who follow me about like puppies
and listen to me like I'm the greatest thing since
sugar melons. All this, Southwind sweet wind. All
this and now. . . . And now. . . ." She laughed and
flung out her arms, embracing the wind that pushed
against her.

"Talking to yourself?" Jevati's contralto broke
through the noise of the wind and water.

Gleia grinned down at her friend. "Talking to
the wind, little fish." Jevati was plumper these
days with a silver sheen to the delicate blue-green
of her skin. Once again she was a cherished daughter instead of a sick and neglected wife. Once again
she danced in waters with her own, filled with joy
and lightness. Gleia dropped onto her knees and
watched Jevati struggle up the side of the rock.
The seaborn were not made for climbing.

Breathing in quick short pants, Jevati fell into a
tired sprawl beside Gleia. She sat in silence, staring out into the wind until a line of vandars flew
overhead, strong wings cutting into the wind, eerie cries counterpointing the continual brush-brush
of the water. She twisted round and rested a
webbed hand on Gleia's shoulder. "You're not content here any more, my mammal. You want to
leave us."

Gleia curved her neck and rested her cheek briefly
on the hand. Then she straightened, looked down
at hands opening and closing. "I don't know, little
fish." And knew as she said it, it was a lie. She was
silent again for a while. The wind coiled around
them, warmer than the rock, smelling of summer
and green growing things. Off to the south a small

boat was running before the wind, heading for the
harbor. She watched the white triangle of sail grow
larger as the crew brought the boat skillfully past
the Grinders and into the channel. "Where would I
go?"

"I thought you might want to go home. Temokeuu . . ."

"Home!" Gleia threw herself recklessly back on
the rock, arm flung across her face to protect it
from the sting of hard blue Hesh. "Home." The
word was muffled by her sleeve. Even more softly,
she said, "I've never had a home, just temporary
resting place, even with Temokeuu."

"I don't understand you." Jevati stroked her hand
along the arm that passed over her friend's face.
"You've got a home with us. Always."

"I know." Gleia felt a sudden weariness. Jevati
said she didn't understand, but didn't mean it.
The friendship between us is real and deep. But
this is a part of me she can't possibly understand.
Where was I born? When? Of what parents? She
moved her arm a little so she could see her friend's
face. A sudden revulsion for her wallow in self-pity
brought her sitting up with a sharp laugh. "Southwind's making me itch, that's all." Then she looked
past Jevati. She sucked in her breath, jumped to
her feet, waved wildly.

The figure standing at the tiller waved back,
beckoned to another, jumped overboard. Moments
later Tetaki was clambering awkwardly up the
rock. He collapsed grinning beside the two women
"This penchant of yours for sitting atop rocks,
Gleia-my-sister." He chuckled and shook his head,
scattering drops of water over her arm and leg.

"Tetaki, what're you doing here?"

"Visiting my sister."

"Idiot."

"Well then, we're here to set up some things for the thissik."

"How did they winter?"

"Might have been better. Most of them lived. They're starting to wake the sleepers. Got most of the houses cleared out, but they need help with growing food and harvesting the sea." He grinned again, nacreous pointed teeth gleaming bloodily in Horli's read light. "Month or two from now, the Keeper and I . . . remember the Keeper?"

Gleia snorted. "No winter ice in my head, brother. I remember the Keeper. What about him?"

"He's bought into a trade circuit with Temokeuu-my-father. We're going to hit the ports and cerns south of here far as the Drylands." He reached out and took her hand. "Temokeuu'd like you to come home with me."

Jevati stirred, gave a small sharp cry quickly cut off. A protest. Gleia saw her troubled face and felt a pang of regret. Then she moved her shoulders impatiently and turned back to Tetaki. I'm not ready yet, brother." She looked past him toward the Grinders. "You came from the south."

"Got a message for you."

Gleia stiffened, a fluttering in her stomach.

"Juggler was mad as hell when you disappeared."

"So?" She looked down and found her hands clenched into fists. She straightened out her fingers and rested them on her thighs. "That was a long time ago. There's a winter between us now."

"Well, I calmed him down by explaining about Jevati's widow journey."

"Then he knew where I was. He could have been here if he wanted to." Again she looked down, feeling a growing chill that made her tremble in spite of the day's warmth and the soft pressure of the wind.

"The thissik needed him. So he stayed."

She closed her eyes, remembered the worn cynical face of the Juggler. "That doesn't sound like him."

Tetaki laughed. "You knew him—how long? Three days? Four?"

Gleia shrugged. "You said you had a message."

"Right." He flipped a hand at the boat rocking beside a pier, sails taken down, the seaborn crew sitting on the pier, legs dangling, waiting for him. "We're just back from Thrakesh. Left the Juggler there. He said for you to come if you want, but get there by the end of this month or don't bother." He bent down and touched her cheek. "That's it, sister." He straightened. "Got work to do. See you when." He eased himself over the edge and began climbing down the rock.

Jevati dropped her head onto her crossed arms a moment, then looked over at Gleia. "What are you going to do?" Her voice was soft and sad, her mouth drawn down into a gentle droop.

"You know it already, little fish." She got to her feet and stood looking to the south. "Shove everything into the *Dragonfish* and go. Help me?"

Jevati rose and moved across the rock to stand beside Gleia. After a minute she slid her arm about Gleia's waist and leaned against her thin nervous body. "I don't want to. I will, of course."

Gleia hugged her affectionately. "Little fish."

"Will you be back?"

"Don't know. I won't forget you, Jevati. That's all I can be sure of." She felt the seaborn trembling. "I'm sorry. I can't help it."

Gleia left Jevati staring wistfully after her as she sent the *Dragonfish* quartering the wind, her heart as light as the wisps of cloud skimming over the spring blue of the sky.

For a week she sailed south and west, keeping the great black cliffs on her right, each day much like the one before. Occasionally one of the seaborn would surface, wave a greeting and sink under again. Sometimes one would swim alongside the boat to talk with her awhile. She was amused to find herself something of a hero among the seaborn because of her part in turning the stranded thissik from slavers to a vigorous new market for seaborn trade. Her very small part. But there was a rising excitement among the seaborn about Tetaki's coming trade circuit.

On the eighth day the wind was suddenly gone. The sail slapped idly against the mast and the boat rocked up and down, creeping south along the Sestatiri ocean current. Gleia grimaced at the empty sky. Horli was high and Hesh had moved behind her so that the day was hot and still and red, but free of Hesh's dangerous bite. The sluggish current took the boat along, bobbing like a long slim cork on the purple-tinged water. As the day crept on, she stripped off her cafta and went over the side. The water was cool, moving in long slow-rolls. She swam along beside the boat until she was tired, then pulled herself back inside, stretched out naked and unprotected in the bottom of the boat and let the sun dry her body. Sun-bathing was rare on Jaydugar. Hesh would take the skin off any fool who tried it. The rocking of the boat lulled her into a heavy sleep.

The creaking of the sail against the mast jerked her awake. She sat up, clutching at her head as a dull pain throbbed behind her eyes. The wind was back, coming from the north this time. Gleia uncleated the mainsheet and let the boom swing out so the sail filled with wind. The little boat began skimming southwest again. She breathed a sigh of relief, glad to be free of the calm.

Horli was low in the west, half of her red circle gone behind the stone. Gleia felt the wind pushing at her, cold fingers pushing through her sweat-stiffened hair. In spite of the growing chill in the wind, she felt sticky and uncomfortable and nervous for no reason she could discern.

The sun vanished completely, leaving streaks of crimson and violet along the horizon. By the time these had faded, Aab was already high in the sky and glowing like a crescent of milky opal. Gleia looked about. She wasn't sleepy, and the night was bright enough. She decided to sail as long as she could into the night to make up for the day's lack of progress.

Later, when Aab and Zeb were both close to setting, the wind turned erratic, eventually circling around until it swung north to south and back to north. Curls of fog began peeling off the water. Gleia sighed with regret and brought the nose of the boat into the wind. After lowering the sail, she dug out a blanket and settled herself to sleep. She drifted into a series of nightmares, dipping in and out of sleep as the fog thickened and closed in around the *Dragonfish*.

A dull thud and a jarring impact that sent the *Dragonfish* rolling violently woke her. She jerked up and looked about hazily, her mind dulled by sleep. She heard shouts, saw dim figures bending over the railing of a ship looming out of the fog like some ancient monster of the sea. Splashes and a thud; men overside, one in the boat, others in the sea beside her boat. Hands closed over the side. They were up and in. Catchvine slapped around her arms and torso. The misty figures stood

over her a minute then were shouting for a line
from the ship.

That night she woke in darkness with her wrists
hurting. Groans and stenches filled the hold-section
around her as the other captives cried out in their
sleep, broke wind, or let overburdened bladders
find relief. She pressed her wrists together, trying
to quiet the pain. She had struggled to force her
hands through the cuffs until her flesh was scraped
raw and her muscles strained, then leaned back
against cushions that smelled of old sweat and
other less pleasant things.

Cushions. Thinking about them amused her
briefly. She folded her hands in her lap, smiling
into the darkness. When the Captain had looked
over the plunder from her boat, the caftas and
uncompleted work the men had dumped in front
of him, his eyes had sparked with greed. He knew
the worth of what he saw. His scorn altered
instantly. He looked from the embroidery to her.
"Your work?"

When she nodded, he grunted with satisfaction
and beckoned to one of his men. Gleia was led off
and taken down into a forward hold. Inside the
black and stinking enclosure, the seaman's lantern
threw a flickering light over a mixed clutter of
chained bodies. Two catmen, drugged into dull-
ness to keep them from fighting against the chains
until they killed themselves. A leather-skinned
Drylander blinking watery eyes at the light that
was painful for him. Six or seven women of various races.

As Gleia waited unhappily, toes curling up off
the slimy floor, a luscious young girl with a pretty,
sullen face was kicked unceremoniously off the
cusions and chained farther down on bare boards.

Gleia was shoved forward and chained in her place. In the uncertain light she was dismayed to see the girl's rage and jealousy.

Now she looked into the thick blackness toward the place where the girl lay. *So dependent on the valuation of others.* She shook her head. *Better to be gifted than pretty.* Chains rattled as she lifted her hand to rub again at the brands on her cheek. *A plain brown thing with a face badly marred. The Captain's first opinion. Not worth selling, barely worth raping. The skill made the difference. Shining gold on the hoof.* She jerked about on the cushions, itchy with annoyance and frustration. Plans shipwrecked. *Something has to be done. A woman who simply wants to be left alone to do things her way should be left alone. As it is she's prey to any lout with the strength take her. Me. I am prey. Aschla curse them.* She moved her hands again, listening to the clink of the metal. *Slave. I'm tired of having to work myself loose over and over again.* With a sigh she lay back on her meager cushions and closed her eyes.

She woke again to the sound of shouts, violent and continuous, muffled somewhat by the walls of the ship but still audible. She listened a moment, then grinned into the fetid darkness. The Captain was arguing with a Thrakeshi official about wharfage rates. This went on for a while longer, then the voices dropped to a conversational level as they reached agreement. When the sounds outside diminished, she began to hear chains clinking as the other captives awoke and sat up.

Some time later she heard several loud thumps then blinked as a square of light opened above them and bold yellow light flooded the hold, shocking tears from her. When she climbed out on the deck the first in a chain of five, she stood blinking at black cliffs looming over the ship.

The markets of Thrakesh were famous. The stalls were barges moored in the ever-warm waters of the harbor. On market days the blue circle was a magic world of color and noise. The wharves and warehouses, inns and taverns, the decaying hovels and more substantial homes, all these were built on a narrow crescent of land circling the horse-shoe bay and backing up against the mighty cliffs. The city itself perched on that sheer stone rise, a hundred meters over the commercial area.

Following the irregular curve of the cliff, a thick stone wall shut off from view all but the bright gilded roofs of the great houses of the lords of Thrakesh and of the merchant masters. The human sea-wrack that came to land here where the hot springs on the harbor bottom made life easy during the long winter, the ragged boatmen, the longshoremen, the hired officials, the visitors, the traders: these outsiders could look with envy and awe and resentment at the roofs, but none of them dared climb the twisting paths that led up to the gates in that wall, gates that stayed mockingly open all day and half the night.

The black cliffs that looked so formidable were riddled by blowholes and bubbles. Some of these were used to store food against siege, others emerged to the air high up on the cliffs and housed barrels of oil that could be heated and dumped on attackers.

The traders of Thrakesh were notorious for their scrupulous honesty and for the outrageous prices they charged for that honesty. The market was the safest place on the coast—if the trader or traveler had enough money and cared to pay the price of safety.

Waiting to be told what to do next, Gleia continued to look about. *I've heard a thousand stories
about this place*, she thought. *And for what I can
see, I think most of them are true.*

The seamen prodded the slaves into longboats, a
chain to each boat, and started ferrying them out
toward the market, cutting solemnly through darting water-taxis moving about on the calm blue of
the bay like brilliant water beetles, filled with city
folk from above, with visitors staying in the inns,
with others from the many ships at the wharves or
anchored out by the breakwater.

Other than the cerns, which were closed to all
but the seaborn, and now perhaps the thissik,
Thrakesh was the best anchorage for hundreds of
stadia along the coast. Many of those converging
on the market barges were ship captains and master traders looking as often to exchange complete
cargoes as to buy outright. Most of the breakwater-
side barges were rented to those outsiders.

As the longboats moved through these, Gleia
looked around with intense interest. The somber
gray structures of the rented barges were silent,
all the drama and color confined inside the walls,
the only signs of life the dozing boatmen hunched
under their bright canvas awnings, and the more
alert seamen keeping an eye on their masters' boats.
Under the Captain's grunted orders the rowers sent
the longboats working into the stream of traffic
moving toward the inner lines of market barges.
Then the longboat she was in emerged into a stretch
of open water.

Some distance to her right she saw a crowd
gathered on a flat, open barge with a platform in
the middle and an orange-and-blue canvas roof
stretched out like a huge tent. In the center of the
crowd, on the stage a meter above their heads, a

gaudy figure postured and turned, a man with long red hair flying in the erratic breeze. Shimmering blueness swung up and down, sometimes replaced by glimmers of gold that vanished and returned to blue as they touched his white painted hands, swinging up and around the blankness of his white-painted face. Shounach. He was too far for her to make out his features, but it had to be Shounach.

She moved her hands and the chains clinked. She frowned down at them. He was so close. She slid her eyes cautiously around. No one was paying any attention to her. Without the chain she could be over the side and away. Without the chain. So close and so far away. She looked wistfully at the tiny colorful figure as the boat slid between two tall barges, blanking out the scene.

Gleia sat in a wooden straight-backed chair, shut into a small bare room with a single barred window set high in the wall. The chain was off her neck. She was free of any restraint at all. Simply she could not leave the room. She'd expected—well, she didn't know, something more like Carhenas when several ships were new in port and celebrating their temporary victory over the treacherous sea. But the slave market she saw was extraordinarily decorous. She wasn't exposed naked on a block. There was no auction with cold-eyed buyers prodding and poking her.

The Captain had greeted the barge master as an old acquaintance. The small sober man had inspected the chains of captives, nodding, shaking his head, clicking his tongue, muttering offers as he moved. Occasionally the Captain had argued. Occasionally the murmured price was raised. When the barge master reached the end of the chains, the slaves were led away to be cleaned and re-clothed.

When she was clean, with her hair washed and towelled as dry as possible, then combed neatly back from her face, a tiny Mariti slave handed her a fresh cafta with narrow vertical strips of black and white. The material was coarse, unpleasant to the skin, but it was clean, and Gleia accepted it with a gratitude that annoyed her when she became aware of this sneaky surrender of her body.

In the little room she sat mute as the barge master brought in a series of men to look at her and at her work. They all dismissed her with a glance but her work held them. She surprised herself with the intense pride she felt when she saw their appreciation.

Then the barge master led in a man, he treating him with extravagant deference. Despois Lorenzai, the little man called him. He was a big bulky man but looked solid—with the strength of a mountain tars and something of its feral quality. The belly that pushed out the front of his robes was more muscle than fat. He kept a sober demeanor, spoke in low measured tones; but when he stood over Gleia, his eyes brooding down at her, when he arched his heavy body over her to peer at the brands on her cheek, she sensed a wildness in him that was sternly repressed but not eradicated. With this meager evidence she decided that he was a man who might succeed greatly or might destroy himself utterly but taking impossible chances. Amused at her mindleaps, she watched him turning her caftas over in his hands, examining the stitches and designs with a glow in his eyes that the barge master read as quickly as she.

The small man murmured a price. Gleia wrinkled her nose, disgusted. She'd wanted to hear the

price set on her. Though she had no intention of
remaining a slave, fetching a respectable sum would
soothe her pride and give her something to laugh
about with Shounach later on.

Lorenzai raised a heavy eyebrow and turned to
leave. Hastily the barge master plucked at his sleeve
and began talking again in low swift mutters. The
merchant looked over his head and met her eyes.
The laughter in them challenged him, and he began bargaining in earnest.

She waited in the small room until Lorenzai's
housemaster came for her. He was a short brown
man whose head topped out at Gleia's chin. He
had a round wrinkled face like an ancient, evil
baby. With a smirk on his face he bent over her
and snapped a slave ring about her neck. When
she stood, he looked evilly at her and stalked out,
leaving her to follow as best she could.

Gleia carefully suppresed a smile as she moved
through the narrow corridors to the landing where
the water-taxi waited. She was forever barred from
his favor by the length of her head.

The water-taxi was square-ended and narrow,
roofed with bright colored canvas stretched flat
over a rectangular frame. There was a seat for one
person at the bow, a second seat in the center of
the boat, and a third for the boatman at the stern.
It glided smoothly from the landing and slid toward the end of the line of wharves. Gleia pushed
back her hood and let the breeze wandering over
the water flow through her hot sweaty hair. The
little room had been airless and dull. She sighed
with pleasure, not caring if Ussuf heard.

Hesh and Horli were approaching zenith, Hesh
visible as a tiny bead of blue on the side of Horli.
It was coming up high heat so the bustle of the

morning was dying to a drowsy amble. Gleia glanced toward the tent barge as it came into view, but the crowd was breaking up and the stage empty. She was disappointed, then surprised at the extent of her disappointment. He's finished for the day, that's all. He'll be back, I hope. . . . Days before the month ends. Days yet.

When the one-eyed boatman reached his customary mooring, he swung the boat against the ladder and waited. Ussuf swarmed up onto the pier, tossed him a silver coin, then stalked away. Gleia snorted with amusement, pulled up her hood, and hauled herself onto the dock. Then she sped along the worn planks toward Ussuf who was waiting impatiently at the start of a switch-backed scratch that wound up the black stone to one of the smaller gates.

The trail was too steep to climb comfortably. Ussuf kept altering his pace, slowing abruptly until she nearly bumped into him, then speeding up until her legs ached from trying to keep up with him. Her temper began fraying, the anger boiling in her to match the heat radiated by the black stone. She kept stumbling on the carefully roughened track; at times she was forced to stop and wipe the sweat from her face so she could see where her feet were taking her.

By the time she reached the top, she was trembling with fatigue and fury, but she looked into the housemaster's small bright eyes and smiled, so angry that acting was no effort at all. His sly glee dissolved. Disappointed, he wheeled and stumped through the gate in the wall, the ends of his headcloth fluttering out in small wings beside his ears. Gleia clamped her mouth shut and followed.

There was a guard lounging against the planks of the gate. Startled, Gleia stared at him. His leath-

ers were decorated until no inch remained untouched His eyebrows were gilded and his moustache twisted into fierce points that extended
beyond the wings of a headcloth stiff with gold
thread. The cloth was held on his head by gilded
cords whose tasselled ends hung down beside his
ear, brushing against his shoulder each time he
moved.

Ussuf was waiting impatiently at the end of the
alley that led from the gate into a wider street.
She hurried toward him, but couldn't resist a final
look back at the guard. He preened as he met her
eyes, obviously convinced that he'd stunned her
with his magnificence. Gleia followed Ussuf along
the broad inner street, looking with interest at the
elaborate façades of the great houses. They were
built of the same black stone as the cliffs and
carved as thoroughly as the guard's leathers. There
were few people in the street, all of them in the
black and white stripes of slaves. Gleia shook her
head, puzzled, wondering if Thrakesh's boasted
strength had gone hollow in the middle. That ridiculous guard.

Humming softly, Gleia bent over the fragile
material, her fingers sliding the needle in and out
with quick precision. The oil lamp threw a steady
glow over the sleeve bands with their scrollwork
of leaves and vines in olive and ocher. One lay
beside her on the table, its design completed. The
other was close to being finished. She yawned, set
the work aside and stood up. Rubbing at the brand
scars on her face, she strolled across the small
room and leaned into the window embrasure.
Small Zeb was a skinny crescent swimming
through a light mist, while Aab was an opaline
nail-clipping on the horizon. Gleia sighed and

moved her shoulders until she rested comfortably
on crossed arms, looking out across the harbor of
Thrakesh.

Aab edged higher, lighting up the tips of the
waves with her thinning crescent of silver. *Slave.*
Gleia grimaced at the shimmering water. *Tomorrow,*
she thought. *Somehow I'll get out and find him.* She
ran her eyes over the dark bulk of the market and
the pinpoints of light that marked the positions of
the ships anchored out by the breakwater. *Wonder
where he is now.* She sighed again and pulled away
from the window.

As she settled at the sewing table and took up
her work, she thought about the heavily carved
outer walls of the merchant's house. *I could climb
down on those carvings,* she thought. *Have to get
over the wall, though. That'll take a bit of doing.* She
chuckled as she considered Lorenzai and his proba-
ble attitude toward her plans, then sobered. Not a
man to be taken lightly, her new owner. *Once I'm
out, I better keep going.* She set the last stitches then
held the band up close to the lamp, checking to
make sure the work needed no final touches. He
would tolerate sloppy work as little as he would
being cheated. She nodded. It was good. Simple
but effective. Wrapping the sleeve bands in muslin,
she set them aside, then stretched and yawned. A
long day. Lifting the chimney, she blew out the
lamp and wound the wick down. In the new darkness Aab's light painted a square of silver on the
door close to the floor. She made a face at it,
glanced at the bed and groaned. Then she went to
the door and opened it, stood listening. No sound.
No sign of anyone in the hall outside. She went
out.

A single oil lamp burned where the corridor met
another running at right angles to it. Some light

trickled into the gloom beyond the small circle of brilliance. Gleia frowned, closed her eyes and sought the memory of how she was brought here, then she straightened and reached out for the wall. Her fingers trailing along the stone, she moved slowly off down the corridor.

Slowly, carefully, she worked her way into the maze of corridors and through the slave dormitories under the roof, then went down the narrow flight of stairs toward the floor below. And found the way blocked by a grating with a large clumsy lock. *Very sensible of Lorenzai,* she thought. *Must sleep better at night. Slaves aren't known for their kind thoughts about their masters. May he walk Aschla's seventh hell for messing up my plans.* She stood a moment fingering the lock, her mind going back to her childhood and the lessons Abbrah had forced on her. *Too long ago? Have I forgotten the touch? I've got no tools.* Sighing, she turned and started back up the stairs, not that displeased at having to sleep instead of explore. She was very tired.

A pounding on the door jerked her from a heavy sleep. She sat up, groaning and bleary-eyed. In the fuzzy red twilight she pushed reluctantly onto her feet and stumbled to the battered table propped against the wall at the foot of the bed. With both hands she lifted the heavy ewer and poured a dollop of water into the bowl. The night had given the water a pleasant chill that stung away the last wisps of sleep.

When she was finished she poured the water from the bowl into the slop bucket then sat on the end of the bed and began combing her hair. Nothing up here. The comb scraped on the slave ring. She worked a finger under the ring and ran it around inside the curve. Have to get rid of this thing somehow. Her mind flew back to the spring before when the thissik had locked her into another neck ring. *At least this won't explode. I wonder what you're doing here, Juggler. Wish I was out of this and with you.* She dragged the comb impatiently through the last of the tangles, tied her hair back from her face with a scrap of material, then slid into her slave cafta. She wriggled the cafta into place and went out to breakfast.

As she'd half-expected, the other female slaves were still taking their attitude from Ussuf, giving her surreptitious pinches and glowering looks. *A little man who resents anyone taller than him. Especially a female slave with privileges.* She looked briefly around at the sullen faces, then kept her eyes on her dish, eating the porridge with a quiet concentration its taste scarcely deserved. Again her solitude was driven home to her. There was no one here she could trust, no one to laugh with, to tease and quarrel with. She bit into a section of quella fruit beside her bowl. *I've grown soft, never used to need any company but my own. Never even wanted it. Tetaki. Temokeuu-my-father. Jevati. Shounach. You've spoiled me, my friends.* She washed her fruit down with a last swallow of cha, trying to wash away the thorns of loneliness with it.

She spent the hours after breakfast in the sewing room allotted to her, sketching designs and waiting to be summoned. When the morning was half gone, a slight blond girl came drifting into the room and beckoned to her. Gleia saw the ring around her neck and was abruptly angry. The child winced as she saw the flare of anger, and Gleia hastily controlled herself. "What is it, little one?"

The girl touched her lips, shook her head, then

beckoned again. Gleia rolled up her designs, thrust them in a pocket and followed her.

At the entrance to the wizard maze an aged Mariti male, tongueless and blind, wrapped soft white cloths about their faces and led them into the maze.

The wizard maze filled the large room beyond the bare anteroom with sliding panels and dead ends. Whenever Lorenzai ordered it, the route was changed by sliding the panels about and locking them in place to open new ways and close the old. The maze was the only entrance to the master's private quarters.

Her determination fueled by a growing annoyance, Gleia put to work a skill she'd learned almost before she could walk. Her sense of direction and her direction-memory never missed. She kept track of turns and twists, silently counting her steps as the mute led her along. When they came out into the bare room on the far side and the mute took away the blindfolds, she knew she could retrace that route whenever she wanted.

Amrezeh, Lorenzai's wife, was sitting up in her wide bed, dressed in a lacy green bedgown. Her small pointed face was alive with interest. "You're the new one."

Gleia bowed her head. "Yes, mistress."

"Lorenzai says you do beautiful work. He says he set a task for you yesterday to see how I would like it. Did you finish?"

"Yes, mistress." Gleia bowed her head again and extended the sleeve bands.

"Bring them closer." As Gleia stepped froward, Amrezeh noticed the scars on her cheek. She gasped and pressed a small hand against her mouth. Then she pulled it down, her eyes bright with curiosity. "What happened to your face? Bend down." She touched velvet fingertips to the letters burned into Gleia's flesh. "Brands. What do they mean?"

Gleia was silent a minute. The brands were like talismans to her and she was reluctant to speak of them. She found it harder and harder to act out the slave's part. She was silent too long. Amrezeh's brows began to lower; she didn't like having to wait for a slave. Gleia forced her reluctant hand up and touched the oldest brand. "This marks me a taken thief, bonded to serve where they told me, mistress. The Kadiff put me under bond to a cafta maker who beat my skills into me." She touched the second scar. "And made it possible for me to buy my bond. This marks the cancellation."

"And now you're a slave again." Amarezeh sighed, but her eyes were shining. "What stories you must have." She dropped. "I was shut up in my father's house and only left it to come here." Gleia caught a flash of blue as Amrezeh peeped slyly at her, assessing the effect of her words. "Not that Lorenzai has been unkind. It's just I get so bored! Enough of that." She pulled her knees up and rested her arms on them. "Let me see the bands. Sit down there where I can talk to you without shouting." She pointed to a low footstool beside the bed.

As Gleia settled herself, Amrezeh began examining the bands critically, drawing her fingers over the stitches to see if they were small and firmly set, examining the design itself. "You completed this is one day?"

"It's a simple design, mistress. And I worked late. Master said I was to finish the bands before sleeping."

"Um." She pulled the lengths through her soft pale fingers. "Simple but charming. In one day."

Her voice trailing off, she fixed her vivid blue eyes on Gleia. "What do you call yourself, girl?"

"Gleia, mistress." She lowered her eyes and moved her shoulders cautiously. Playing submissive was making her back ache and starting a pain behind her eyes. She found Amrezeh's friendliness extremely seductive. It crept through her defenses and teased her to respond with equal warmth. But she'd learned her skepticism on the streets of Carhenas where trust was a quick way to pain or death. The parchment design sheets rustled as her hand brushed them.

Amrezeh pounced on that. "What do you have there?"

"If mistress pleases." Gleia put the roll in the outstretched hand. "While waiting to be summoned, I prepared several other designs."

The tough translucent parchment rustled crisply as Amrezeh unrolled the drawings. The first sheet bore a design of waves and fish, highly stylized, the curves squared off. Color values were indicated by ink washes—the palest gray to solid black. The values passed through the angular forms with a rippling grace. "Ah. Unusual and delightful." Amrezeh flashed a smile at Gleia. "You really are gifted." Then she set that sheet aside and examined the second.

That design was an abstract pattern of interlocking, irregular shapes, not too impressive in the black and gray of the ink washes. Amrezeh tapped her fingers thoughtfully on the parchment, then closed her eyes, a faint smile on her lovely face. She turned abruptly to Gleia. "You flatter me."

Gleia dropped her head. The surprise she felt wasn't exactly the flattery that Amrezeh thought. She hadn't expected that design to mean anything to an untrained eye, had done it to please herself.

"No, mistress," she said softly. Pain beat in long slow pulses behind her eyes. She was annoyed at herself for bringing the designs, only prolonging this miserable interview.

The small blonde woman smiled and put the second sketch aside. One glance at the third was all she needed. It was a simple design of spring flowers with nothing really interesting about it. Amrezeh pulled the first two back in front of her and went over them again, then she tugged on the bell rope.

The frail child came gliding in and sank onto her knees, bending over until her forehead touched the carpet. "Go to the storeroom," Amrezeh said crisply. "Bring the blue-green avrishum and the white katani. Understand?"

The feathery blonde curls flipped about as the child nodded, then she stood with careful grace and slipped out of the room.

Amrezeh picked up the sea design. "This first, I think. I can't wait to see it realized. How long do you think it would take to complete a cafta? Do you cut?"

"Mistress, I can't say for sure until I've worked on it a little. And if you have one who cuts for you, perhaps it would be better for that one to continue. I was not taught cutting."

The small slave was almost lost behind the big bolts of cloth as she stumbled into the doorway. She hesitated there, waiting for permission to enter. Amrezeh smiled and said pleasantly, "Bring them here, child, and put them on the bed beside me. Then wait outside until I call you."

The avrishum was a grayed blue-green with a subtle darkening where folds touched the light; it was beautifully suited as a background for the sea design. Gleia was startled by this casual glimpse into great wealth. A body length of that material would probably sell for more than her purchase price. Beside it the white katani, also a rare material, looked almost common. It was a crisp fabric, katani, so fine it was translucent.

"The avrishum, I think. The katani might serve for the abstract." Amrezeh turned to Gleia, eyebrows up, waiting for her comment.

Gleia could see the harsh bright colors and shapes contrasting with the delicacy of the katani. The garment would have a rich barbaric flamboyance. She glanced at Amrezeh. Might be too strong for her. I don't know her. Is this only an act she's putting on for me? If so, why does she bother? Something in her that makes it necessary to conquer everyone around her before she discards them? What could have done that to her in the sheltered life she's led? Or was it so sheltered? There was something exaggerated about her behavior that shouted to Gleia of a weakness too strongly compensated for. Habbiba had looked like that when she was trying to impress a highborn customer. How young I was then, but I could smell it when Habbiba was faking it. And I can smell it now.

Amrezeh ran her thumb across a corner of the avrishum. "You'll need thread." She slipped out of the bed and padded a few steps to a cluttered dressing table. Opening an elaborate jewel case at one end, she dug about inside then brought out a handful of gold coins. "Come here, girl."

Gleia came round the end of the bed and took the coins.

Amrezeh tilted her head back to look up into Gleia's face. "I want you to go down to the market and get that thread; I wouldn't trust any other eye than yours for that. Mind you, don't stint on quality; but don't be uselessly extravagant. What you have there should be enough." She paused, frowned.

"No. Wait." She wheeled and went through a door Gleia hadn't noticed before. Minutes later she was back with several silver drachs. You'll need these for the boatman. One drach to take you out and back. Don't let him take you for more. Be back in time for the midday meal." Her smile widened suddenly; her blue eyes twinkled. "Don't yield to temptation, my dear. Sad though it is, you have no chance of escaping."

Gleia passed the guard, who smirked at her until she wanted to kick him. Halfway down the track she stopped and leaned on the safety wall and looked out over the bay. She could just see the pointed top of the tent roof over the stage. With a sigh, she wiped the sweat off her face and continued on down.

The boats at this last pier were a bedraggled lot. There were patches of decay in the canvas tops and paint peeling from the wood. The worst-looking one had a skim of water over the floorboards. The boatmen matched their craft, ugly and infirm. But slaves had nowhere else to go for transport; these were what they had if they needed a water-taxi to run their errands. Gleia went down the pier, stopping at the one-eyed man's boat. She brought out a silver drach.

The one-eyed man recognized her, she saw that. He shook his head. "Two."

For a moment she was tempted. It wasn't her money, better he had it than the pampered Amrezeh, but let the man cheat her now and she had nothing but more of the same to look forward to the rest of her time here. She raised an eyebrow. "One."

"Two." The boatman sneered toward the other boats. "If you want to swim. . . ."

"One. Swimming doesn't come into it if I want to walk a little."

The boatman grunted and held out his hand. Gleia tossed the drach to him. In spite of his missing eye, he caught it with no difficulty. With a neat economy of motion he swung onto the back seat and brought the boat around so that it was parallel to the dock.

Gleia went agilely down the ladder and settled on the middle seat. "The shop of Shahd the thread-seller."

When the taxi passed the open space, the crowd was back and Shounach was performing. Gleia lifted a hand. "Wait. Take me over there." She pointed.

The boatman complied silently. He brought her to the landing and waited until she stepped out. Gleia dug into her sleeve and tossed him a second drach. "Wait here till I come back. Then I want the thread shop."

He shrugged and settled down to sleep until she chose to return.

She stood looking down at him a moment, fingers stroking the house badge sewn on her right shoulder. That was what made them all polite to her. In an odd way she had the power of Lorenzai behind her. She rubbed at her nose as she turned to inspect the crowd around the stage.

It was loosely packed on the outside. Gleia managed to work her way through spectators, mostly men, as they laughed and yelled their appreciation. As she got nearer the platform the crowd was denser and quieter. It was harder to push through them. She wriggled and shoved, mostly ignored, as they stared in fascination at the stage. At last she broke through and came up against the edge of the platform. She closed her hands around the outer plank, pushed back with elbows, bumped her body about until she'd moved the staring men aside enough to have breathing space. Then she looked up and met Shounach's eyes.

Swallowing a growing excitement, she pulled back her hood so he could see her face better, then she clicked her fingernails against the slave ring.

He nodded, his painted mouth stretching into a quick grin. And he never missed one of the blue spheres circling his head.

She watched him for a while. He began spinning slowly on his toes, turning round and round without missing one of the growing and shrinking number of glowing spheres. When he faced her again, the blue spheres expanded suddenly to head-sized blurs that flickered in and out of existence, changed suddenly to smallish gilded dragons that snorted and cavorted and shot out miniature tongues of flame as they rose and fell around his masklike face. Then one by one they changed to crimson jewels catching the light of the suns in dozens of facets and shining red rays out into the crowd and up at the canvas overhead, dancing red light flickering and darting over dazed faces. The balls kept circling and changing. The Juggler was on his toes, then sitting cross-legged, then circling slowly, then whirling. And the spheres kept circling. . . .

Gleia blinked and wrenched her eyes from the firgure. Time was passing, time she couldn't afford. She looked up. Hesh was peeping from behind Horli and both were two-thirds of the way up the eastern arc of their day. Sighing she began pushing her way back through the crowd.

The boatman swung the taxi against the ladder. Gleia climbed up, clutching her packet of thread. She smiled at the man, flipped him a third drach,

then walked slowly down the pier and hesitated at
the base of the cliff. After one look at the winding
track, she rebelled. The morning's play-acting had
worn her out. There was a little time before midday,
a little time before she had to return to confine-
ment and irritation. She stepped back on the pier
and looked along the crescent toward the middle.
A lot of activity there, water-taxis darting about,
groups of men gesticulating, snatches of music coming out of the taverns. She began walking along
the wharves, heading toward the taverns in the
center of the crescent, looking down the short side-
alleys as she moved past them. Behind the great
warehouses, hovels cobbled together from drift-
wood and whatever scraps of refuse were usable,
clustered like starlings' nests against the stone.
She saw occasional drunks sprawled in and around
these places. Otherwise there were few people this
far from center.

The wharves were mostly empty, the ships having discharged their cargoes and retreated to the
breakwater where anchorage was much cheaper.
Many of their captains and master traders were
engaged in marathon bargaining in the rented
barges out in the market. What ships were left
creaked slowly in the rocking water and the erratic breeze with drowsy watchmen curled up in
the few patches of shade on deck. There were sneak
thieves among the sea-wrack living in the hovels,
driven by desperation that made them disregard
the death-by-torture of the captured thief.

This end of the crescent was still and somnolent
in the growing midday heat so it was startling
when a hoarse voice called, "Hey, girl."

She looked around. For a moment she saw
nothing, then a waving hand caught her eye. A
large fat man was sprawled in the meager shelter

of a warehouse doorway. His face was moon-round and sweating. There was an amiable grin on his whiskery face, a twinkle in his bloodshot blue eyes. Wisps of greasy white hair stuck out in a dirty halo around his face. His grin widened as he met her eyes. He lifted a wobbly wineskin. "Want a drink?"

"Why not." She strolled across the planks into the narrowing shade under the eaves of the warehouse. She glanced back over her shoulder at the suns. "You'll fry your brains, bareheaded like that."

He chuckled. "Got it figured." He slapped meaty knee tenting his tattered robe. "I don't gotta move 'fore I run outta juice." He handed her the skin and watched as she drank. "You new here?"

She slapped the stopper home and gave the skin back. "Thanks. Yes, I'm new. How'd you know?"

"Thought so. Why I yelled. Only one kinda woman down that way. You too new here to figure that. Thought I'd let you make up your mind 'f you wanted that kinda game."

She settled herself cross-legged beside his feet, looking down along the crescent to the activity in the middle, then shivered. "I owe you, old man. I wouldn't like that." She started and blinked as a gong note boomed out over the water. "What's that?"

The old man grimaced and squirted more wine into his mouth. "Openin' the Big Gate," he grunted. He sniffed. "Look up, you'll see yourself a sight."

Gleia tilted her head back, shading her eyes with her hand.

The massive gilded gate split in the middle and the two leaves turned slowly outward as she watched. The heavy structure above the gate was swinging slowly over and down while a broad wooden platform slid out from inside the gate. The platform was ornate with carved and gilded railings. The gong sounded again and as the reverberations died away she saw dark figures visible as little more than black shapes jutting above the gilded rail. Two of them picked up a third and tossed him over the side.

His screams wheeled around the harbor as his body plummetted toward the buildings at the center of the crescent. Down and down. Until there was a crunching noise, then a sudden silence.

Gleia pressed her hand against her mouth and closed her eyes. *Why?* She pulled her hand away. "They threw him over. Why?"

She could hear the wine slosh as he took a long drink. She looked around to see him cuddling the limp skin against his chest. He rubbed his face with his free hand, producing a papery rasping sound. "Ayandar's figurin' to come down. He don't walk like ordinary folk. Got that madardamned lift. Don't trust it either. Says the stone want blood, don't want it to be his, so he give it some."

"That's crazy."

"Well, so's he. But don't say that in front of anyone up there." He waved the wineskin vaguely in the direction of the cliff top. Then he dabbed at the sweat on his face. "He gettin' crazier by the day. Now he meddlin' with the merchants' guild. They take a lot. Not that. One a these days they get together and toss him over the cliff like that one." He waved a broad meaty hand toward the center. "You listen to them down there. . . ." He stopped and drank some more. "They'd kick him over tomorrow if they weren't shit-scared of the Ayandar's Apartas, those guards of his."

She took the skin from him. "You're talking too much, old man."

He grinned at her, vaguely amiable, not quite

present any longer. "You gonna tell on me, sweet thing?"

"Of course not."

"Anyway, who pay attention to a headrot like me? You don't want drink, give that back."

She sighed and handed the wine over, then dug in her sleeve, pulling out a handful of change she had left from buying the thread. With a second sigh she flipped two silver drachs onto his billowing stomach. "Enjoyed the talk." She rose to her feet, stretched and yawned. "Time I was getting back."

He fished the coins out of the folds of his robe. "Girl, they'll have your hide, you come back short. Here."

She waved his hand away. "Mistress didn't bother counting. Keep the damn money; better you than her, old man." With a laugh she went back along the wharves.

As she leaned into the climb, she thought, *this whole place is going to explode soon. Madar! Got to figure a way out. And money. Or something I can turn into money. Tonight. I'll work on that tonight.*

Late that night she set the avrishum aside and rubbed her eyes. Then she stood and walked to the window. She leaned into the embrasure and looked out. *Fog is heavier tonight.*

Aab was a ghost of herself, shimmering through a dozen veils. The water was velvet black except for faint blurs from the ship lights. Once again she wondered about Shounach. What was he doing in Thrakesh? Juggler. Not waiting for me, I'm sure. Curiosity was like an itch between her shoulder-blades, irritating and in a place she couldn't scratch. She sighed and left the window. Forget Shounach. Time to get to work.

She crossed the room and tapped fingertips

against the wood. Hard. Small tight grain. Good.
She opened the door a crack and shut it again on
the weaving needle she'd salvaged from the sewing room, using the wood as a vise to hold the end
as she bent the rest toward her and used a metal
darning egg to hammer it flat. Several times she
took out the needle and examined the bend until
she was satisfied that she had a reasonably right-
angled turn. She dealt with the other two needles
the same way.

During the afternoon she'd fashioned some muslin into a crude bag. With a grin she slipped its
strap over her shoulder and patted it down against
her side. Back to beginnings. Thief before, now
thief again.

With her picklocks tucked into her sleeve pocket
she slipped from the room and made her way to
the grating. Her old skills came back faster than
she'd expected as fingers remembered how to feel
with the probes and force back the wards. It took
her about five minutes to get the lock open and
only two to lock it behind her.

She flitted down the stairs breathing hard. At
the bottom of the flight she stopped and pressed
her hands hard against her chest, struggling to
calm herself.

When she felt steadier, she took a candle from
her bag and lit it at one of the wall lamps. The
halls down on this floor were much better lit than
those in the warren above. She wrapped a rag
around the candle to catch most of the drippings
and looked around. Loose on the family floor. Curiosity was almost as big a drive as her need to
finance her escape.

She wandered through the halls, poking into
sitting rooms, several empty austere rooms that
were merely spaces for housing bodies temporar-

ily while they waited to talk to Lorenzai, and finally Lorenzai's public office. Which turned out to be as empty of interest and value as that depressing series of waiting spaces. She thrust her head into a series of sewing rooms. They were all the same, bare and uninteresting. She turned a corner.

The door to the anteroom before the maze was an uncurtained archway. She was in front of it before she realized where she was. She froze. But the mute slave was gone. The room was empty. After her heart slowed and her breathing steadied, she blew out the candle, ran on her toes across the small room, and entered the maze. Eyes closed, counting her steps, she let body memory help her thread through the complicated turns.

Light touched her eyelids. She jerked to a stop and opened her eyes. The exit to the maze was near, one more turn and she'd be out into the other anteroom. She listened. Not a sound. She strained against the wall, holding her breath, listening with all the intensity she could summon. Nothing. She edged past the corner.

The room was empty. On her right there was a shallow alcove. On the couch inside, the mute lay, eyes shut, breathing steadily, a thin blanket over his legs and torso.

Not daring to breathe, she padded across the room and stepped into the corridor. Legs shaking, heart pounding, a pulsing pain in her temples, she leaned against the wall and let the air out of her lungs.

When she was calmer, she went soft-footed down the carpeted passage, trying doors as she came to them. One or two were locked. One led to a library with stacks of scrolls resting on wide shelves. She poked about in there for a few minutes but little light trickled in from outside and she didn't dare relight her candle for fear of leaving splotches of wax behind. She went out again and stood in the corridor looking at the turn close ahead. Amrezeh's bedroom lay around it. She rubbed at the scars on her face, then shivered and started forward.

Amrezeh's bedroom. The door was open a crack. A lamp was burning inside. She could see the glow. She dropped onto her stomach and edged the door open a little more. Holding her breath she pushed her head through the opening until she could see most of the room. It was empty. The bedding was turned back, the side door swung half-open, showing a small sliver of another lighted room beyond it. Still on her stomach, she eased inside.

All senses straining, her stomach knotting and unknotting, she went rapidly and neatly through the jewel case. Leaving the more spectacular jewelry untouched, she slipped two from the small hoard of coins into her loot bag, then several heavy gold chains twisted together and pushed into the back of Amrezeh's jewel case.

The half-open door itched at her. She fidgeted from foot to foot, her eyes jerking back and forth between the two temptations. Leave now or go on? With a small gasp she danced on her toes to the wall and stood just beside the opening, listening intently. Nothing. She stroked her scars, sucked in a breath, then dropped to her stomach and worked her head slowly through the space between door and jamb.

Another bedroom, also empty. A simpler room, with massive furniture and somber colors like the robes Lorenzai wore. His room *His kind of self-discipline*, she thought. *He does this more to rule himself than to fool others*. Letting the air trickle out of her lungs she went limp, lying on the carpet, chin propped on her fist, resisting an urge to giggle. Layer on layer on layer. That man. Breath puffed from her nose in tiny whuffs. She pulled her hands away and buried her face in the carpet to stifle her laughter.

When the fit passed, she sighed and snaked into the room. She stood, hands on hips, inspecting it. Then she stiffened. Voices. Muffled. Coming from beyond heavy portiers. Must open into a room there. On her toes again, she ran to the drapes and listened. The voices were louder. Lorenzai and Amrezeh. Quarreling or close to it. She edged the paired drapes apart and put her eye to the crack.

The room beyond was large with elaborately carved panels masking the stone of the walls. Big leather chairs scattered about. A rack of scrolls. In the center of the room, a table—a heavy slab of wood polished to a high gloss. On it, near one end, a round metal tray holding a cha pot and two used cups. Thrown in a crumpled heap beside the tray, a soft leather pouch.

Lorenzai wasn't talking anymore. He sat behind the table, bending over a small wooden box with the lid turned back. Whatever it contained was shining erratically, turning his face into a pattern of harsh black lines and shifting planes of light.

Amrezeh was stalking back and forth in front of him, scowling, her bedgown whuffling about her, her small bare feet kicking at the carpet's thick pile. She glared at him repeatedly, then stalked on, chewing at a knuckle, her eyes glittering, the blonde hair flying out in wisps from her face. She wheeled and slapped her hands down on the table. "How much longer?" She threw her weight on quivering arms, every muscle tense. "How much longer are you and those cursed merchants of yours going to sit around talking? HOW MUCH LONGER

DO I HAVE TO SMILE AND SMILE AND LET THOSE BITCHES TREAT ME LIKE...."

"Like what you are, the Ayandar-before's bastard daughter got on a concubine they despised." Lorenzai lifted angry eyes to meet hers. Then his face softened. "Rezeh, sit down. Let me work."

Behind the curtain, Gleia stifled an exclamation. I've walked into something all right. The old man knew what he was talking about.

Amrezeh thrust her hands into her hair and pulled, expelling her breath in an angry hoarse cry. Once again she slammed her hands on the table. "I want them dead. Now!"

When he didn't answer, she backed away, flung out her arms in a gesture that should have been absurd but was not, mainly because of her real passion. "Why the hell did I marry you?"

Lorenzai surged to his feet, his massive body knocking the table several inches forward. "Your loving father," he shouted at her. "He wanted his bastard daughter out of sight before she made scandals even he couldn't swallow."

She shrieked and leaped at him, fingernails striking at his eyes.

He shoved her hard away from him, but Gleia was astonished to see that he aimed her carefully at one of the large leather chairs.

Amrezeh bounced, then sat staring at him, trembling, tears trembling in her eyes, slipping out one by one and sliding down her face. Her breasts heaved. Her breathing rasped hoarsely in new silence. Lorenzai watched her sit up and rearrange her bedgown, his face somber. "Catch your breath, Rezeh. There's time. There's plenty of time." His brief burst of anger was already under control.

She let her head fall back. "Yes," she said tiredly. "Too much time."

Lorenzai resettled himself in his chair. He pulled the table toward him, the legs groaning over the carpet. With a quick glance at Amrezeh, he thrust his hand into the box and pulled out a small egg-shaped crystal. He snapped it from hand to hand, called, "Rezeh! Look up. Careful with this." He tossed the crystal to her, smiled as she let it drop in her lap. "Get it to the Ayandar tomorrow. He's been after me for months to provide him with an Eye. Do it discreetly. Your neck on it and mine."

She nodded absently and stared down at the crystal in her lap.

Behind the curtains Gleia could read a familiar fascination and revulsion in her face. Amrezeh touched it, jerked her hand away, touched it again, began stroking it. The veils of color shimmered about her, starting to coalesce into forms.

With an exclamation of horror, Lorenzai leaped across to her, knocking the table askew in his haste. He wrenched the Eye from her and dropped it on the carpet beside the chair. She tried to twist away, but he forced her back and held her against the leather until her struggles subsided.

She blinked and moved her lips. Then lifted her hands and passed them one after the other across her face. She was shaking. "Madar!" She shuddered. "Lorenzai. . . ."

He shifted her from the chair and held her against him. Carefully he swung around and sat down, still holding her. "Thought you knew better," he said softly. He began stroking his hand over her hair and down her back. Over and over until she stopped shaking. Then he slipped from under her and settled her back in the chair. With a last touch on her cheek he went to the table and perched a hip on it. "All right?"

She smiled. The smile widened to a yawn, then

her eyes began to glitter again. "Dear darling half-brother, he won't be able to put it down if I know him and I do know him. How long before it eats him?"

Lorenzai shrugged. "You felt the power. Two days. Three. Maddib and Chayl have arranged to send in some slave girls to the Apartas three days from now. They'll have more Eyes with them. Sadh-Mahar is working on the girls now to see that they do what we want, then forget everything. Once the Apartas have the Eyes, we move." With a quick loud snap he shut the lid on the box, then picked up the leather sack. "You wanted to know how long. Four days. Satisfied?" He tossed the pouch to Amrezeh. "Hang on to that a minute." Reaching behind him he scooped up the box and slid off the table. He crossed to a side wall and pressed the center of a salt-flower carved along the side of a panel, one flower in a cluster of five or six. A small square popped open, revealing a dark cavity. Lorenzai slid the box inside. After snapping the panel shut, he crossed to Amrezeh, took the sack from her and stuffed the Eye inside. He pulled the drawstring tight and held the sack out to her. "This is important, Rezah. The Ayandar may be crazy, but he's not stupid. We've got to take him out before we can move."

"I can get it to him." She took the sack and set it down on the arm of the chair. "He hates all his sisters, wouldn't tell them he's breathing if they thought him dead. Suspects them all of trying to poison him, especially the Ayandara. Only reason he tolerates me is because he thinks I've got no way I could take him out." She giggled, stopped as the giggles grew shrill. "The fool!"

Lorenzai caught her flying hand and held it. "Won't be long now. Be patient, love."

With her free hand she touched his cheek. "Won't he be surprised. And he did it to himself when he married me to you instead of throwing me over the cliff. He thought of doing that. I don't know why he changed his mind." Her hand threaded through his hair in a gentle caress, then she ran the back of the hand down his face and touched it to his lips. "Dear brother."

"You were lucky in your mother." As she flushed and tried to snatch her hand away, he closed his fingers hard. "Don't be a fool, Rezeh. Think a minute about your half-sister Lahalla who's Ayandara now because she poisoned her crazy mother. Would you want to be that half-mad bitch whose only sustained interest is running after adolescent boys?" He laughed and pushed onto his feet. Still laughing, he stretched his arms over his head, groaning as he worked stiff muscles. He brought them down and grinned at her. "Or the Ayandar, degenerating by the day. Be glad you're what you are." He backed up and rested his buttocks on the edge of the table. "Back to business. Zuwayl is bringing in the last shipment tomorrow. He'll be here at low tide. Said he'd have the rest of the Eyes we need and the last load of arms. Four days and you can kick those half-sisters of yours off the cliff if you want." He canted his head, winked at her. "Satisfied?"

She yawned, brought her legs up and curled in the chair like a sleepy cat. "Yes. I want to see Lahalla bounce." She opened her eyes wide suddenly and was out of the chair, running to him. "No." She smoothed her hand down his body and leaned into him. "Come to bed."

Gleia jerked back, poised to run across the room and out. Then Lorenzai's words stopped her. "Down there," he said huskily. "Come down to the armory with me."

Gleia leaned to the slit. He was off the table, leading Amrezeh toward a wall. She looked a bit dubious for the first few steps, then her eyes glazed as the thought of making love amid spears and swords began to excite her. Gleia shivered. *He knows her.* She shook her head, put her eye back to the crack.

Amrezeh was dancing impatiently from foot to foot as Lorenzai pushed at the centers of three salt-flowers. A long narrow section of wall gaped open suddenly. Lorenzai wriggled through first and Amrezeh followed, clinging to his thick robe.

Gleia hesitated a minute, then brushed through the curtains. With a glance at the tantalizing gap in the wood, she circled the table and ran to the place where Lorenzai had stored the box. After a little fumbling about she managed to open the small cavity. She took out the box and turned back its lid.

Ranga Eyes. Her tongue flicked around her lips. Their lure tickled at her, calling her. She hugged the box against her breast, staring down at the nested crystals. Hesitantly she touched them with the fingertips of her free hand, waking in the Eyes the veils of color and in herself an urgent desire to know if these would take her back to the world of beauty with stilt houses and butterfly people dancing in the air under a butter-yellow sun and daisies big as trees. The crystals warmed under her fingers. She flattened her palm over them, then lifted one out. As it nestled in the hollow of her palm she began to hear whispering voices, to see forms within the veils.

"No!" She slammed her hand against the wall. The pain broke the spell. She dropped the Eye

back in the box, hastily counted them, then snapped
the lid shut. Fifteen eyes. Fifteen souls sucked from
their bodies. She pushed the box back into the
cavity and clicked the panel shut. Rubbing at her
hand, she crossed to the secret door. A little light
penetrated from the lamps in the room and she
could see the beginning of a spiral staircase. Curiosity pulled her in a step or two, then she shook
her head and backed out.

She moved into the center of the room. Turning
slowly, she examined it, then shook her head again.
Nothing from here. I'm not going to fool with that
man. Ranga Eyes Madar! She giggled. Ranga eyes
to power a coup. Still laughing she ran out, heading for the maze.

Lighted candle in her hand, she slipped into her
room. Humming a lilting tune, she lifted the bag
from her shoulder and tossed it onto the bed, laughing at the dull chunk chunk of the coins as they
bounced. She carried the candle to the lamp on
the sewing table, lifted the chimney and lit the
wick.

And heard the chunk-chunk again of the gold
coins. She wheeled.

Shounach was sitting on the end of the bed emptying the loot bag onto the cover. He looked up
and grinned. "Busy little thing, aren't you."

"Fool. I near strangled on my heart."

He came off the bed and walked over to her,
took hold of the slave ring, slipping his fingers in
between the ring and her neck. "You're in a rut,
girl."

She pulled away from him and sat down in her
sewing chair, leaned back, trying to look relaxed,
watching as he sauntered about the room. He

glanced briefly out the window then sat down on the bed again.

"Not me."

"What?" He lifted his legs onto the bed and stretched out, head resting on laced fingers.

"In a rut. Not me. Men. They seem to have only two ways for dealing with stray females. Rape them and slave them. Or both. Preferably both."

He pushed up and looked about the small cozy room. "You seem to have landed soft enough this time."

"Seen from the inside of this, it's not so soft." She tapped the slave ring with her thumbnail. "How'd you get in here?"

"Flapped my wings and flew through the window." His changeable eyes were bright green with amusement.

"Oddly enough, Juggler, I think I believe you. Why?" she caught the green glint again and hastily amended her question. "I thought you'd given up on me. Why bother coming here?"

"Why'd you leave Cern Vrestar without a word to me?"

"Tetaki told you."

"I wondered if you'd panicked and run from me."

"No."

"Gleia, you told me how it is with you."

Her hand came up and rubbed at the brand scars. "No," she repeated. "I didn't want to go. But I pay my debts."

"Companion," he said softly. His eyes, cooled to a silver gray, held hers.

She shifted uneasily. "I. . . ." She couldn't finish.

"I thought that was a promise." The silver eyes were like ice.

She swallowed, then grew angry. "What did you

expect! Jevati needed me. You . . . Juggler . . . when did you ever need anyone?" She pushed at her hair, then pressed the heels of her hands against her burning eyes. "Madar! Shounach, it's been a long hard day for me. What do you want here?"

"To get you out. If you want. Do you?"

She stared at him. "No," she said, startling him and startling herself. "Not yet." Then she threw back her head and glared at him. "Do you think I can't get myself out whenever I want?"

"Still prickly." He relaxed, a smile touching the corners of his wide mouth. "My turn. Why?"

Gleia jumped to her feet and went quickly to the window, thrusting her shoulders in the embrasure. She stared blindly out, struggling to bring into order some of the things that revolved in her head. The plot, Shounach, the Ayandar and his crazy ideas, Amrezeh and Lorenzai, and most of all, the Ranga Eyes. With a new resolution she jerked out again and turned to face him. He was stretched out flat once more, waiting, eyes on the ceiling. She crossed to the bed and settled herself beside him, one hand going out to rest on the hard muscles of his chest where the gaudy jacket fell open. "How long can you stay? I've got a story you might like to hear."

Gleia woke feeling obscurely happy. She moved slightly, thinking to feel Shounach's body against hers; but she was alone in a narrow bed grown suddenly too large.

He was standing by the window, the faint starlight silvering the planes of his face, painting heavy black lines from nose to mouth. He looked remote and sad, lost in the contemplation of some old pain.

"Shounach?"

He turned quickly, stared at her, came to her. Bending down he drew fingertips gently along the side of her face. "Time I went, Companion. The Cat's eyes are high and Horli-rise is close."

She caught his hand, held it between hers. "Shounach, why do you want the Ranga Eyes?"

He straightened, pulling his hand free. "I don't."

"Why go after them, then?"

He was silent so long she thought he wasn't going to answer. At last he said quietly, "I'm hunting for the source."

"And?"

He looked down at hands closed into fists. "I'll destroy it, I'll wipe all those...." Wheeling, he crossed the room in two strides. Without stopping, he dived headfirst into the embrasure and disappeared.

Ignoring the chill of the air, Gleia scrambled from the bed and ran to the window. The fog had sunk to a woolly blanket over the water. By the time she located the Juggler's plummeting body, he was a dark blotch sinking into the haze. She stared and shook her head. "I don't believe it. I see it and I don't believe it."

The morning dragged. She worked on the cafta, trying to restrain her impatience. The front panels were finished. She began work on the strip around the bottom. The avrishum caressed her fingers and took the thread with a hunger that continued to amaze her.

About mid-morning she tucked the needle into the design then sat stroking the material. "Stupid. I can't...."

With a shaky grin, she carried the cafta to the large mirror. She shook it out and held it up in front of her. Giggling at her foolishness, she stripped off her slave dress and pulled the avrishum over her head. She smoothed it down, shivering with delight at the touch of the material on her skin. When the hem was in, the cafta would be too short for her. So would the sleeves. But the allowance was so generous the sleeves came to midknuckle and the bottom brushed the floor. She stripped the rag from her hair and shook soft curls loose about her face. Then she held out her arms and examined her image in the mirror.

She caught her breath. She looked taller. There was a copper sheen in her dark brown hair. The glow of the avrishum was reflected in her eyes, changing the brown to hazel. Even the brand scars on her face took on an exotic charm. She stroked her hands over her breasts, down her sides to the curve of her thighs, delighting in the way the material took the touch and transferred it to the skin beneath. Almost as if some other hands were touching her. She turned slowly, twisting her neck to keep her eyes on the mirror, enjoying her fleeting moment of beauty.

Reluctantly she pulled it off. After the avrishum, the coarse material of the black and white cafta felt doubly harsh on her skin. She settled back at the sewing table, moving her shoulders irritably before she took up the needle. When I go, I'm taking this. She measured the distance from the band of embroidery to the edge of the material. I can widen these bands when I let down the hem. She rubbed at her eyes and started work again.

At mid-afternoon, Gleia heard a commotion in the hall and wondered without much interest what was happening. Then she heard a flurry of tinkling laughter and slow-drawled words. A tall, thin blonde woman came through the door. She was elegant and angular with an arrogance so total that lesser mortals simply accepted it as they would accept a force of nature. Behind her were coarser copies circling around her. Hastily, Gleia rose to her feet.

The other women were tall and willowy with the same almost-innocent pride of caste. The resemblance between them was strong. Amrezeh came in behind them and stood to one side, stiff and awkward, a miniature version of the others. When her eyes flicked up, the hatred momentarily visible in her face was identification enough. The Ayandara. And the rest are Amrezeh's half-sisters and cousins. She looked quickly from Amrezeh to the others and back. A lifetime of scarring. Madar, I never thought I'd be glad my life was what it was.

The Ayandara drifted over to her, followed by her fluttering court. The ice-blonde tilted her head and examined Gleia's scarred face. "Ugly," she murmured. Shuddering with distaste, she traced the brands with her fingernail. "Bonder from up north, isn't she?" She stepped back. "But you said the merchant didn't buy her for her looks." With a ripple of laughter, hastily echoed by the others, she went on, "A lusty bull like Lorenzai might find a fascination even in this thing. You better watch her." The tip of her tongue traveled around her lips and there was a glazed look in the milky eyes. She slid those eyes to Amrezeh. Her thin lips stretched into a faint smile.

She's enjoying this, Gleia thought suddenly. *She knows exactly what she's doing to Amrezeh.*

"She's what? I forget."

Amrezeh closed her eyes. After a major effort she subdued her rage and said softly, "She designs and embroiders, Ayandara."

"So. What is she working on now?"

"Hold up your work, girl. Show the Ayandara." Amrezeh was calm again, seeming resigned.

Gleia held the cafta so it fell in graceful folds from her hands, the front panels carefully displayed.

"Ay-ai!" The Ayandara abandoned her teasing and stared at the panels. She snatched the cafta away from Gleia and held the work closer to her short-sighted eyes. She fingered the stitching. "A treasure. Rezeh, give her to me." She dropped the cafta on the floor as she turned imperiously to her half-sister. Gleia quietly retrieved it.

"I want her," the Ayandara repeated.

Gleia held her breath, the avrishum dripping from her hands. Not now. I can't leave here now. Not before tonight.

Amrezeh sank into a deep curtsey, her head almost touching her knee. "Though despois Lorenzai bought her for me, I don't own her. Lorenzai is master of this house. I dare not give away anything of his without his consent."

Gleia began to relax, silently cheering Amrezeh on. In a tiny way the small blonde was getting a touch of her own back. Anything the Ayandara asked for would get the same soft answer that said nothing except refusal but said it in such a way that the refusal was hard to counter even by the Ayandara.

The thin blonde was not accustomed to resistance. "We are displeased," she said icily. "We begin to think you don't want us to have this slave."

"I only have to ask," Amrezeh went on smoothly. "I am sure he is as eager to honor the Ayandara as I. The girl will be sent to you tomorrow."

Her lower lip trembling with petulance, the Ayandara said, "We are seriously displeased." She swept toward the door, her women parting hastily before her. In the doorway she turned, glared at

Amrezeh, her eyes taking on a hard glitter foreign to her pose of elegant languor. "We will be more than displeased if that slave isn't in our hands by tomorrow morning." She sailed out, the women following, cautiously silent, though more than one of them darted contemptuous and rather startled glances at the stubborn little figure kneeling in the center of the sewing room.

When they were gone, Amrezeh rose stiffly to her feet. She took the cafta from Gleia and stroked her fingers over the stitching, then gave it back. "Continue," she said abruptly and went out.

Gleia was still working, sitting at the sewing table in her room, when Shounach slid in through the window. He dumped his bag on the floor and stood scowling at her. "You'll end up blind."

She folded up the avrishum, wrapped it in muslin and stuffed it into the loot bag, along with extra thread and needles and her scavenged gold. She smiled at him. "It helps steady me." She slipped the strap over her shoulder and smoothed the bag against her side. "I'd have gone crazy waiting for you with nothing to do. Had a little trouble this afternoon. The Ayandara covets me, nearly walked off with me. Would have, if Amrezeh hadn't stopped her." She shuddered. "Let's get out of here."

At the entrance to the maze she took his hand. "Madar grant they haven't changed the pattern," she whispered. Then she closed her eyes and began counting the turns.

When they stepped into the corridor on the other side, Gleia went more boldly. Lorenzai would want no witnesses to his activities this night. Outside Amrezeh's bedroom, she dropped to her stomach and signed Shounach to lift the latch and ease the door open. When the room proved to be empty, she jumped to her feet and slipped in.

Grinning at her, Shounach sauntered through the door and started for the one leading to Lorenzai's room. Gleia caught hold of his sleeve. "Wait," she whispered.

"There's no one in that room."

"How do you know?"

"No questions, Companion." He frowned. "Why not get rid of this?" He touched the slave ring. "Stand still."

She heard the faint clicking of the probe, was intensely aware of his strong nervous hands brushing against her neck and shoulder, aware too of a suppressed irritation of her nerves, an impatience with herself and with him that they hadn't taken care of this in some safer place. Then the lock clicked open. He broke the ring and pulled it away from her. As she rubbed at her neck, he dropped the ring and kicked it under Amrezeh's bed. She sighed with relief as it vanished, then looked up as his hands came down on her shoulders. He dropped a light kiss on her lips then turned her about and pushed her toward the other room. "Time to move."

He stopped by Lorenzai's table. "The Ranga Eyes. Where?"

Gleia crossed to the wall and stared at the carving. It was harder to remember the right spot than she'd expected. She fumbled exploring fingers over the sprays of salt-flowers, then gave a small gasp of relief as the panel popped open.

Shounach reached a long arm over her shoulder and scooped out the box, startling her because she hadn't heard him come up behind her. He turned back the lid and stared down at the Ranga Eyes. "You said there were fifteen?"

She looked over his arm. "They're getting busy. Five left." She shrugged. "Why don't you leave them there?"

"You know why." He snapped the box shut and slid it into his bag. "How do we get down?"

Sighing she moved along the wall and began hunting out the flowers that opened the hidden door.

"Need light?"

"Lorenzai didn't bother . . . ah!" The door swung open. She took a deep breath and stepped into the passage.

Six turns into increasing darkness. Then a sudden graying ahead. She hesitated, felt Shounach's reassuring hand on her shoulder. She touched it briefly then edged around the turn. The stairs opened into a twisting hole that turned steeply downward. A knobby fungus growing in patches on the walls glowed with a cold greenish light. A deceptive light. She stumbled uncertainly. It was hard to judge distance without shadows. When she reached out to steady herself, her fingers brushed against the fungus. It had a rubbery warm texture, almost like living flesh. She wiped her hand vigorously on her sleeve, then looked back over her shoulder.

Shounach ducked down as he left the stairs, too tall to stand upright in this claustrophobic wormhole. With a rueful smile he motioned her forward.

She nodded. Better to get out of this discomfort as soon as possible. She went on as fast as she could, wondering how Lorenzai managed his bulk in this cramped place.

As she negotiated the difficult dips and turns, her excitement rose until her heart nearly choked her. She was working free of this trap, using her

wits and luck to outwit man and circumstance.
She felt light-headed, soaring with elation. Poor
Lorenzai. Standing down there waiting for his ship
to arrive. She giggled. Waiting for us though he
doesn't know it and a bump on the head and being
stowed away where Zuwayl can't see him while
we take his place. . . . She giggled again then
frowned. After several more turns of stumbling
and swaying and knocking into walls, she became
aware of a faint sweet odor. The fungus. She tottered along, wiping at her face with trembling
hands, struggling to bring her mind and body back
under control.

The wormhole wound down and down until a
low sound began to merge with the near inaudible
slip-slip of her feet. The sound quickly grew louder
until it was a rhythmic booming that bounced
around the hole with deafening force. Then she
was out of the blow hole, tottering on a narrow
scratch carved from the side of a great echoing
bubble in the stone whose top was lost in shadow
and whose bottom was drowned in rocking black
seawater. The fungus grew over the wall, thicker
here because of the salt damp. The track, wide
enough for two large men to walk side by side, had
no guard wall or anything between her and the
drop. It angled steeply down to a short pier whose
planks were sodden with the salt water which was
just backing off it as the tide fell. She walked to
the edge and looked down. The black water washed
against the black stone far below. At least fifty
meters. Looking down so far with nothing for her
hands to grasp made her dizzy. She retreated,
bumping into Shounach as he came up behind
her.

He chuckled, wrapped his arms around her, edged
her around and released her, then was off down

the scratch ahead of her, his booted feet silent on the stone.

Gleia pressed the back of her hand against her mouth, biting down hard on her finger to stifle her annoyance. He was taking over her escape. She watched him flit down the track, an absurd figure in his crimson trousers and the loose blue jacket that was flying open to expose its gold lining. With a reluctant smile she started after him.

A spark of light angled along the rock some distance below. In the treacherous cold light of the fungus she saw a dark shadow, solid and large, carry the small flame along the pier toward the end, footsteps heavy and dull on the water-soaked planks. A torch flared. The candle flame moved to the other side of the pier and a second torch was burning.

Gleia blinked. The sudden brightness of the flame killed the feebler glow of the fungus and her dark-adaptation at the same time. The cavern was suddenly black except the small area of torchlight where Lorenzai stood, elbows out, fists socked into his sides, staring out into the darkness. Gleia shut her eyes and waited a moment, trying to re-adapt. As she began creeping downward again, Shounach stepped onto the pier and started toward Lorenzai.

"Lorenzai!" The shriek burst into the silence, was echoed and re-echoed around the bubble. "Lorenzai . . . renzai . . . zai . . . ai . . . ai . . . ai."

Gleia wheeled. Amrezeh was plunging recklessly down the track, her face twisted with fury. She must have been up there all the time . . . followed us. . . . Gleia jerked back but Amrezeh was on her, biting and scratching, whining in her eagerness to hurt and punish. Her fingernails furrowed Gleia's cheeks. As the clawed hands drove for her eyes again, Gleia twisted away. She pulled her head down and slammed her fist into Amrezah's diaphragm, driving her back, choking and gasping, stumbling, finally falling hard on her buttocks.

Scrambling frantically, Amrezeh caught herself before her head cracked against the stone. Eyes glazed over, hands clawing, she was up immediately, driving at Gleia, knocking her back against the wall, mashing her against the patches of fungus, grinding the slimy stinking mess into Gleia's shoulders and hair.

Bleeding and nauseated, sick as much from the stench as from the violence, Gleia brought up one leg, planted a foot on Amrezeh's stomach and shoved blindly.

For a frozen moment Amrezeh tottered on the edge of the track. Her eyes opened wide. Her mouth gaped soundlessly. Then she fell back, tumbling over and over in eerie silence until just before she hit the water. A brief tearing shriek. A splash. Silence.

Dabbing at her face with her sleeve, her stomach churning, her hair clotted with the mashed fungus, Gleia staggered to the track's edge and looked down. The black water was lapping lazily at the stone, the surface rising and falling like the side of a panting beast. "No," she whispered. "No. . . ." She dropped to her knees and vomited until there was nothing left in her, until she knelt trembling with fatigue and soul-sickness.

"Gleia?" Shounach's shout and its echoes jerked her back to reality. She got shakily to her feet and looked down.

Shounach stood over a dark mound, his body tense. He relaxed a little when he saw her but called again to make sure. "Gleia?"

The word broke into fragments as it echoed around the bubble. She winced and tried to scrape some of the fungus off her hair. "It's me, Juggler," she called. She scrubbed at her face with her sleeve then tugged at the cloth that was sticking to her back. Then she went slowly and unsteadily down the track. A few moments later she met Shounach on the pier.

"You stink, Companion." He wrinkled his nose and backed away.

The look on his face surprised a short laugh from her. "I know, Juggler. I'm closer to it than you." She squeezed sections of her hair between thumb and fingers, then flung the mess into the water beside the pier. "Is he dead?"

"No." He nudged Lorenzai with his toe. The body fell over to lie with arms and legs tumbled awkwardly. "Just out cold. He went berserk when Amrezeh fell off the track."

Gleia dropped to her knees as her legs gave way with relief. The man's chest was rising and falling steadily; she could hear his rasping breath. Not dead, Madar be thanked, he isn't dead too.

Shounach sniffed. "As I remember it, you swim."

She looked up. "Yes, why?"

"Swimming seems a good idea right now." He grinned at her. "We've had enough melodrama, love." Grimacing with distaste, he picked her up before she could protest, strode the length of the pier, and dropped her off the end into the cold salt water.

Half an hour later, scrubbed pink, hair clean and damp, back in a soggy cafta, she stood beside Shounach over the bound and gagged figure of Lorenzai. She winced away from the fury in his eyes and turned to the Juggler. "Where are we going to put him?"

"I'm thinking about it." He began playing with the pouch of gold he'd taken from Lorenzai's robes, juggling it from hand to hand. From somewhere he produced the large and clumsy key to the armory's door and began tossing them both up and catching them, managing effortlessly the two radically different weights and shapes.

Gleia watched, exasperated. "Must you fool with those?"

One eyebrow arched up. "Why so serious, Companion? Life is only as grim as you make it. Relax." He caught the pouch and the key and slipped both into his bag. "You take his feet. I'll get his shoulders. Up there." He pointed up the track to the point where the worm hole broke into the bubble. "No one's likely to look for him there."

After an exhausting struggle that Lorenzai hampered as much as he could, they dropped him on the stone and stood a moment to catch a breath before returning to the pier. Gleia leaned against Shounach smiling down at the merchant. "We'll see you get your weapons, Lorenzai. I'm sorry about Amrezah." She closed her eyes a moment, feeling sick as she saw again Amrezeh tottering on the rim of the track, face ugly with horror. "We didn't plan to hurt anyone; it just went wrong." Shaking herself out of her sudden depression, she moved away from Shounach. "We'll have your smuggler stack the weapons in front of your armory. You can still pull your coup. Not my business but I think you'll do a lot better at running Thrakesh than those crazy Ayandari." She smiled tentatively but the rage on the merchant's face failed to abate. He humped his body about, struggling against his bonds, then fell back, gasping for breath around the gag.

Shounach tossed the armory key down beside him. It rang on the stone, bounced, settled against Lorenzai's arm. "Forget him." He took Gleia's arm.

"You're not going to reach him now. Let's get back out there."

An hour later they stood together between the torches, watching a line of small boats come into the light. Gleia plucked at the still damp material of her cafta and glanced up at Shounach. He was frowning slightly, his eyes moving from the six rowers to the man sitting at the bow of the front boat. She tugged at his sleeve. "Zuwayl?"

"Probably."

"You know him?"

"No."

She scowled at the nearing boats. "Five, Shounach. A lot of men."

"We don't intend to fight them. Words, Companion. They'll get us a lot farther than swords."

Gleia examined the man they thought might be Zuwayl. "Wag your tongue carefully, Juggler."

Zuwayl stepped from the boat onto the pier. He looked at them, looked past them at the empty pier, raised his eyebrows and turned to face Shounach. "Who're you?"

"Passengers."

"Hoh! Not that I know. Persuade me."

Shounach tossed five pentoboloi at him, one at a time. "Let these whisper in your ear."

Zuwayl grinned and clicked the coins in his left hand. "They have sweet tongues, friend. Welcome aboard." He jerked a thumb at the boats rocking in the water by the end of the pier. "I had a deal."

"Still got it. Our friend who shall be nameless gave me the money for the shipment. Have your men haul it up and dump it in front of the armory door."

Zuwayl's mouth split in a wide grin, folding the

skin of his cheeks into a dozen small wrinkles on each side of his mouth. "You seem like an honest man, friend." He snapped thumb and forefinger together. "Me, I gotta check myself to see I don't sell my skin. The gold, friend."

Shounach dipped into his bag and produced the pouch of gold. He tossed it to Zuwayl.

"Now that's style." Zuwayl wheeled, casually turning his back on them. "Jorken, take our passengers out to the ship. Herler, the rest of you, start unloading. Move it. Tide'll be in before we finish, we don't hurry."

Gleia stepped into the boat and settled herself somewhat nervously between two of the villainous-looking oarsmen. Shounach stopped for a last murmured word with Zuwayl, then settled in behind her.

The stone bubble's wall swept quickly down to another wormhole dripping seaweed and slime. They wound quickly through the short tunnel, then were out under the open sky and heading for a dark bulk barely visible in the dusting of surface mist. Gleia looked around, her curiosity back stronger than before.

They were outside the breakwater in the open sea. She glanced up and back, catching fugitive gleams from the gilded roofs of Thrakesh. She moved her shoulders impatiently. That part of her life was irrevocably over. *Over.* She laughed silently, remembering the crazy rage in Lorenzai's eyes. *Better to get away far and fast.* She looked around at the men bending their backs in practiced unison as they drove the boat across the waves toward the ship anchored in deeper water. *Far and fast. The both of us.*

She stared to turn to the Juggler but changed her mind. *Time for that later. Time to find out who and what he is. Shounach the juggler. The thissik Keeper called him Starfox. Hunting for the source of the Ranga Eyes. Should be uncomfortable but interesting.* As the longboat's bow cut across the incoming waves, rising and falling in bumpy swoops, she began to feel a similar swooping in her spirits.

She ran her hands through her hair and sniffed the wind. Southwind again. *Southwind.* She laughed aloud, drawing astonished glances from the rowing men. *Southwind my mother, here I go again. Jumping into the dark. I wonder what will happen this time.*

FIFTH SUMMER'S TALE
(PART TWO)

Companioning

"Damn him. Five days and not a word." Gleia stabbed the needle through the soft black material, pricked her finger, and jerked it away before blood could stain the cloth. Sucking at the small wound, she laid the shawl aside and swung around on the window seat where she'd taken her work to save on lamp oil, using instead the pale red light from Horli that struggled through the heavy layer of clouds. She propped her elbows on the windowsill and gazed out at the busy street below. The pattern of silver and green on the shawl heaped beside her was nearly finished. Another day and there'd be coins plumping out the limp money pouch she'd left on the table by the bed. *One more thing to worry about. That and Shounach. Damn him for not letting me know whether he's alive or dead.*

She was still chuckling at that absurdity when an iron bird swooped past to hover over the street. As she watched, it darted back and forth over the suddenly quiet people, then soared back to hover in front of her, humming like an outside insect, wings a foot long, moving slightly but constantly, the red light from cloud-hidden Horli sliding along crisply modeled features. The ball-head's single eye set above a needle beak scanned her, small flickers of red light stirring in the depths of the dark lens. The thing made her shiver—a parody of a living bird. Deel called it an iron bird, the Lossal's iron bird, though it was made of a shining metal more like polished silver than black iron. *It's only a machine*, she told herself, *not a creation of some devil sorcery*. As it swung suddenly and whirred off, she shivered again. *Temokeuu-my-sea-father, I wish you were here to tell me it's only a machine.* She continued to watch as it soared inward over the middle city, dipping finally out of sight behind one of the Family Houses that dominated the center of walled Istir.

She rested her chin on her hands and looked dreamily out the window, thinking of her adopted family of sea-folk, wondering how Tetaki-her-brother was coming with his new trade route, wondering whether Jevati-her-friend had married again. Snatches of music from neighboring taverns drifted up to her; street sounds floated around her—men's voices as they passed along the street, arguing, talking, laughing; the clop-clop of horses' hooves on the dark stone paving, a whinny or two and some snorts; the distant blended noise of huckster cries coming from the markets on both sides of the Strangers' Quarter. Sharp smells floated on the lazy breeze—frying oil, fish, cooked meats, urine, horse manure. Her eyes dropped; she studied the people passing by, feeling a comfortable familiarity with a mix much like that she'd grown up with in Carhenas across the ocean—drylanders in silent groups; hunters; hillmen; boatmen from the highland rivers; an enigmatic group of veiled and armored women who seemed to call out hostility in the men around them. Gleia blinked, frowned as they passed out of sight followed by curses, uneasy laughter, obscene gestures.

Once the women were gone, Gleia lost interest in the street and turned back to wondering about Shounach. *How is he? What's he doing now? What's he been doing the last five days? Why doesn't he send word out?* She scratched at her arm; living with the Juggler was making her itchy. *Companion. What's that mean? That red-haired cow, the Lossal's daughter. . . .* She flexed her fingers, then began rubbing at the line of her jaw. It was difficult. She wasn't used to fitting her actions to someone else's needs. *If he isn't back by tomorrow, I'm getting out of here.* With a feeling of relief, she let her hand drop into her lap. Relief and anger and uncertainty.

Relief because she was going back to the comfortable simplicity of living alone; she could feel her taut muscles relaxing.

Anger because she hurt at the thought of leaving him. She didn't want to allow him that much importance in her life. With an involuntary smile she remembered the long, lazy nights on the smuggler's ship that had brought them across the ocean from Thrakesh to this new land—new for her if not for Shounach—long lazy nights crawling north along the coast, city to city, waiting while Zuwayl did his deals, moving on again, in no hurry to get anywhere. She remembered the painful, clumsy beginning of intimacy. Remembered his patience and skill—a skill she teased him about later when she'd regained some of her assurance—as he taught her body to respond. She clenched her hands into fists and beat on her thighs. *The Lossal's daughter. He's with her. Five days, five damn days. . . .* The thought was fire in her blood. She pushed at the pain, trying to deny it, and sat for some minutes, the heels of her hands pressed against aching eyes. As her breathing steadied, the anger altered to uncertainty.

Uncertainty because she wanted to stay as much as she wanted to go. Because she had no place to go to if she left. Rubbing absently at the brand on her face, she leaned her head against the end of the shutter and wondered what she was going to do.

A rippling laugh from the street pulled her from her painful musing. She caught hold of the sill and leaned farther out.

A cloaked figure was slapping at the hands of a Harrier, one of the mercenaries hired by the six Families to act as guards and as a small private army if necessary. The long slim arm, the fluid movement looked familiar. The woman laughed again, called back a last cutting comment to the Harrier as she moved along the street with a free, flowing swagger that sent the ends of her cloak flying. Gleia smiled with pleasure, leaned down and waved. "Deel?"

The dancer looked up, pushed the hood back off her head. Raising her voice over the noise of the street, she called, "He back yet?"

"Not yet." Gleia coughed to clear her throat, then yelled, "Going somewhere?"

"Work." Deel wrinkled her nose, twisted her mobile face into a comical grimace. "New bunch of boatmen in from upriver. One-eye sent word I was to get there in half a breath." She shook her head, her tight thatch of brown-gold curls glinting in the pale light. "Good money, but I hate those sorry slobbering bastards. Have lunch with me tomorrow?"

"I'd like that. Meet here?"

The dancer nodded. Gleia watched her swing off until she was out of sight, then pulled her head in and slid off the window seat. Making sure the needle was tucked securely into the material, she folded the shawl neatly and set it on the table by the bed, smiling as she remembered her meeting with Deel. *Five days ago I didn't know her and now I have a friend.*

In the Square of the Cloth Merchants, Shounach stood on a platform he'd rented, the blue glass balls circling his white painted face, changing in number and shape as he turned slowly to face the traders and sellers, shoppers, market women, other entertainers, scattered Harriers, and a number of pickpockets and other thieves that pressed about the four sides of the platform. Gleia sat on the coping of the market well, watching what she could see of Shounach past the heads of the onlookers. A constant stream of people moved by her, edging along the fringes of the crowd, going on to stop at one or another of the small open-faced shops that lined the square.

As Shounach's routine neared its close, she felt a brief tugging at her cafta, heard an angry yell, then a boy's shrill, rapid protest. She looked around. A Harrier had a small boy by the nape of the neck. Behind him a tall woman muffled in a long cloak stopped to watch, stiff with disapproval as she saw the Harrier drag the boy back to Gleia.

"Had his hand in your pocket." He scowled at the boy. "Fork over, schlop."

"I din' do nothin'," the boy shrilled. He wriggled, trying to pull away from the Harrier's cruel grip. "I din' do nothing'."

Eyes on the child's tear-streaked face, Gleia thrust her hand into her pocket. Her handkerchief was gone, nothing more. She smiled up at the glowering man. "You're mistaken, despois. The boy took nothing. Let him go."

The Harrier grunted, hesitated a moment, then loosed his grip on the boy's skinny neck. He watched the child dart away, then stalked off, muttering about fool women.

"You might want this back."

Startled, Gleia looked over her shoulder. The woman who'd been watching was smiling at her, holding out her handkerchief.

"It's a beautiful thing; whoever gave it to you must think a lot of you." The woman smoothed out the square of katani with its wide band of white-on-white embroidery, her fingers lingering over the exquisite stitching.

With a laugh Gleia waved the handkerchief away. "If it pleases you, then keep it. It's no gift, merely my own work and my own design."

"I couldn't." The woman's dark amber eyes glowed as she touched the delicate pattern.

"Please do. I have others."

Smiling with pleasure, the woman tucked the handkerchief into her cloak pocket and settled beside Gleia on the well coping. "Why did you let the boy off?"

She was a tall woman with high cheekbones and almond-shaped eyes, a wide mobile mouth that flashed easily from smiles to frowns. Her skin was a silky red-brown that looked poreless and fitted smoothly over elegant bones. Her hair was a disciplined foam of tiny curls only slightly darker than her skin. Underneath the cloak she wore wide amber silk strips arranged to flow around long slim legs. "My name's Deel. I dance at the Horn of Sandar in the Strangers' Quarter. You're new in Istir, aren't you. Why did you let the boy go?"

"I grew up in the streets myself." Gleia touched the scars on her cheek and met amber eyes bright with interest and understanding. "Not here. You're right about my being new." She flipped a hand at Shounach. "I came with the Juggler; we've only been here a few days." Reaching out, she touched Deel's hand. "My name's Gleia."

"I've been watching him the past few days. He's damn good, your Juggler." They sat in friendly silence as Shounach began putting away his paraphernalia.

A litter carried by four brawny men eased into the square and moved through the scattering crowd toward the platform. The litter was gilded and profusely carved, its occupant hidden behind pale-blue curtains.

Gleia frowned. "Who's that?"

"Trouble." Deel wrinkled her nose. "Toreykyn, the Lossal's daughter; that's the Lossal's sigil stitched on those curtains." She looked up, pointed. "Yeah, has to be her in there. Lossal's iron birds are keeping watch on her."

Two glittering metal bird-shapes were circling over the square. Gleia squinted up at them, trying to see them more clearly. "Iron birds?"

"Lossal's spies." Deel's mouth twisted, turned down at the corners. She tapped her polished nails lightly on her silk-covered thighs. "You've lost your man for a few days. Until she gets tired of him."

Gleia hid a smile as she watched the litter stop in front of Shounach. *The Fox's luck has turned*, she thought, remembering his frustration as he paced the room, cursing the insularity of the Families that shut the Lossal away from him. Now he would be riding in with the Lossal's daughter. She looked down. Her hands were closed into fists, fingernails cutting into her palm. After forcing her hands open, she glanced at Deel, and said with outward calm, "We do what we have to. No point in staying here any longer. Going back to the Quarter? Come and have a glass of wine with me."

Shounach snapped the lid off the solvent and poured some on a rag. Kneeling beside his bag, he wiped the paint from his face, then began on his hands. His eyes moved restlessly over the scattering crowd; he was impatient with this waiting time, wanted to get on with his search for the source of the Ranga Eyes. He saw Gleia talking to a strange woman, felt a touch of irritation that she'd hadn't bothered to watch his performance. He scrubbed at his hands, annoyed at the way the white paint clung around his fingernails, jabbed the rag at the stubborn paint in the creases. At the same time he fought against the rising waves of rancor that threatened to explode into shapeless, unreasonable anger spilling over anyone or anything around him. *It never ends*, he thought. He looked down at his hands, flexed the fingers, then put the solvent and the rag back in the bag.

He saw the litter approaching and remained on his knees waiting to see where it was going, holding his face calm as excitement rose within him when he recognized the Lossal's arms on the curtains.

The litter stopped in front of him; a slim, bangle-laden arm came through the curtains. With a flourish of clanks and tinkles, a delicate hand weighed down with many rings pulled the curtain back, retreated. Inside, the woman smiled up at him; she was stretched out, leaning on one elbow, pale-blue cushions piled around her; the hand that had drawn the curtain back now played with long strands of red-gold hair flowing over large firm breasts which thrust against the silver-shot white avrishum of her long, loose dress.

Red hair. Red-headed women. He shivered, then smiled to cover a surge of rage mixed with contempt. *In my mother's honor*, he thought, then bowed his head and waited for her to speak.

The big brown eyes focused on him began to blink nervously, the hand caressing the hair stiffened. *Stupid cow*, he thought. The soft smiling mouth drew into a pout. "Juggler!" Her voice was sharp, petulant. He got the feeling she'd expected more response from him than a polite bow. *Lossal*, he told himself. *A way in. Don't be more of a fool than you can help.* He widened his smile and let his eyes travel slowly over her, lingering on the slim curves barely concealed by the clinging material.

"Juggler." She was smiling again, her voice caressing. "The Lothal wanth you to perform." Her long lashes fell, then lifted, as she lisped the words, the command in them smothered in sugar. "I am motht interethted in your performanth, Juggler," she murmured. Her plump little hand closed tightly around cloth and hair. "Come with me now, Juggler. To my father." She stretched out her hand, more as a token of intent than as an offer of touching.

Shounach jumped easily down from the platform, the jacket swinging open to show the flat, hard muscles of his chest. He slipped the strap of the bag over his shoulder, slapped it into place against his side, then walked the two steps to the woman's

side. "My pleasure, lady." He reached out and
almost touched her, letting his hand hover over
hers for a moment as he smiled into the dark
brown eyes. Her red hair fluttered gently as the
litter moved toward the gate to the market. She
lisped banal and impertinent questions, her eyes
moving over him with the possessiveness of a herds-
man assessing a prize bull. At the gate he looked
around and saw Gleia watching him, an odd expression on her face, a gentle, vulnerable look as
fleeting as a moment's thought. She turned and
moved away with the tall, dark woman beside her.
He glanced back again a moment later, saw the
cluster of soft brown curls held high, saw a brief
arc of cheek as Gleia turned to talk to the strange
woman. A sharp note in the voice of the Lossal's
daughter brought his attention back to her. He
listened, then answered her as they walked along
the broad avenue leading to the Families' quarter,
walled in, apart from the rest of the city.

Gleia picked up the pouch, poured the coins into
her hand, frowned as she counted the diminishing
supply. With a sigh she dumped them back in the
pouch, jerked the drawstring tight, slipped the loop
over her head, dropping the pouch inside her cafta
to dangle between her breasts. She brushed off the
bottoms of her feet, slid them into sandals, ran a
comb through her tangled hair, tossed the comb
on the bed and went out. She grimaced with disgust as she locked the door and slipped the key
into her pocket; given a bit of bent wire she'd be
inside with no trouble at all. *Good thing there isn't
much to steal.*

Outside, she looked up, shading her eyes with
one hand. The sky was clear, blue Hesh edging
past fuzzy red Horli. She pulled the hood of her

cafta up over her head. The respite was over. With Hesh emerging from behind Horli she'd have to watch her exposure; ah, well, she was used to that. She stepped back and stood waiting as clusters of men moved past her, some strolling, others walking briskly.

Deel came rushing up, her cloak fluttering about her long legs. "Thanks," she gasped out. "For waiting. Merd had some time off this morning and I couldn't get away earlier."

Gleia turned, began walking along beside the dancer, threading through the thickening crowd as late sleepers joined those already moving, blending into the same mix as before, even to the compact group of veiled women. Gleia nodded at them. "You know who or what they are?"

Deel followed the nod and saw the women. "Never mind them," she said hastily. She sounded uncomfortable.

"Why?" Gleia caught hold of Deel's arm. "Who are them?"

"They call themselves Sayoneh," Deel said reluctantly. "Some folk call them trail women, some witches, unnatural creatures. They live together, won't let men in their compounds; lot of funny stories about them and I don't mean ha-ha. Come from somewhere upriver like the boatmen, no one knows really where they live, they just show up. Some say they steal women and babies, girl babies to raise, boy babies to sacrifice or eat, Madar knows what." Deel looked after them and shivered. "Best to keep far away from them."

With Gleia silent, thinking over what she'd just heard, and Deel too disturbed to talk, the two women wound through the streets toward the row of cook shops in the shadow of the outside wall.

After buying meat pies and mugs of cha, Gleia

and Deel moved outside and sat down on a shadowed bench in a quiet corner where the massive
outer wall turned to follow the line of the River.
Deel finished the meat pie quickly, lifted the cheap
clay cup to her lips, her amber eyes sweeping over
Gleia. "Still no sign?"

"No." Gleia sipped at her cha, then settled back,
pushing the hood off her head with a sigh of
pleasure.

Deel chuckled, unfastened the clip holding her
cloak around her shoulders and let it fall away.
She shook the springy foaming curls haloing her
head, pushed straying tendrils off her face. "He
must be something special, your man." She raised
an eyebrow. "Most of Toreykyn's fancies don't last
this long." Her mouth turned down again. "If she
gets too taken with him, the Lossal will open the
eyes he keeps shut. Then, well, good-bye Juggler."

Gleia folded both hands about the coarse clay of
her cup, sipped at the cooling cha. The clay clicked
dully against her teeth. Her hands were shaking.
After a moment she rested the cup on her thigh,
feeling the spot of warmth through the material of
her cafta. "What choice do people like us have?
We do what we must to stay alive."

Deel leaned back, her eyes narrowed, her long
legs like polished wood coming through the slits of
her costume. "Istir's no place for a woman on her
own. You should look around, find yourself a
protector." She grinned at Gleia's grimace. "No
need to make faces, girl; it's the truth and you
know it."

Gleia's mouth twitched. She rubbed her thumb
under her lower lip, then stroked the scars on her
cheek. "No," she said quietly. "Deel, I've been on
my own since I was born, almost. I wouldn't know
how to act with a protector." She took a long

swallow of cha, lowered the mug back to her thigh. "And I don't want to learn."

"What about the Juggler?"

"That's different."

Deel snorted. "It always is."

Gleia scowled stubbornly. "You don't know." She examined Deel's face over the edge of the cup as she lifted it for another sip. "What happened to your eye?"

Deel grimaced. "Merd. His captain's been riding him hard the past few days so he takes it out on me."

"And you want *me* to find a protector. No thanks, friend."

Deel spread out long slender arms, her narrow elegant hands turning in quick flashing gestures. "Lot worse about than Merd. Me being a dancer, I keep running up against creeps who think dancer's another name for whore. Some of the bosses're worse than the drunks hanging round the bar when I dance. Since I've been with Merd, both types leave me alone. He got physical with some hecklers and clods hard-timing me a while back." She chuckled. "He's half as big as a house and a Harrier besides. No one wants to get the Families stirred up. It's worth a few lumps. Anyway, he's not so bad." She shrugged, stroked her finger along the clean-cut curve of her upper lip. "You wouldn't be bad looking if you covered up those scars. Why don't you let me give you some stuff I have? I'll show you how to fix yourself up."

Gleia shook her head, then grinned at Deel. "I don't give a damn about trying to change myself, my friend. I know how I look. I like how I look."

"Dumb." Deel leaned forward, spread her hands out in front of Gleia. They were meticulously manicured, the nails polished a dark plum that matched the gloss she wore on her lips. "Put your hands by mine."

Gleia spread her smaller hands beside the dancer's. Short fingers, short nails, the tip of her middle finger and the side of one thumb rough as sandstone from repeated needle pricks.

Deel clucked with distress. "Didn't anyone ever show you how to take care of yourself?" She lifted one of Gleia's hands and turned it over, scowling at the dry skin of the palm. "You got any money left?"

"A little." Gleia gently freed her hand. "I've almost finished embroidering a shawl. A couple hours' work left on it. I could use some help finding a reasonably honest merchant to buy it."

"Got it, hon." Deel frowned, tapping the tips of her nails lightly on the amber silk covering her thighs. "I'll see if I can talk Merd into coming. With him along, no merchant's going to cheat you more than reasonable. If the Juggler's not back by tomorrow morning we can grab a bite to eat and hunt out a couple of men I know of. What're you going to do once you've got the money?"

Gleia was silent a long moment. Finally, she smoothed her hand across her eyes. "I don't know," she said slowly. "Last night I thought I'd leave. Now . . . I don't know. I. . . ." She stopped talking, shook her head, sat frowning at the dregs of cha in the cup. "Deel, what's happening here in Istir? What's got people so stirred up?"

The amber eyes studied her, then the dancer nodded. "Right. You and your Juggler picked a bad time to come here." Deel crossed her arms over her breasts and leaned forward until her head was close to Gleia's. "The Stareyn's getting feeble, so I hear. They don't let it out, the Families, I mean, but a lot of people work in the Kiralydom and go home to their families when their hours are done. So people know more than the Families think. And Merd had duty in the Kiralydom twice a week. He tells me the Stareyn drools and goes to sleep in the middle of what he's saying. He's a Sokklaun, the Stareyn, I mean. The Sokkla have held the Stareynate for the past three Stareyns which means they've ruled Istir and the Istraven for years and years. But the Lossalni are prowling around ready to take it from them soon's they figure out how." She looked cautiously around, then leaned closer and whispered, "Rumor is they have. The Stareyn's Lot is supposed to be tamperproof, pure chance, but men keep saying the Lossal's found a way to change the odds. Me. . . ." She glanced about again, but none of the men moving past seemed interested in them. "Me, I'm thinking hard of getting out of here, maybe going south to Zindaira. Summer's almost over, got to find a place to winter somehow. I've got friends there. And I'm a damn good dancer. I won't starve. Why don't you come with me? You said you were thinking of leaving. Two women would be safer than one."

"What about Merd?"

"I'll miss the big idiot, but I'd miss my head a lot more. If the Stareyn goes, he'll be on duty till he drops. What I see, there's going to be trouble. When powerful families fight, the little people get stomped. Like you said, you can feel the tension, even here in the Strangers' Quarter. Any day now the mess starts. One of the reasons Merd's captain is so edgy." She giggled. "One of the reasons I got this eye." She looked up. Clouds were beginning to thicken over the suns. "Damn. It's going to be a wet night. On top of everything else that means the Horn is going to be wall-to-wall boatmen, Hankir Kan's Hands like lice on a beggar's hide."

She hitched her cloak back around her, fastened the chain and pin. "Think about what I said, Gleia. The Juggler's got himself in a real sticky spot. That little viper the Lossal would poison half the city to protect his daughter. He'll never admit even to himself that she sleeps around worse than any whore. Six days now." She shook her head. "I don't think you'll see him again." Sighing, she stood and pulled up the hood of her cloak. "I've got to go. Merd's coming back later this afternoon and he expects me to be home. Think about it. If you want to leave, come with me."

Gleia watched her swing off then looked down at the skim of cha left in the mug. With a sharp cry of pain and frustration, she tightened her fingers about the mug, then flung it against the wall where it crashed into crumbly shards that pattered softly on the stone pavement. She dropped her head into her hands, her dilemma intensified by Deel's offer. "Shounach, Shounach," she whispered. "What should I do? If I knew what was happening to you . . . if I knew . . . why me . . . why do you try so hard with me . . . if I knew . . . if I knew what I . . . Madar curse all Ranga Eyes." She lifted her head and stared down at her hands. *Ranga Eyes. Worse than any drug. Those that make laws . . . every place I know, they say it's death to be found with one, death if you're caught trying to sell one. But men do. And men buy them. Ranga Eyes. Ranga dreams. They bait us with dreams. Until we can't look away. Until we die of hunger and thirst . . . and longing.* She cupped a hand and saw in it the colorless egg-shaped crystal she'd stumbled over in that street in Carhenas. Her Ranga Eye. She remembered holding it, letting it warm in her hands until it folded her in veils of bright color, until it showed her a world unlike her drab, gray

surroundings, a world where tree-sized flowers
bloomed under a butter-yellow sun, a world where
men flew on great bright butterfly wings, dancing
their delight in soaring swoops. They called to her,
called her to come, whispered to her that she had
only to let go, let the Eye take her and she would
be with them soaring on transparent wings under
a single yellow sun. Gleia shivered and let her
hands drop. *How many times do I have to say no?*
She rubbed her hands on the cafta, trying to rub
away the feel of the crystal egg. *Death to be found
with them, but still the traders carry them. And fools
buy them. Ranga Eyes. I wish Zuwayl hadn't told
you where he got the Eyes, Shounach. If it wasn't for
those damn Eyes you wouldn't have gone off with
her . . . and left me . . . I think you wouldn't have
left . . . Madar bless, I don't know . . . I don't
know . . . I don't know. . . .* She jumped to her feet,
jerked up the hood, walked quickly away.

Late that evening when she came back to her
room, tired from wandering aimlessly about the
market quarters, she shut the door and turned to
find rain drifting in through the open shutters.
With an exclamation of annoyance, she ran to the
window and reached out to unhook the braces, the
rain misting into her face.

Four large men came trotting down the street,
rain painting highlights on their oiled bodies and
running down the sides of the gilded litter they
carried. Gleia recognized the blue curtains, stiffened,
wondering whether she was glad or not to see it.

Shounach slid out, shook his bright head as the
misting rain settled on his hair, pressed a lingering kiss onto the small, plump hand thrust through
the curtains after him. Ignoring the rain slanting
down harder now, he watched the litter move off,

then looked up. When he saw Gleia, he grinned, waved, ran into the building.

Gleia swung the shutters to and dropped the bar-latch into its hooks. She moved to the bed and sat down, shoulders bent, feeling strange. All the pain, anger and uncertainty was back.

He rapped on the door. "Gleia, open up."

She slid off the bed, kicked off her sandals, padded to the door. After a moment's hesitation, she turned the key in the lock and retreated to the windowseat. Her body tucked into the corner where the walls met, she sat with legs pulled up, hands resting on her knees.

Shounach stepped inside, shut the door, looked around. The only light in the room came from the torches in the hall, trickling in through the cracks around the door. He was a nervous shadow in the darkness. She could hear him moving about, could feel his annoyance in the jerky movements. He dropped his bag beside the bed. "Gleia?"

She closed her eyes. Accusation, bitter complaints, questions boiled inside her, all of them futile, it seemed to her. Without speaking she watched him light the lamp. Her hands were shaking again. She folded her arms across her breasts, hugging the cafta tight against herself, waiting for him to speak.

"Sitting in the dark?"

She examined his face, still saying nothing. He looked tired and irritated, but the grinding frustration that had been wearing him down was gone; he'd found out what he wanted to know. She swallowed and let her eyes drop.

"Sulking?" He dropped onto the bed and began pulling off his boots. "Come here." With a grin he patted the bed beside him. "Got some good news."

She pulled her legs up farther, pushed back into the corner. "No."

He slipped out of the loose jacket and threw it on the floor by the boots. "What's eating at you?"

Sucking in a long breath, she fought with the urge to spill her anger over him. She swallowed repeatedly, finally burst out, "Five damn days and not a word."

"You know where I was." He started undoing the fastenings of his trousers. "And why I went there."

She heard the anger in his voice as he snapped the words at her; it sparked her own anger. "So?" She wriggled out of the corner and swung her legs off the windowseat. "It couldn't have been that hard to get a word, one word, out to me. Let me know you're still alive. How do you think I feel when I hear how jealous the Lossal is of his daughter, that he'd poison half the city for her?" She leaned forward, her hands closed tight around the edge of the seat. "I saw her; she's beautiful. I never knew why you took up with me; you could decide to pack it in any time." She lifted her head, stared at him, the anger draining from her. He looked tired and unhappy. His shoulders slumped. He wiped a hand across his face, dropped the hand on his knee. Gleia closed her eyes a moment, opened them again, said, "You did forget me, didn't you."

"You finished?"

"No. But what's the point of saying more?" She shrugged. "I planned on leaving tomorrow, when I thought you weren't coming back."

"And now that I have?"

"I don't know."

Gleia was leaning back against the shutters, her face lost in shadow. The loose cafta fell about her body, concealing it, but her hands were restless, fingers twitching, palms brushing over her thighs, shifting across the wood of the windowseat. Shounach suppressed a burst of anger, felt instead a frisson of fear as this repeated an old pain. He was afraid of his anger, afraid of what it made him do. She'd wriggled in under his skin without knowing what she'd done, had stirred up emotions he'd thought dead—happily dead. He rubbed his hand across his face again. He was tired, sick with a self-loathing born of his pandering to Toreykyn's fancies, sick too from the ancient anger that drove him after the Ranga Eyes. He watched her hands a minute, then asked, "What do you want to do?" For the first time in far too many years he found himself caring about what another person decided; he could feel parts of himself unfolding painfully. Trying to shut those vulnerabilities away as he waited for her answer, he crossed his arms over his chest and stood watching her.

For several minutes she said nothing. Her hand lifted, her fingers moved slowly over her scars— her talismans. "I don't know."

"You said that before." He smiled briefly, let the smile fade when she continued to stare past him.

"I said it to myself a lot the last few days. Until I was sick of hearing it." She sat up, bringing her face into the light. "I don't know if I can run double; that's the truth. Not when there's pressure on like now."

"I see." He looked down at his boots, at the jacket falling over them. He looked at her again, turned away. After stepping out of his trousers, he carried bag, boots, and clothing to the wall pegs where Gleia's bag already hung, its canvas sides bulging. He touched it, looked over his shoulder. "You're ready to go. All packed."

She thrust her fingers impatiently through her hair. "I told you."

"So you did." He dropped the bag and boots, hung jacket and trousers on the pegs, then came slowly to the bed, stretching and yawning as he walked. She watched without moving. He stripped the quilt back until it pooled at the foot of the bed, then lay on his back, pulled a pillow under his head, folded it, wriggled about until he was comfortable. "Come here, Gleia. I'm tired of yelling across a room at you."

Smiling reluctantly, she shook her head. "I don't trust you, Fox. You could talk a tars into skinning himself for you."

"That windowseat looks uncomfortable and it gets cold before dawn." He rolled onto his side, propped himself on an elbow and held out his hand. "Don't be silly, love. Come here and listen to the story of my life."

"Damn you, Fox." She slid off the windowseat. "Five days in that bitch's bed. I should kick you out that window." She jerked her head back at the shutters, then began pulling off the cafta. Her words muffled, she went on, "You don't know how tempted I am." After draping the cafta over the unfinished shawl on the bedside table, she blew out the lamp, then stretched out beside Shounach, lying on her stomach, her head resting on crossed arms. "The story of your life?"

"A part of it." He smoothed his hand slowly down the curve of her back, her flesh cool and taut under his fingers. "I had a brother once." Catching hold of one of her curls, he drew the silky length between thumb and forefinger. "A long time ago. A half-brother really, although we grew up almost like twins."

She pushed his hand away, turned slightly on her side. "I'm making no promises. Tell me what you want, but remember, it won't mean I have to

stay. I'll make up my own mind; I won't be pushed."
She settled back. What he could see of her face
was set in stubborn lines.

He turned on his back, stared into the shadows
thick on the ceiling. "Remember how we met?"

"On that ship the Thissik took over. Why?"

"You told me you couldn't remember your
parents. I. . . ." He lay silent a moment. The noise
from the tap room filtered up the stairs and hovered over them. Shounach could feel Gleia resisting him. She was moving away, stiffening. He stared
into the darkness, scratched at an arm. "When the
Thissik brought you in and dumped you on that
bunk, I thought I'd been fooling around too much
with the Eyes. I saw my brother. . . . you could
have been his twin."

"Your brother?" She pushed up from the bed,
swung around until she was sitting cross legged,
looking down at him. "Your brother? All this time
you've been making love to your brother?" There
was anger and revulsion in her voice. She started
to slide off the bed.

He caught her ankle. "Don't be stupid."

"Let go." She kicked her foot, trying to shake
him off.

He hesitated then released her. "Go if you want."
He rolled over, turning his back to her, waiting
tensely to see if his gamble worked. There was
silence for several minutes then he heard the sheets
rustling as she stretched out on her stomach again.

"Well?" The word was sharp, almost spat at
him.

"Well what?" He grinned into the darkness, relief and happiness stirring his blood, but he kept
amusement out of his voice.

"What has your brother got to do with anything?"

"Ummph." He turned on his back again, punched

the pillow up, angled his head so he could see her. Her face was lost in shadow, her curls tumbling forward until all he could see was the curve of her jawline. "Half-brother," he said. "Same father, different mothers; my mother was a red-haired witch with a curse on her. She. . . ." He stopped abruptly, finding after all he couldn't talk about the mother who'd abandoned him. "Never mind. My brother had a temper like yours, Gleia. Lava-hot one minute, gone the next. I was different. I held grudges a long, long time. Far beyond any reasonable point. My father tried to teach me better, but as the story goes on you'll see how little luck he had with that. My . . . my mother sent me a present one day, a Ranga Eye. I was watching the river flow past when a man came along the road behind me, told me he had something for me, a present, like I said, from my mother. He juggled it a moment then threw it in the water. I fished it out. If you're interested, that's the river that comes to sea a little south of Carhenas."

Gleia made a soft startled sound. He shifted onto his side, smoothed the hair back off her face, touched the scars on her cheek. "Strange to think we might be related," he said.

"I thought you were off-worlder. You let me think that."

He smoothed his hand over her back. "I don't talk about this much. I killed my brother."

"Shounach." She wriggled around, caught his hand—she drew back, peered through the darkness at his face, her skepticism returning.

He closed his hand about hers, taking strength from her. The next part was painful, no matter how he struggled to distance himself from the memory, he could still see his brother's emptied face. "I was about six-standard that spring. And

angry with my brother. We'd played some trick, I
can't even remember what it was, and he'd told on
us, got us both punished. Why I was sulking down
by the river. After that stranger disappeared, I fished
the Eye out of the water and sat turning it over
and over, fascinated, as it began playing its dreams
for me. You know. Before it could get too strong a
hold on me, the bell rang for the evening Madarchants. I hid the Eye in the roots of a tree and
went inside. And things got worse. After supper I
quarreled then fought with my brother and I was
punished and he was cosseted. That night I set
the Eye beside him, then went to bed, pleased
with myself, figuring he'd play with it all night so
he'd be spanked for oversleeping. He must have
been especially sensitive. In the morning he was
already lost. Eaten hollow." He pulled his hand
free, moved away from her, lay staring up into the
shifting shadows. The ancient anger was growing;
he struggled to control it as he finished the story.
"I ran away because I was afraid of what they'd
say and do to me. I couldn't face that, couldn't
face myself. I ran into the mountains, came near
dying half a dozen times. Met an Offworld thief,
went with him until he died. Wandered about,
never coming back to Jaydugar, running away from
myself as much as anything. Taught myself not to
feel deeply about anything. But something happened not long ago—that's another story, I'll tell
you sometime—that sent me back here."

"Hunting Ranga Eyes."

"Hunting," he said harshly. Turning his head to
her, he half-smiled, a quick upward jerk of a corner of his mouth. "I told you I hold grudges a long
time." He reached out again, took her hand.
"Something else you need to think about, Gleia.
Thanks to my . . . my mother . . . when I say long

time, I mean a very long time. All that. . . ." He searched her face, uncertain about how she would take what he was going to say; he'd been burnt too often by the bitterness and jealousy of lovers and friends when they stumbled on the truth about him, that he would live on much the same while they aged and died. For many reasons he needed to be honest with her, as honest as he could manage to be. "All that happened a hundred years ago. Jaydugar years not years-standard. If we are related, it's so remote there's almost nothing there."

Outside, the rain hissed down, drumming steadily against the shutters. Voices from the tap room below rose and fell. In the silence that followed, Shounach could hear curses as a man was thrown out into the wet, then his pounding feet as he ran for another shelter. Beside him Gleia shifted restlessly; she pushed up on one elbow and flattened her free hand on his chest. She was smiling a little, the whites of her eyes gleaming softly in the half-light. "What happened these past six days?" Catching a bit of flesh between thumb and fingernail, she pinched hard. "And don't brag about your conquest. I don't want to hear about it."

He laughed, happy with her, his relief as great as his joy; he squeezed her hand until she squeaked and tugged it away. "You delight me, my vixen. How I've missed you."

She slid back a little. "No promises, Fox." Her voice was cool; she wasn't about to let him play on her sentiments or talk her into forgetting her doubts. And, at least for the moment, she wasn't bothered by the implications of his age.

He laced his fingers behind his head, crossing his ankles. "What happened? I performed for the household and for the daughter of the House. In between times I wandered about, asked a few questions, listened a lot, and found out nothing about the Lossal and the Eyes. Though I listened to more than I wanted to hear about the Lossal and his ambitions." He yawned, stretched as he lay, loosening cramped muscles.

He slid carefully from the bed, stood looking down at the sleeping Toreykyn, filled with soul-weariness and self-loathing. "Whore," he whispered and didn't mean the woman snoring slightly, her face slack, empty for once of the greed and fretfulness that marred its prettiness. He stood a moment, eyes closed, then turned away from her, trying to throw off his weariness of body and spirit.

Aab's light crept through the curtains, turned the darkness into a pearl-gray shimmer. Shounach dressed quickly, then knelt beside his bag, reaching through the membrane into the hyperpocket for his tools; he hung a tingler in his ear, a pear-shaped red gem that would warn him of electronic spying. The Lossal's iron birds had startled him; they had no place in this pre-industrial society. As he slid the finder ring on his thumb, he wondered idly about the source of the birds. Offworld trader probably. He turned the gray-white stone inward, his lips tightening as he saw a faint glimmer in the dull gem. The finder was tuned to Ranga Eyes. For the first time he had evidence of their connection with the Lossal. He transferred lock picks, a small stunner, a cutter, and a laser rod to his pocket, then closed the bag.

Toreykyn stirred, muttered. Holding his breath, Shounach went quickly to her. She was still asleep but moving restlessly. He touched her temples, concentrated, sent her deeper into sleep. Straightening, he drew the tips of his fingers down his jacket. She was snoring again, soft little whistles.

She even lisps in her sleep, he thought. His revulsion had passed away and he felt only pity. She was, after all, a stupid woman without enough imagination to be evil.

He left her and moved to the window. For the past two days he'd been trying to get into the room the Lossal called his library. He'd tried every avenue he could discover, had returned again and again at various times during the day and night; there were guards around all the time, people going in and out at all hours. There was one last thing he could try—going in from the outside. He slipped through the heavy drapes and went into the window on his stomach. The wall here was nearly two meters thick and the window embrasure narrowed as it went outward, but it was still high enough for him to sit upright when he reached the outer opening. He wriggled around until he was sitting with his legs dangling among the vine tendrils, the over-sweet perfume of the vine fruit strong around him.

The garden below was silent, filled with a peace that seemed to mock him. The shrubbery and trees were dark areas separated by the paler grass and the silver glint of streams converging on the fountain in the center. Beyond the garden, the wall that shut in the privileged part of the city was dark and sullen, the crenellations etched against the torchlight from the market quarter beyond. He started to push out of the window, then stopped as he saw three figures moving at a rapid walk from the Strangers' Quarter, heading for the inner gate. He watched with considerable curiosity, high enough so he could look down into the wide street but too high to see much more than dark shapes. As the shapes disappeared behind the wall, he felt heat against the palm of his hand. He looked down, excitement cold in his stomach. Slowly he unfolded his fingers, uncovering the finder gem. The glow was strong and hot. Ranga Eyes. A lot of them. Close.

As the three appeared on the near side of the gate, a pair of iron birds swooped from the eaves to circle around the gate towers. Shounach frowned, then pushed out from the window and floated down close to the wall, dropping through wavering vine tendrils, his eyes fixed on the birds.

He landed crouching, scrambled back into the shadow close to the wall. The vine stalks were ancient, twisting monsters with loose, fibrous bark that curled away from the inner wood and came loose at the slightest touch, clinging to the material of his trousers, even to his bare feet and hands. He brushed cautiously at the itchy fragments, looking out through the skim of leaves at the birds.

One of them hesitated in its circle, then came soaring around over the garden. Shounach slid his hand into his jacket pocket, closed his fingers about the laser rod, silently cursing the bird. He had to get a look at those men, had to know who was bringing the Eyes to the Lossal. The smell of the vine fruit was stronger down here, near stifling. The leaves whispered, the vine stalks groaned and thrummed in the rising wind. In the trees and bushes he could hear a few night birds crying, night insects creaking and chirking. And over the small night sounds he could hear the humming whine of the iron bird.

It circled the garden and came back along the House wall. Ruby light shot suddenly from the eye and began sweeping along the wall's base. Shounach waited tensely; once he used the laser, he'd have to get out fast. The red light splashed on stone and leaves, moved swiftly toward him, left him wishing passionately for Stavver's chameleon web, though that was long gone, having died with its master.

The gate in the garden wall swung open and the three men came through. Two were Lossalni Harriers, the third a boatman from upriver. *Important man, judging by his strut.* An ugly, arrogant man hugging a large leather pouch against his barrel belly. Shounach stared greedily, his ring hand clenched in a fist, the ring-fire burning into his palm. *Madar be blessed*, he thought, echoing the formula of his childhood. *Fox's luck, as Gleia would say.* Forgetting about the searching bird, he stared at the man, fixing the blunt, scarred features in his mind.

The boatman looked up, saw the bird. "Get that damn thing away from me." He stopped walking, glared stubbornly at the Harrier. "Not another step till that abomination is gone."

Shounach started, then held himself very still as the bark and leaves rustled against the stone; he cursed the obsession that made him forget the danger he was in. He eased his head around and glared at the bird. The red light had stopped moving about two meters from him and the bird was bouncing up and down in the air as if it rode invisible waves.

"It senses something or someone in the garden. I'll. . . ." The Harrier broke off as the bird hummed away from the wall and darted back to the gate. "Must've been nothing. Come on. No talking once we're inside. Not till we're with the Lossal." The boatman nodded and the three men walked rapidly across the garden to the recessed door with its small flight of steps. Shounach crouched in the shadows, not daring to follow them, watching them go with a sick feeling of futility. Shaking with anger and frustration, he pressed the heels of his hands against his eyes, trying to convince himself that he had all he needed. *He's a boatman and I know his face.* He leaned against the stone, dizzy from the fumes of the vinefruit, too tired to force himself farther.

"I went back to the room, tucked things back in the bag, slept hard until Toreykyn woke me the next morning and kicked me out." He yawned, turned on his side, trying to make out her features in the darkness.

Gleia pushed her hair back from her face, raised on one elbow. "A boatman." She swung up, sat cross-legged, elbows on her knees, chin braced on her hands, her curls falling forward around her face as she focused her eyes on him. "You've got the next step. What now?" She hesitated a moment, then went on. "Deel says the Stareyn is close to dying."

"Deel?"

"You saw her—that time you went off with Toreykyn. The dancer standing next to me. She says when the Stareyn dies, the Families lock the gates and don't let anyone in or out until the Stareyn's Lot has been cast and the new Stareyn installed. That could make problems for you."

"For me?"

"Deel's leaving soon; she asked me to go south with her."

"I see. Will you?"

"I don't know." She started laughing, straightened her back, stretched extravagantly, then folded her arms across her breasts. "Stop pushing, Fox." She yawned suddenly. "Madar, I'm tired." She patted at her mouth, yawned again. "In the morning. We can talk this out in the morning."

*   *   *

Gleia jerked upright, dazed with sleep, as the door slammed open and a Harrier stalked inside. Shounach came awake like a startled animal, diving off the bed in a swift movement that changed into an awkward scramble as the quilt twisted around his legs. He kicked it away and ran for his bag.

The Harrier yelled an order and Shounach came to an abrupt stop, a sword at his throat. A third man came in, an archer. He stepped away from the door, a bolt ready in his crossbow, his dark cynical eyes turning between Gleia and Shounach. The leader of the three waved a hand; Shounach was backed into the center of the room where he stood, narrowed eyes searching for an opening. The lead Harrier tossed Shounach's clothing at his feet. "Get dressed," he said. He turned to Gleia. "You too, girl. On your feet and put something on." While Gleia pulled the cafta over her head and smoothed it down, he moved about the room, poking into its meager furnishings, tossing the two bags onto the bed, throwing the unfinished shawl over them. Shounach fastened his trousers and slipped his arms into the sleeves of his loose open jacket, watching grimly as the burly lead Harrier thrust his arm through the two straps and shrugged the bags up against his side. He turned to frown at Shounach. "The Lossal wants you. Don't try nothin'. Herv there can wing a gnat." He nodded at the archer. "We can tie you on a pole and haul you to him like a side of meat. Or you can walk. Up to you."

"I walk." Shounach held out his hand. Gleia took it and together they walked out the door, the leader ahead and the other two Harriers following close behind.

The rain had stopped; the pavement glistened wetly in the starlight that had broken through the tattered clouds. The torches were extinguished in front of the taverns and all the buildings in the Strangers' Quarter were dark and silent. In the near distance she could hear the shouts and other noises of the produce carts coming into the produce market. The only other sound was the shuffle of their feet on the wet stone.

The Library was a large room, filled with racks of scrolls and layers of flat pages sewn together. Among the piles of books, the piles of scrolls, sat small statues, vases, objects that glowed with color. The corners of the room disappeared in red-tinted gloom as the dawn light fanned through the line of long narrow windows in the outer wall, red light with motes dancing in the beams like points of fire. The Lossal sat behind a massive table in a low-backed massive chair. He was a small man with an exuberant nimbus of white hair, touched dramatically with crimson by the light pouring in the window just behind him, haloed in crimson light so that his features other than the pale glint of colorless eyes were lost in shadow. He sat waiting for them, watching them intently as the Harriers escorted them into the room. The leader set the two bags on the table in front of him. "As ordered, Lossal-vas."

The chair and table had elongated legs so the old man's eyes were on a level with theirs though he was sitting while they stood. His pale eyes moved past the Juggler, stopped on Gleia. "Why'd you bring the woman?"

"She was in bed with him, Lossal-vas."

Gleia shivered as she saw him frown, then glance upward. *Deel's wrong*, she thought. *He knows about Toreykyn's fancies. He knows about her and Shounach.*

The Lossal leaned forward and hooked Shounach's bag toward him. He flipped the top back and pulled out the contents—the blue glass balls, the red crystals, three small gilded dragons, a gilt dancer balancing on one foot, some bits of faceted glass, cheap jewelry, some crumpled scarves and dingy rags and fragments, other odds and ends. He upended the bag, shook it, then set it aside. Pushing the balls about with his forefinger, he smiled tightly at Shounach. "These look a lot better by torchlight and at a distance. Like you, Juggler." Sweeping everything from the table back into the bag, he dropped it beside his chair, then began investigating Gleia's possessions. As he fingered her spare caftas and reached for the unfinished shawl, Gleia forced herself to stay quiet, anger burning in her at this invasion of her privacy. He unfolded the shawl, touched the design, fingered the needle, then swept the shawl aside and took up the two handkerchiefs. He spread them out on the table before him, ran his fingers over the fine stitching. He dug through the rest of the things in the bag—her bag of thread, her book of needles, the tambour hoop, the small thread-knife with its razor-edged half-inch blade and horn casing, a ragged brush and some cakes of black ink, some parchment for sketching designs. He unrolled the wrinkled parchment, examined the scribbled sketches. After contemplating these for several minutes, he pushed the other things aside and pulled the shawl back in front of him. Smoothing the soft black triangle out on the table, he ran his fingers slowly along the band of silver and green embroidery above the elaborately knotted fringe.

Fuming and impotent, Gleia hugged her arms across her breasts and refused to look at the old man. The room was still; the only sounds were the soft rasp of his chalky fingers over the black cloth and the steady breathing of the man beside her. There was a dry, dusty smell to the room, a dusty smell to the old man as if he sat here like a withered spider, touching the threads of his plots.

The Lossal dropped the shawl and leaned back in his massive chair, dominating it and the room by the cold intensity of his colorless eyes. "Bring the woman closer."

Gleia jerked her arm away from the Harrier's hand, marched up to the table and stood glaring at the Lossal, too angry to give in to the fear that was clutching her stomach.

The Lossal leaned forward, frowned. "Turn your face." His eyes opened a little wider. "Show me the marks."

Reluctantly, Gleia turned her head. She moved stiffly, forcing an outward calm she was far from feeling. Her fingers twitched; her hand stirred, started to lift to her face. She stiffened her arm, brought her hand back to her side.

"Carhenas marks. Thief?"

"Yes." Though he waited, obviously expecting her to expand her statement or justify herself, she said nothing more.

He placed his hands palm down on the shawl. "Your work?"

"Yes."

"You're his woman?" He pointed at the Juggler.

Gleia stirred; she glanced at Shounach's blank face, then she shrugged. "For now."

He reached over, picked up the limp money bag,

his eyes on her, a small tight smile curving his thin lips. "You don't need this now." His smile widened and he tossed the pouch to the leader of the Harriers. "A small bonus for a good job, Ciyger."

Gleia clenched her hands, watching the money she and Shounach had worked hard to earn thrown so negligently away. Anger and a growing fear alternately burned and chilled her. Once again her skill was saving her neck; her fear wasn't for herself. What she'd begun to understand on Zuwayl's ship was coming clearer to her. What happened to Shounach happened to her; she was vulnerable in a way she'd never been before. The thought dismayed her, made her more uncertain than ever about what path she should take in the future.

"Move aside, girl." The Lossal's impatient command brought her from her unhappy thoughts; hastily she moved from in front of him and stood watching as the Harriers brought Shounach forward.

She stared. He looked furtive, cunning; his shoulders were rounded, his head thrust forward, an ingratiating smile twisted his mouth upward. Unconsciously she relaxed, realizing that the Fox was fitting himself into the Lossal's image of him, intending that the Lossal despise him and in despising him underestimate his capability. She glanced at the Lossal, saw him watching her, began to feel uneasy again. She clasped her hands behind her and tried to keep her face blank.

The Lossal shifted his gaze to Shounach. "Juggler." His voice was silk sliding easily over the ears. Gleia heard amusement crouching behind the softness and felt a lump of ice growing in her stomach. His next words weren't a surprise, she'd been waiting for them since the Harriers had broken in on them. "Tell me what you were doing in the garden last night."

The smile was wiped from Shounach's face; he looked startled and increasingly nervous. He rubbed a shaking hand over his mouth and stared at the floor. Forgotten for the moment, Gleia began to enjoy his performance. *Nothing overstated*, she thought. *He's another person.* "The bird spotted me," he muttered. He shivered, his eyes turning and turning, visibly searching for some escape from this difficulty. The Lossal waited, fingers tapping on the table. Shounach seemed to collapse in on himself. "I'm a thief," he said sullenly. "Too many people in the halls, couldn't lay my hands on anything worth the trouble. I went down the wall, meant to come inside on this floor, see if I could pick up something worth putting my head in the strangler's noose." When he finished, his words were coming fast, piling out one on top of the other, but the last words trailed off under the Lossal's cool and skeptical gaze.

Reptilian lids dropping over pale eyes, the Lossal studied Shounach's face. "You could be the trash you seem." He waved away Shounach's protests. "No matter. I'll find out." The jerk of his hand brought the lead Harrier to the table. "Take that downstairs; tell Ottan Ironmaster to play with him a little, find out what he knows. I don't think he'll find anything interesting so he doesn't have to waste effort trying to keep it alive. Leave one of your men here to take the girl."

Gleia swung around, her hands pressed briefly over her mouth, then pulled back to her sides. Shounach went without further protest, without even a look at her. *It would have worked*, Gleia thought, *it would have worked except for Toreykyn*. She turned back to face the Lossal. His hands were folded on the table; a small, satisfied smile pulled his thin lips into a tight arc. She suppressed a shudder. She must have made a sound, though she wasn't aware of it; he swiveled his head and examined her, his smile widening as he enjoyed her distress. He began touching the shawl again, watching her intently as he pinched and smoothed the material. A faint flush bloomed in his cheeks; the tip of his nose reddened. Gleia began sweating. She swallowed, nauseated by the feeling that his hands were moving over her body.

He pushed the shawl away and leaned back. "You're gifted with your hands, girl."

She stared at him.

"No point in wasting that talent." He got up, smoothed his robes down over his small round belly, walked across the room to the guard. "Put her in a room in the servants' quarters, away from the others, put a guard outside to see she stays there. See she's fed, bring me the shawl when she's finished with it." He strolled out leaving Gleia seething behind him.

The Harrier reached for her. She jerked away. "I need my things," she snapped.

He scowled at her. "Don't take all day."

Gleia moved around the table without arguing. For the moment she was too tired to keep fighting. She folded her things and put them back into her bag, ignoring the Harrier's impatient muttering. When she leaned over, reaching for one of the handkerchiefs, she kicked something on the floor. Shounach's bag was sitting beside the Lossal's chair. She folded the handkerchief with shaking hands and slipped it into her bag. *Unarmed,* she thought. *Ay-Madar, what will he do?* The Harrier was fidgeting by the door, paying little attention to her. She caught the strap of Shounach's bag and slipped it over her shoulder, then covered it with the strap of her own. Holding her bag in front of the other, she walked slowly to the door, her shoulders slumped in weary acceptance of her servitude, trying to hide her nervous anxiety.

The Harrier grunted impatiently and urged her out of the room, too much in a hurry to bother about what she carried. She walked ahead of him along the high echoing hall to a pair of swinging doors. On the far side of the doors the hall was smaller and a great deal rougher. A few horn lamps lit the undressed stone of wall and ceiling; the coarse matting on the floor was worn but thick enough to muffle footsteps. They passed several closed doors then came to a busy kitchen. Gleia's stomach cramped as she smelled the scent of cooking food. She stopped walking. The Harrier went on two steps before he realized she was no longer with him. He wheeled, grabbed for her. She evaded his fingers. "The Lossal told you to see I'm fed. Food and candles. I need both." She faced him, her head up, her eyes defiant. For the moment she didn't give a damn about anything.

Reading this in her face, he backed away. "Wait here."

He left her standing in the hall outside the kitchen. She was tempted to slip away but she couldn't leave Shounach. She hugged his bag against her hip, wondering what was happening to him, then shied away from the thought. *He can't die. It would be absurd for him to die now.* Even as she thought this, she knew that anyone could die any time, absurd or not.

The Harrier came back with a covered pannikin and a handful of candles, thrust both at her and hustled her on down the hall. After turning several corners, he caught her arm and shoved her inside a small room. After he slammed the door and stalked off, she tossed the two bags onto a narrow cot and looked nervously about. There was a small barred window, and a table holding a battered candlestick clotted with wax. She put the pannikin and the candles on the table, stretched, then went quickly to the door and pulled it open.

A Harrier was coming down the hall, not the one who'd brought her. He speeded up to a trot, opened his mouth to speak. She shut the door.

There was a narrow space between cot and table, just wide enough to let her walk back and forth. She paced nervously, angry, confused, and afraid, worried far more about Shounach than she was for herself. Back and forth until her legs ached. Back and forth, rubbing her sweating palms up and down her sides, feeling the rough material of her cafta riding up and down against her skin. Abruptly she kicked the stool from under the table and sat, taking the lid off the pannikin. There was a hunk of bread soaking in a thick stew. It smelled good and re-awakened her hunger. She fished the spoon out of the gravy and began eating.

The morning dragged by. Again and again, she went to the door, but the guard was always there. She tried talking with him. He told her to get back inside and stay there, said nothing else. She worked on and off at the shawl, stopping when her hands began to shake, paced awhile, sat down again to send the needle dancing in and out of the material as her mind circled endlessly and futilely around and around Shounach and her own uncertainties.

Once Shounach and she were loose—she wouldn't think of any other outcome to this mess—she could let him go off on his obsessive quest and strike out on her own. In a way that was the easiest road, the most comfortable choice. She wouldn't have to

change at all, just go on the way she always had.
She could sell the shawl or trade it for passage to
another city where she could keep herself with her
skill. There were times when this path seemed
irresistible, when she was sick of trying to adapt
herself to another person's needs, friend or lover.

Deel had asked her to go south with her. The
dancer was brisk and practical; she represented a
way of life that was strange and exotic to Gleia.
The dancer fascinated her both as a person and as
a symbol. Most of all, she would be someone to
talk to, to share things with. The need to share
was growing on Gleia, perhaps because she'd been
getting more practice at it. It fought with her urge
to autonomy, it was a contradiction to all she
thought she wanted, but she couldn't deny that
need.

Or she could go on with Shounach, trying to
learn the rules of pairing, finding herself forgotten
again and again as he pursued the source of the
Ranga Eyes, moving in and out of danger with
him, living in pain and fear and confusion.

Late in the afternoon she was sitting on the edge
of the cot, the shawl on her knees, her mind milling in its endless circle. She jerked her head up,
tried to smile as the door clattered open and Deel
swept inside. The dancer shut the door, leaned
against it, her arms crossed below her breasts.
"Some mess you got yourself in."

"How did you know?" Gleia tucked the needle
into the material and folded the shawl into a neat
square.

"Merd." Deel laughed, left the door and went to
sit beside Gleia. She dropped a hand on Gleia's, a
brief comforting touch, then wriggled around until
she was leaning against the wall, her long legs
tucked to one side. "He got me in here to dance for

the Lossal. Guess he figured he could make points if they liked me. They stick us artists with the servants." She laughed again. "Unless like your Juggler we're sleeping with the masters. Anyway, the servants, they're buzzing like a bunch of night-crawlers about you and your friend." She wiggled long fingers at the door. "The guard out there, he's seen me with Merd so he let me in. Why the hell'd the Juggler go fooling about in the garden?"

Gleia ran her hands over her curls, shook her head. "He had good reasons. You said it right. Some mess. You better keep away from us."

"Get away's a better way to say it." Deel sucked in her lower lip, bit down on it with small white teeth. "The servants got other things to talk about. They say the Stareyn is laid out, barely breathing, that he could go any minute. Look, I'm not going to be penned up in this stinking city while a bunch of power-hungry families fight for the Stareynate. Bad enough if I was sworn to one of the families. I figure people like you and me, we're going to get squashed. We could get out of the city tonight, go south like I said. It's tonight, I think, or not." She narrowed her eyes, swept them over Gleia's face. "I don't suppose you'd care to forget the Juggler?"

"Not while he's in here." Gleia rubbed nervously at her scars. "You know where they've got him?"

"I can find out."

"Be careful."

"You're telling me?" Deel grinned. "I'll be so damn careful nobody'll know I'm around. Can you use a knife? I could get us a couple."

"Deel, I grew up running the streets. Four summers. You know what that means."

"Yeah, too well." she pushed up off the bed. "I'd better get back, I have to be dancing soon. It'll be late when I come, better that way, I suppose; most of the place should be asleep. Just you pray to whatever gods you know the Stareyn doesn't die on us before we're ready." She touched Gleia's cheek, then swirled out of the room with a flutter of her favorite amber silk.

The candle was guttering in the gusts of cold air coming through the window. Gleia paced back and forth past the table, her distorted shadow jerking dramatically on the wall. She wheeled and faced the door as she heard voices, then a choking sound and a thud. The door opened and Deel stepped in over the body of a Harrier. She bent down and took hold of one of his arms. "Help me. Quick."

Together they pulled the dead man into the small room. As Gleia shouldered the two bags, she looked down at the Harrier. He was very young; she hadn't noticed how young he was before. He had a wispy blond moustache, a scattering of pimples on his nose and cheeks, a reed-thin neck. Deel pulled her knife loose, wiped it on his trousers. She looked up at Gleia. "Had to be."

"I know. I don't have to like it." Gleia shifted the straps to settle the bags more comfortably then took the knife Deel handed her. With a last glance at the dead boy, she followed the dancer out of the room, pulling the door shut behind her.

Talking softly as she walked, Deel said, "Far as I can tell, there won't be any Harriers down below. The Lossal left with a bunch of them not so long ago. There's no one in the halls, not in this part of the house anyway. Feels like they're all shivering in their beds. Matter of hours before the Stareyn goes, I expect. Piece of luck for us since that keeps the old viper busy." Her hand on Gleia's arm, the dancer pulled her along the hall and around the corner. "The stairs to the cellars are just ahead.

We better not talk after this." She stepped briskly ahead of Gleia, pulling her dark cloak tight against her body. Stopping in front of a heavy door, she swung it open enough to slip through. Gleia followed, eased the door shut behind her.

She found herself on a small square platform at the top of a steep stairway, one side against the wall, the other a precipitous drop to a floor some distance below. Gleia moved quickly to the wall side, refusing to look down again. Deel glanced at her, grinning, her teeth glistening in the uncertain light from the torch burning smokily halfway down the stairs. Fingertips of one hand brushing the wall, Deel ran down the stairs, surefooted and silent, her dancer's body balancing easily. Gleia followed more cautiously. The darkness off the side spread into a vast silent cellar under the floor of the House, dark and eerie, amplifying the slightest sounds until the whisper of her feet on the stone came back to her like the breathing of some great animal.

At the bottom of the flight Deel stopped her. "Cells just ahead," she whispered. "Through there." She pointed at a torchlit arch a few feet farther along the wall. "I'll go in first, distract the guard. When you see a chance, take him out." She stripped off her cloak, handed it to Gleia, patted at her hair, moistened her lips, shook her arms, took several deep breaths. "Don't wait too long, hon." Without staying for an answer she moved toward the arch, hesitantly at first, then with her usual swinging swagger.

Gleia hurried after her, feeling it almost like a shock to the heart when the dancer vanished through the opening. At the arch, she dropped to her knees, edged forward until she could see what was happening.

Deel was smiling at the only man in the room, a hard-faced thug with a hairy bare chest, short bowed legs encased in greasy trousers, knotty bare feet. He wore a leather apron stiff with old stains. Deel touched his bulging arm with a teasing giggle, dancing back as he grabbed for her.

He scowled at her, moved around the table where he'd been sitting, stopped in front of her. "Who you, girl? What you doin' here?"

Deel circled closer, ran her slim red-brown fingers up his arm. "I wanted to see the strongest man in Istir." She danced around behind him, running her fingers over the massive muscles of his shoulders, reappearing on the other side of him, pulling him around so his back was to the arch. "Show me how strong you are."

The man lunged clumsily at her, his meaty hip knocking aside the table. He was at least half-drunk. There were two empty bottles on the floor and a third rolling across the tabletop. It smashed against the stone as Deel danced away before the Ironmaster, smiling and flirting her eyes at him, narrowly avoiding his groping fingers, the slotted skirt swirling around her long slim legs, her light teasing laughter bringing the blood to his face. He lumbered after her, caught her arm, pulled her against him.

Gleia slipped the straps from her shoulder, was up and on her feet, running for him. As he held Deel helpless against him, his mouth avid on hers, Gleia drove the knife between his ribs, slamming the blade home with all her strength.

With an animal bellow he threw Deel sprawling and turned on Gleia, his animal strength as awesome as his ugliness. She fled, terrified.

Then he faltered, his face went blank, he coughed, spat blood, crumpled to the floor, falling on his face. Feeling a little sick, Gleia looked at Deel. The dancer rose slowly to her feet, walked to the Ironmaster, scrubbing and scrubbing at her mouth. She thrust her toe in his ribs. He gurgled, moved his hands slightly. Deel beckoned impatiently to Gleia. "Come on. Help me turn him over." The dancer caught one of the man's thick wrists in both hands. "Hurry, I don't know how long we got. The keys, Gleia. We need his keys. And take your knife back."

They labored several minutes, finally got the heavy body on its back. Gleia ran her bloody knife under the leather thong that held his key ring, cut it free, then while Deel stood watch at the arch, she ran along the line of cells.

In the third cell a dark figure lay sprawled on a rough plank bench. "Shounach?"

The figure stirred, tried to sit up, collapsed. Hands shaking, breath harsh in her throat, Gleia tried the keys until the lock finally turned over. When she slipped inside, he was trying again to sit, using the backs of his hands to push against the planks. He looked up, moved his battered mouth into a slight smile. "What took you so long?" The words were slow and blurred so badly it took her a while to understand what he was saying. He lurched heavily and was finally sitting up. She reached out.

"No!" The word was whispered but vehement. She waited, biting her lip, hugging herself, as he got slowly and painfully to his feet. In the dim light from the torches outside the cell she saw that he was naked, his body covered with cuts and bruises, his face distorted into a crude mask hardly human. He stretched out one trembling arm. "Let me lean on you, love. I'm a bit sore for hugging." Again his words were indistinct, spoken slowly

and with difficulty. His arm came down on her
shoulders until she was supporting much of his
weight. "Not too fast."

Deel gave an exclamation of horror when they
emerged. She brought the Ironmaster's chair and
helped Gleia ease Shounach into it; then she stepped
back and raised an eyebrow. "Juggler, you're a
mess." Gleia bit her lip, ran to the arch.

She came back with the garish bag hugged
against her breasts. When he reached for it, she
gasped. The inner side of his fingers and both
palms were seared black, the skin charred and
cracking. She looked from the bag to him, not
knowing what to do.

Shounach examined his hands, grimaced. He was
badly beaten, his face bruised and swollen, his
back raw with lash marks that circled around his
rib cage and ended in ragged purpled cuts. There
were marks of the hot iron on his groin and flat
stomach. His mouth moved in a painful smile.
Swollen and reddened, his changeable eyes glinted
green. "Companion," he murmured. He brushed
her hand with the backs of his fingers. "You are a
delight. Hold the bag open in front of me. Deel?"

"What?" The dancer glanced anxiously at the
arch, then back to the battered man.

"See if you can find my clothes. They should be
somewhere around here." As she swung off, he
scowled, opened and closed his savaged hands,
then reached into the bag.

"Fox, can't I do that for you?"

"No." Sweating, his face twisted with pain, he
pulled a small leather case from the bag and
dropped it onto his thighs. He reached in again
and pulled out a thick roll of bandage, then leaned
back carefully, closed his eyes and said, wearily,
"Put the bag down and open the case for me."

The case opened easily when the two sides were pressed apart. Following Shounach's instruction she tipped a pale blue wafer from one of the vials and slipped it between his lips.

While he was resting, waiting for the drug to act, Deel came back with his jacket, trousers, and boots. She dumped them on the floor beside him. "Can't we hurry this? I'm having a fit every few minutes when I think of someone finding us here." She waved a hand at the arch.

"You can leave if you want." Gleia began smoothing a thick white liquid over Shounach's cuts, bruises, and burns. Sighing with impatience Deel began helping her. Together they covered his burns and other wounds with the pain-deadening antiseptic and began wrapping the gauze bandaging around his body, finishing with his hands, wrapping the gauze neatly over the palms and, at his whispered instructions, around each of his fingers so he could use them. When they were done, he stood, swaying a little at first, working his fingers stiffly.

He dressed as quickly as he could, more in command of himself than Gleia would have believed possible, even for him. When he'd stamped his feet into his boots, he looked around, his eyes pale gray with effort, glittering with the effects of the pain and the drug. Gleia watched, worried, then went slowly to the arch to fetch her own bag. When she returned, he was kneeling beside his bag.

He pulled out one of the blue spheres, got to his feet with a grunt of effort.

"Shounach?" She touched his arm, but he ignored her and walked away from her, stumbling a little, then stopped by the body of the Ironmaster. He dropped the ball on the man's chest, watched as it rolled down the slope of his belly and came to a stop between his legs. Gleia shivered at the expression on his face. *I hold grudges*, he said, *I hold grudges a long, long time.* She closed her fingers about his wrist, careful not to squeeze the burns. "Shounach?"

He blinked at her, awareness slowly returning to his eyes. His face was shiny with the liquid she'd spread over his bruises, his long red hair was matted, dark with blood and sweat. She chewed on her lip, then went back to the bags, slipped both straps over her shoulder.

Deel fidgeted in the archway, fastening and unfastening the clasp of her cloak. "You two ready?" she said, her voice a whisper filled with urgency. "We're really pushing our luck, hanging around like this."

"I think so." Gleia moved to Shounach's side, offering her shoulder as a prop.

With Deel striding ahead, Gleia and Shounach following more slowly, they went up the stairs and eased into the servants' quarters. The rough, narrow hall was deserted and dark, most of the horn lamps blown out.

A few steps past the silent empty kitchen, Shounach called softly to Deel, dragged Gleia through a door into a small, empty room. Deel followed, startled and a little annoyed. "What. . . ."

"Quiet." Shounach leaned against the wall and closed his eyes. "Someone's coming."

For a moment they heard nothing, then confused footsteps and deep voices as several men strolled past. The sounds faded but the Juggler continued to wait, pain and weariness showing in his face. Finally he opened his eyes and pushed away from the wall. "All clear. Let's go."

Deel turned those glowing amber eyes on him as he settled his arm on Gleia's shoulders. "You're something else, Juggler. For a while there I thought I'd made a big mistake." She grinned and swung out, the swagger back in her walk. Gleia saw a flicker of appreciation in Shounach's slitted eyes; she poked him in the ribs. He grunted, grinned down at her, wincing as a cut on his lip reopened. "Vixen."

She sniffed. "Fox."

Deel thrust her head back inside. "Come on, you idiots."

They moved swiftly through the dark, silent house. Just inside the door to the garden Shounach stopped them again.

Deel leaned close, whispered, "Someone outside?"

"No. Those damn iron birds." He closed his eyes a moment, pulled his arm from Gleia's shoulder, leaned against the wall, the false energy from the drug beginning to melt away. Eyes still closed, he said, "Gleia, bring my bag here and hold it open for me."

"You all right?" As she held the bag up, she watched him anxiously.

"No." He reached into the bag, sweat gathering on his forehead. "Silly question." He pulled out a small rod, handed it to her, glanced over his shoulder at Deel who was fidgeting with curiosity and impatience. "Hang on a minute, dancer."

"This is the slowest escape I ever heard of. Good thing the Lossal's busy in the Kiralydom." She twitched her cloak higher on her shoulders.

Shounach shifted his attention to Gleia, touched one end of the rod. "Twist this a half-turn and be damn careful what else you touch." When she'd done that, he continued. "The black spot is a sensor. If one of the iron birds shows up, point the rod at it, touch the sensor, slice the beam through the bird. Don't use it unless you have to." He looked bleak for a moment. "I hate to see that here. I hate seeing those damn birds on this world." He watched as Gleia twisted the cover back over the sensor. "Be careful with that. Deel, lend me a shoulder so Gleia can keep a hand free."

"About time."

They moved across the garden and stopped in the shadow of the wall. Deel looked up. "Hope you've got a few more tricks, Juggler. I don't think I can climb that." She watched him expectantly, waiting for him to come up with another bit of magic, Aab's light turning her into a statue of many-textured blacks and grays too exotic for the austere and formal garden.

Gleia held the rod tight in a sweaty hand, her eyes fixed on him. "Can you do it?"

"Maybe." He rubbed the back of his bandaged hand along her cheek. "You first."

"No."

"Don't argue. Help me sit. Stretch out flat once you're up. You hear?"

She nodded then eased him down until he was sitting cross-legged on the grass. Then she moved close to the wall. "Ready, Fox."

She felt something grip her body, something like a tight second skin. It held her, lifted her. She rose slowly up the wall. When she reached the top he shifted her to the right a few inches then turned her loose. She stumbled, went to her knees. Then she stretched out flat, her body in the shadow of the crenelations. Below, Deel gasped and rose into the air. In seconds she was flat beside Gleia, temporarily speechless.

When Shounach reached the top, he let go suddenly and slammed into the stone hard enough to send the air from his lungs in a small puffing sound.

Gleia touched his arm. "Fox. . . ."

His answering whisper was slow, broken by the air he was sucking in. "Be . . . all . . . right . . . in a minute . . . look around . . . iron birds?"

The sky was still empty. "Nothing," she whispered. "Some torches by the gate, guards there, I suppose. No birds."

"Help me up."

As soon as he was standing, he moved away from her to lean against one of the stone uprights. He looked down then beckoned her into the opening beside him. "Ready?"

"Ready." She stepped off the wall, felt the skin catch her and lower her gently to earth. As soon as she was down, he sent Deel after her, finally dropped himself beside them. He folded onto his knees, stayed there, unable to get up. Gleia knelt beside him, helpless and frustrated; she could do nothing except stay futilely at his side. In Aab's light his face was ashen around the purpling bruises. Deel began walking up and down, six steps each way, the hem of her cloak flaring out around her strong slim legs. Across the street this section of the Market quarter was filled with the noise of the produce carts rumbling in, louder than ever because the wagons from the surrounding farms were bringing in the harvest of tubers and grains. There were several streets of small shops between them and the open stands of the central market, shops that were shuttered and deserted, the shutters barred also on the living quarters above them.

Shounach lifted his head, let it rest a moment against Gleia's shoulder. He watched Deel pacing, her body crackling with suppressed energy. Gleia met his eyes, grinned. "We better start moving again," she murmured. "Before she succumbs to spontaneous combustion."

With Deel flitting before them, running ahead and returning, they moved slowly along the narrow side street past the folded-in shops. By the time they reached the end of that street, Shounach was shambling along, leaning heavily on Gleia as the battering he'd taken began to overcome the drug. He stopped, looked at the busy noisy scene in front of them. "This isn't going to work. Let me sit a minute. I need to think."

With a grunt of pain, he settled on the third step of a flight of stairs rising up the side on one of the shops to the family living space above. Gleia dropped beside him. Deel came swinging back and stood leaning on the shaky railing, looking down at both of them. Shounach opened his hands. The gauze showed dark stains near the crease lines. "Hand me the bag." His voice was hoarse, strained.

Gleia held it open for him while he fished inside. When he brought out the leather case, she took it from him, opened it and found the vial of pale blue wafers. She touched it, hesitated. "Just how dangerous is this stuff, Fox?"

His eyes glinted blue in the torchlight. He looked past her at the black bulk of the Lossal's house looming against the paler clouds; there was a crazy glare in his eyes for a moment, then he looked back at her and the glare faded. "About as dangerous as staying here and letting myself be caught." As he swallowed the drug, a great gong note reverberated over the city. Gleia jumped to her feet. Deel's hands tightened on the rail. She looked sick.

Shounach stood. "Deel. That an alarm for us?"

She shook her head. "Look." She waved an arm at the chaos developing in front of them. For a moment the drivers had frozen. Now they were whipping their teams, racing for the gate giving on the wide main street, ignoring everything and everyone between them and the exit. When Deel spoke, her voice was nearly drowned by the clangor of the great gong as it was beat continually, each stroke blending into the next until the air itself shuddered. She leaned closer, yelled, "Our luck's run out. That's the Knelling. The Stareyn's dead and they're sealing the city off. Once the gates are shut nobody's going to get in or out."

Shounach looked past her at the city wall, rising high above the roofs on the fire side of the market. "Will there be guards walking the walls?"

Understanding wiped the despair from Deel's face. She lifted her head, her eyes glowing with excitement. "Not yet. Not yet," she chanted, then danced away only to stop and stare at the monstrous confusion in the long rectangle of the produce stalls. The noise was appalling, the wagons, carts, teams, merchants, drivers, all involved in an intricate tangle. She looked back at the Juggler, raised her eyebrows. He walked slowly past her, scanned the confusion, began walking along the edge of it, heading away from the main gate, his tall form fitfully visible in the light from the market torches. Deel looked at Gleia, eyebrows raised. Gleia shook her head. "Don't know," she yelled. "He's got some kind of idea." They started after him, Gleia tired and feeling a bit grim, Deel excited and beginning to enjoy herself, her long legs scissoring in her dancer's swagger.

Gleia shifted the straps on her shoulder then ran after Deel. She saw the dancer take Shounach's arm and move along beside him. *Complications. At least she doesn't look like the brother he killed. I wonder, is that an advantage or a disadvantage? Damn them both, let them keep each other company. I can get along without either of them.* She rubbed at the back of her neck; it was starting to prickle.

As if someone were staring at her. The prickle grew to a tingling apprehension that grew stronger as they neared the wall. She walked faster, coming up on Shounach's left side. He was sweating again; the glazed look of his eyes bothered her. She touched his hand. Even through the gauze she could feel the heat in his flesh. *Fever.* She rubbed her neck again, looked up anxiously. A ragged layer of clouds rushed across the face of Aab, then past Zeb. The little moon was higher, adding its small fraction to the light pouring into the street. Gleia shivered. *Too much light.*

The gonging stopped. Behind them the confusion around the market sheds seemed to be sorting itself out. Even that noise was muted. The shutters of the dwellings above them were beginning to open. Gleia saw several heads thrust out, felt curious eyes following them.

A man called down to them, cursed when they didn't answer. The buzz of voices grew louder.

Shounach stopped in the deep shadow at the base of the great wall. He drew in a breath, let it out, looked down at Gleia. There was a question in his eyes and a great weariness. "I don't know...."

"I think you can do it, Fox." She looked back. "I think you'd better."

Deel tilted her head back, looked dubiously at the height of the wall, then over her shoulder at the people leaning out their windows staring at the strange three. "Any minute now, one of those gogglers is going to think of making points by turning us in."

Shounach set his back against the wall, eased himself down until he was sitting cross-legged on the dirty stone pavement. "Get as close to the wall as you can, love."

The skin tightened around her, lifted her. It wasn't

the easy glide of the inner wall. She could feel the effort he was making as she rose and paused, rose and paused.

When she finally reached the top, she stumbled again as he released her; for a moment she tottered on the edge of the wall, then sank onto her knees and looked down. Shounach was breathing hard, his shoulders rounded, his head swaying.

Deel stepped close to the wall, rising in the same fitful increments. When she was high enough, Gleia caught her around the waist and dragged her onto the wall.

Below them the street was beginning to fill as the watchers came running down the stairs to stand about chattering and staring at the Juggler on the ground and the two women kneeling on top of the wall. As Gleia watched, a man broke away from the crowd and began running down the street. Her heart bounding painfully, she whispered, "Come on, Fox. Come on."

He began to rise slowly, his body taut with effort. He sank back a little, rose again. The crowd surged closer, excitement changing into disapproval. He continued to rise jerkily. Two men came closer, then ran at him, leaping to catch hold of his feet. He strained higher; their hands brushed his boots, then the men fell back.

Gleia and Deel caught him as he rose above the wall, rolled him onto the stone beside them. Overhead, the clouds thickened and darkened. As Shounach lay trembling and panting, a few drops of cold rain came splatting down. Gleia knelt beside him, touched his face. It burned her fingers.

"He's in bad shape." Deel lifted her head, jumped to her feet and went to look at the angry muttering crowd below. "If we just had a bit of rope."

"Well, we don't." Gleia settled back on her heels

and tried to pierce the growing gloom over the
city. More rain fell, a short flurry of large drops.
The wind was rising; it pushed the heavy material
of her cafta against her body, tossed her curls
about until they tickled her face. It seemed to her
that she saw torchlight reflected against bits of
metal in the sky, bits of metal circling and soaring
like wind-caught sparks. She fished in her pocket,
found the small rod, looked up again. "Deel."

"What?" The dancer came back from the edge of
the wall, the stained amber silk whipping about
her legs.

"Help me move him."

The two women shifted Shounach until he was
stretched out at the base of the crenelations. "Stay
with him," Gleia said. She moved away from them,
stood in the center of the wide wall, peering tautly
into the darkness, the sense of danger rising within
her. She fingered the rod, hoping it was the magic
she needed, afraid, terribly afraid of the demon
birds, birds that were not birds, birds with talons
like crescent knives. She drew on her store of
stubbornness, her anguish, and even her fear, drew
on all she'd learned from the seaborn who kept
longer memories of their technology. She held the
image of her adopted father in her mind. "It's only
a machine," she whispered. She heard Deel stirring behind her and ignored that. She heard shouts
from the crowd, stones striking against the wall,
ignored that. Kept scanning the black sky for the
circling sparks, waiting for one or more of them to
come closer. "The Lossal is back in his house," she
said.

"What?" Deel's voice was sharp; she was strung
taut again with the waiting. "How do you know
that?"

"The birds are out." Gleia pointed at the flecks

of crimson riding through the darkness, coasting on the surging winds. There was a strained silence behind her then she heard Shounach and Deel talking quietly, heard a scraping on the stone as the dancer helped the Juggler sit up.

"Gleia."

"I've still got the rod, Fox. You rest." She bit her lips, rubbed at her eyes. One of the sparks broke from the pattern and glided to the wall. It started toward them, skimming over the stone about five feet off the surface. She faced it, twisted the cover off the sensor and aimed the rod at the flicker of red and silver.

"Good, vixen." Shounach's voice was calm, steady, feeding her confidence. "Don't touch the sensor yet. Wait a little . . . wait . . . now!"

Gleia touched the black spot with her forefinger, nearly dropped the rod as a beam of intensely white light about as big around as her finger cut through the air. She steadied the rod, brought the beam up until it woke glitters in the polished metal of the bird's body. She moved the beam until it touched the bird, cut across it. She gasped. The bird melted, then blew apart, fragments tinkling like distant rain on the stone. Hastily she twisted the cover back over the sensor, awed and a little frightened by the power she held in her hand.

"Help me up." Shounach's struggles brought her around. Muttering protest, Deel was propping the Juggler against the stone upright. He shook her off. "Gleia." His eyes were glittering with fever.

She came to him, touched his face, shook her head. "Not this time. You go first. Once you're down you can bring us."

He reached for her. She backed away. "No."

Deel shivered. "Dammit, do something. We got to get out of here."

Shounach looked past Gleia at the House. He smiled suddenly, a smile more like a snarl. "A minute more," he muttered. "A minute. Minute . . . minute. . . ." He broke off, shook his head. "Right." Turning unsteadily, he stepped off the wall.

Deel gasped. "He's falling like a damn rock. Ahhh . . . all right now. He stopped himself just before he was going to splash." She glanced at Gleia. "He's waiting for you."

Gleia rubbed wearily at burning eyes. "No, you next. There's another bird coming. I have to deal with it."

Deel looked down, then at the bird. "Oh well, it'd be a quicker and easier death than the Lossal would give me." With a flourish of her arms, she stepped off the wall. A moment later Gleia heard a startled cry and knew the dancer had reached ground safely.

The second bird came more slowly than the first, wavering erratically from side to side. She couldn't keep the rod aimed at it, couldn't anticipate where it would be next. Pressing her lips together, she waited until it reached the spot where the other bird had exploded, then she touched the sensor and swung the beam in an arc, cutting through the bird, feeling an intense satisfaction as it fell apart and rained fragments on the pavement below.

She waited a moment longer, searching the sky for more of the birds, then twisted the shield back over the sensor and thrust the rod into her pocket as she ran to the opening in the stone. Shounach was leaning on Deel, both of them looking anxiously up. "Coming," she cried. She stepped off the wall. For a terrifying time she fell, the wind whipping at her, then she felt the skin tighten around her, slowing her fall. In spite of this she landed heavily, going to her knees, the breath knocked out of her.

Deel helped her to her feet, then gasped with fear. Gleia followed her gaze and saw more iron birds circling the place where she'd been standing. She fumbled in her pocket for the rod, turned to question Shounach.

He was standing, swaying a little, the wind tugging at his matted hair, a wild glittering triumph in his fever-glazed eyes. "Shounach," she called. He didn't hear her. Or he ignored her. She didn't exist for him, only the wall and the birds existed for him.

She sank to the ground, pulled her knees up against her breasts, tired of fighting, waiting now. Waiting with Shounach for whatever he expected to happen. Deel walked past her, cloak whipping about, silk slapping against her long legs. Not too far from them the river was a shimmering rippling surface whispering past low stone piers toward the sea, opening below the city into a wide estuary where a number of large ocean-going ships were anchored. Smaller boats were tied up at the piers, their owners joining the crowd milling outside the gates. Deel turned. She came back and stood in front of Gleia. "One of those ships could take us anywhere. If you're worried about passage money, I've got plenty."

Gleia looked up at her, then over at Shounach. *This is the crux. I can't drift anymore.* She closed her eyes. *Shounach, Deel, or neither? If I take the easiest way and go on by myself, what will my life be like—day and day and day with no surprises. No pain, no fear, well maybe no fear, no anguish. No highs either. It could be very comfortable. I could go back and live contentedly enough with Temokeuu-my-father. And die a little every day. End up hurting both of us. No. I turned my back on that. What's the point of going back? Deel. I like her. Friendship without the complications of sex. I've had that too. Jevati-my-sister.* She smiled with affection as she remembered the slim silver-green seagirl. She glanced up at Deel who had turned again and was looking out to sea. It was tempting, yet. . . . She shook her head and turned to Shounach. *I've been playing games with my head. There was never any real question. I just didn't want to admit it. I need him. I've never needed anyone before. I don't like it. It's hard, trying to be a companion. Harder than anything I've done before.* She shivered. *Scares hell out of me.* Stiffly, slowly she pushed onto her feet and walked over the stony earth to Shounach.

She touched his arm. The fever in him burned her even through the heavy material of his jacket sleeve. She frowned at him, the fever beginning to frighten her; his intensity frightened her also; he seemed unaware of anything but the city, didn't even feel the touch of her hand, didn't even know she was there. *Oh Fox*, she thought, *how am I going to deal with this? How do I reach you when. . . .*

The sky above the city seemed to open; springing from behind the wall a blue flash fanned out, searing her eyes, covering a large portion of the sky. A moment later there was a sound like fifty thunderclaps; the blast deafened her. Beside her Shounach started laughing. She couldn't hear that laughter, but seeing it was bad enough. Again she heard the thing he'd told her yesterday night; the words echoing in her mind like the gong strokes of the knelling. *I hold grudges. I hold grudges a long, long time.* She closed her eyes and saw again his face when the blue ball rolled down the Iron-master's belly to sit rocking between his legs.

He slapped his arm about her shoulders still

laughing, then she felt him sag against her; when she looked at him, the strained madness was gone from his face. He said something, but her ears were still ringing and she couldn't understand him. She swallowed, swallowed again, felt the ringing diminish. Wriggling around until she was more comfortable under his weight, she settled herself then smiled up at him. "What'd you say, Fox?"

"Coming with me?"

"If you can put up with me." She hesitated, added, "It won't be easy."

"I know. We make a cranky pair, my Vixen." He tugged her around until they were facing the smaller piers at the far end of the line of landings. "We need a boat before I wash out. Once I crash, love, I'll be out a good long while."

With Shounach leaning heavily on her, Gleia started walking slowly to the east, angling toward the riverbank. She heard a patter of quick steps, a flurry of silk, then Deel was beside her. "You've made up your mind."

"I'm going upriver with the Juggler." She watched Shounach with considerable anxiety. His eyes were glassy; he was stumbling along in a daze, close to doing what he called crashing. "If we can reach the damn river."

Amber eyes narrowed, Deel moved swiftly ahead, gliding easily over the barren dirt as she walked backward, examining Shounach, measuring what strength he had left. Then she nodded, shifted to his other side and slid her shoulder under his arm, helping Gleia support him. "Mind if I come with you?"

The scattered flurries of rain merged into a steady drizzle that the wind drove fitfully against their backs. Gleia looked across Shounach at Deel. "If you want." She smiled. "At least you won't be bored." She thought a minute. "Wet, cold, hungry, scared, sore, but not bored."

Deel burst out laughing, continued to chuckle at intervals as they slogged through the rain toward a quiet eddy where several small boats rocked unattended. As they stopped beside the best looking of these boats, Deel glanced back at the still glowing city, then up the river. The clouds were matting heavily across the sky, blocking out moonlight and starlight until the river flowed into a heavy darkness. She chuckled again as she helped Gleia maneuver Shounach into the boat. "No. With the Juggler around, we certainly won't be bored."

FIFTH SUMMER'S TALE
(PART THREE)

Currents

Bursting from the constraints of the Chute, the River spread itself in wide serpentines across the wedge-shaped plain, sucking into itself the rich black earth, growing swollen and dark and powerful until it swept into the Istrin Estuary, a fresh-water ram half a mile wide.

Slowly losing intensity, the storm blew inland along the River, its turbulent winds countering and crossing the massive flow, teasing the slick surface into cross-hatched wavelets, shattering them again with intermittent gusts of rain.

Buffeted by wind and water, sail taut-bellied and near to bursting, a small boat edged out from a crumbling pier and began clawing its slow way upstream, leaving behind Istir and the destruction spreading like blue rot within the walls.

*   *   *

Deel crouched beside a bunk that took half the space in the small crude cabin yet was too short for the suffering man, fretting at her inability to help him, struggling to learn the feel of the boat as the floor pressed up against her buttocks, fell away, rose and fell in a jagged counterpoint to the Juggler's hoarse labored breathing.

Though the darkness was intense inside the cabin, now and then the winds tore the clouds apart long enough for the larger moon's milky glow to wake amber gleams in her dancing silks and summon to the Juggler's sweaty face a fugitive luminosity.

Lightning walked. When the blackness closed in again, she still saw him, red hair twisted into spikes about a puffy, battered face. In the moment of light his bandaged hands clenched into fists, he groaned, then his fingers slowly uncurled. Blinking, her eyes watering, dazzled by the harsh glare from the repeated flashes of lightning, she heard rather than saw the cycle repeating itself—fist, groan, opening fingers, over and over as if something in his fever-dream tormented him.

A vindictive man he'd called himself. Deel drew the back of her hand across her eyes, then blew her nose, memories of the events of the night troubling her.

Shounach moaned. She pulled herself onto her knees and groped for his face. The heat in him startled her. He's dying, she thought and felt a touch of relief. Dying had to be easier for him than living with the memory of what he'd done, the slaughter of all those innocents he neither knew nor cared to know. Her own part in those deaths made her sick, though she kept telling herself that there was nothing she could have done, she'd known nothing of the Juggler's intentions. Even now she didn't quite understand why she'd involved herself with the silent brown woman out there guiding the boat and, through her, with the Juggler. A moment's warmth, revulsion at the thought and sight of torture, a sudden deep loneliness—and here she was.

She drew her fingertip across the heavy silk where it was pulled taut over the curve of her thigh. *Should change; I don't want to ruin this.* Bracing herself against the jerk and shudder of the boat, she stretched across the floor and hooked her bag to her. The rain was drumming steadily now on the low roof; the cabin was tight enough, though several icy drops splattered against her face and arm as she wriggled into a damp, wrinkled cafta. She rolled the silks into a tight bundle and pushed it to the bottom of the bag, her hand stilling when she touched a familiar shape, the shell comb that was the only thing she had left from her brief marriage. Shaken by that sudden and unexpected surge of memory, she snatched her hand from the bag, tied the flap down with quick jerks of trembling fingers. Shoving the unwelcome memories away, she yanked the ties into a bow-knot and tossed the bag at the other two piled against the end of the bunk.

More lightning. The Juggler lifted his head a few inches; his eyes opened and stared blindly at nothing. His tongue dragged across dry lips. New sweat beaded his forehead. After a moment he collapsed again. Water. He needs water. Shivering at the thought of facing the icy rain beating against the low roof, she rubbed bits of crust from the corners of his mouth, moved her fingers over his face, feeling the flutter of his eyes under their closed lids. The husky rasping note in his moans woke a sympathetic dryness in her throat. *I could*

just open the door, I suppose. Her lips twitched.
And let the storm rain on him. She sighed again.
And on me. Oh well. She groped for her cloak,
swung it around her shoulders, fought the door
open and struggled out onto the deck.

Her arms aching, Gleia fought to keep hold of
the tiller bar and the sodden straining sheet. The
rope rasped at her cramped fingers burning her
palm and the bar slipped through her hand like a
thing alive, slamming into her or wrenching away
as wind and water battled for control of the boat,
while the continual changes of direction and the
need to strain through the gloom for the uncertain
line of the bank (her night-sight lost over and over
to the walking lightning) kept her strung tight.
Then the boat rounded a wide bend and nosed into
a stretch where the curves were shallow enough
to permit her to run before the wind without fear
of ramming into one of the banks. A sharp slamming cut through the howl. When she lifted her
head, blinking water from her eyes, she saw Deel
come from the cabin, her cloak whipping about
her slim calves, one hand holding her hood in
place. The Dancer stood a moment bent into the
wind as she adjusted herself to the rise and fall of
the boat, then she straightened and shouted something Gleia couldn't make out as the wind tore the
words to fragments. Fear for Shounach was a
moment's catch in Gleia's throat, but only that. The
Dancer looked too buoyant to bear that sort of news.
As lightning flickered and the wind snatched the
hood from her clutching fingers, whipped her aure-
ole of tiny tight curls into a wild tangle, the Dancer
crossed the planks with quick light steps and tumbled in a heap by Gleia's feet. She looked up,
grinning, scraping the water off her face with one

hand, leaning on the other. "You look beat," she shouted.

Gleia nodded, smiled tightly, alternating her gaze between the Dancer's face and the water in front of them. "Shounach?" When her voice cracked, she cleared her throat, then waited with returning anxiety for the Dancer's reply.

"He needs water." Deel pushed herself higher, rested one hand on the seat beside Gleia. "Let me take over here. You tend him." She nodded toward the squat blotch where the cabin walls projected a double handspan above the front half-deck.

Gleia flexed the fingers of one hand, then the other, felt weariness like a blanket smothering her. Fighting it back, she dipped her head closer to Deel's. "You've handled small boats?"

Deel grinned again, wiped water from eyes that were lit with mischievous enjoyment. "Island born," she shouted. "Swam before I could walk."

Too tired to resist any longer, Gleia slid from her place, hanging onto tiller and sheet until Deel took them from her. Uncertain about how well her legs would carry her, she crawled to the water bucket, pulled it loose from the spring-catch keeping it in place. Clear cold rainwater was sloshing out over the wooden sides as the boat jerked and heaved. She spilled more away until the bucket was half empty, then tumbled inside the cabin, surrounded by rain-laden wind.

Once the door was closed the darkness in the cabin was profound. She moved uncertainly about on her knees until her groping fingers found Shounach. She knelt by the bunk, eyes closed, forehead resting on the hard mattress, hearing Shounach's struggle to breathe, feeling the heat from the arm pressed against the top of her head. With a struggle of her own, she pushed up, unclipped the dipper, filled it, lifted his head and held the dipper to his lips. She got a little water into his mouth; more ran down his neck. She raised his head higher and tried again, her tension draining away as she felt him swallow. When the dipper was empty, she settled his head onto the small hard pillow, turning away quickly to sneeze twice. Sinking back to sit on her heels, she plucked at the front of her cafta, the chill from the sodden cloth seeping into her bones.

She stripped off the cafta, threw it into a corner and pulled another from her bag, along with a scrap of katani left over from a handkerchief she'd embroidered and sold. When she was dressed again she crawled back to Shounach. She wet the cloth and bathed his hot puffy face, dipped it into the bucket again, wrung it out and laid it on his forehead. It was all she could do; it made little difference as far as she could see but it was something to do while she waited to see if he'd live or die.

After a while she dropped her head on her arms and knelt beside him in a half-doze while her body slowly warmed.

When her knees began to cramp, she lifted her head and eased her stiffened body around, listening to Shounach's breathing as she sought a more comfortable position, trying to convince herself that it sounded more natural. She touched his face. It was cooler. She smiled, then turned about so she was sitting with her back against the bunk, her knees drawn up. Sipping at a dipperful of water, she listened to the noises outside. Like Shounach's fever, the storm seemed to be abating. The boat was moving smoothly, the dip and lift under her nicely rhythmic. The Dancer was handling it as well as she handled her body. Gleia felt a touch of jealousy, made a face at her foolishness, dropped the dipper back into the bucket and wriggled around to smooth the sweat-sticky hair from Shounach's forehead and run her finger along the line of his long nose, the curves of his upper lip; except when they were making love, he didn't like to be touched so she felt defiant and a bit uneasy at indulging her own needs when he couldn't take note and defend himself. *You scare me, Fox. You bother me.* She sighed and hoped he wouldn't remember too clearly what he'd done this night. *Reason to control rancor, that's what you said to me before we slept. I've had three hundred years to learn that lesson, that's what you said. Reason to control rancor—until the Ironmaster and the fever and the pain beat reason out of you. I wonder what you'd do to me if I made you angry.* She shivered, yawned, scrubbed her hand across her eyes. With a last glance at the dim blur of his face, she tucked herself into a corner with her bag under her head, the rocking of the boat easing her into a deep sleep despite the bruises on her body and the hardness of the floor.

When she woke, a broad beam of red light was streaming through one of the window slits and painting a horizontal crimson rectangle on the wall above her. She yawned and stretched out cramped legs, wincing as pains shot from her knees. The boat was lying at rest in water that gurgled slowly past its sides. She could hear bird song and the rustle of leaves and small scrapings as something scratched the boat's side. Wondering why Deel hadn't bothered to wake her, she sat up, groaned as stiff sore muscles protested, rolled onto her knees and crawled to the bunk.

Shounach lay deeply asleep, his chest rising and

falling in long slow breaths. His skin was cool and
dry. The puffiness was gone and the bruises were
rapidly fading. A corner of her mouth curled up.
*How much more do I have to learn about you, Fox?
An ordinary man would have the courtesy to spend
at least a week recovering from hurts like those. One
day, hunh!* She stroked gentle fingertips across the
flat taut planes of his face. *All that worrying. A
waste.* Feeling a little foolish, she sat on her heels
and looked around. The bucket was gone; a locker
low in the forward wall had been broken open. *I
missed that?* The cabin door was unlatched, tap-
tapping against the jamb in time with the gentle
rocking of the boat. After a last look at Shounach,
she climbed into the crimson dawn.

Deel had turned the boat's nose downstream
and used the current to wedge it in among a thicket
of suckerlings, young shoots growing from the
drowned roots of an ancient horan. Five fingered
leaves were dark green spangles marching in pairs
up the lengths of the reed-slim suckerlings, brushing against each other and the sides of the boat in
spasmodic whispers, dancing in the thick red light
from the great red half circle on the eastern horizon.
High overhead a falcon cried out, the harsh wild
sound snapping her head up; the bird was gliding
through overlapping loops a crisp clean silhouette
against the red-violet glass of the cloudless sky.
The morning air was fresh and invigorating, sharp
with a thousand smells and songs. Her blood sang
in her veins and she laughed aloud with the sheer
joy of being alive. Almost dancing, she walked to
the bow where the boat was tied to the huge old
horan. Its trunk was lightning-split into two great
limbs, one more or less vertical, secondary branches
providing abundant concealment for the mast and
raised boom. The second limb sprang away from

the trunk in a low arch, supporting part of its weight on the steeply rising riverbank, providing a natural bridge from boat to land. Sobered by the implications of what Deel had done, Gleia swung herself onto the low limb and ran along the springy rebounding arch. She stopped where the limb touched the earth, looked up the bank to a small clearing where Deel was kneeling beside a bed of coals, humming a lazy tune as she stirred something in a blackened pot. Her thicket of sorrel curls was neatly combed, her dark skin was taut over the bones of her face, glowing with the sheen of hand-rubbed hardwood. She tasted the mixture in the pot, wrinkled her nose, dusted a pinch of salt or some other seasoning across its surface. Gleia stretched and stepped from the limb and started walking toward the fire, her sandals rustling through sun-dried grass, crunching over debris-strewn earth.

Deel sniffed at the fish stew, lifted the pot from the coals and replaced it with a kettle filled with water. She heard footsteps, swung around, relaxed and smiled. "You're looking better."

"I'll live." Gleia raised her brows at the kettle and the other things piled in a ragged heap by the fire. "You've been busy. The locker in the cabin?"

"Uh-huh. How's the Juggler?"

"His fever's gone. He's still asleep." She glanced over her shoulder at the patches of the boat visible through the suckerlings. "I don't know. . . ."

Deel dipped stew into a metal plate. "Here. Eat some of this. Takes a full belly to make the world sit right." She held the plate out, nodded as Gleia dropped beside the fire and sat looking dubiously at what she held. "Only fish stew." She brushed aside a rag, lifted several small tins and found a second plate. "Once I got the boat tucked away, I poked around a bit. Found that." She rested the plate on her knee while she waved the dripping ladle at a ragged net hanging to dry on the lower branches of a gnarled bydarrakh. "And the rest of this junk." She grinned. "I made enough noise. You and the Juggler—you didn't wiggle a finger." She filled her plate and settled back, tucking her legs under her. "There's a spoon by your knee. Toss it, will you?" She caught it, dug into the stew. "Not bad, considering what I had to work with."

The breeze stirred the foliage over their heads, stripping a last few raindrops from the leaves, spattering them with scattered touches of icewater. Though the frosty nip had lingered longer than usual for this time of year, the air was slowly warming as Horli climbed higher with blue Hesh like a wart poking from her side. *Bad storms and cold mornings already*, Deel thought. *Likely a hard freeze coming up.* She laid her spoon down and gazed pensively at the barrow section of glassy green water she could see sliding past at the bottom of the slope. *An early winter—and a bitter one if the signs don't lie. I can't keep drifting like this.* She scratched at her nose. *How do I get myself into these things? A wintering place. Not Istir.* Her lips twitched and she swallowed a gurgle of laughter. *Definitely not Istir. What's left? Jokinhiir? Gahhhh— not for me, not with Hankir Kan drooling over me.* She blinked, startled out of her reverie as Gleia's spoon clattered loudly enough on her plate to scatter into flight several small brown birds scratching through the rubble not far from them.

"Why did you stop here? And tuck the boat away like you did?" Gleia's forefinger was tracing the brands on her cheek, something she had a habit of doing when she was disturbed. She pulled her hand down, stared at it a moment, then got to her feet and turned her back on Deel. "You think someone could be following us from Istir?"

"After the Juggler blew away half the city? Not likely." Arm resting on one raised knee, hand dangling, Deel watched the shifting patterns of steam on the kettle's sides. "Once it got light enough I could see around me, first thing I saw was the Mouth of the Chute. I wasn't about to sail past the watchtower there in a stolen Handboat. Not in daylight anyway." The coals began hissing as the water boiled and steam blew out the kettle's spout. Deel grabbed at the handle, snatched her hand away, pulled her sleeve down over her fingers and lifted the kettle from the fire. "And not even at night unless it's raining and blowing hard enough to keep the Hands there more interested in their fire than what's happening on the River." She set the kettle down, twitched the lid off and dumped in a handful of cha leaves. The lid back in place, she jiggled the kettle, sloshing the water about for a moment, then put it aside to let the leaves settle out.

Deel settled herself more comfortably and watched with some amusement as the nervous brown woman moved restlessly about, glancing at Hesh and Horli as the double sun rose above the treetops, glancing repeatedly at the boat, stopping by one tree to rub her fingers along its bark and sniff at them, touching a brittle bydarrack leaf, pulling it between thumb and forefinger. She snapped the leaf away and marched back to the fire, her cafta hem jerking about her ankles, collecting leaf fragments and bits of grass. Deel poured cha in a mug and held it out to her.

Gleia shook herself as if she was trying to shed

some of her urgency. She dropped onto a patch of
grass, facing Deel, took the mug and wrapped both
hands around it. "Watchtower?" The corner of her
mouth jerked into a very brief half-smile, a dimple
danced in her unmarred cheek. "Start with the
basics."

"Know what a Hand is?"

Gleia sipped at the cha, considering the question.
"You don't mean the thing that grows on the end
of an arm?"

Deel chuckled. "Right." She pushed onto her knees
and scraped a rough oval of ground clear of debris,
then she straightened, looked around vaguely.
"When I got to Istir a couple of winters back,
Gengid—my boss, the creep—made me hustle for
drinks when I wouldn't whore for him. I was broke
and new in the place and I didn't know Merd yet,
so. . . ." She frowned, looked about again, caught
up her spoon, wiped it on the grass, reversed it,
fitting the bowl into the curve of her palm. "Hand.
Comes from Svingeh's Hands, because they put
the touch on anyone trying to get past Jokinhiir
without paying toll. Well, I sat at a lot of tables
listening to a lot of Rivermen, Hands mostly, slobbering on about their problems. I heard a lot more
than I wanted to know about Jokinhiir and how
the Svingeh runs things." She bent over the cleared
spot and used the spoon's handle to scrape a line
in the dirt, ending with several swooping curves.
"The River." She continued drawing until she had
a crude map of the Istrin plain to the west and the
hinterlands to the east. The Plain was a blunt
wedge driving into the mountains. From the point
of that wedge she scratched two lines parallel to
the River. "The Chute." She jabbed the handle at
a spot near the lower opening. "We're here." She
looked up. "You sure you want to go on? Once we

get in the Chute, we're in Hand territory with
nowhere to go but Jokinhiir." She tapped the map
at the top of the Chute. "There. That's Jokinhiir."
Muscles beginning to cramp, she wriggled around
until she was sitting with her legs crossed in front
of her. "Well?"

"No choice," Gleia said curtly. "Reasons I can't
talk about until I talk with Shounach."

"Mmmph. Like I said, Hands are the Svingeh's
enforcers. Lot of trade travels the River." She flicked
her fingers at the wiggling line, then gathered in
the lands beyond the Chute with a quick curving
gesture. "Knives and tools from Kesstave, cloth
from the weavers of Maytol, horses bred in Ooakalin
on the Plains, you get the idea. Anything that passes
Jokinhiir, the Svingeh takes his cut. Nothing—no
pack trains, no free-boats—nothing goes through
the Chute either way without paying toll. Hands
see to that. Hankir Kan told me once what they do
to smugglers." Deel shuddered. "His way of getting me into bed. Hankir Kan. The Big Fist." She
tried to smile. "Makes my skin crawl." A nervous
laugh. Hands combing through her hair, passing
over the back of her head. She nodded at the boat.
"You know what we did? We stole the head Hand's
boat. I should've known it, he tried hard enough to
get me on it. We stole Hankir Kan's boat and now
we're sailing it right back to him." She scrubbed
her palms hard along her thighs, trying to wipe
away the memory of his groping fingers. "I'd really rather keep away from Jokinhiir."

Gleia started tracing her brands again. After an
uneasy silence, she murmured, "I wonder. . . ." She
looked around, her brows drawn together. "Describe
him."

Deel scanned the still, brown face then sighed
and settled back on her heels. "He's a little worm.

I could set my chin on his head if I was so inclined, which I'm damn sure not. Looks fat. Isn't. It's mostly muscle. Personal experience, he tried using it on me till Merd tied him in knots one time. Black eyes. Straight black hair. Full of himself. A strut like he owns the earth. Scar from here to here." Starting at her hairline just above the cheekbone, she ran her finger across her cheek, grazing the end of her mouth, slanting across her chin. "Wide and deep as a bit of binding twine." She leaned forward again, watched Gleia's unresponsive face. "know him?"

"Not me." Gleia shoved at hair falling across her eyes. "Maybe Shounach. Ask him. I'm just along for the ride." She sat watching the water glide past. "We're here till dark—no, until the storm breaks. If there's a storm tonight."

"It's the season."

Gleia nodded absently. Lost in thought, she got to her feet, drifted down the bank and across the arching limb. Deel heard the soft splat as she jumped onto the boat, the scraping of her sandals as she crossed to the cabin. Then there were other sounds rising above the resonant susurrus of the River—fragmented laughter, shouts, the snorting of horses, a steady scraping.

Deel glanced around the clearing. Where she was anyone coming up the River could see her. She ran to the bydarrakh, scrambled up it and settled herself in a limb crotch, her back against the knobby trunk, concealed from the River by a thin screen of stiff dark-green leaves. A barge slid into view, drawn by eight massive dapple-grays, their creamy feathers rippling, their heads bobbing up and down as they plodded steadily along the tow-path cut into the opposite bank of the River. On the deck of the long barge men were scattered about, talking or gambling in small groups, some asleep among their barrels and bales. Isolated at one end, a group of players laughed together, worked on costumes, exercised, a vibrant splash of color against the duller hues of the merchants and their wares. "Hah," Deel breathed. "I forgot. Jota Fair at Jokinhiir." She scratched thoughtfully at her upper lip, feeling a rise of excitement and just a little awe. *Juggler's luck*, she thought. Kan used to bitch about the fair. About using his men to handle drunks and prod a bunch of slippery merchants into paying the tollage. He'll be calling them in from the towers, if he hasn't already. She settled against the trunk with a sigh of relief, smiling drowsily at the antics of the players until the barge passed out of sight.

Hesh and Horli were almost clear of the treetops when she slid back down the bydarrack. She brushed away shreds of bark, thinking she should get some sleep. She glanced toward the boat, shook her head, twisted at the waist, winced at the protest of sore muscles. Stringing wordless sounds into an airy melody, she started working the knots from her body. After a short series of stretches and bends had raised a sheen of sweat on her skin, she began dancing about the clearing, her worries forgotten in the demanding joy of movement.

Finally, the shadows growing shorter and the heat thickening about her, she hunted out a sheltered spot where she curled up on thick, sweet-smelling grass and went to sleep.

The air quivered under the hammering of the double sun when she woke. She sat up slowly, licked dry lips. *About the middle of high heat. Why couldn't I sleep through?* Rubbing at her throbbing temples she got to her feet and stumbled toward the River, her eyes closed to slits in a futile effort to shut out the glare that seemed to stab through the deepest shadow.

Collecting the bucket on her way she stopped at the River's edge, then waded carefully into the water, testing each step before she committed herself. River bottoms had a way of acquiring sudden holes and a night of fighting the River's current had taught her respect for its power. She worked her way to an eddy moving in slow circles between two huge roots, dunked the bucket into the water and upended it over herself, gasping with pleasure as the cool water splashed onto her head and ran down her body.

Bucket filled to the brim in one hand, splashing dollops of water onto her legs and feet, Deel ran along the arch of the limb and dropped onto the boat; it rocked under her, the suckerlings swaying languidly in the steamy heat as it pressed against them and they pressed back. The deck was drowned in violet shadow, the thick foliage of the ancient Horan protecting it from Hesh's claws. The cabin's door was propped open to let a little air creep through to those inside. Deel set the bucket down and crossed to the door.

The Juggler was still sleeping. Gleia sat with her back against the side wall, her face shiny with sweat, her eyes glassy with fatigue. She looked around as she heard Deel, tried—not too hard—to smile, lifted a hand in a limp, half-hearted greeting.

"How's he?" Deel settled herself in the doorway, dabbing at trickles of sweat on her face and neck with the hem of her sleeve.

"The same. No fever. He just keeps sleeping."

"It's an oven down here. Come up on deck with me."

Gleia frowned, gave a slight shake of her head.

Deel caught her arm. "Don't be an idiot. Does he look like he needs you?" Smiling with satisfaction when Gleia yielded, Deel pushed her out, then moved past her to the bucket in the bow. She scraped up a dipperful of water, swallowed some of it and emptied the rest over her head. "Ah, that's good." She filled the dipper again and handed it to Gleia. "How'd you meet him?"

Gleia drank greedily then settled herself beside the bucket. With the dipper resting on one knee, she stared past Deel at the River, narrowing her eyes against the glare. The River was molten metal in the blinding light of this end-of-summer high heat. "I was living with the seaborn," she began, then her voice trailed off. She was smiling a little, as if at some gentle memory.

Deel stretched out beside her, her knees raised, her cafta pooling in folds across her pelvis. She was restless and bored, unaccustomed to so much inactivity. Getting Gleia to talk about herself was a game she could play to make the hours pass. She lifted her brows, lifted her head a little. "Seaborn?"

Gleia dipped her sleeve into the water, mopped at her face. After a moment she began absently tracing the letters burned into her skin. "When I was working to lift my bond, I thought it would be marvelous to have someone take care of me, to get whatever I needed without having to fight for it." She lifted the dipper and drank slowly, then rested her head against the railing, her eyes closed. "Temokeuu-my-father taught me—many things— gave me a comfortable home, affection, even interesting work. I had friends and freedom and anything I wanted. And after two winters of this I was starting to climb the walls. I left—with my father's blessing. He understood me very well. I left, got picked up by some people scrounging for slave labor who'd picked up Shounach before they came on me, we escaped, split up, got together again and ended up in Istir."

Deel closed her fingers about Gleia's ankle, shook it. "Slavers? Why? How did you get away? What happened?"

Gleia yawned. "It's too hot for anything that complicated."

Deel wrinkled her nose, sighed loudly. "What else have we got to do?" As the silence continued, she patted a yawn while she watched a few puffy white clouds float out from behind the horan's crown and drift across the sky's glassy, blue-violet dome. She laced her fingers behind her head, chewed on her lip, a restless itch crawling about inside her skin that kept her fidgeting, jiggling her feet, moving her buttocks in small nudges back and forth across the planks. "Told you I was island-born," she said when she was unable to endure the silence any longer. Hoping to tease more out of Gleia, she dug into her own past, something she usually avoided like a bad case of sun-itch. "A stretch of islands a long, long way south of here. The Daraghays. You think this is hot, you should be on one of the Daraghays at midsummer. Families were scattered along the islands but my people lived on Burung, the big island. It had a small mountain range with caves in the biggest mountains. When it got too hot outside, everyone—from all the islands, not just Burung—everyone packed up food, clothes, and household goods and moved into those caves. We'd sleep days and at night we'd eat and drink and dance on the sands. When the fall storms started, the people moved back to their homes, but we had a giant feast before they left and drank up all the shua wine we had left, married off all the new couples, said good-bye to some we wouldn't see again for maybe two years-standard when the next summer would be on us. We got some wild storms in winter but no snow." She rolled onto her side, fixed her eyes on Gleia, willing her to speak.

Gleia looked away but yielded finally to the pressure of Deel's steady gaze. "I don't know where I was born or who my people were." Her mouth worked as if she tasted something unpleasant; she drank, emptying the dipper and dropping it back in the bucket. "I sometimes have this nightmare. It starts out with a lot of noise and ugly faces, some kind of raid, I think. A woman screaming. I never see her face clearly, it's always blurred. My mother? I don't know. There's a man struggling and yelling as other men hold him down. I don't see his face. My father? Don't know. He's killed. I'm somewhere in that room, hidden I think. It's confused and bloody and I'm terrified." She stared down at hands clenched into fists, forced them open and rested shaking fingers on her thighs. "My first real memories, I'm on my own in Carhenas, about five-standard I think, running with a gang of street kids. A lot of us died that winter." She shivered. "I don't know why I'm alive, except I fought like an animal to survive. The next years—I can remember begging, digging through garbage piles to beat the scavengers to bits of bone and half-rotten fruit. I was hungry all the time, I was always too hot or too cold, I couldn't trust anyone much, though there was one girl . . . until she died. The gang . . . I was the littlest, the skinniest, and in a lot of ways the smartest, so they boosted me into windows in rich men's houses, windows they couldn't wiggle through. Sometimes I hunted up another window and let the boys in, sometimes

I just took whatever I could carry and passed it out to them. Locks . . . there was a shaky old derelict who lived in one of the falling-down houses, Abbrah our gang leader said he was his brother, anyway he taught me about locks. I had a few scares. . . ." She grimaced, her fingers moving over the letter branded on her cheek. "Guards caught me inside a merchant's warehouse one night. I was branded and bonded . . . sold. . . ." Her voice trailed off, her hand dropped into her lap and she sat brooding over the old memories.

When it became evident that she wasn't going to say more, Deel swung her legs around and pushed up. She sat scratching idly at one palm, a small muscle jerking at the corner of her left eye. Things were coming back to her too, things she hadn't thought about in years, things she didn't want to think about. The suckerlings behind her stirred, leaves rustling as they brushed against each other. At first she thought her movements had tilted the boat into them, then she felt a breeze tugging at her hair—little more than a sighing against her face that came and went. Snatches of birdsong came from the trees and a coughing bark from somewhere near the cliffs upriver. The molten glow of the River was beginning to soften. The interminable day was after all falling toward its end. Deel stopped scratching, smoothed her palms over the sweat-slick skin of her thighs, her cafta still bunched around her hips. "I was a four-winter bride," she burst out. Gleia's head came up. She leaned forward, her brown eyes bright with interest. Deel pressed her palms together. "Only fourteen years-standard when I married Alahar." She touched her tongue to her lips, leaned against the boat's side, her eyes closed. When she spoke again her voice was soft and dreamy, she felt like she was floating outside her body. "All of us in the islands married young," she said. "After all, what else was there to do? No one had to work very hard to live a good life, the islands were generous that way. Alahar was my cousin, tall and strong and beautiful and I wanted him terribly. He chose me, I think, because he liked the way I danced. He loved dancing almost more than anything. We went to live on a little island not far from Burung. Tattin it was called. It had a few trees, a spring. You could walk across it in a sneeze and a half. Our families built us a house. We had a feast. Then we were alone. Alahar taught me to dive and handle the fish-boat for him. He found a good spot for pearls. We never worked very hard, diving was more like playing. I found a big kala shell washed on the beach one day. I put it on a shelf. After a few months it was heaped with pearls, all sizes, shapes and colors. We used to play with them and dream wild dreams about what we would buy with them." She stopped, swallowed, went on. "Between the trips to Burung, the drinking and dancing and the games we played at home, I was so happy ... so happy ... and marrow-of-my-bones-sure this happiness was going to last forever." She sighed, opened her eyes. "Well, I was very young."

"Young," Gleia said wistfully. "I don't think I was ever young. Not that way."

Deel rubbed at her nose. "I was pregnant by the time we started getting ready to move to the Caves. Well, I'd been married over two years by then and was beginning to wonder. I was far enough along that I was glad I was going to be with my mother for the next few months. Alahar was getting rest-less too; he wasn't sure he wanted the baby, it interfered with our good times, I couldn't go swimming and diving with him anymore and I was starting to get nervous about being out in the fishboat. We had our first serious quarrel, made it up, but I was moody and unsure of myself and our second quarrel followed fast on the first. We made that up, but it wasn't the same between us. One day when we were packing up the fishboat a couple of Alahar's friends came by to tell him a trade ship was anchored in Burung's Bay. They stood there on the sand ignoring me, talking a hundred words a breath, slapping each other's forearms, jigging from foot to foot, laughing, excited. After the friends took off Alahar was going to leave me alone and sail the outrigger to Burung. I yelled at him and cursed him and drove him away when he tried to convince me that he needed a new knife and he wanted to buy me a mirror to celebrate our baby. All I could think was he was leaving me alone. In the end he got angry too, jerked the outrigger into the water and took off." Deel stopped talking, dropped her head onto arms crossed over her knees.

With a soft exclamation, Gleia crossed to her and sat beside her, closing warm strong fingers about her hand. She said nothing, but Deel relaxed under the strong current of sympathy flowing to her. She lifted her head. The story wasn't finished yet. Painful images boiled in her. She had to get rid of them before she could be at peace again.

"I didn't worry that first night when he wasn't back. Besides, I was still on the boil because I knew he was fooling around with his old gang, bragging about this and that, maybe flirting some, drinking the shua wine he liked a little too much. When the second night came and went without him, I lost my temper again and took the fishboat to Burung.

"The tradeship was putting out to sea when I sailed into the bay. I ran the boat up onto the beach and went steaming about Barangash hunting for Alahar. Lots of people had seen him, some had talked to him. Several said he'd been showing pearls to one of the traders off the ship. But no one had seen him since yesterday morning. When high heat came on, I went into the council house to wait it out. I sat in a corner, refusing to talk to anyone. My anger cooled as the heat rose. I was beginning to be frightened. I could understand his staying to drink and dance, but why hadn't he come back to me so we could unsay the things we said and be happy again?

"At dusk I walked along the beach, kicking through the foam edging the incoming tide. I didn't know what to do. One time I stopped and looked back. I could hear the drums and the shell horns and some laughter, someone singing, could see the glow of the bonfires built on the sand. I didn't go back. I felt better when I was moving so I just kept walking. I came to a place where a lot of rocks had tumbled down the mountainside and spilled onto the beach and into the water.

"Alahar was there, sitting with his back against one of the rocks. He was dead, of course. Crabs were starting to nibble at his legs, birds had eaten his eyes. A mirror lay beside one knee, laid flat so it wouldn't break. His hands were locked tight about something. I couldn't bear to touch him, but all I could think was I had to find out what he had in his hand. I pried his fingers open and watched a small crystal drop from them and roll over one foot. A Ranga Eye. He'd traded our pearls for my mirror and a Ranga Eye. It lay on the sand glowing in the moonlight. I looked down at it, started to kick at it, but stopped my foot, afraid if I touched

it, it would eat me too. I got down on my knees,
the child was heavy in me, so it was hard, but I
did it. I took a rock and killed the Eye. I beat it
into slivers and dust. When I'd finished it, I got
back on my feet, took hold of Alahar's wrists and
dragged him across the beach and gave him to the
sea. It was a stupid thing to do; I should have gone
back to the village for help, but I didn't even think
of that. I waded back to the beach, got on my
knees again and smashed the mirror, grinding the
shards into the sand with the fragments of the
Eye. Then my pains started. I tried to get back to
the village. I didn't make it. A courting couple
found me before I bled to death. My mother took
care of me, gave my baby to the sea for me and
tried to comfort me. I wouldn't be comforted. I
hugged my grief to me like it was my baby. As
soon as I could get around I pestered everyone in
Barangash until I had everything they could remember about the trade ship, its captain and the
trader Alahar had talked to. I loaded up the fishboat
and took off early one morning for the mainland. I
was going to hunt down that trader and kill him. I
did manage to get there, the mainland, I mean—
luck of the crazy, I suppose." She slipped her hand
from Gleia's, started scratching absently at her
palm again. "I never found him, of course. Since
then . . . since then, I've stayed alive."

"Ranga Eye." There was an odd note in Gleia's
voice.

Deel swung around, startled. "What?"

"Nothing. Never mind." Gleia stood. "I'm sorry."
She spread her hands helplessly, turned and walked
toward the cabin.

Gleia knelt beside the bunk watching Shounach
sleep. *Three of us. Spaceman, southron, and me. All*

of us brought here, three currents meeting, sucked in by that horror. She drew her fingertips gently along his jawline. *Deel said she killed it. I never thought of them being alive. Leeches, that's what they are. Sucking at us. Shining egg-shaped stone, like solidified water, green-tinted mountain water, nestling into the curve of her palm. Weaving pictures of her heart's desire. She held it, seduced by its whispers and the images it wove from veils of colored light. Held it and forgot the world outside, forgot to eat, to wash, everything—until she recognized the trap and wrenched herself free. . . .*

And still felt the pain at that loss—even now, even after almost ten years-standard had passed. Remembering, she shuddered. *They weave wonders for us to hold us while they eat.* She took one of Shounach's hands. The bandages felt dry and brittle; the skin she could see looked pale and healthy. She began working at the knots. *While they eat,* she thought and felt sick. *Madar bless, we'll find their source and destroy it. Then maybe both of us can find some peace for a while.*

Deel stirred from a dream-ridden doze as the sound of voices drifted to her from the cabin. She yawned, listened drowsily to the crackling tension in the broken tones. *Arguing about something,* she thought. She lay watching the clouds pile up overhead, darkening and dropping lower as the double sun started its long setting and the wind blew strongly along the boat, rippling the worn cloth of her old cafta against her body. *Storm tonight.* She yawned again and wondered idly what the Juggler had done to stir up Gleia's temper. When the cabin door crashed open, she sat up hastily, shaking down her sleeves and twitching the hem of her cafta over her knees. The Juggler was scowling over his shoulder at Gleia who stood with her back braced against the overhanging roof of the low cabin. "So you're finally awake," Deel said.

"So it seems." He crossed the space between them with two long strides, his face smoothing between one foot-fall and the next, and stood smiling down at her, eyes darkening to a cool gray-green and gleaming with appreciation as they moved over her. "I owe you, Dancer."

Her pulse quickened and she felt a familiar ache in her groin. Surprised, she started to smile, then remembered where she was and who he was and looked away. "I'll settle for an explanation."

"Of what?" He started to look at Gleia but checked the turn of his head. There was a sudden taut stillness about him that reminded her of a tars she'd seen once, motionless except for the tiny jerks of his tail—then he changed. His eyes warmed and he relaxed; in the next moment he was focused so intently on her that she had trouble breathing.

I don't need this, she thought. "Where we're going and why. What's driving you." She got to her feet and glared at him, using her surge of anger to fight off the effect he was having on her. "I'm tired of walking in a fog." She folded her arms over her breasts and hugged them tight against her. When she felt resistance draining from her with her anger, when she found herself wanting to smile, to reach out and touch his face, she dropped her eyes and turned her shoulder to him.

Gleia stood where she'd been before, a faint line between her brows. She was tense, her temper roused by the exchange in the cabin and by what she saw happening in front of her. Deel felt a sudden kinship with her, an urge to join with her against the man. Whatever his reasons the Juggler was being deliberately provocative. To both of them. Deel took a step backward, felt the railing touch her legs. "Well?" she said sharply. "You going to give me an answer or not? That all your fine words are worth?"

He moved past her and stood in the bow, looking out over the River, one hand resting lightly on the horan's papery bark. "Let it lay, Dancer." Light from the setting suns swept across his face. She noticed for the first time the network of very fine lines written across his face, noticed also that there was no sign remaining of the cuts, bruises and burns that had been there last night.

Deel stared. *How old? And healed already? What is he?* As if he read her thoughts, he glanced back at her and smiled. She shivered at the heat he could rouse in her. *No*, she thought, *not again. You don't distract me that way again.* "No," she said. "I can't let it lie. Give me an answer."

"Tell her."

Deel swung around. Gleia's face was strained, the brands on her cheek harsh black lines on the matte brown skin as the slanting light deepened the shadows.

"You can't use her without her consent, I won't. . . ." Gleia pressed her lips together. When the Juggler continued to say nothing, she jerked her head up and back, her eyes glittering, her nostrils flaring.

Boom, Deel thought. *Hit the bastard hard.* She suppressed a grin, then sobered, stood frowning. *Use me?*

"The three of us," Gleia said. Her voice was harsh, angry. "We've all been burned. Ranga Eyes—they're what drives him; he's tracing them to their source. They brought us to Istir, now they're tak-

ing us upriver. When we find that source, we're
going to blow it to Aschla's dark. You lost a hus-
band to an Eye. Shounach lost a brother. Me, I
had a brush with one that almost. . . . well, never
mind that. He thinks Hankir Kan holds the key to
the next leg of our journey and he wants to dangle
you in front of him as bait for a trap." She glared
defiantly past Deel at the Juggler. "I told you I
was going to tell her. Live with it."

The Juggler was furious. His eyes were narrowed
to slits, muscles knotted at the corners of his wide
mouth. Gleia stood stiff and silent now, scowling
back at him, her hands closed hard over the edge
of the cabin roof. Deel thrust her fingers through
her hair. "Bait?" She looked from one to the other.
"No! Kan? Let him . . . no!" She ran across the
deck swung onto the arching limb, ran across it
and up the bank.

The wind whipped clouds past overhead; moonlight flickered in nervous gleams as shadows flitted across the clearing. By mutual consent the
three avoided the confines of the boat while they
waited for the storm to break. The Juggler sat
with his back against the old bydarrakh, watching
the silver gleams of moonlight on the dark water.
Deel and Gleia sat talking, short exchanges separated by long silences.

After one of these silences Deel jumped to her
feet and began prowling through the trees around
the clearing, the wind snatching at her cafta, snarl-
ing her hair, tossing long canes of pricklebushes at
her, their red-tipped barbs threatening to snag and
tear the cafta. On impulse, she began dancing with
the canes, coming close, then swaying back, sometimes a step or two, sometimes a slow whirl, dancing with them like a lamia worshipping her serpents,

moving through the trees and back into the clearing, flitting in and out of moonshadow.

Music behind her startled her into stumbling. She swung around. The Juggler sat as before by the bydarrakh, his legs crossed in front of him, his bright hair whipping in the wind, but now he was turned from the river and playing a shepherd's pipe, his long fingers dancing over the stops as he searched for the rhythm of the storm that wouldn't come down, teasing a music from the wind and from the River and the rustle of the leaves—and from her. She stood watching him, her feet hesitating with him, her body moving in slowly augmented oscillations until she matched herself to the pipe's song as it firmed into a melody. She flung her arms out. Forgetting her restlessness, her fears and her anxieties, she danced with the wild song of the pipe, glorying in the play of her muscles and the beat of her feet against the ground— until she collapsed beside him, laughing, panting, dabbing at the sweat on her face and arms.

He set the pipe aside, pulled her down until her head lay in his lap and began smoothing wisps of hair off her face, each touch a caress setting her on fire with need for him. With a sharp cry she rolled onto her side and pressed her face against the bare skin of his chest where his jacket fell apart, her arms closing about him, holding him. He smoothed his hand along the side of her head, then his fingers began playing in the tiny hairs at the base of her skull and sliding lightly along her neck and shoulder, back and forth, very softly until she shuddered under them.

Gleia stood watching Deel dance around the small clearing, catching the wind and turning in it, her cafta pasted one moment against her long body,

then billowing away, concentration turning her
face into a mask of strained serenity—around and
around, playing with the wind, defying the wind,
teasing it into partnering her, catching the thread
of the pipe music and weaving it into the wind.
Breath caught in her throat at the wonder she was
watching, a dull pain under her heart at the ab-
sorption on Shounach's face as his eyes followed
the Dancer, Gleia stood on the horan's arching
limb and felt the crackle of the brittle papery bark,
the brush of the five-fingered leaves, the heavy
wood shifting under her feet, the wind-driven limb
swaying against her hand, felt everything around
her with an intensity indistinguishable from pain.
She wanted to run along the limb and join them,
she wanted to climb down onto the boat and shut
herself in the cabin until she could face the two of
them again. She didn't move. Stirred profoundly
by the beauty of dance, dancer and music, she
watched until Shounach put his hands on Deel's
shoulders and pulled her down against him. Then
she wrenched herself around and jumped onto the
boat. Crouching at the rail, she stared past the
suckerlings at the sliding dark water, refusing to
think, driving away images that tried to surface
until she felt like a spring wound so tight a touch
would send her flying apart.

Lightning glared momentarily. As she pressed
her hands over her eyes, thunder crashed so close
overhead that she tottered, her heart racing, then
tumbled back onto her buttocks. As she picked
herself up and knelt beside the rail again, she
heard a soft thud behind her. She twisted around.
Deel stood by the horan, her face a blur with dark
eye smudges. "I suppose you expect me to tell you
I'm sorry," she said.

Gleia made a shapeless, meaningless gesture with

one hand, then turned back to the River. "I expect nothing."

"I didn't mean that to happen."

"I don't suppose you did." Gleia winced as she heard the bitterness in her voice. She didn't feel especially bitter. More than anything else she was simply tired. Too tired to keep on being angry. Especially at someone who was as much a target of the Juggler's malice as she was. Besides, it was true enough. Deel had planned nothing. She knew her well enough by now to understand that. The Dancer was a leaf in the wind, reacting to what happened around her, following her impulses without much thought of the consequences of her actions. Gleia scraped the hair out of her eyes and turned to face Deel. "Where is he?"

"Back there somewhere. I don't know." Deel moved quickly past her. A moment later Gleia heard the Dancer's voice, muffled by the cabin walls, singing a melancholy minor song in a language she didn't recognize. Not sure what she was going to do, not even sure what she was feeling, she left the boat and walked slowly up the bank to stand shivering in the center of the clearing with lightning jagging across the sky and thunder crashing around her. She looked up, sighed. The air was damp and heavy, but there was no indication that the storm was going to break any time soon.

The wind teased at her hair, blowing it into her eyes and mouth as she turned slowly. The clearing was empty. No Shounach. She felt cold and lonely and uncertain. *Cha. Something warm.* She built a small fire and sat watching the steam patterns form and dissipate on the soot-blackened sides of the kettle. The warmth from the fire eased away some of the soreness and woke a restlessness in her that brought her back onto her feet. Stretching her arms out, she began moving in slow circles, her cafta belling out around her as she swung around. Humming a snatch of the song Deel had been singing, she danced a bit, beginning to feel more comfortable with herself until she opened her eyes and saw Shounach watching her.

She stopped, so angry she couldn't speak, stood staring at him, her hands curled into claws. If he'd started toward her, touched her, she'd have thrown herself at his throat in that all-out mindless attack she'd learned early on the streets of Carhenas, biting, kicking, clawing at his eyes. But he stood a shadow among shadows, his pale face catching stray gleams from the fire, floating like a mask in the darkness under the trees, his eyes unreadable smudges. She turned her back on him and stood gazing blindly at the River, still trembling, rage mixed with shame that he'd seen her awkward attempt to imitate Deel. She heard his feet brush through the dry grass and debris, tightened her fists until her fingers ached. She would not turn to face him.

"Vixen," he said softly. She pressed her lips together, scowled at the ground by her feet. He walked around her. "Gleia, listen to me." Cupping his hand under her chin, he forced her head up.

She jerked away. "Don't touch me."

As they stood glaring at each other, the clouds over the clearing ripped apart and sudden strong moonlight flooded around them. Filled with wonder, Deel's voice came suddenly from the horan. "You could be twins. Did you know? Except for your coloring you could be twins."

Gleia's shoulders slumped, her hands opened, anger subsiding. "What?"

Deel pushed away from the trunk, balanced along the limb and stepped onto the bank. "You and the

Juggler. The set of your eyes, the slant of your bones, the way your lips curl, especially when you're mad, you're alike. I didn't see it before, not till the moonlight stripped your coloring away." As she started up the bank toward them, the break in the clouds flowed shut and lightning cut through the resulting gloom, followed by a crack of thunder loud enough to shatter the sky. Deel looked up. "Dammit, why don't you rain?" With a disgusted snort she moved past them to the small fire; it was flickering erratically as water bubbled from the spout of the kettle. She snatched the kettle off the fire, dumped a handful of cha leaves into the boiling water, then sat back on her heels. "You know how far a fire can be spotted once it's dark? From a height like that watchtower ahead? This was dumb. Juggler, get me a bucket of water. The sooner this is out." She tumbled the stack of pots over, upended the biggest over the fire.

Rubbing at her arms, Gleia watched Shounach walk away. "I wasn't thinking," she muttered. "Sorry, Deel." She turned and walked slowly to the Dancer, stopped beside her. "You're seeing things. I'm nothing like him." She took the mug Deel lifted to her and curled the fingers of both hands around it. She stared down at her hands, realizing they were shaking only when the hot cha slopped over the rim of the mug and burned her. The shaking moved up her arms. Waves of shudders passing through her body, she dropped clumsily to her knees. When she tried to lift the mug, her hands shook too badly and she lowered it until it rested on her thigh. That she couldn't even drink a mouthful of cha was a last burden added to all the others piled on her shoulders until they were more than she could bear. Blinded by a sudden flood of tears, she flung the mug away with a nervous flick of her hand, huddled lower, crying and trying to regain control of herself, frightened by the surges of wild emotion, ashamed of giving way to them, unable to stop crying no matter how she struggled.

Deel patted her shoulder, slow comforting touches that left Gleia more confused than before. When she was too tired to cry anymore, she sucked in a long wobbly breath, then felt warmth against her hands as Deel closed her fingers about a fresh mug of cha and helped her raised it to her lips. The hot liquid was pure pleasure sliding down her throat; she gulped it down until the mug was empty, then picked bits of cha leaves from her tongue. Finally she looked up. "I never cry."

Deel chuckled. "No, I see that." She shook her head. "Nothing wrong with a good hard cry; cleans the system out."

Gleia scrubbed her sleeve across her face, looked wearily around. "Where is he?"

"Supposed to be getting water to douse the fire. Avoiding this . . ." She reached out and drew a finger along Gleia's damp cheek ". . . is more likely."

"Sorry about the fire."

"Can't be helped. It's done. I just hope no one happened to be looking this way."

Gleia rubbed at the nape of her neck, her eyes on the boiling clouds that showed no sign of releasing their burden. "Let's get out of here, take a chance on the tower."

"Mmmh, might be a good idea." Deel looked past her. "He's coming. Finally." She rose to her feet with a graceful economy of motion that made Gleia sigh as she struggled up to stand beside her.

He handed the bucket to Deel. "Here's your water, Dancer."

"You took long enough." She kicked the pot over and emptied the bucket over the coals.

In the next series of flashes, Gleia saw his face with exaggerated clarity. He looked tired but calm, purged of his annoyance at her. In that moment she understood him more clearly than she had before or perhaps would again. As the moonlight had stripped away the differences of coloring between them, so fatigue cleared away the emotion that blurred her view of him. Absorbed by her sudden insight, she forgot Deel, forgot where she was, and spoke slowly, softly. "I wondered what you might do to me if I got you angry. Companion, you said. You don't even try. You were punishing me, weren't you."

Deel's stifled exclamation brought her head around and she realized wearily that she'd inflicted hurt without meaning it. "I shouldn't have said that. I wasn't thinking. But he needs you, Deel. And he knew I was watching. You might as well face that." She turned back to Shounach. "You're using us both, aren't you. As you'd use anyone and anything to get at the source of the Eyes. You don't give a damn about either of us." Oppressed by the futility of more words, she fell silent, listening to the rustle of Deel's feet as the Dancer fled the clearing and the uncomfortable confrontation there.

"It's not so simple as that."

Gleia lifted her head.

He stood gazing down at hands held open a little, fingers curled up, his clever juggler's hands. He looked up, changeable eyes paling to a silver gray that gave him a blind look. He took a step toward her. She started back. He closed his hands over hers. "No one ever has a single reason for any of the things he does to other people. Gleia. . . ." His tongue moved along his upper lip, touching the small beads of sweat gathering there. His hands trembled. It cost him to wrench his armor open and let her see the creature inside. "Since my brother . . . no, since the man who raised me . . . since he died, I haven't let anyone get close to me . . . close enough to hurt. We're alike that way, Gleia . . . whether Deel's right or not . . . when the thissik threw you in with me and I saw my brother's face—your face—for the first time in . . . oh god, Gleia."

Gleia looked down at the hands holding hers, believing against her will the pain in his voice. She was right about him, but she found herself thinking he was right too. She was confused and miserable but the anger was draining away.

"Old habits die hard," he said. His fingers tightened about hers until she winced. "You're right. I'll use you, but I'll use myself as ruthlessly. You are . . . when you pull away from me, when you go against me like you did with Deel, I. . . ." He coughed, then stood waiting, saying nothing more.

Gleia drew in a long ragged breath. "You really are a bastard, Fox. Playing with me like the things you juggle. A while there I could have murdered you and danced on your corpse." She tugged her hands free. "Do you know what humiliates me most? I can't even keep on being angry with either of you. How am I supposed to act? Tell me. I've got no experience in this kind of thing."

He caught one of her hands again, held it loosely, small square and dark against the long pallor of his own. After a moment he lifted it, touched his lips to her fingertips. "Act? How do I know, Vixen?" He held her hand against his face, his breath warm on her wrist, then he set the hand gently by her side. "My bitch mother saw to that when she passed her curse on to me. I learned the hard way what to expect. You'll start by resenting me and end hating me—unless I leave before then. That's what I have to offer, Vixen. A rough ride and a miserable end. But I need you. For a while at least I need you."

"Stop juggling, Fox." She sighed. "Just ... I don't know. Don't push. And I reserve the right to yell a lot if I don't like what you're doing."

Shounach drew his hand along the side of her neck, gently caressed her throat with his thumb, a softness on his face she'd not seen before. He pulled her against him, his hands playing in her hair.

"Look here, Juggler." The deep voice with its slight lilt was amused and contemptuous.

Shounach pushed Gleia gently from him and turned to face the man standing at the edge of the clearing, several other forms dark in the shadows behind him.

"Good boy." The speaker was a short broad man with black hair, black eyes, dressed in tunic, trousers and boots, all black, a black tabard buckled across the bulge of a pot belly, a red hand with its fingers spread appliquéd on it. Gleia stiffened. *The fire. That damn stupid fire.* In the flickering lightning a long thin scar was a black string slanting across his face. *Hankir Kan.* He walked forward two steps, stopped, snapped short thick fingers.

Deel came stiffly from the shadows, gray-faced with terror, arms wrenched behind her by another of the Rivermen, a knife at her throat. A third Riverman walked beside her, a crossbow aimed steadily at Shounach. A skinny rat-faced man slipped from behind him and went to hover at Hankir Kan's elbow, restless eyes shifting from Gleia to Shounach, past Shounach to the gaudy shoulderbag leaning against the bydarrakh, its glossy sides catching and throwing back the flickers of lightning.

His eyes swept round the clearing, then he ran quickly to the bag, squatted beside it, tipped the flap back and started rummaging through it, pulling the contents out item by item, examining and dropping them.

"You kicked shit out of Istir, Juggler." Kan smoothed his hands down over the bulge of his belly. "I got word you climb walls without ropes and some other fancy tricks. You going to tell me about that?" There was a conspiratorial, almost friendly, gleam in his eyes. Gleia shuddered as she remembered Deel's face when she'd talked earlier about Kan and his pleasures.

Deel, she thought. *I forgot about Deel.* She turned from the silent contest between Kan and Shounach and scanned the Dancer's face. What she saw there frightened her.

Deel's eyes were glazed, unfocused—or rather, focused inward on nightmare. Her earlier stiffness was beginning to change. Her sagging face muscles tightened, her head lifted; she was visibly nerving herself for desperate action. Gleia stroked her brands, not sure what she could or should do. Deel had survived a lot, but she'd survived not because she had the strength to endure, but because she simply got away from the trouble and put it immediately out of her mind. Killing herself to escape the pain and degradation she knew was waiting for her would be just another flight, an impulse yielded to with little consideration for its consequences. When Deel's lips parted slightly and her body tensed, Gleia tensed also, shouted, "Deel. Don't."

The Hand holding Deel needed no warning. As soon as he felt the thrust of her body, he whipped the knife aside and sent her sprawling with a powerful shove that stretched her at Kan's feet. Gleia closed her eyes a moment, went to stand at Shounach's side, feeling a little sick as if she had somehow betrayed her friend.

Deel lay still, dazed, resolution draining away, then she moved, blindly, hesitantly. She flattened groping hands on patches of grass and tried to push herself up, but her arms were shaking and too weak, her hands slipped on the tough grass and she fell on her face. Before she could try again, the silent Hand was kneeling beside her. He slipped a strangling cord from a belt loop, pulled her arms behind her and tied her wrists.

Kan turned suddenly; Gleia met his assessing gaze, saw him dismiss her, jerk a thumb at her, saw the Hand nod and get to his feet. She knew she should be happy that the man had underestimated her so badly, it gave her an edge on him, but she couldn't help preferring a healthy respect on his part for her lethal potentialities even if he had no use for her as a woman. She felt a fleeting amusement at herself in spite of her overriding fear and anxiety, looked out of the corner of her eyes at Shounach to see how he was taking this.

Face expressionless, body relaxed, he stood waiting in apparent passivity for events to progress around him. She wasn't fooled by that, though she hoped Kan's lack of perception would extend to him. She lifted her face to the clouds, eyes almost shut against the glare of the lightning. A few raindrops blew at her, but the storm still refused to break.

The Hand walked toward her, cord dangling from his stubby fingers. His unbroken silence was acquiring a powerful *presence*, it even extended to his walk. He was a chunky man with short, thick legs but his booted feet made no noise at all on the twig- and leaf-strewn earth. He was a shade, about as noticeable as a single stone among a hundred others in an ancient wall, but with that ponderous silence he drew over himself a kind of dignity. He held her wrists behind her as he wrapped the cord around them and pulled it tight, his short strong fingers quick and deft at their work.

When he stepped away from her, Kan jerked his thumb in another silent order, this time at Shounach. The silent man slipped another noose from his belt and moved behind the Juggler. Shounach stiffened then forced himself to relax. Breathing again, unwilling to witness the Juggler's mingled frustration and desire as his eyes followed Kan about, Gleia examined the four Hands, trying to assess their strengths and weaknesses as best she could.

Kan—a power eater, he wanted Shounach's abilities under his control, and he wanted that intimacy that could link torturer and victim. *Poor Deel*, she thought.

Rat-face by the bag was greedy, tricky and—as far as she could tell—negligible.

The Silent Man was disconcertingly competent, perceptive, quick and to a large degree unreadable. From the feel of the cords around her wrists—her hands were already swelling, stiffening, as the cords cut into her flesh—he took a more realistic view of her aptitude for creating difficulties. He frightened her a little because she couldn't think of any way to reach him.

The Bowman bothered her too, but in another way. She'd seen crazies like him in her sojourn with the street gang, had learned to walk very carefully around them, to avoid them if it was at all possible.

The Bowman's hair was long and light and in the flares of lightning it looked crimped as if, freed,

it might curl as exuberantly as Deel's. He had it
pulled tightly back and tied with a strangling cord,
but short hairs escaped to coil with absurd delicacy about his long bony face. He was taller than
the other Rivermen and put together differently,
all legs with no body to speak of. He fidgeted
nervously, kicking at the debris on the ground,
adjusting his tabard, fiddling with the bow. His
light eyes were slightly protruberant and he had a
habit of opening them wide every few moments,
showing white rings about the hazel iris. She had
the feeling that anything could touch off the violence pent up inside him—even something as triv-
ial as a leaf fluttering against his hand. A dangerous
man—but Kan had him leashed. Gleia saw the
fear in his staring eyes whenever they turned to
the Head Hand. He was competent enough as a
guard; the point on the bolt never left Shounach
and however much his eyes shifted about they
never left the Juggler long enough to matter.

"Anything interesting?" Kan was watching rat-
face as he pawed a last time through the things
from Shounach's bag.

The skinny Hand scooped up the clothing, gear
and juggling paraphernalia and stuffed it back into
the bag. He stood, kicked at the bag, then slouched
sullenly back to Kan, disappointment on his wizened face. "Junk," he snarled. "All junk."

"Mmm. He does funny things with that junk.
Saw him in the market in Istir a while back." Kan
smiled genially at Shounach, patted his arm as
one would pat the head of a favorite dog. "We'll
talk about that, you and me." He stepped away
from Shounach, stopped beside Deel. The Dancer
sat with her legs tucked beneath her—but the para-
lyzing terror that had seized her was gone; she
was slowly coming back to life. "Don't let him

near that bag, Gabbler," Kan said. The silent man—
Gabbler—nodded. Kan looked over his shoulder at
Shounach, one eyebrow raised. "Tricky shit," he
said. He hooked a hand under Deel's arm, lifting
her to her feet with a casual ease that was an
eloquent testament to the strength in that round
body.

Gleia moved her shoulders, bit down hard on
her lip. The Dancer had humiliated Hankir Kan
too many times in the past, sometimes in front of
his men. She remembered Deel's shudder, her nervous laugh, and felt sick.

Pushing Deel along in front of him, he took two
steps, turned and scowled at the Bowman. "Raver,
keep your hands off. He's mine and I want him
delivered to me in good shape." He glanced at the
clouds, then fixed a hard eye on the Bowman's
working face. When Raver nodded his grudging
assent, he turned to the silent man. "Get him to
the Roost fast as you can. I can't give you more
men, most of them've been called to the Fair, you
know that. That means there'll be plenty mounts
for you, anyone give you bother on that, let me
know. Six days and I expect you. No more. Me, I'm
taking the boat. Turp. . . ." He jabbed a forefinger
at the scattered pile of pots and cooking things by
the embers of the dead fire. "Get those onboard
and don't take no year doing it."

Deel jerked loose from the light hold he was
keeping on one arm. She smiled calmly enough at
Gleia though horror lurked in her eyes. "Been fun,"
she said, then she turned and began walking with
quiet dignity toward the boat. Chuckling, obviously pleased with the Dancer's show of spirit,
Kan followed her. At the horan he turned again.
"Don't lose him, Gab. I'll have your hide for a rug
if you do."

*   *   *

Gleia shifted cautiously, trying to find a more comfortable way of sitting the saddle; her cafta was hiked past her knees and provided no protection for the tender skin on the inside of her thighs while the horse's barrel seemed to grow wider with each jolting step. Being city-bred, she knew little about horses and less about riding; she felt horribly precarious perched this high off the ground. It seemed to her she was continually on the verge of leaning too far back or bumping her nose on the cropped mane or sliding to one side or the other in danger of tumbling off. Gabbler had tied her hands in front of her when he found she couldn't ride; she clutched desperately at the saddle, her fingers cramping as she used her hands to compensate for her deficiencies in balance. She was terrified of falling—yet, with all this, she was almost grateful to the beast since fighting to stay on his back kept her too busy to fuss much about what was happening to Deel.

The cliff at the Mouth of the Chute loomed in front of them, a granite wall grooved with deep vertical wrinkles. A narrow trail crawled up the face, pleated in repeated switchbacks. The rain now hammering against the stone collected on that trail and cascaded from pleat to pleat. Not something Gleia felt she could reasonably be expected to ride up.

When her mount stopped moving, she sighed with relief, tried to ease herself a little by standing in the stirrups. This started the horse sidling and tossing his head so she lowered herself before she fell off, wincing as chafed flesh burned as soon as it touched the saddle's rain-soaked leather.

The two Hands were muttering together. The Bowman shrugged, turned and shouted an order

that the gusting wind and rain shredded until Gleia
heard only the last word. *Down*. She watched with
weary admiration as Shounach, his hands still tied
behind him, leaned back, balanced, swung one long
leg up and over, balanced again as he sat sideways
on the horse, then slid off. He landed on his toes,
swayed, straightened, his face impassive. Gleia refused to move.

Scowling, the Bowman cantered back to her; he
jerked her hands from their grip on the saddle and
pulled her off the horse, wrenching her shoulder,
almost throwing it out. When he let go of her arm,
she went heavily to her knees. Behind her she
heard the creak of leather, the splat of feet in the
mud, gasped as the Bowman grabbed her and
slashed the ropes from her wrists, hauled her to
her feet and shoved her toward Shounach who
was already free, rubbing at his wrists, his face
carefully blank. At a gesture from Gabbler, she
followed Shounach up the track, her feet slipping
in the icy water racing down it. The horses were
left tethered to trees; apparently the tower was
close enough for someone to come later and re-
claim the beasts.

Raver Bowman walked behind her, almost stepping on her heels, touching her repeatedly, grossly,
laughing at her shudders, adding to the nightmare
of the climb. Heights bothered her but this was
the worst she'd had to face. In the howling darkness of the stormy night the path seemed hardly
wider than her feet, though she knew the horses
would come up it later. Before she was halfway up
the cliff, her legs started shaking and her head
swimming so badly at times that she had to stop,
and when she stopped, she had to endure more
handling from Raver until she could collect herself
enough to go on. Finally, Shounach drew her up

beside him. By the time they reached the top of the track, he was nearly carrying her.

When a last flicker of lightning broke the heavy blackness of the night and the rain, she saw forest blocking the view to the south, a forest that stretched from horizon to horizon. To the north, on the far side of the river, the cliffs were lower; she could just catch a glimpse of treetops when the lightning walked. Ahead, a little way off, a squat cylinder stood, a few hazy, nondescript outbuildings near its base. Shounach slid his arm under hers, bent suddenly, swept her feet from the ground and started walking toward the tower.

Deel sat in the hot dark cabin, her back against the wall, the broken locker's latch poking into her. Even when that small annoyance turned painful she didn't move—it kept her from dwelling on what was waiting for her and from sinking back into the numbing horror that robbed her of the will to resist. She moved her shoulders, curled her fingers; both ached from the forced backward pull and the bite of the cords around her wrists. When her nose started itching, she tried rubbing it against her shoulder, then drew up her legs and scrubbed her nose across the cloth stretched tight over her knees. For the moment eased, she sat with her head resting on her knees. *Ay-Madar I'm in a spot.* She swallowed, swallowed again, trying to control the nausea that cramped her stomach and soured her mouth. *If he touches me. . . .*

Kan slammed the door back and ducked inside, bringing with him a gust of wind and rain. Deel straightened. He forced the door shut and lit a small lantern, hung it on a wall hook and turned to contemplate her. Hysterical laughter rose in Deel's throat; he seemed ridiculous to her as he

came at her on his knees, the cabin roof low over
his dripping oily hair, his right hand slipping along
the sidewall to help him balance against the leap
and fall of the boat, a five-tailed scourge in his
left, the metal bits knotted into the tails clattering
and skittering along the floor. Ridiculous—yet the
serpentine swaying of his body was oddly mesmerizing. She stared at him, the urge to giggle
gone as bile rose in her throat.

He settled onto his heels, smiled at her, mild
and unhurried and almost detached. Tucking the
scourge handle under the hem of her cafta, he
eased it upward, his face set in that slight smile,
his eyes flicking from her legs to her face to her
legs again. He slid the cloth down her thighs until
it lay in folds across her groin. Then he shifted the
scourge to his right hand and cupped the left over
her knee. "I promised you a boat ride, Dancer." He
rubbed his hand in slow circles for a moment then
slid it down her thigh, his fingers hot, quivering a
little. She heard his breathing quicken.

Her body jerked, then she was bending forward,
heaving up the contents of her stomach, spewing
the half-digested food over herself—and across the
shelf of his belly, across the red hand stitched on
his tabard.

He recoiled, cursed as his head slammed into
the ceiling. In ominous silence he stripped the
straps from the buckles and tore the fouled tabard
over his head. He threw it away from him, caught
up the scourge and brought it down on her head,
her shoulders, whatever was available of her body.

She screamed as the metal bits cut through her
cafta and into her flesh. Slipping and sliding she
tried to get away from the awful pain, the bite of
the cords, was driven back until she huddled in
the corner between bunk and wall, alternating

screams with whimpers, pleading with him in broken words until she forgot about words and simply screamed until her throat was too raw to scream any more.

With a grunt half of satisfaction, half of disgust, he dropped the scourge on the bunk. Deel heard a snapping then a soft slither then felt cold steel pressing against her cheek. She trembled, lay still, sure she was about to die, knowing she ought to do something, anything, did nothing but lie with her face pressed against the wood, caught in the sweet seduction of passivity. She heard a bark of laughter, then the cold moved from her face to her wrists. "You won't do this again," he said. His words came to her from a great distance. "Get this place cleaned up," he said. He cut the cords binding her wrists. Her arms fell apart, across her back; her hands thumped lifelessly against the slimy floor. She didn't move, even when she heard the brushing slide of his knees as he crossed the cabin, the slam of the door behind him.

The sweetish stench in her nostrils broke her apathy a little; she stirred, pushed around, sobbing as each movement sent pain burning through her. When she bent her wrists and tried to close her fingers into fists, the bite of returning circulation was almost more than she could bear. She moved somehow along the bunk until she was close to the door, sat awhile working her fingers, rubbing at her wrists until she could use her hands again. Slowly, carefully, she eased the bloodstained cafta free from the wounds on her legs, worked it under her buttocks and with great difficulty over her head. She dropped her arms with a sigh of relief and held the cafta crumpled in her lap a moment, then she let it fall away as she struggled onto her knees, briefly thankful that the front of

her body was relatively untouched. She flattened
one hand against the heavy planks of the door,
rested her forehead beside it, fumbled at the latch
with her other hand.

To her surprise the latch moved easily enough.
In his certainty that he'd beat the fight out of
her, he hadn't bothered to secure the latch. *Clean
the place, he said. Clean the place. I'd like to . . .* For
a moment anger seared through her, then she
slumped back into apathy. The wooden bucket was
pressing against her thigh. She grasped the bail,
slipped the latch and staggered outside.

The rain was coming down hard, the wind driving it almost horizontally, the drops pelting her
like small stones. Indifferent to her nakedness and
to the gaze of the two men in the stern, dragging
the bucket beside her, she crawled across the deck
to the place where the bucket usually rested in its
spring clip, a small coil of rope cleated beside it.

When she reached the side of the boat a hand
twisted in her hair, jerked her head back. She
blinked rain from her eyes and stared blankly into
Kan's threatening face. She licked her lips, faltered.
"You said clean."

He held her a moment longer, then stepped back,
scrubbing his hand across the soaked black cloth
of his tunic where it stretched over the jut of his
belly.

Taking his silence as permission to get on with
what she was doing, Deel shook out the coils of
rope. One end was knotted about the cleat, the
other attached to a snaphook. She thumbed the
hook open, snapped it over the bail, rested the
bucket on the rail, holding it there with one hand
while she pulled her aching body up beside it.
When she was on her feet, she stood a moment
gathering herself.

Kan came up behind her. "Don't even think it."

"What!" When he only smiled tightly at her, she shrugged, winced, turned back to the rail. Standing with her feet spaced to help her keep her balance, she began lowering the bucket to the black glide of water below.

For a moment the bucket bounced wildly, then the lip bit into the water and the current seized it. She cried out, whipped her hands hastily away as the rope hummed taut against the rail with enough force to tear off a finger or two. The boat slewed at the sudden grab of the current as the bucket acted like an anchor. She caught hold of the rail to steady herself, then was thrust aside with a curse at her stupidity as Kan grabbed hold of the rope and began pulling it in hand over hand, muscles working powerfully under the clinging black cloth of his tunic, his strength as awesome as the River's.

Shaking with reawakened fear, fascinated by the play of muscle in back and arms, Deel stared at him for what seemed to her an eternity until she heard the bucket slam against the side of the boat. She moved to the rail and looked at the glassy surface of the water. Without thought of escape, without thought of dying, simply letting the River's call take over, she tumbled over the side and fell into the black water.

She heard a roar of rage, broken shouts, then the water closed over her head. She was helpless against its power, paralyzed by the sudden, intense cold, surrendering without the least attempt to resist as it swept her along faster and faster—until her lungs began to burn and the realization seeped into her that she'd got away, she'd really got away from Kan and all he meant. The River had her, but water was no enemy to her, never something to be fought or mastered, but a capricious friend to be

teased into doing what she wanted. Holding her
arms tight against her body, straightening herself
until she paralleled the current, she began kicking,
using her strong dancer's legs to drive her up until
her head broke surface and she could breathe again.
Still letting the River take her where it wished,
she gulped air into her straining lungs, then continued kicking just enough to keep out of undertows
and as near the center of the main channel as she
could. After a little while she risked a glance back.
The boat had swung around; sail furled, slowed by
the opposition of the powerful storm wind blowing inland, it was coming after her.

For a moment she despaired, then she had no
time for despair as she was swept into the long
shallow plunge from the Chute. Arms wrapped
around her head, legs drawn up, she was whirled
along the crazy twisting current of the rapids, scraping again and again against scattered boulders,
losing more skin to the stone, her tattered flesh
bleeding into the water, sucking in as much water
as air whenever she dared snatch a breath until at
last the River left the Chute, spread wider and
began its long series of serpentines.

On and on the eerie flight and pursuit continued
while the storm began to abate and the rain to fall
more gently. Deel grew aware that she had to try
to ease herself free of the River or face rolling out
to sea and making a meal for crabs; she tried a few
slow kicks and was distressed by the leaden response of her legs; they were heavy, so heavy,
worse than after a dozen days of dancing. She
forced herself to kick harder, using the sweep of
the current around an approaching curve to push
her close to the bank.

As she struggled painfully shoreward, gaining a
grudging few bodylengths, she saw torchlight as a

red-gold glow coming toward her, but didn't understand what she was seeing until she knocked into something hard, floundered a moment and was sucked under. When she fought her way up again, she was being dragged along wooden planks. She struck out blindly. One hand slapped against a thick hawser, a mooring line. She clutched desperately at it, managed to wrap her body around it and cling there, gasping in lungful after lungful of air, only air, no strangling water. A moment later she heard shouts and twisted her head around.

The boat came nosing past the curve, the two men dimly visible in the stern. Overhead, on the deck of the barge, she could hear men stirring, a few sleepy complaints, nervous questions. Hastily, hoping she hadn't been seen, she lowered herself into the water and used the hawser to launch herself into the quieter eddies underneath the up-slanting rear of the barge. She kicked wearily to the bank and reached up, intending to pull herself from the water. Her hands clutched weakly at the capstones, slipped, caught again, but her arms had no strength left. She raised herself slightly then dropped back, her hands slipping, the gentler current dragging her slowly along the stone facing of the cut. She reached up once more, fumbled for a hold on the mossy stone.

Small, strong hands closed over her wrists. "Help me, Seren." The words were a sibilant whisper, unmistakably female, as were the hands. Deel was weakly surprised, then relieved when this reached through her despair. Then other hands were on her arms and she was being pulled from the water.

"Sssah! Look at that." Gentle fingers touched her back and she groaned, unable to bear any touch, no matter how gentle.

"Is she alive?" This was a soft contralto, little

more than a whisper over the rustle of wind and the susurrus of the water, a crisp command in it nonetheless.

"Just, I think."

"That's a Hand-boat coming up on us." A third voice, this one with an eerie hoarse quality, almost like a growl.

"Remember the compact. No men in our quarters, even Hands." The murmuring contralto was calm, encouraging, sustaining. *This one is the leader.* Deel thought about opening her eyes and looking around, but she didn't, she lay stretched out on the gritty stone feeling like a lump of dough, her brain like day-old mush. Over her she heard the rubbing of cloth against cloth, the grating of sandal-shod feet on the paving of the horseway. "Get her in the tent before someone on the barge comes over to see what we're fussing about. Better if we can deny seeing her." A pause, then she said, acid in her voice, "Don't stand there like lumps. She's going nowhere by herself."

Hands closed around her body. More hands than could belong to the three voices. She started to moan but a small palm pressed down over her mouth. Other fingers brushed sodden hair off her ear. She felt cloth against her face, warm breath and the vibration of soft lips against the ear. "Be still." The whisper was a thread of sound, she had to concentrate to catch the words. "You've endured much, hold on a little longer."

They carried her into a large tent lit by a single lamp and laid her belly down on a thick warm rug, someone's sleeping rug. Someone lifted her head and held a cup to her lips. Drinking was difficult with her neck so sharply bent, but she managed several mouthfuls of the thick sweet wine, sighing with pleasure as a soothing warmth spread through her chill, sore body. The one holding her took the cup away then eased Deel's head on to her thigh. She bathed Deel's swollen eyes and wiped them with a soft clean rag, smoothing away the mucous and clotted blood, then she eased Deel's head around so the Dancer could see the other women in the tent. They clustered about the entrance, bent forward slightly, whispering now and then, listening intently to what was happening outside. They wore long loose robes of home-spun cloth dyed blue and green, ocher and umber and a deep rich russet—and blue veils completely concealed their heads. Deel shifted her gaze; metal and leather armor piled along the tent wall confirmed her guess about the identity of her rescuers. "Trail women," she croaked.

"Hush." The small hand came down again on her lips. "Sayoneh," the soft voice breathed after a moment. "To ourselves we are Sayoneh, the delivered ones."

Deel stiffened as a too-familiar voice sounded just outside the tent. Kan. The small hand stroked her cheek, passed gently over her hair, touched her lips, reassuring her and reminding her to keep quiet.

"A woman. A smuggler. In the River."

"No stray females here, Hand. Look for yourself." The contralto voice was polite with a hint of cool distaste. "The watchers would have reported any such occurrence immediately."

"The tent, Saone?"

"You heard what I said, Hand." The voice was really chill now. "And you know our strictures."

"I heard you, Saone. The watchers would have reported to you, hah! I notice you carefully didn't say if they had. One day, Saone. I'll remember this." Deel shivered at the anger in Kan's clipped words and began to feel guilty for drawing these women into her troubles. Kan stomped off, clearly refusing to waste his breath arguing and for reasons she couldn't understand, equally unwilling to use force. She let herself relax, the rug under her wonderfully soft, the thigh beneath her aching head soft and firm at once, the robes of the small saone smelling pleasantly herbal. Distantly, through the waves of sleep that were washing over her, she heard the scrape of sandals coming toward her. Sighing, she forced her heavy eyes open once more.

Enigmatic behind the long blue veil with its embroidered eyeholes, a tall woman stood looking down at her. "Now, Dancer," the contralto voice said crisply. "Perhaps you'll explain what this is about."

Gleia winced as Shounach laid her on a shelf bed supported by rusty chains that groaned and rasped when her weight settled on the worn planks. The only light in the narrow cell came from the torches flickering and smoking in the icy drafts that swept along the walls of the cellar outside, a cellar filled with well-oiled, well-used objects of sinister purpose. Shounach touched her cheek, winked down at her, then straightened and turned to face the closing door. "Hand."

Gabbler ignored him and slammed the heavy door shut. Gleia saw Shounach's hands close into fists, then open, wondered what he was up to. He rounded his shoulders, shambled forward a few steps. When he spoke again, he was using the whiny beggar's voice that turned her a little sick though she knew well enough what he was doing once the performance began, having seen him playing a fawning, worthless vagabond for the Lossal the day he faced a spy's death. Saved his life with it though he couldn't save his body from the Lossal's malice.

"Noble Hand," he whined, "if you remember, the noble Hankir Kan requires me whole." Gabbler's face appeared in the small barred opening in the door; he was frowning but he was listening.

Gleia smiled. *Play him, my sweet Fox, tease the shirt off his back.* Shivering again, this time from the cold, the movements of her body setting the chains to creaking, she tugged at her sodden cafta, hugged her arms tight across her breasts. *I could use that shirt.*

"I'm wet, noble Hand, I'm cold and hungry. I'll die, noble Hand." Shounach's whine was louder, tainted with a weak insolence. "I'll be dead come morning if I don't get dry clothing. And blankets. And hot food."

Gabbler listened with stolid indifference. Intermittently visible behind him, the Bowman radiated contempt and muttered continually into the Gabbler's ears. The Silent Man refused to be hurried. He moved his eyes slowly over Shounach who stood shivering and looking miserable enough to underline his words. He glanced past Shounach at Gleia, then without a word or any other apparent response, he moved away.

Gleia shivered again, pulled her legs up and raised herself until she rested her back against the wall. She sat rubbing at her arms as she watched Shounach straighten his shoulders and flex his fingers, then cross the few steps to the door. He stooped to look through the opening (though it was head-high for the Rivermen, not excepting Bowman Raver, it hit him below his shoulders) and gazed out at the room beyond. Abruptly he stretched, yawned, set his compulsions aside for the moment and came toward her, his face shadowed, the torchlight creep-

ing in from outside touching the curve of a cheek
and lighting up one of his long narrow hands. He
dropped beside her, his legs stretched out before
him, his arms lifted, his hands laced together behind his head.

"Think that will do any good?" In spite of her
effort to speak casually, her voice shook and her
teeth clicked together.

He swung around, touched her face, began rubbing her hands gently, warming them with his.
His body felt furnace hot, but oddly not feverish, a
different quality in the heat. "Might," he said. "If
not, I'll chance fetching my bag."

She raised her brows.

"Raver chucked it down under a torch on the far
side of the cellar, sweet man that he is." His eyes
darkened with amusement. "Vixen, shame, remember how I got you over the walls?"

She laughed then, a chattery uncertain laugh,
sobered. "Hope hard Gabbler doesn't think of that."

He pulled her up, opened his jacket and held her
against his chest, the warmth of his body seeping
through the soggy cafta and into her shuddering
flesh. She sighed with pleasure and lay against
him, limp and drowsily content. "Madar bless,
Fox," she said after a few moments.

"For what?" He sounded as content as she felt
and as sleepy.

She rubbed her cheek against his chest, yawned,
murmured, "You didn't need any of those things.
What if he turned the Bowman loose?"

His slow chuckle rumbled under her ear. "Go to
sleep, love."

The thin blonde woman pushed the brazier into
the cell and backed out again, carefully avoiding
the Bowman. In spite of this he shied away from

her; eyes white-ringed, a crazy hatred twisting his long face. Roused from a deep sleep by the scraping of the brazier across the stone, Gleia watched this byplay with drowsy interest, then looked around for Shounach. He stood by the end of the bed, arms folded over his chest, leaning against the wall, his face lost in shadow.

The woman came back, struggling with a large basket, holding it in front of her with both hands, straining back to balance the weight of it. She had thick almost white hair standing out from her head in a ragged untidy bramble crimped into tiny tight curls. Her long pale face was scarred by sun-itch, some of the skin still flaking from the newer cankers. Long thin arms poked from the minimal sleeves of a dirty homespun shirt, a milky white like her face, scarred like her face; she had no pigmentation to protect her from Hesh's bite and that shift certainly wouldn't. Gleia's mouth tightened. The Rivermen didn't need chains to keep her kind at the towers. No more expression on her face than a wooden doll might have, she set the basket on the floor by the brazier and left, edging around Raver. The Bowman's body-type, height, facial structure and hair shouted of shared blood; the revulsion the woman woke in him was a measure of his hatred of that blood, his rejection of that blood. The door creaked shut, the iron bar shrieked as the Bowman dragged it through the staples. With a last kick at the planks, he stalked off.

She woke again late at night. The storm was over and the cell was filled with silence, the darkness broken only by the dying flicker of the torches outside. Shounach stood at the barred opening in the door. She pulled the blanket closer around her shoulders and lay watching the man, warm enough though there was very little red left in the brazier's coals. She started to call out to him but changed her mind. He was intent, straining, all his will and thought focused on something outside the cell.

A dark bulk rose before the opening. The faint glow from the brazier woke fugitive green gleams in the shiny side of Shounach's magic bag as it hovered before the cell door. He reached through the bars and caught hold of it. Tipping back the flap, he thrust an arm deep inside, reaching, she knew, into that eerie magic place that somehow seemed to hold more than the bag itself could contain. When he pulled his hand out, the dim red light touched a dull rod held between thumb and forefinger. As he dropped it into his jacket pocket, she sucked air between her teeth, making a small hiss that brought his head around. He grinned at her but said nothing, then he was fishing in the bag again. This time he brought out a rectangular leather case. She'd seen that before also, it held the drugs that had kept him moving after his torment in the Lossal's cellar. He eased it through the bars, slid it into his pocket. Once again he tensed. The bag slid away. A few minutes later she heard a gritty thump then a soft exhalation from Shounach.

As he came toward her, she saw that he was very tired, that only his will kept him on his feet. His will and her need. With a sudden flood of warmth, she let herself believe finally that she was important to him. She brushed a hand down along her body under the blanket, touching the loose long tunic, the black Riverman tunic worn threadbare over the elbows, the trousers torn on one knee, almost transparent on the other but dry and warm in spite of this. His jacket and trousers were dry; he was warm. He'd be warm in the middle of a snowdrift. He hadn't needed any of this, but he'd risked a lot to get the food, clothes and blankets for her.

He moved her legs closer to the wall, making a space for himself on the plankbed. Then he was bending over her, pushing the tunic up until it was bunched about her waist. He began undoing the laces on the trousers, his fingers warm against her skin, each fleeting touch sending small thrills through her. She murmured a protest when he eased the trousers under her buttocks and pulled them off entirely.

"Hush, love," he murmured. "Let me take care of this." On the inside of her thighs the raw flesh had hardened over and started cracking while she'd been asleep; when he touched those chafed places, she bit down hard on her lip to hold back a moan. Then the hurting touches stopped. He straightened and his shadow slid down from her head and shoulders. She heard a small snap, then the shadow flowed back as he bent over her once more, spreading coolness along the inside of her legs, a salve with an herbal bite to the vapors rising from it. She sighed with pleasure, then lay quiet as he set the case on the floor, his shadow now a swooping blackness running across the stone. Then his hands were stroking her legs, moving slowly up, heating her as they moved. His lips touched the shallow curve of her stomach, moved upward as he helped her ease the tunic over her head.

The morning air was chill on her face when she woke for the last time. She was dressed again, though she couldn't remember pulling the tunic and trousers back on; the blanket was tucked carefully around her. The cell was filled with a cold gray light that drained color and life from everything visible, even Shounach. He was listening to voices that came to her as unintelligible fragments of sound. His hands in the pockets of his jacket, he lounged against the cell door, one corner of his mouth twisted up, a sardonic look on his lean face.

Gleia sat up, keeping the blanket pulled around her. She yawned, pushed at oily tangled hair.

Shounach looked around, grinned impudently at her, last night's tenderness something left to memory.

"He-goat." Chuckling softly, she flexed her legs, wiggled her toes, and had to admit that the salve had worked a small miracle on her legs, though— she wrinkled her nose as she discovered them— she'd managed to collect some other bruises and aches from last night's exercises on the hard planks. She yawned again. "Unh! Do I need a bath."

The voices outside were growing louder. She couldn't make out the words, but the anger, malice and bitterness in the tones made her acutely uneasy. She drew her feet up, tucked them under her to warm them again. "What's happening?"

"Arguing. Bowman wants you along as his personal playtoy. Gabbler says you ride like a half-empty sack of grain and you'll slow us down. He wants to leave you here."

"Some choice." A small black speck crawled from her sleeve onto the back of her hand. She stared at it, grimaced and pinched it between the nails of her thumb and forefinger, scowled as she felt dozens of other small tickles, making her uncomfortably aware she had lots of company under the blanket. She unwrapped it hastily and dropped it to the floor. Her fingers busy under her tunic, hunting the small lives crawling about on her skin, she watched Shounach as he continued to listen to the argument outside. "What are you going to do about this mess?"

"Wait."

"What about me?"

"Sit and scratch."

"Hell I will." She swung her legs over the edge of the plankbed, then groped under it for her sandals. As she buckled them on, she said, "Don't expect me to stand about and admire your tricks, Fox. Madar!" She pinched another black speck off her instep. "I've had enough of being handed around like lumpy baggage."

He lifted a brow. "Lumpy?"

"You know what I mean."

"Oh?"

"Fool."

"Bless you, child." He rubbed at his nose, suddenly serious. "They're coming. Think you could push Raver into jumping you?" He stepped away from the door. "He might get his hands on you before I can take him out."

"I expect so." She frowned, remembering the Bowman's hand pinching and groping at her on the track last night. Absently she popped another small life. "Playtoy, hunh!" She smiled grimly. "There's a button I can tromp. I'll poke him hard, Fox."

Gabbler dragged the bar free. One end hit the floor with a reverberating clank as he leaned it against the wall. He hauled the door open, stepped back a body-length from the cell and beckoned Shounach out.

Hands in his pockets, Shounach strolled through the door. When Gleia started after him, Gabbler waved her back. Across the cellar, standing on the lowest step of the short flight leading up to ground level, the Bowman snickered, giving her the excuse she needed. "Laugh, you horse's ass," she snarled. "You son of a crimp-head whore. Your ma was too dumb to know wet from dry."

With a howl of rage, the Bowman cast his weapon aside and lunged at her, everything forgotten but his need to get his hands around her throat.

Sputtering a curse, Gabbler leaped for the bow, but pulled up when a fingerthick rod of light touched it and exploded it to ash. He turned slowly, glancing as he did at Raver who was writhing on the floor, screaming and clutching at a leg that was gone from the knee down, vaporized as the bow had been vaporized. Gabbler fixed his flat dark gaze on the small rod in Shounach's hand. "What now?"

With a tug of admiration for the man's calm acceptance of this series of misfortunes, Gleia jumped over the Bowman and moved to Shounach's side, stumbling a little as the trouser legs unrolled and threatened to trip her. She knelt and began rolling them up again. Shounach touched her head; she paused in what she was doing to look up. "You wield a wicked tongue, Vixen," he said.

"My pleasure, Fox. What do we do with them?" She nodded at the silent Gabbler and the howling Bowman.

Tugging at a stray curl, laughing as she jerked her head away, he said, "Through the hoop for you. Just for you." Still chuckling, he turned to face Gabbler. The squat dark Riverman had wrapped his ponderous silence about himself and stood waiting with an exaggerated patience that was a reproach for their frivolous waste of time and energy. He was waiting, it seemed to Gleia, with the patience of a stalking Tars for them to make a mistake. But he hadn't tried taking advantage of Shounach's apparent inattention, perhaps he didn't care to lose a leg as Raver had. "In." Shounach jabbed a thumb at the cell. Gleia dusted off her knees as she rose from her crouch. "Drag that with you."

Shounach nodded at the cursing, whimpering Bowman.

Gleia slammed the door shut behind them and helped Shounach slide the bar through the staples. She stepped back, frowning at the arrangement. "That won't hold them any longer than it takes to yell someone down here."

"This will." Shounach twisted one end of the rod, inspected it a moment, then stood slapping it against his palm, eyeing the door. Abruptly he shrugged and pressed the rod against the point where the bar touched the staple. The light this time was a murky red. The iron boiled and flowed together and congealed again when he took the rod away. The bar was welded to the staple and it would take a heavy maul, perhaps even a steel chisel to break it loose. He fingered the other staple, shook his head and dropped the rod into his pocket. Gleia watched, puzzled. Something was bothering him about the rod but she didn't know enough to tell what it was. She started to ask, shut her mouth again as he stepped to the opening in the center of the door. "Hand," he said.

"What now?" Gabbler's voice was expressionless, but Gleia shuddered and hoped she'd never fall in his hands again.

"I've fixed it so you won't get out of here without time and hard work. Too late to catch us. You could try sending the Watchman after us. Give you one guess how much chance he'd have of bringing us back. If I stood in your boots, once out, I'd head for distant parts where Hankir Kan couldn't get his hands on me." He waited a moment but Gabbler said nothing. Patting a yawn, he crossed the room, retrieved his bag and started for the stairs. Gleia trailed behind him, unhappy at the thought of climbing back on a horse, any horse, swearing under her breath as her trouser legs started to unroll again.

"Seren." There was a gentle reproof in the small saone's voice. "Let her rest. She's almost asleep now."

The tall woman moved a hand in an abrupt, angular gesture of denial. "A Hand, Chay. That Hand. We have to know what and why. Know it now, little Chay. So we can plan. Dancer, do you hear me?"

Deel sighed. Flattening her hands on the rug, stifling a groan as the stiffened muscles of her arms and back protested and scabbing wounds cracked, she pushed herself onto her knees, eased back until she was sitting on her heels. "I'm no smuggler." She croaked, her throat burning as she tried to speak, the sounds she could make as painful to her ears as to her throat. "I'm a dancer, you know that," she managed.

"Why is Kan so hot after you?"

Deel looked away from the elaborate eyeholes turned on her. With that veil hiding the woman's face, talking to her was like trying to talk to a hole in the ground. "I turned him down too often and too hard," she whispered, her voice breaking and vanishing as she struggled with the words. She closed her eyes a moment, forced them open again when sleep threatened to drown her. It was hard to think, hard to know what she should say. She swallowed, then pressed a hand against her neck. The saone Chay poured some more wine in the cup and held it out. Deel gulped down several mouthfuls, relaxed a bit as warmth spread through her, chasing away—for the moment, at least—some of the soreness in her throat. She clutched at the cup, wondering just how much silence she owed Gleia and the Juggler and and how much explanation she owed the Sayoneh for rescuing her from Kan. It was a hard choice and she didn't feel like trying to sort out the rights and wrongs. Still, Seren was waiting with growing impatience for an answer. "He got me on that boat," Deel whispered. "When he got amorous, I was sick all over him."

Chay giggled and several others, anonymous among the clustering veils, chuckled with appreciation. Deel smiled a little, warmed by this bit of sister-sharing as she was warmed by the wine she was sipping. "He beat me." Sympathy flowed from the blue veils—it was eerie, those veils staring at her. "No faces," she said, her eyes blurring and watering as she turned her head from one set of fanciful eyeholes to the next.

Seren moved her hand in another of her angular gestures. Deel blinked. The hand was brown, square, small for her size but conspicuously competent. "Your hands are like hers," Deel said, pleased with herself for seeing this likeness between Seren and Gleia. That small hand made her feel comfortable and secure.

"Her? Who?"

Jolted a little out of her drifting rumination, Deel stared at the veil, started to shake her head, but stopped that when she nearly fell over. "You wouldn't know her. A brown fox, secret. Secret. No face. Don't need a veil. Turn it off."

Seren snorted. "You're drunk, Dancer."

"Uh-huh." Deel smiled dreamily at the purple-red film staining the bottom of the mug.

"Pay attention." The saone's voice was sharp, annoyed. "How did you get away from Hankir Kan?"

"Threw up all over him."

"You said that."

"Said that. He said clean up. Fetch water. Went to fetch it." She lifted a hand, swooped it out and down in an unsteady arc. "Whoop. Over the side." She giggled. "Stupid. Him. Letting me drop that damn bucket in the River." She sighed. "Wasn't thinking, me, just did it. Boat went crazy. I went over. He come after."

"I see. Did the Hand take you out of Istir?"

"Don't want to talk about that."

"Why?"

"Friends in it. Not your business."

"Mmm. Well, we'll leave that till later when you're sober again. Dancer."

"Huh?"

"Listen if you can. We're going to Jokinhiir to join our sisters at the Jota fair. You'd better come with us; you're not in any shape to set off by yourself."

"Jokinhiir." Deel touched her tongue to her lips as she considered this. "She's going to Jokinhiir if she gets away." She scrubbed her hand across her face. "Him too." Thought of the Juggler warmed her blood. She coughed, swallowed. "Kan will be in Jokinhiir."

"You don't have to see him."

Deel shivered, suddenly cold, suddenly awake again, all her aches and general exhaustion flooding over her. "Go with you." She shivered again. "Poison," she said, not fully aware she was speaking aloud. "I'm poison. Alahar first, then. . . ." She stopped, blinked. "Kan will have your skin for this and don't think he won't find out." She swayed, jerked herself upright again.

Chay caught her arm, supporting her. "Seren, that's enough."

With the small saone helping her, Deel stretched out on the fleecy rug, on her stomach again so the fleece wouldn't get into the wounds. She heard the slither of Chay's robes and a murmuring exchange with another saone, then she twitched as gentle fingers spread a cool lotion over the bruises, scrapes and cuts, wiping away the pain. "Sayoneh, the delivered," Chay murmured as she worked. "The broken, the beaten, the rebels, they find refuge with us." The voice began to fade in and out. "Pass through ... stay ... you can stay ... want ... stay ... wider, warmer home ... place to be ... belong...." Deel heard nothing more, drowning deep deep in sleep.

The next four days were a floating shapeless dream as Shounach's drugs helped her endure the endless riding and the pain that otherwise would have immobilized her. They rode double all night through storm and frost and all day except for the few hours of high heat when they dipped into the forest to avoid the hammering of the suns, Gleia pressed against Shounach's back, holding tight to him, separated from him only when he stopped to switch horses, having ridden the one they were on into exhaustion. When they came to watchtowers, they herded the Watchman and his servants into the holding cell each tower was equipped with. The guards usually there had been pulled away to police the Fair, only one man being left behind to hold the tower, soured and made careless by having to miss the Fair and spend Fairtime sitting out in the middle of nowhere.

They left the fourth tower early in the evening. Gleia relaxed against Shounach's back, gratefully free of drugs for the first time, her body having toughened enough to support the effort of the ride; she was beginning to respond automatically to the horse's motion, was beginning almost to enjoy the ride, though the rain was beating down on her and the growing cold was eating through the heavier clothing she'd liberated from a watchman's wardrobe. The storm cleared away sometime after midnight and the clouds blew apart, unveiling crescent Aab and a great swirling sweep of stars. Gleia sucked in the frosty air, snuggled against the warmth of Shounach's lean body and felt content, even happy.

In the dark hours just before dawn, Shounach pulled the last of the stolen horses to a stop. "The Roost," he said.

Clutching at him, she leaned out and looked around him. The tower was a black cylinder cutting into the starfield, twice the girth and twice the height of the other watchtowers. Though there were a few sparks of red near the base where torches burned at guardposts, the rest of the tower was quiet and dark, those inside apparently all still asleep. Shounach tapped her hands. When she loosed her grip, he slid to the ground and reached up for her.

Gleia eased her head above the step and wrinkled her nose as her eyes confirmed what her ears had told her. A corseleted guard paced steadily back and forth in front of an elaborately carved door, a regrettably alert sentry far different from the two men supposed to be watching the tower's entry, both of them drunk and intent on the leaping bones and the piles of coins in front of them. Up here on the top floor of the tower, Kan's own roost within the Roost, everything was different. She watched the guard pace then looked around the wide open space in front of the door. It was bare of cover and lit by at least a dozen shell and pewter lamps; the only shadows visible were those multiple shifting shapes pooling around the feet of the pacing guard.

She crept carefully back down the steps to the floor below, tensing at each accidental sound. She pushed open the door to the unused room where he'd left her. The lamps in the corridor were burning low, it would be dawn too soon and at dawn the tower would turn into a trap. Her sandals creaking on the stone, she paced back and forth over the gritty flags, circling around the broken, three-legged chair that was the only furniture in the room, too restless and worried to sit or even stand at the window.

Shounach came back after what seemed an eternity though the darkness outside was as thick and still as ever with no sign of the approaching dawn. She whirled when she heard a noise at the door, relaxed when she saw him, lifted a brow at his burden—a large metal tray with a pewter pitcher sitting in the middle, a ragged hunk of bread on one side and an equally ragged lump of cheese on the other. He set the tray in the window embrasure and shook out the wad of cloth he'd carried pinched between arm and ribs, a servant girl's shift, cleaner than most she'd seen in the other towers.

"What's that for?" She glanced from the shift to his face. "I almost hate to ask."

"You. I want you to distract the guard for me. He won't be suspicious. No sane person would invade this tower."

Gleia chuckled. "Sane? Neither of us qualifies."

He held out the shift. "Get into this."

Scowling, she shook her head. "Look at me. Smell me. I smell more horse than woman."

"You don't have to seduce him. Use your tongue, Vixen."

"What? Oh." Ignoring his sudden grin, she reached around the shift and snapped a finger against the shoulderbag riding his hip. "Use the light-blade on him. It'd be quicker and quieter."

"Can't. Not enough charge left to light a match." At her puzzled look, he shook his head. "Never mind. It's used up for the moment, that's all. You can do this, Vixen."

"But I won't like it."

Laughing he moved to the window and stood gazing across the chasm at the dark bulk of the Svingeh's Keep sitting high above the sleeping Fair. Shivering as the damp chill pervading the desolate little room touched her skin, she stripped off the tunic and trousers and smoothed the shift down over her body, regretting already the warmth she'd discarded; the sleazy material of the shift provided little protection against the cold. She joined Shounach at the window, rubbing briskly at the cold-bumps on her arms. The starlight glittered on patches of frost that shone white against the black of the stony earth far below. "Winter in a few months," she said. "Have you thought. . . ."

"Time for that later, Vixen." He lifted the tray and carried it to the door.

She took it from him and stood back to let him open the door for her. "I'm an idiot to do this. You be sure you're close behind me."

Shounach smiled down at her, drew fingertips gently along her cheek, lingering over the brands. "See if you can get him to turn his back to the stairs."

"Talk about your one-idea minds." Shaking her head, she went out, walking slowly, intent on keeping the unstable pitcher from tipping over and dousing her with the beer it held.

"What you doin' here, girl?"

Her head down, her eyes on the rocking pitcher, she ignored the guard's snapped question and moved several more steps toward Kan's door. With a muttered curse he rushed at her, grabbed at her arm and jerked her around. The pitcher rocked precariously but didn't quite tip over. She held her breath until it settled, then stood with her eyes lowered, refusing to look at the guard, trying to present him with a picture of sullen stupidity. "Orders," she muttered. "Tol' me, bring this here."

"He's sleeping." The guard kept his voice low though there seemed little chance that many sounds would penetrate that massive door or the equally massive walls. "He don't want no food now. Get your butt down those stairs before I kick it down."

She stood stubbornly silent.

Breath hissed between his teeth. His fingers closed painfully on her arm; he jerked her around, sending her into a stumbling run toward the stairs, the tray wrenched from her hands. It bounced on the floor with an appalling clatter, the pitcher rolling away in a lopsided arc, spilling beer in a frothy stream across the flags.

Then the guard was folding down to lie with his face in a puddle of sour beer, Shounach standing over him. He grinned at Gleia who stood rubbing at her bruised arm and scowling down at her beer-soaked sandals. "About time," she said.

"You know you did good, Vixen." He crossed to the door, lifted the latch and shoved. "Barred inside." Eyes narrowed, body taut, he concentrated a moment then shoved at the door again, smiling as it swung ponderously open, silent on oiled hinges. He beckoned Gleia to him, sniffed as she came up beside him. "Horse and beer are not a pretty mix."

"You should be as close to it as I am." She moved past him into a huge dark room with scat-

tered divans, their piles of silken pillows gleaming
liquidly in the faint light from a single lamp. She
started across the room, expecting to hear Shounach
following behind; near the middle she turned, raised
her eyebrows as she saw him back outside, stoop-
ing beside the unconscious guard. He dragged the
man inside, went back for the pitcher and tray,
swung the door shut and dropped the bar into its
slots. "No use getting anyone excited."

Kan's breathing filled the bedroom beyond, a
steady rasping not quite a snore. Starlight and the
meager gleam from Aab's shrunken crescent came
grayly through the window hole cut in the thick
outer wall, through the double panes of its glass,
just enough light to darken the shadows and fuzz
the outlines of the room's furniture. Her sandals
whispered over layered furs as she crossed to the
wide bed where Kan sprawled alone among scattered pillows, quilts twisted around him until he
looked like a dark moth emerging from a tattered
cocoon. He lay on his stomach, his face turned
toward her, drooping open, quivering with each
noisy breath. She glanced up at Shounach. "The
sleep of the just," she said acidly, not bothering to
lower her voice.

His eyes darkening with amusement, his teeth
gleaming in the ghost-light, he touched her shoulder, then bent over Kan, startling her by slapping
his open hand against the man's neck.

Kan grunted, tried to fight out of the quilts,
collapsed onto his back; he stared glassily up at
them, a dark disc clinging leech-like to his neck.
Shounach watched him a few minutes, eyes narrowed, measuring the changes in his face, then he
retrieved the disc, slipped it back in his pocket.
"Hand," he said sharply; he slapped him, his hand

cracking against the plump cheek. "Hand, tell me your name."

"Hankir Kan ycon y-sannh." His voice was thick and slow; a line of drool dripped from the corner of his mouth.

"Do you carry Ranga Eyes into Istir?"

Kan's eyes opened wide; for a moment a flicker of awareness brightened in them, then his face went slack again. He said nothing.

Shounach frowned, then nodded. "Right. Did you carry Ranga Eyes into Istir?"

In a dull, blurred voice, Kan said, "I did carry Ranga Eyes into Istir."

"Where did you get the Eyes?"

Gleia moved closer until she was pressed against Shounach's side, his arm shifting to rest on her shoulder as he waited with more patience than she could muster for the answer to this question.

"The Svingeh."

Suppressing an exclamation of disgust at the let-down, Gleia pulled away from Shounach and began wandering about the room. With more understanding of the limitations of the drug, Shounach continued his questions. "Where does the Svingeh get the Eyes?"

"Hell-bitches."

Two of the walls were covered by large tapestries, their colors swallowed by the cold light, the woven images fading into blotches of gray and white. She wandered over to one of them, ran exploring fingers along its surface.

"Explain Hell-bitches."

"Sayoneh. Trail women."

Gleia pulled the tapestry out from the wall, raised her brows when she saw the small alcove it concealed.

"Where do they get the Eyes?"

"Don't know."

Gathering the tapestry into folds to let the meager light filter past her, she peered into the alcove. With a soft exclamation she dropped the tapestry and groped across the small space to the two bags piled in a back corner, her bag and Deel's. She took one in each hand and pushed back out into the main room.

"Where is their settlement?"

"Don't know."

"Who does know?"

"No one. They keep it secret."

Gleia stripped off the beer-stained shift, glad to be rid of it. She dug into her bag, found one of her caftas and pulled it on; it was wrinkled and damp but she felt more like herself.

"When do the Sayoneh bring the Eyes to Jokinhiir?"

"Ten days before the Jota Fair."

"They've already delivered the year's shipment?"

"Yes."

Gleia hauled the two bags across the room and stopped beside the bed. She touched Deel's bag, considered interrupting Shounach to ask about Deel, decided that she could wait a little longer.

"What do the Sayoneh buy with the Eyes?"

"Protection."

"Protection?"

"Come and go, buy and sell, Svingeh keep hands off, make everyone else keep hands off."

"When the Sayoneh leave the Fair, do they go off together?"

"Sometimes."

"Sometimes they leave in separate groups, go in different directions?"

"Sometimes."

Gleia looked down at the man's slack face, then

up at Shounach. She rubbed slowly at her arms. Kan was sweating copiously, little ripples of twitches running repeatedly across the flaccid muscles of his face as if in some deep part of his mind he fought this invasion of his private thoughts. Gleia chewed on her lip, feeling uncomfortable at the probing, feeling also a degree of satisfaction at seeing him struggle helplessly as he must have made Deel struggle.

"What direction do they take when they leave together?"

"South along Skull-crusher."

"What is Skull-crusher?"

"River."

"What river?"

"Cuts between Roost and Svingeh's Keep."

"In the chasm?"

"Yes."

"Anyone tried following them?"

"Not far."

"Why?"

"After the first time, Svingeh forbade."

"Why?"

"No more Eyes."

Gleia scratched at her nose, glanced at the window, frowned when she saw the faint rosy tinge to the gray light. She laid her hand on Shounach's arm.

The muscle under her hand jerked, he twisted around and frowned at her. "What is it?"

"Deel."

His face went blank, then he passed a shaking hand across his eyes. "Sorry. I forgot."

"I know." She touched his cheek. "You do that. One track at a time."

He shook his head, then bent over Kan. "Where's the Dancer?"

"Gone."

"How gone?"

"In the River."

Gleia sucked in a breath, held it, waiting tensely for the next answer. Shounach's mouth tightened, his hand closed hard around hers. "What was she doing in the River?" he asked quietly.

"Swimming."

Weak with relief, Gleia leaned against Shounach. Once again he absently rested his arm along her shoulders and held her close. "Did she get out of the River?" he asked.

"Don't know."

"Is it possible that she got out of the River?"

"Yes."

"How?"

"Hell-bitches could have pulled her out."

"Sayoneh. Where were they?"

"By the Mouth of the Chute."

"What were they doing there?"

"Riding a barge to the Jota Fair."

"Why do you think they got the Dancer?"

Kan's mouth fell open, worked moistly; his face twisted into distorted shapes. For a moment Gleia thought he wasn't going to answer, then the distortions smoothed out. "Too . . . too uppity," he said dully. "Daring me . . . to . . . to do . . . something. Hiding her . . . know it . . . they got her."

"How long ago was this?"

"Five days."

"When will the barge reach the Fair?"

"Tomorrow . . . day after."

Gleia moved restlessly, happy that Deel was probably alive and safe, increasingly worried as the red tinge strengthened. She came back to Shounach. "Not much time left, Fox. Sun's up."

He nodded. "In a minute. Kan."

"Yes, I am Kan."

"The Dancer. What are you going to do about her?"

"Get her. Make her sorry."

"How will you get her away from the Sayoneh?"

"Make an excuse, get in the bitches' tents. Spot her anywhere veil or not." His face twisted again, the hate in it naked, undisguised by the masks custom and caution imposed. Gleia shuddered and stepped back. "Fox. . . ."

"I know." He slid a hand into his pocket—and paused, frowned down at Kan, his eyes unfocused, his face troubled. After a moment, he shrugged and brought out the disc. He thumbed the dials to a different setting and slapped it on Kan's neck. He straightened, smiled at Gleia. "What I'm using on him is outlawed just about everywhere. For good reason. And available just about everywhere. For the same reason. It's a powerful conditioner." Gleia raised her eyebrows; he flicked her cheek with a long forefinger. "Means I can tell him what to do, what to think, what to say—and what to forget. I can shape his mind and memory like a sculptor shapes clay."

"And when he wakes up?"

"The shaping holds. One thing. . . ."

"What's that?"

"I like Deel."

"I noticed."

"No, not just that. She has ... generosity of spirit." He smiled at Kan, a harsh unlovely grimace. "I don't. There's a very appropriate side effect of the drug. Females are passive, their senses dulled to nonexistence. Males are affected more strongly that way and are temporarily impotent."

"Lovely idea; let the punishment fit the crime."

Shounach chuckled. "What sharp teeth you have,

my Vixen. Shall I watch my cha?" He didn't wait
for a response, but bent over Kan and began speaking in soothing tones, drawing from the mumbling
muzzy man the responses he wanted. Gleia strolled
to the window and leaned into the embrasure,
listening to Shounach lay the geas on the Hand—
forget about Deel, forget about them, leave the
three of them alone, and, as an afterthought, the
Sayoneh had done nothing to thwart him, he was
to be neutral to them, neither welcoming nor
harassing.

Currents, Gleia thought. *Poor old Kan, if he wasn't
so awful, I'd feel sorry for him. Poor old monster,
caught up in the currents we generate without the
faintest idea what's happening.* Red streaks were
spreading across the sky, blocked in part by the
bulk of the Svingeh's Keep across Skull Crusher's
chasm. She backed out of the embrasure, started
to speak, then stared. Shounach wasn't on the bed
any longer, he was standing by a hole in the wall,
scooping coins into his bag. She patted the bags
hanging heavy on her own shoulder, started again
to speak, then stiffened.

A faint sound of excited voices floated through
to her, the door boomed as someone pounded on it
with a sword hilt. There was a lot of yelling, muffled by the thickness of the planks, but audible
enough, Kan's name, demands to know if he was
all right. Hastily she started fumbling with the
window, looking for its catch. Behind her Shounach
bent over Kan, closed his eyes with a quick brush
of his hand. "Sleep. Wake in three hours. Say you
understand."

" 'nerstan.' "

Gleia got the window open. Shounach boosted
her into the embrasure and crawled in behind her.
When she reached the outer end of the hole, she

looked down, gasped. The tower was built on the edge of the chasm and she was looking straight down at the roaring white water of Skull Crusher. Shounach caught her around the waist. "Out you go."

"Madar!"

"No time to argue." He shoved her out, jumped after her.

They dropped like stones, the chill air whistling past them. She clutched at the bags, her eyes screwed shut, the sound of the tumbling water roaring up to her louder and louder until she was rigid with terror.

A familiar skin closed around her plummeting body, a rubbery second skin that tugged at her, slowed her, and finally set her on the ground gently as a falling feather, then loosed her.

She stumbled, started to fall, but Shounach caught her, held her, warming and comforting her, until her shaking stopped and the strength came back into her body.

She stiffened her arms and pushed away from him. Over the noise of the water that bounded and rebounded from the granite cliffs, she yelled at him, "Don't you do that again. Don't you ever do that to me again!" He grinned at her, mimed repentance that she didn't believe for a moment. She flounced around and started walking toward the glassy slide of the River a short distance away where the Skull Crusher's ravine opened out and a more subdued tributary joined the larger flow. They'd landed on a rocky stretch of ground between the cliff and the edge of the water, difficult walking with the stones turning under her feet. She shifted the bag straps to a more secure position on her shoulder and shortened her strides.

Shounach caught up with her and strolled easily beside her.

As they rounded a slight bend, she saw a flat-bottomed ferry bobbing on the water, winched against a landing built of massive planks. Thick hawsers swayed in the breeze, swooping in shallow curves to the far side of the river. There was a man on the landing, sitting with his back against the windlass, his legs stretched out before him, his head hanging forward, chin on chest, his mouth open. A hand rested on an overturned jug. His snores were lost in the river noise.

Gleia stopped. "Almost a shame to wake him."

Shounach dipped into his bag, pulled out a few coins from Kan's hoard and clinked them together, smiling. "Kan's paying our way, we can afford to be generous."

Her hand on his arm, she frowned up at him. "What now? After we get across the river, I mean."

"Find a way of going on." He looked around. "Wait for Deel." He shrugged, laughed, lifted her onto the landing and jumped up beside her. "Right now, I want food and a bath." He rubbed gently at the curve of her neck. "Let's enjoy the Fair for the next few days and leave worrying to Kan when he wakes up."

SUMMER'S END

Old Acquaintances and New

On a dew-wet morning Shounach and Gleia strolled down the steps of the ferry landing and along the warped planks of an improvised walkway, the wood squeaking underfoot, the River a whispered roar beside them. Gleia knew she was forgotten for the moment as the Juggler focused on the peacock scene before and around him, sorting the parts, assessing the possibilities; he was a peacock figure himself, crimson clinging trousers, the skirts of his sky-blue jacket fluttering back to show the bright gold lining, red hair blowing in the wind, pale skin like ancient whitewashed leather even paler in the thin red morning light. A sort of camouflage, all that—she'd seen it work when the Lossal in Istir dismissed him as a negligible fool and later when the Hands had let their contempt for him undermine their vigilance; she expected to see it happen again.

He moved with a smooth swinging stride that made
her hustle though there was no hurry to him; he
looked relaxed and casual, but Gleia knew he was
far from being as calm as he looked. The hand
resting on the magicbag sometimes smoothed over
the silky green surface, the red and blue stars,
sometimes drummed restlessly and soundlessly,
sometimes fingered the steel rings that connected
the strap to the bag. Never still. Alive with the
tension he would not show otherwhere.

Endings. Summer's end, quest's end. She was
tired. And like all the humankinds and otherkinds
on Jaydugar, her body and mind were responding
to the signs of ending. It was time to prepare for
wintering, for dormancy, for life encysted and
slowed; it was, urgently, a time for searching out
shelter. She slanted a quick glance at Shounach,
then frowned at the walkway. He seemed to have
escaped these urgencies by his long absence from
Jaydugar. How long really? Could she really believe the tales he fed her? She smiled at the splint-
ery planks, a sudden rush of affection warming her
though she had few illusions left about what would
happen if she got between him and any of his
obsessions. Ranga eyes. He'd tromp over her or use
her as ruthlessly as he'd planned to use Deel. And
she didn't mind that much as long as he didn't try
to make a fool of her. She hated and feared Ranga
Eyes and approved of eradicating them from the
face of Jaydugar, yet for her it was a willed
detestation, not the fire that burned in Shounach
and drove him on. It was expiation for him, a
righting of an old wrong, the wrong that had bitten into him, water into rock, until he had to find
some way of atoning or cease living.

Ahead of them the cliffs swung back from the
River in a great arc that softened into rolling high-

lands with forests that were a blue-purple band as
Horli pushed up above them. Shadows were long
and indistinct, coming at them across the muddy
ground where sun-dried grass was trampled into
the slop by the split hooves of various sorts of
cattle, the ironshod hooves of various sorts of riding stock. Most of the herds were across the River
where the cliffs of the Chute were gone completely,
the land opening out to the north, rolling prairie-
land with scattered herds dotted thick on the grass,
dark above the pale yellow grass, waiting for the
abattoirs to reduce them to pieces suitable for the
smoking racks and the salt barrels, waiting for the
barges and packtrains to take those pieces and
barrels away to cities and steadings stocking up
for the winter. The herd-owners from the inland
ranches and their drovers were finished with that
part already, their herds sold for whatever they
could get for them, good prices or not; it wasn't
worth driving them back and finding feed for them
over winter, or butchers and barrels enough to
store their meat.

The beasts on Jokinhiir's side of the River were
breeding stock. There were black-and-white milkers,
lankier and taller than the broad-backed dun gavha
that were raised mostly for meat and leather. There
were small mountain cattle with short curled horns
and slender legs and long shaggy coats that the
mountain folk wove into a heavy coarse cloth that
could be treated to repel water. Haywains trun-
dled down the aisles between the open-face sheds,
men standing on them forking hay down to the
mangers.

On the nearest of the wains a man over two
meters tall with a shaved head and blue-black skin
that glistened with amethystine highlights in the
thin red morning light was pitching hay into the

mangers of a shed that held the tiny mountain cattle. He straightened, wiped sweat from his face. In strongly accented parsi, he called to the man in the next lane over, whose charges were the black-and-white milkers, "Who gonna buy those eaters of fields, freeze into statues one puff a winter?"

Grinning, the short dark man dug his fork into the hay, leaned on the handle and yelled back, "How d'ya keep track a those mice? Let 'em run loose in the walls all winter?

The black man's voice had been lazily amiable, the answer was equally amiable. Old friends, despite their differences, as accustomed to trading insults as they were to trading mugs of beer. Gleia heard the belonging in all this noise and sighed. Even among the seafolk this was something she'd never known. And with a sudden insight she realized it was one—though only one—of the prods that drove her from safe havens into the unknown, this hunger for the kind of camaraderie these men had without effort. She listened as the retreating cliffs echoed with their noise, the words blending with birdcalls, the lowing of cattle, an occasional bellow from the carefully separated bulls and the powerful basso whisper of the River, the shriller broken boom of the tributary Skull Crusher.

The haymen stopped to stare at Shounach with a curiosity that they were too cautious or perhaps too courteous to express, but went back to their raucous exchanges once the strangers were safely past.

The sounds muting behind them, Shounach and Gleia left the cattle sheds and moved on to the corrals and stalls where the horses were, where the noise was more subdued, the tension greater.

The horses were already fed. Handlers were leading some out for exercise on the track visible behind the barns. Others were washing down or currying their beasts, braiding manes and tails with wired ribbons. Riding beasts, racers, huge draft animals like those that towed the barges upriver and a few exotics, tiny beasts smaller than dogs but perfect in their conformation, all brought to be haggled over and sold.

While the hired hands worked, the owners walked through the sheds or huddled in small groups gesturing nervously or with an exaggerated calm that fooled no one, talking in short bursts, their eyes continually assessing their own stock and that of their rivals. Much depended on the auctions and the private deals they made here at the Jota Fair. The men with the racing stock were especially alert; they had guards around their prizes. Betting was heavy and men had been known to interfere with favorites if given the opportunity—not a healthy shortcut to wealth; the Svingeh had several maimers skinned and swung from gibbets to discourage this kind of thing, but the breeders still took no chances. The money earned here and the supplies hauled home could make the difference between a comfortable wintering and a winter of dead children.

The day was beginning crisp and cool. The hay was a crackling and a stinging in her nostrils, the grain in the boxes had a more subtle tang with a hint of bread about it; the fine leather harnesses and saddles and the rest of the gear, the manure and mud and sweat and oil combined into a dark rich smell thick with life and energy, oddly pleasing in its pungency. Gleia breathed deeply and smiled, looked up to see Shounach watching her, his eyes green with laughter. She laughed aloud, walked on, deeply content, refusing to think about what lay ahead of them.

They left the stock sheds behind, walked through a thin line of trees and emerged into another space where a number of weathered flimsy structures poked like gray fingers from the crumbling cliff-face. At the far end, in the shadow of the cliff, there was a large shapeless opening she thought looked rather like the toothless mouth of a sea slug. Yawning, stretching men and women were emerging from the mouth and strolling toward the walkway laid above the mud.

A tall thin man in black velvet robe crudely embroidered with silver wire, bits of faceted glass and many small mirrors came sauntering toward them; as he reached the walkway, he glanced casually at Shounach, looked away, looked back, stopped and waited for them. "Juggler," he said. "Never thought to see you this side of the ocean." He had a thin face with delicate features that gave way to the dominance of thick straight black brows, a square black beard and rat-tail moustaches that curved around his mouth to meet the beard. Gleia examined him with a fascination she didn't try to hide, this bit of flotsam floating up from the past that Shounach wouldn't talk about.

"Zidras," Shounach said coolly, "I might say the same." He slowed a little and moved over to give the man space to walk beside him.

"Finger of fate." Zidras waved a hand airily, an absurdly delicate hand, little more than soft white skin stretched over long thin bones.

"How's the crowd? Tight or easy?"

"Tight. Early days yet." Zidras was smiling and chatty, relaxed and comfortable enough with Shounach to hint of favors exchanged until the balance was fairly equal between them. "They smell a bad winter coming early," he went on. "The meat auctions ended yesterday. That should liven things a

bit. But the races start tomorrow and that'll draw
the day crowd away from the market booths and
the players' pitches. Even from the cat-pits, though
there are some as likes the blood too much to be
interested in such tame entertainments. Night now,
that's getting livelier, but too many Hands about
to make it profitable as we'd like. And they keep
reminding folk of the Svingeh's cut, enough to
sour hullu wine." He shivered, pulled his robe
tighter about him and looked over his shoulder.
Gleia followed his eyes, disciplined herself not to
flinch when she saw what was bothering him. A
Hand stood watching them. Zidras' gaze rested on
her face a moment too long, so she knew he'd
sensed her wariness, but he said nothing for several more paces, then spoke to Shounach with a
seriousness that rested uneasily on him. "One thing,
Juggler. Don't set up till you've fee'd the Svingeh.
You're used to working free and easy. That don't
go here. You get us all busted, you try shafting the
Svingeh. They just looking for the excuse to use
those cords on us."

Shounach nodded. "So I hear. Anyone else we
know working the Fair?"

Zidras grinned, his dark eyes flicking to Gleia's
face then up to Shounach's. "Trina and Shaur."

"Ashla's hells," Shounach grimaced. "Hasn't
forgot, has she."

"She forget when she dead. She'd throw fat on a
fire that was burning you." He slid another of his
too-knowing glances at Gleia who apprehended
what he was saying by trying so obviously not to
say it. She kept her face impassive, uninterested.
Go play with yourself and leave me alone, she
thought. "Won't be around for long," he went on.
"Leaving first light tomorrow. Svingeh wouldn't
license her. Said the last seer made too much trou-

ble for him and was a fraud anyway and he
wouldn't believe in it even if she told him the
names of his eldest ancestors, so Shaur's had to
work the crowds, but a Hand almost caught him
. . . mmmh. . . ." He gazed at Gleia, assessing the
brands on her face. ". . . transferring the wealth,
one might say. He a dainty shade of green since
and afflicted with a palsy most awful."

Shounach snorted. "You haven't changed."

"Never thought you'd notice, love." He patted
Shounach's arm, then sighed, fluttered long curling eyelashes. "Such a loss. Such a loss, my limber
lovely friend." Chuckling, he stroked his beard. "I
come up with a band of players, earn my cut being
musician, cashman and costumer, anything the
manager can think up to make life miserable. You
need a bit a music, give me a call. Remember
about the feeing?"

"Eh-Zidras, I hear you, enough. Any rooms left?
Price is relatively no object. We chanced across a
smallish windfall."

"I would not say the room you get is much better than any of the local trees. They quarantine us
degenerate player types in that thing you see me
coming out of. There's a room or two left, got roofs
and walls, 'bout all you can expect." He turned
and faced the way they'd come. "Svingeh's man,
he sit in a hole by the door. Shell out what the
viper ask and don't argue or you get labeled trou-
blemaker and first excuse you rolling back down
the River with a swole face and a black line about
your neck. Hands they been busy with strangling
cords." His eyes shifted to Gleia and swiftly away.
"I be late, manager get nasty, think up more slop
for me to do. Come see us. Not bad, could be
better with a better audience; these mud-heads
want it broad or not at all." With a quick nod, a

flip of his hand, he moved off at a pace just short
of a trot.

The Svingeh's man shuffled off, leaving them in a
wretched stale-smelling enclosure that qualified
as a room only because the walls were more or
less upright, the floor had no obvious holes, there
was a semblance of a roof overhead and a flimsy
door with a lock on it a child could open with spit
and a whistle. There was a shock of fairly fresh
straw in one corner, a torn dirty canvas pulled
over it. It was an end room with two walls exposed to the winds that crept along the cliff-face
and whistled in through cracks wide enough to
show daylight. The single window was broken, the
hole stuffed with moldy rags. A tree growing too
close to the building tapped continually against
the remaining glass and the wall, blocking what
little light might have managed to trickle through
the filthy glass. There was enough light in the
room to show patches of moss on walls and floor,
suggesting that the roof was somewhat less than
watertight.

Gleia wrinkled her nose at the smell and the
damp. "Just as well we won't be staying long."

Shounach laughed. "They should be paying us."
He slipped his bag off his shoulder, reached deep
into it, into the magic pocket she despaired of understanding no matter how many times he explained
it, the pocket that produced miracles on demand—
at least at prudent moments when no strangers
were about and no crossbow bolts threatened. This
time he brought out a faceted bit of yellow glass
with a muted oily sparkle. He tossed it up and
caught it and she remembered seeing it before,
when they were prisoners of the thissik. Checking
for eyes and ears, he'd said. But this was Jokinhiir,

the Svingeh was a self-glorified thug who controlled a strategic stretch of water and squeezed everyone going past, there wasn't likely to be anything about more complicated than spy holes and thumbscrews. He tossed the glass bit from hand to hand some more and then she wasn't much surprised when he put it away, and brought out a familiar short rod.

"I thought that was used up."

"Almost. Enough left for one more small service." He fiddled with the rod a moment, then pointed it at the canvas. When he touched the sensor, the light that came out was no longer hard and white and confined to a long thin rod, but a pale violet fan. He played the fan across straw and canvas, once, twice, the light beginning to fade on the last pass, then returned the rod to the bag.

"What service?"

"Delousing." He walked to the straw bed, the bag swinging against his calf, settled himself, his back against the wall, held out a hand. "Come here."

"And spoil the rod's last gallant effort? Better delouse me first. I picked up friends in the watchtowers."

Gleia wakes in the soft light of late afternoon. Shounach is seated cross-legged, his eyes unfocused, his face relaxed. She feels again the slow pulsing calm radiating from him. The room is light and dark and light again as clouds drift past overhead, the air is like water flowing, the drafts flowing over her without insistance or check. She feels herself closer to him, drifting closer to fold around him and be enfolded in his, a paradox that pleases her but doesn't assert its nature, only is, as she only is, as he only is. This too has happened before, they were put together by the thissik and he makes himself this space and she comes toward him but not so close then. She was frightened then but is not now, is more at ease with this merging because she is more at ease with Shounach.

Time passes.

He blinked and came up from the depths where he floated. She came with him, came swimming up warm and content, that contentment ruffled by the need to face once more the jars of everyday living, the drive of his obsession. For a moment he sat smiling at her, a gentled softened look on him she'd seen only once before. As if he too lingered in that limbo he could create, that he now shared with her, as if he too was unwilling to break into the moment's peace.

But it was not a thing that could be held beyond its time. Gleia sighed, rubbed at her back. Shounach reached over to the floor in front of him, scooped up a pair of earrings that lay there—she was startled to see them, she hadn't noticed them until he moved to pick them up—and dropped them into the bag slouched open beside him. Large copper hoops threaded through irregular lumps of amber. Barbaric things but beautiful in their way. Gleia started to ask him about them, but the softness was gone from his face and she was too contented and comfortable to feel any real urge to disturb herself. She pulled her own bag to her, sat holding it, yawning and blinking, getting herself together enough to face the need for washing herself and the rest of her clothing.

Shounach helped her up. "While you slept, I arranged the license. You hungry?"

"When I wake up enough." She ran a hand through her hair. "Any chance of promoting some hot water and soap?"

"There's a bathhouse along the River a little."

"Can we afford it?"

"Bless Kan when you're rubbing in the soap."

"Poor old monster. Wonder what he thought when he woke."

"Likely too confused to think." He slid the strap of the magicbag onto his shoulder. "Bath first, then food."

They went down the stairs in companionable silence, strolled along the mucky path toward the boardwalk.

"After bath and dinner, what?" she said.

"I negotiate for a place to perform, you locate the Sayoneh camp." He set his hand on her shoulder, a light touch quickly removed, a reassurance as much for him as for her. "I didn't want to leave you sleeping alone too long so I didn't do more than glance around." They left the frowsy Inns behind and started toward the noise and confusion ahead, the tents and booths of the market cluster, the performance stands of the players. "I know you can take care of yourself, but you were sleeping."

She chuckled, patted his arm. "Poor old Fox. All that gallantry wasted on one who doesn't particularly need it."

The sayoneh tents were set up in the shadow of trees on the far side of the Fairgrounds, apart from the rest of the fairgoers, patrolled lackadaisically by sour-faced Hands. There was a corral with a large herd of horses, riding stock and sturdy packers, a ring of tents whose peaks showed behind a canvas wall tacked from tree to tree. All those that came out from behind the canvas wall wore blue veils with embroidered eyeholes but not the leather and metal armor of those Gleia had

seen in Istir. Several of the veiled women were
hauling water to the horses, others were forking
hay into a manger, some were sitting with stacks
of gear, oiling it or repairing broken bits, yet more
were flitting about on errands that seemed to involve a lot of giggling, chasing about and teasing
slaps. There were many happy shouts, much laughter, women's voices, altos and contraltos, mezzos
and sopranos, here and there growls of ruined
throats, blending into a pleasant noise like the
song of birds and the brush of the River.

In a small clearing beyond the walls and the
corral, several young sayoneh had hitched up their
robes to leave their legs free and were playing a
game with a leather ball and much laughter, more
sweat, and a lot of scrambling around.

Gleia drifted through the trees, avoiding the
guards and the working sayoneh, and stopped to
watch the girls play. She wore a clear cafta, a
gray-green with a row of embroidered leaves about
the hem, sleeves, and neck. The hood was pulled
back and lay in folds under her hair, hair that was
clean and moving softly in the morning breeze,
tickling at her face, whispering across the silken
fabric of the hood; she felt refreshed, capable of
anything, the strains of the struggle upriver dissolved for the moment. She leaned against a tree,
watching the game, wanting to laugh at the un-
complicated pleasure of it, but keeping silent so
she wouldn't disturb the players. One of them had
a way of moving she knew too well for her own
comfort; she didn't need the flash of long mahog-
any legs to confirm her identification. Deel. Alive
and obviously well.

A tall saone came quickly up to Gleia, beside her
before she was aware she was no longer alone.
"Your intent, Despina?" The voice from behind

the veil was a pleasant contralto but the crisp delivery demanded a response.

Gleia turned to face her. The veil was an irritation. Here in the shadow of the trees, the saone's eyes were a darkness as opaque as the blue cloth that hid the rest of her face. Gleia smoothed a hand back over her flyaway hair, feeling as if her mind was half-muffled, her senses smothered. She hesitated, but there was no help for it, she had to speak or leave. "You have a friend in your tents. Deel. I need to speak to her."

The saone watched her, that much Gleia could tell, but it was several moments before she spoke again. "We do not recognize the outclan names of those who join us."

Gleia stiffened. "You speak double, Saone. Deel has not yet joined you, that I'm sure of—though I grant you the possibility she may at some later time. She will want to see me. There are things we must say to finish off what lies between us." She was annoyed at the saone's resistance and at the same time pleased by it. Deel was well-guarded. She fixed her eyes on the shadows behind the embroidered openings, silently demanding consideration while she spoke what she was thinking. "I am pleased my friend is so well protected. But I will speak to her. With your consent or without it."

The saone said nothing.

Once again Gleia passed her hand over her hair, stood elbow out, clasping the back of her neck trying for a posture of casual determination. "This much concession. I'll give you time to talk with Deel. See what she wants if you have any honesty in you. I'll return here in an hour."

*   *   *

She came back with Shounach.

The tall saone was rigid with affront. "Go away. There's nothing here for you. Either of you." Her voice sounded like she wanted to spit in their faces. "Leave. Or I'll call Hands to take you away."

Gleia glared at her, sputtering in her fury. "You lie," she yelled at the blue veil. "You're worse than Hankir Kan, keeping Deel prisoner."

Shounach dropped his hand on her shoulder. "Quiet, Vixen." He faced the tall woman. "Saone," he said. "This heat is stupidity. You've questioned Deel about us enough to know we're not her enemies or yours. If you have any fondness or understanding of her, you must know how angry she'll be at this interference. Old hates are ruling you; forget them and think, Saone. We don't ask to enter your tents. Let Deel come here. The three of us will say what we have to say, then we'll leave you to your own concerns. More recalcitrance on your part must lead to assumptions that justify drastic action."

"You threaten?"

"No. We state. We'll take Deel from you."

"And if I call the Hands?"

Shounach shrugged, said nothing.

"You're either ignorant or a fool."

"I could say the same of you if I were inclined to insult."

"Wait here." She turned and stalked toward the canvas wall, vanished through a narrow opening.

Gleia paced restlessly through the trees, turning to look again and again at the grassy playground where nothing was happening. Finally she came back and stood in front of Shounach. "Will they?"

"Trust Deel, Vixen. Wait and see."

"Ashla's hells. Ah!"

A veiled figure hardly taller than a child came

through the opening, followed by two more; together the three of them walked toward Shounach and Gleia, the strut of the center figure identification enough. The two Sayoneh kept Deel between them with such grim determination there seemed no point in asking them to go away, though there was much Gleia needed to say to Deel that was not for outside ears. She sniffed with disgust, rubbed her hands down her sides.

Shounach moved until he was standing behind her. He put his hand on her shoulder, the warmth of it comforting and steadying her. He kept silent, leaving the talking to her. She sighed. "Deel?"

"Uh-huh. You got away."

"Juggler played his tricks soon as they left us alone."

Deel chuckled. "Me, I threw up on Kan and went into the water."

"I heard. Deel. . . ." Gleia scowled, ran her hand through her hair, wiped it across her brow. "Did you say anything about. . . ." She moved her hand in a brief arc to include the tents and with them the other Sayoneh who had trickled out after the three and hung back now close to the canvas wall, watching them and whispering together. "To them?"

Deel fingered the veil. "About you? Not their business. How'd you know about Kan and me?"

"We weren't going to leave you in that monster's hands. We went after him to get you away. And. . . . and there was that other thing." She hesitated, then relaxed and smiled at the Dancer. "Deel, you don't need to hide behind that veil. Juggler played games on Kan's head and he's forgot you. Us too. Count on that."

Deel pulled the veil off, bunched it and tossed it high into the air, ran to Gleia, hugged her, swung around her, hugged Shounach, then stepped back, breathing deeply, her wide mouth stretching into a glowing grin, relaxing, stretching again as if she couldn't help it. She looked from Shounach to Gleia, then sobered abruptly. "And the other thing? Did you find out what you needed to know about it?"

Gleia felt Shounach's fingers tighten on her shoulder. She put her hand over his. "A little. Enough to go on with."

"Then you'll be leaving the Fair."

"Soon."

"Oh." Again her eyes traveled from Gleia to Shounach to the Sayoneh and back around, her face wrinkled into a painful scowl.

"We're going to winter over at Ooakallin," Shounach said. Gleia tilted her head back to look up at him, suddenly worried. She was so attuned to him that he was less and less able to hide his intentions from her. He was acting now, lying with ease and grace, and she was disturbed because she didn't know why he was doing this. "Why don't you winter with the Sayoneh," he said. "Come spring you should know what you want. Meet us at the Ooakallin Horse Fair. Or send us word you're not coming." Gleia kept her face still; she wasn't ready to challenge him, not in front of the Sayoneh.

Deel turned to the tall one, smiling broadly, her happiness shining all over her. She started to say a name, but the saone lifted a hand, stopping her. She nodded. "Saone," she said carefully, "could I?"

After a lengthy silence the saone nodded, a brief twitch of her head. "Yes, little sister. Be welcome for the winter and for as long after as you wish. By the Motherheart of the Madar, I swear you will be free to stay or leave as you choose."

Deel's grin glowed again. "Thank you, Sister."
She swung round. "Thanks, Juggler. The Ooakallin
Horse Fair come spring. If I don't show . . . well,
you know."

Gleia laughed, relief untying a few knots in her
stomach. "We're not leaving all that soon. We've
got to work, Dancer. Takes money to suppy the
trip and buy us shelter for the winter."

Shounach reached into his bag and brought out
a small box of dark polished wood, a red-brown
wood very near the color of Deel's skin. "I saw
these yesterday and thought of you, Dancer."

Deel opened the box, exclaimed with pleasure
when she saw the earrings. She took them out and
held them up, the red sun shining through the
lumps of amber until they seemed drops of molten
butter. She laughed happily and hung them in her
ears, then danced about, singing a song, clapping
with it, moving her head about so the earrings
swung and caught the suns' light, started her white
robe swinging, catching the suns' colors and merging them into violet shadows that shifted and
danced with her. The short saone laughed with
delight and took up the clapping and the young
sayoneh hanging back till now came swarming
around, clapping, laughing, dancing their own
dances to the song.

The tallow candle flickered and guttered, attacked
by the drafts that wandered about the room. Gleia
shook out the blankets she'd bought that afternoon
while Shanouch was performing, spread them over
the canvas and thought about Deel. Deel and the
earrings. She didn't trust the Sayoneh no matter
how many heart-oaths they swore. And she trusted
Shounach even less. She watched him. He was
pacing about the room, a scowl on his face; the

next leg of the search was clear to both of them, but until the Sayoneh left the Fair, there was no way he could start on it. Waiting was rubbing at him, turning his temper sour.

Gleia settled herself on the canvas. "Nothing you do is what it seems," she said suddenly, unwilling to cater to his black mood, not caring at the moment if she put him in a rage. "What are they, those earrings?"

He glared at her, his eyes a flat silver. He said nothing, scooped his bag up and stomped from the room, slamming the door so hard it bounced open again. After a while she got up and shut it.

She went back to the canvas and sat watching the candle burn lower, the stink of tallow strong in the room. She was awash with contradictory emotions, angry and oddly happy and frightened and more sure of herself, somehow, than she'd ever been. The room was growing colder as night settled down over the Inns and the winds grew stronger and blew storms at them, but she was cold for other reasons. *He left because he couldn't trust his temper and was afraid he'd hurt me. He values me. He left because he didn't want to try justifying himself to me. Because he knew he couldn't and didn't plan to change what he was doing.*

He's using Deel again. Using her without her knowledge or consent like that time before when he meant to dangle her as bait for Hankir Kan. No wonder he was happy to leave her with the Sayoneh. He's got a way of tracing her as long as she keeps the earrings with her. Setting her up to betray the women who saved her life, who shelter her still.

Gleia clasped her hands over her knees and stared at the dying flame. She had little regard for systems of morality. Most of them, from her experience of them, seemed merely ways for a few folk to run the lives of many. The Madarmen had drubbed the Madarchants into her, but they only put words into her head, not beliefs. She didn't like killing, but she'd done it before and would again without remorse as long as there was clear necessity. She stole with equally little remorse; most wealth, as far as she could see, was stolen in one way or another, only not so directly and honestly as she would do it. And she avoided promiscuity at first because she found sex painful and unpleasant, avoided it later because she'd gained a sense of her own worth. Shounach had taught her the pleasure of her body and his, but that was so bound up with who and what he was to her she didn't know if she could repeat that pleasure with anyone else. Everything else was vague and shifting and had little meaning to her; law and custom, manners and politics, none of these touched her life. But there were two very specific rules she'd followed longer than she could remember, even before she could speak enough to put them in words. Help those who are hurting and never ever harm a friend. In a sense they were the same. Help those who are hurting because their hurt hurts you; don't harm a friend, because you harm yourself that way.

Not easy rules. If she told Deel what she suspected, she would be hurting Shounach who was friend and more than friend. If she kept silent she hurt Deel and herself in the same way, made them partners to the betrayal of women already too often beaten and betrayed, women who had done only good to both of them. Nor was that the only knot for her to unravel. What this revolved about was a real evil. Ranga Eyes. Whatever else they were, whatever else they did, the Sayoneh were responsible for the soul-deaths of countless men, women and children who'd never heard of them, let alone done them any harm. The Sayoneh traded in this subtlest and most horrible of betrayals. However admirable their conduct otherwise, they undercut whatever worth they had by their remorseless pimping for death. And yet—and yet, they were targets of hatred, villification, persecution. Without the freedom the Eyes bought for them, how could they continue to exist? She wanted them to exist. How many times since her first memories had she been victimized simply because she was female and alone? How many times had she been furious because she'd been treated as prey not person? Among the many reasons she had for valuing her Fox, he was the first of her kind to rate who she was higher than what she was. She understood better than Deel that the Sayoneh were a refuge for women who could no longer endure the lives they were forced to live. In helping Shounach destroy the Eye-source, would she be destroying them?

She stared at the flame and tried to sort out the aspects of the problem, but finally knew she could not. There were not clear rights and wrongs here, but a weave so tangled she couldn't separate the threads. The Sayoneh refuge. Deel's self-respect. Her own self-respect. Shounach's need. His acts in servicing that need. Ranga Eyes. What they bought and what they did. She sighed and turned to the consideration of her choices.

She couldn't stop Shounach, only lose him. Might be close to losing him now. How much would he take from her? His brother's face or no, how strongly was he tied to her? Last night she would have sworn the bonds between them were forged of steel, this night she knew they still existed but they seemed weak as wet paper.

She wasn't about to tell the Sayoneh anything. She owed them nothing except what she owed any person—to refrain from causing them harm. But if she stayed with Shounach, she must harm them; there was no way of avoiding it. She had to live with that. She hated having to make the choice but she couldn't and wouldn't evade her responsibility. The Sayoneh would have to find another way to protect themselves.

There was one thing she must do. She had to tell Deel about the earrings. She had to let the Dancer decide what she wanted to do. She couldn't be Deel's conscience. Or Shounach's. When she told him what she'd done, he would rage, he would . . . she didn't know what he'd do. She was afraid, but she couldn't afford either fear or hesitation. She'd warned him once before that she'd do what she thought was right no matter what. She'd meant it then. She had to mean it now. If their relationship couldn't stand the strain, well, so be it. She gazed at the door as the candle guttered out. He won't be back tonight, she thought and was glad of that. Better not to say anything to him until she'd talked with Deel.

Zidras was tootling a bouncy tune on a tin-whistle while Shounach juggled a cabbage, two eggs and a tuber of some sort, using hands and feet in a comical skipping dance, teasing his audience with absurdities of fear and doubt and astonishment at the impossibilities he was accomplishing with an understated ease. The crowd was large and happy, laughing, a little drunk, enough to loosen them up, not enough to make them mean. She stayed a moment to watch. Even with Zidras sharing the

take, they'd get a good pile of coin from this bunch.
Reluctantly she moved on, winding through busy
aisles toward the grove where the Sayoneh had
their camp.

In the grassy glade where the young Sayoneh
had played ball, Deel was teaching six of them to
dance. She seemed so happy Gleia almost went
away, miserable at the thought of disrupting that
serenity; she felt as if she stood on quicksand,
every way she moved promising disaster. The
Dancer lived in presenttime, ignoring past and
future whenever she could. She had a wintering
place and folk to care for her, food and shelter and
friends, so she was as joyous as any kitten playing
games with its shadow. Not the worst way to live.
Gleia watched the lesson, listened to the music,
putting away for the moment the dreary task that
had brought her there. She smelled dust and sweat
and bruised leaves and liked the smell, and liked
the vigor and honesty of the girls before her, liked
their intense concentration on what they were
doing.
Then a saone tripped and others fell with her in
a tangle of arms and legs and flying robes.
Deel stood laughing at them, hands on hips,
then she waded into the mess to sort them out and
help them to their feet. When that was done she
looked around, saw Gleia, waved to her. She sent
the young Sayoneh scurrying off and came over to
the trees, wiping at her face, scraping off dust and
sweat.
"Looks like fun," Gleia said.
"Mmm," Deel said. "Hot for it, though."
"Come for a walk. Can you?"
Deel wiped her hands down her sides. "They'd
rather I didn't. Not dressed like this, even without

the veil. Folk get mean." She moved her shoulders impatiently. "I don't see the problem if we keep away from drovers and the market. Come on."

They threaded through the trees until they were walking along the River's bank in shade thick enough to protect them from Hesh's bite. For a while Gleia said nothing. Finally, without looking at Deel, she broke her silence. "Shounach drugged Kan, made him talk about the Eyes. About who brought them to the Svingeh." She moved out on the bank until she could stand looking down into the eddying water.

Deel came to stand beside her. "I'm not going to like the answer, am I."

"If you think about it, you already know it."

"Uh-huh. Sayoneh."

"Right."

"I wondered why Kan backed down so fast after they pulled me out of the water." When Gleia looked at her, the buoyancy had gone out of her. "I wish I thought he'd lied," Deel said. She brooded a while. "I wish you hadn't told me." She bent with sudden energy, scooped up a bit of rock, flung it at the water. "They don't know. The young ones."

"Probably not."

"Why did you tell me? Chances are I'd never have found out and would have gone on content." With a soft gasp she reached both hands up, cupped them over the copper and amber earrings, pressed them against her head and neck. "Juggler," she said, her voice a sad whisper. She took the hoops from her ears and stood gazing at them. "He never gives up, does he. What do these do?"

"Maybe nothing."

"You don't think that. Or you wouldn't be here."

Gleia sighed. "I don't know anything, I suspect

there's something in them that lets him follow you."

Deel gazed at the earrings a bit longer then flung them far out into the River. "Aschla bite him."

"Where it hurts most."

After a while, Deel smiled, With a reluctant admiration she said, "Tricky bastard."

"Uh-huh."

"He'll be mad enough to bite nails when he finds out you told me. What's he gonna do to you?"

"Don't know. Not going to think about that if I can help it. But I couldn't. . . ."

"Yeah." Deel rubbed her hand across her forehead. "They were so good to me. I thought I'd stay with them, I really did."

"They mean hope for a lot of women. Deel?"

"Huh?"

"If you want to tell them or stay with them, don't bother about Shounach and me. You know us. One way or another, we'll get where we mean to get."

"I like them, I really do, but. . . ."

"Ranga Eyes?"

"If it'd been anything else. Anything."

"I know."

"I can't forget Alahar. How he died."

"Deel?"

"What?"

"You can come with us if you want. Shounach will come around, once he's thought about it some. That's no problem. You'd be better off, though, forgetting the whole thing. Madar knows what we'll run into."

Deel brooded some more, then she shook her head. "I have to bury Alahar's ghost or he'll ruin whatever I try." She fumbled for words, finally she shook her head. "I'm crazy, I expect, but, well, if the Juggler doesn't bite my head off. . . ." She tried to smile. "Anyway, I don't really think I was made to live with just women. I'd probably be climbing the walls by winter's end. Oh . . . come on, let's get it over with. Stay with me while I tell the Saone I've changed my mind?" She went quickly up the bank, stopped and waited for Gleia to come up with her. "I'm a bit scared."

Gleia took the hand she held out and walked beside her. "Will they make trouble?"

"Don't ask me. I've just found out how little I really know about them." She frowned. "Maybe you ought to wait for me somewhere."

"No. Anyway, there's always the Juggler to pry us loose if the Sayoneh turn sticky."

Deel made a face. "You think he'd bother?" She sighed again. "I really wish you hadn't told me all this."

"You said that already."

"I know."

Shounach stopped just inside the door. Gleia was putting the last stitches into the black shawl she'd started working on in Istir. Deel had a brush and a bowl of soapy water and was working over her dancer's silks. He came across the room in a few swift strides, took hold of her chin and tilted her head. "The earrings?"

Deel jerked free, set the brush aside, spread the silks on the canvas beside her. "At the bottom of the river." She got to her feet with a graceful twist of her body, an almost-levitation, and went to stand beside Gleia. "You know why."

Gleia tucked the needle into the soft black wool,

clasped her hands so their shaking wouldn't show. "Deel's a friend, Shounach."

"And what am I?"

"Whatever you want, as much or little as you want, but never my master." She shivered at the fury in him; he was a skin over fire that turned to ice as she watched. She was afraid, not for now but for what his brooding would bring down on her later. "Or my conscience."

"You make yourself mine."

"No. I'm not telling you what to do. How could I, when nothing I say will change your mind? But grant me the right to keep my self-respect, Shounach. If your acts involve me, then I can only do what I see is right with what I know."

"Know? What you know?" There was scorn, even contempt in his voice. She lowered her eyes without speaking when she couldn't look at him any more.

He turned on Deel. "Get out of here."

Deel hesitated, started to speak.

Gleia touched her leg, stopped her. "For now, please? But come back later. Give us awhile to fight this out."

Deel frowned down at her, then fixed angry eyes on him. "You hurt her, I'll carve her name on your ribs, Juggler." She swung away from Gleia, kept wide of Shounach, and bounced out of the room, slamming the door with a crunch that sent it bounding open again.

Shounach scowled after her until the door slammed, then his shoulders seemed to soften; when he faced Gleia again, his mouth was working as he tried to hold in the laughter turning his eyes green, his anger derailed for the moment. "I think she'd do it."

Gleia put the shawl down, got to her feet and

crossed to him. She pushed his jacket aside and
touched her lips to the smooth skin where his ribs
met, then slid her arms around him, the feel of
him so good under her hands she almost couldn't
endure the wanting that burned through her. She
tilted her head back and laughed up at him. "And
you'd have to start wearing shirts, vain man."

When Deel returned, looking pugnacious and
wary, Shounach was stretched out on the canvas,
dozing, and Gleia was back to working on the
shawl. Where there'd been rage and defiance boiling in the room, there was now only contentment
and amity. She looked from one to the other, sighed,
went over to the bowl and brush, picked up the
crumpled silks and settled on the edge of the straw
to continue her cleaning.

The next several days Shounach and Deel performed at his pitch, attracting larger and larger
crowds, including several bands of the Sayoneh,
who watched in silence but never tried to talk to
Deel or persuade her to return to them. At first the
Dancer was nervous, then she put them out of her
mind and just enjoyed herself. Gleia watched them
now and then, not quite able to appreciate their
shared performances, but reluctant to succumb to
the jealous agonies of the time downriver. Most
days she ranged through the Fair, bargaining for
and buying the things they'd need for their journey
into wild country. All but the horses. She knew too
little to avoid being cheated, that was for Shounach
when they were ready to leave.

Tucked away beyond the market booths and tents
was another arena, much smaller than the race-
course, more private. She finished bargaining with
a miller's wife for a sack of flour, winced as a roar

went up from the arena and echoed back from the cliff. "Madar!" She hefted the sack, set it down on the counter of boards stretched between two barrels. "What was that?"

"Cat-pit. I tol Halk I di'un like settin up here." The miller's wife wiped the back of her hand across her round sweaty face, tucked a straying wisp of hair under her coif. "They yell like that, some un or somefin dead. Fights." She spat in the dust to one side. "Slavers, they go catch um some catmen. Out on the grass." She jerked a long broad thumb at the cliff, elevated it, flattened her hand in a wide sweep that was a silent but adequate description of the high grassy plateau beyond the forest. "Set um at each other, killing. Bet on who wins. I tell Halk, I catch um going there, I snatch um balder'n he be." She shrugged. "Men," she said, spat again. She watched as Gleia counted out the coins, took them, looked them over with shrewd care, tucked them away in a metal cashbox sitting on a barrel at the back of the tent. Then she nodded at the sack of flour. "You need help with that, young Arv he just finishin 'is lunch."

Gleia shook her head, winced as another roar went up, swung the floursack onto her shoulder and went back to the room where the pile of supplies kept growing as her supply of coins diminished. She wasn't over-worried about that, Shounach and the Dancer were shaking coin out of the crowd like rain from a stormcloud and Zidras' clever fingers harvested more each night. She set the floursack down, shook white dust off her shoulders and thought about Zidras.

The man had worked loose from his Players and attached himself to the three of them. He was useful, but far too sensitive to nuance for Gleia's comfort, and aware that there was something none

of the three spoke of around him. He was more
complex than she'd first thought, with many ritu-
als which he hid from casual observation, but he
rode his compulsions so lightly and unobtrusively
he seemed a loose and easy man, a waterweed
bending with the current. At first she saw him as
lazy and unambitious, content to keep himself with
a minimum of effort, but as the days passed she
began to understand that was all surface and beneath the surface was something much darker and
more threatening. Shounach seemed unaware of
these depths, but lately she knew nothing about
what he was thinking; he spent little time with her
after that one spate of passion when Deel moved
in with them. Such a brief happiness, ghosts of it
left when he forgot and smiled at her, when he
brushed his hand along her arm or touched her
face. Ghosts only, though. Her confidence began
draining away and she withdrew into herself more
each day. She knew it only made things worse
between them, but she didn't know how to change,
and having Deel there inhibited her until she was
ready to scream—and instead went quieter, more
remote. And saw Shounach reacting to this by
leaving her more and more alone. Days passed,
each one a slipping away from intimacy and joy.
By the time she climbed into the saddle before
dawn and got ready to leave Jokinhiir, she clung
to a single hope. He hadn't left. He hadn't shrugged
them off. He was irritable and secretive, but he
still came back to her. She watched him as he
stood talking to Zidras, tried willing him to look
back and smile at her. He didn't. He mounted,
checked the leadrein of the packer, then kneed his
horse into a walk toward the skim of trees hugging
the base of the cliff. She nodded encouragement to
Deel and started after him.

Zidras was gazing at Shounach's back, his surface thinned until hints of pain and hunger crept out. He heard her horse's hooves and turned to her, his fingers flicking through a calming ritual, his surface intact again. He waved his delicate hand as she rode past, called a fluting farewell to Deel. Before the trees quite closed on her, she looked back. He was still gazing after them.

forest idyll

Morning was reddening the sky when they reached the top of the cliff. A horde of ragged hungry boys ran out from hovels clustered about the base of the massive walls of the Svingeh's Keep and swarmed around the riders, tugging at legs, reins, anything they could get hold of, demanding to be hired as guides through the forest, shouting their skills, begging coins, roaring threats and all the while busy fingers were getting off with anything they could pry loose. It was like being attacked by roaches, none individually dangerous but the horde capable of nibbling them to death.

Shounach thrust an arm into his bag. "Cover your ears," he shouted. He started playing a thin bone-white pipe, producing sounds that ate through their hands and into their heads. The horses bolted, but ran in step like a trained team, leaving the beggars rolling in agony on the stony ground. Gleia lay with her face in the horse's mane, holding on with her teeth, sparing a second's attention to wonder at Shounach's control of the beasts. They blundered blindly into the tangled forest until they stumbled onto a winding track and slowed to a walk, then stopped, heads down, breathing hard.

She twitched as a hand touched her leg, opened one eye a crack, relaxed with a sigh as Shounach eased her from the saddle and carried her to the

side of the track, settling her with her back against
the trunk of a stunted bydarrakh. She looked up
into his anxious face and smiled at him, shocked
out of her retreat and reservations; she reached up
and touched his face, her fingers trembling. He
pulled her to him, held her gentled against him
until she stopped shaking.

When he heard her breathing change, felt the
stiffness come back into her body, he let her go;
without a word he left her and went to tend to
Deel.

Gleia was both angry and jealous, furious at her
own stupidity, furious with Deel for being there,
raging at Shounach for being what he was—and at
herself for being what she was.

Later, as she rode through the reddish half-light
of the forest, she began to understand that this
was how it would always be with them, even after
Deel was longtime gone, even when nothing blocked
them. Moments of closeness so intense it seemed
they wore each other's skins. Longer times of quiet
amity. And times of coldness when anything either
did was wrong.

The Forest was dark and thick with growth in
spite of the heavy crowns of the trees; she soon
saw that much of the tangle was parasitic on the
trees, suckers growing out of trunks and roots,
epiphytes nesting in crotch and crack. The air was
thick with their perfumes, heavy with humidity,
making her head ache. Deel tried singing her
wailing songs, but the air under the trees quenched
them into stillness just as it hushed everything
else.

They rode through the whole of the day even
though high heat turned the air under the trees to
a steambath. The canopy kept Hesh's teeth off
them, and neither Deel nor Gleia complained at

the long day. The Forest made both of them un-comfortable and they wanted out of it.

DEEL

She had very little experience with riding, no occasion for it since she'd kept to seacoast cities until she threw herself into this tangled quest. She was accustomed to training her body to new tasks so she learned the basics of riding easily enough, but the muscles she was using weren't those she customarily used; she was suffering by the end of the day, not thinking, just enduring, images out of memory drifting through her head. . . .

Throb of drums, echoing and re-echoing through the glittering winding Caves of Summerhome on Burung, dancers wheeling past, running nid to nid, singing to the echoes until the Caves rang with the magic, the laughter. . . .

Waves like blue mountains rising under her, about her, the fishboat riding the hills as they rose, dropping as they dropped, seized by water whose power she could not fight only read and yield to, giving herself to Ooaala of the waters, using the best skills she had to keep herself alive, driven not by hate or vengeance but by the more primitive need to survive, to go on and on, an eternity of struggle. . . . Streets, where? no matter, hunger a rat in her belly, confusion of faces and hands, dancing, coins tossed at her, hands pawing her, all the streets fading together, all the same in the end, all the taverns fading together, all the same in the end, all the men fading together, all the same in the end. . . .

*   *   *

Gleia's face shuttered, then open, then shuttered again, on fire with passionate affirmation, freezing with the fury of her determination. . . .

Shounach's face, old, young, enigmatic, exotic, looming over her, tender, angry, fascinating her. . . .

SHOUNACH

They rode past small farms hacked into the Forest, with log forts that housed the livestock as well as the several families living together. Women and children were working in the fields, the harvest just beginning as the days grew colder and shorter. He heard the sound of axes, the crashing of trees, knew the men were deeper in the forest cutting wood to add to the pile rising already over the outlook towers, the greatest need, fuel for the wintering.

He knew when Deel began to suffer from her aching muscles and read Gleia too well for his comfort. She'd gone remote again. He cursed Deel for being there, fought with the growing rancor that was as unjust as his resentment at her presence. If he hadn't sought to use her again, stupidly, viciously, unnecessarily, hating her because he'd wronged her and planned to wrong her again, making love to her not because he wanted her but because he wanted to punish Gleia, if he hadn't been so blinded by malice, she wouldn't be here, she'd be with the Sayoneh, contented, Gleia contented to see her happy. He couldn't understand even now why he'd done it, why he'd expected to fool Gleia who knew him better than anyone had since Stavver gambled his life away two centuries-standard ago. Arrogance, he thought. Because she didn't know what made the earrings work, she wouldn't know what they were meant to do. And all the time he knew how shrewd she was, street-wise, pain-wise. Shounach-wise.

And it was so unnecessary. After the fuss with Deel he'd slipped past the guards and planted stick-tights in the Sayoneh gear, a dozen pinhead beepers, far more effective than those damn earrings that might have cost him more than he was willing to pay. If Gleia left him now, it would be the hardest thing he'd faced since Stavver's death. Love. A fool-ish sickening word. Used mostly for the pull of the flesh. He couldn't say it to her, though he'd tossed it off easily enough a dozen times before. Gleia was ... kin and kind. In flesh and spirit, kin and kind. A wise man would have let her go when she left him the first time to keep her promise to her seaborn sister-friend. But he couldn't help himself, he sent the message by Tetaki. And if she hadn't come, he'd have gone to her. Made a nuisance of himself, or killed her in a rage like he killed his brother. He grew cold at the thought and tried to wipe it away, then tried to wipe away the memory of the times he'd deliberately hurt her. She thought herself plain, marred, awkward. He'd seen her quiet envy of Deel's grace and laughing charm. He knew how many years she'd heard herself called trash, slave, bonder, thief. There were more scars inside than ever on her face. He knew how to hurt her and he'd used that knowledge, frightened by how necessary she'd made herself without trying or even noticing, infuriated by that resilient indepen-dence that was both threat and challenge.

Summersend. Urgency and weariness. End of search. He was tired. He wanted it finished.

Ashla's hells, wouldn't this forest ever end?

*   *   *

Gleia

Her head throbbed. She smelled fear and rage and pain.

There was something behind them. A quick glance at Deel and Shounach showed her that they'd noticed nothing. She rubbed at her temples, pressed the heels of her hands against her eyes, but the prickling wouldn't go away.

Eyes on her. Hate. Blood-hunger. Catman. Arena slave meant to claw the life out of others of his kind or have it torn out of him. Escaped. Pursued. Coming through the trees.

A golden shadow flitting through green-red shadows. An instant he looked at her, eyes new-green like spring buds. Startled. Raging. Then he was past her, silent in spite of the grudging thorn tangles under the trees.

Hounds belling. Coming closer. Their resonant voices dulled by the heavy air, swallowed by the sullen, greedy trees.

Shounach looked over his shoulder, scowling. He reached into his bag and took out the bone pipe. The music he produced this time hurt her ears but not her head; it changed the belling to yelps that faded quickly as the hounds retreated and presumably their handlers ran with them. Shounach played a while longer to be sure he routed them, then put the pipe away; he twisted around, grinned at Gleia, inviting her approval of his minor triumph. She raised her hands, clapped them in polite applause, lifted a brow. With a laugh, he swung back, chucked his mount to a faster walk.

The Forest went quieter and more ominous as night thickened about them; the trees pressed in on them, low-hanging limbs brushing at them, thorny twigs snagging clothing, scraping across skin leaving lines of blood behind. The narrow track felt like a precariously held free-zone, a gap the Forest struggled to close. Shounach pressed on and on into the stifling darkness but Gleia didn't protest or suggest stopping though each time she shifted in the saddle she was more and more aware that her body was one general ache. She hated these trees, they seemed alive and bitterly hostile to anything human, she wanted out of this place so desperately she was willing to ride all night if that's what it took.

But a glance at Deel showed her this wasn't possible. The Dancer was a fuzzy shadow in the blackness, but Gleia could see her swaying like the mast of a small boat in a big storm, her hands wound tight in the horse's mane.

Before she could decide what to do, the Forest drew back from them, a half-moon campsite chopped out of the trees. A small turgid stream wandered across the track and through the burned-out space, managing a subdued glitter or two as it emerged into leaf-mottled moonlight. Gleia sighed with pleasure as she followed Shounach out of the darkness; her shoulders relaxed and she breathed more easily.

She slid down and did a few wriggling hops to loosen up her muscles; it hurt but it was a pleasant sort of pain. Shounach chuckled and got busy throwing down bedrolls and groundsheets, unknotting the small pack of food and cooking things. Deel sat in the saddle without moving, still clutching at the mane, her hands knobby with strain. Gleia rolled over to her, walking on the outside edges of her feet, her knees feeling entirely unreliable, her body light and wobbly. "We stopped."

"Yeah. Tell my legs."

"Tell you what. Just lean and keep leaning, I'll catch you."

Deel snorted. "Hunh! you couldn't catch yourself."

Shounach stepped past Gleia, caught Deel about the waist and pulled her off the horse, stood her beside Gleia then went back to setting up the camp.

Deel clutched at Gleia. Together they staggered over to the pile of blanket rolls and collapsed there, giggling and groaning, sprawled on their backs, luxuriating in the pale gray light seeping down on them through the gaps in the canopy.

DEEL

Deel watched Shounach assembling a small, neat fire, Gleia peeling tubers for the stew. She kept working her legs, bending and straightening them, prodding carefully at the muscles through the heavy twill of her trousers, the tremble and weakness slowly leaving her hands; it'd been a long time since she was so exhausted. Gleia gathered up the peels, pushed onto her feet with a grunt of effort and carried them toward the tangle at the edge of the clearing. Deel raised one leg as high as she could, held it out in front until the muscles began twitching, then let it fall. She started to lift the other.

The brittle bushes in front of Gleia exploded as a limber form burst from them and caught her before she could move, swung her around, pinning her arms to her sides with one of his, his other hand holding a knife to her throat. Gleia stood very still. The catman's bright round eyes peered over her shoulder, radiating rage, pain, and threat. "Chuun!" The word was a spitting snarl. "Auke kaalte chim. Maach?" He shoved Gleia farther into the clearing and Deel got a better look at him.

His tawny fur was barred with slightly darker strips, his ears were drawn back tight against his

head, his snarl lifting his lip to bare curved tearing fangs. He jerked Gleia tight against his body,
drawing an involuntary gasp from her as his claws
dug into her arm.

Deel bit her lip and got slowly and with some
difficulty to her feet, taking care not to startle the
fugitive. "What does he want?" She couldn't take
her eyes from Gleia. The slight brown woman was
relaxed, unafraid. *How does she do it? I'd be
petrified.* Gleia's light brown eyes were fixed on
the Juggler, there was a slight, rather amused curl
to her mouth, a hint of expectancy in the tilt of her
head.

"Food," Shounach said softly, his voice hardly
louder than a whisper. "Keep still." He held out
empty hands. "Maach, damai-shaffiin, chanoyi,"
He turned back to Gleia. "I've told him to let there
be peace between us, that I'll get what he wants."
He started to bend, straightened at a hiss from the
catman. "Ha-shiin, chanoyi, chun tas a hin." He
pointed to the packet sitting beside the shallow
bowl of tubers. "I told him that's meat, but he
doesn't want me to move. Deel, take a step toward
me, let's see what happens."

Deel closed her hands into fists, held her breath
and took a short, hesitant step.

"Baisch. Izhin-usan lim-feh hahshi."

"He approves, says let the woman throw the
meat to him. Keep it slow and easy and we should
get through this with our skins whole."

Deel sighed. "I said it wouldn't be boring with
you around; didn't know what I was wishing on
myself." She moved with slow, unsteady steps to
the packet of meat; Shounach's hand was a warm
strong support as she went to her knees beside the
fire, a necessary support because her body didn't
seem to want to bend. She fumbled with the string,

finally got it loose, unfolded the parchment and
took out a strip of smoked meat. She held up the
meat so the catman could see what it was, then
lobbed it at him.

The hand pinning Gleia's arms flicked out like
the tongue of a toad, snapped the meat and was
curled back about her before she had a chance to
move. He looked down at the strip of meat, his
nostrils flaring, lifted his head. "Zhaish."

"Toss him the rest of it, strip by strip," Shounach
said.

Deel nodded. The meat strips tumbled through
lazy arcs, landing one by one at Gleia's feet; when
the parchment was bare, she settled onto her heels
and looked up at Shounach, suppressing a gasp as
she saw him holding two of the spheres he used in
his act.

He was staring down at them as they warmed in
his hands, their cool blue shimmer reflected in
eyes gone silver. The small breeze that crept along
the stream was pushing his hair about; it carried
to Deel the rank musky odor of the catman, a
smell that made her wrinkle her nose and raised
the hairs along her spine. Shounach looked from
the strengthening glow of the spheres to the nervously twitching catman to Gleia who had a thick
red trickle crawling down her throat where the
catman's knife had nicked her as he caught the
first strip of meat.

"Zhaish." The catman looked down at the small
pile of meat, made a rumbling purring sound,
shifted from foot to foot in a kind of swaying dance,
Gleia swaying with him as she tried to avoid the
edge of the knife.

Shounach began talking in the cadenced guttur-
als of the catman's tongue, making a song of them;
at the same time he began popping the spheres

into the air, turning them into a shining round about his calm and slightly smiling face. Around and around, his voice weaving a kind of magic out of words, playing with them, soothing the catman, relaxing, edging into him so it was a part of him. Deel watched the catman's face lose its snarl, watched his shoulders, arms, hands losing some of their tension, though he still kept the knife at Gleia's throat.

"Hredragh," Shounach sang, weaving the word over and over into the chant like the decade marker on a rosary, soft singing words the beads slipping into the silence until the hush was complete, made so by the single sound of the Juggler's song. "Hredragh, friend, my friend, tush ghusseh, no danger, tush dusseh no threat, tush lameh, no sorrow. . . ." Over and over.

The catman took the knife from Gleia's throat, straightened his arm, the muscles highlighted by the sheen of the short soft fur lying flat against his skin. Slowly he opened his fingers until the knife dropped. It struck the ground at an angle, tumbled over, settled to rest against the heap of meat.

There was tension in the Juggler's face now, rivulets of sweat ran down his nose, dripping from his chin, but he kept the spheres circling in their tranquil round, the words slipped fluidly from his lips. "Tss-sha shau my fire is yours hathya honn hudh my life to your kin hredragh oh friend hredragh ya hredragh."

The catman's arm loosened and dropped away from Gleia, he circled her and came toward the fire in a slow and sensuous dance, ghostly silent, powerful male animal oddly beautiful, the light of the fire running like wild red honey over the sleek, furred body. The Juggler caught the spheres and held them out from him, their glow leaking like oil between his fingers. "Hredragh," he sang again, "ashagya yacha, yach ashai the wind sing free in your ears, your feet run free in the grass, hredgragh anuu ka nuuka ya friend be to me and I do thee, urr-aha, r'adar, uura-ah-ai, chanoyi, sleep brother, sleep you here, grass-son."

The catman stretched out on the ground at the Juggler's feet, his body drawn up into a comfortable curl, his claws retracted, air snuffling rhythmically through the flattened flaring nostrils, long streaks of matted hair dark with dried blood, raw circles at ankle and wrist where the irons had been.

Gleia picked up the kettle and went to the stream to fill it; Shounach squatted, set the two spheres in a tuft of dry grass, their glow almost dead. Deel went stiffly back to the groundsheet and eased herself down, the worst of her aches back magnified now there was nothing to take her mind off them. Gleia returned with the dripping kettle and hung it from the tripod over the fire. Deel began bending and straightening her legs again, working her fingers. When she looked round, Shounach was holding Gleia tight against him, his eyes closed. Her face was pressed against his shoulder. One of his arms curled around her shoulders, the other hand, shaking, smoothed again and again over her fine brown hair. He said nothing, but his face held a tenderness and a vulnerability that for some reason angered Deel so deeply she had to look away from them. She sneaked another look at them. They hadn't moved. Anger gone like a candle blown out, confused and as embarrassed as if she'd stumbled over them naked and coupling on the grass, she fell back on the groundsheet and stared up at the face of the Aab visible through the thin skim of leaves not quite covering the campspace.

Some minutes later Deel heard soft murmurs, then silence, then the rattle of leaves. She sat up. Gleia was gathering the meat strips and brushing them off. The Juggler gazed down at the fire, looked up suddenly, caught Deel watching him and grinned at her, then with a quick limber grace, scooped up the blue spheres and slipped them into the magic-bag. Deel started to speak but he touched his lips and shook his head, then pointed at the sleeping catman. He yawned and stretched, crossed to the sleeper and knelt beside him. "Hredragh," he said softly, "Chanoyi, chanohaya." He snapped his fingers over the dreaming face. "Hredrag friend, damaisheh be at peace. Damaisheh, chanoyi grass-son."

The catman surged onto his feet with a quick twist of his body, looked frantically about, then fled across the cleared space to pounce on his knife. He wheeled to face them, his lip lifted in a snarl.

Deel stopped breathing for a minute, wondering if the Juggler had lost his mind.

The catman sank into an attack crouch, his glistening eyes shifting from one face to another. The Juggler knelt without moving, his hands quiet on his thighs. Deel sat very still, trying to project an all-embracing amity at the frightened and dangerous wild man. Gleia knelt without moving, a strip of meat in one hand, the other held motionless a short distance from her knee. The catman's eyes traveled from Shounach to Gleia to Deel and back, around and around the circle of three, ending always with the Juggler. "Frien'?" he said finally.

"Friend," Shounach said quietly. "Gleia, come here, away from the meat."

Gleia nodded, got to her feet without hesitation, circled round the fire and knelt beside him. Deel

watched with envy the slight brown woman's calm
easy movement and her utter lack of fear.

Shounach pointed at the meat. "Take what you
need, friend. Reyaish y shan, sesh yi tabay, hredragh."

The catman opened his eyes wide. His tongue
flicked about the tearing teeth whose points pro-
truded slightly from under his twin-curved upper
lip and fitted into grooves at the sides of his pouty
lower lip. His dark nostrils flared and his pointed
ears lay back against his head. He stared at the
Juggler for several heartbeats, then relaxed all over
with a rapidity that startled Deel. He slipped the
dagger into the sheath hanging on his wide leather
belt, patted the leather triangle more decorously
in place over his genitals, then came slowly from
the shadows, his head erect, his ears brought
forward, quivering. "Shairesh, G'esh-frien'." He
marched toward Shounach, his palms turned up,
his stubby fingers straightened from their usual
curl, the claws retracted and invisible in the soft
swirling hair on the tips and back of the fingers.
"Phrurr ghl Ruhshiyd od Yrsh-edin."

Shounach stretched out his long hands, touched
the catman's fingertip to fingertip. "Ruhshiyd of
the line of Phrurr of the clan Yrsh-edin, child of
the high-grass, I am Shounach the Juggler, born of
dreamsinger and firewitch, wanderer about the
face of Her." He bowed his head, a sharp jerk
up-down that was matched by Ruhshiyd. He stepped
back, bowed again, then moved swiftly to the meat,
scooped up a thick strip, nibbled at it, passed it to
Ruhshiyd. "Be free to take." With a swift gesture,
he indicated the meat, the fire, the kettle that was
beginning to steam, then backed away and dropped
to a cross-legged seat on the ground beside Gleia.

The catman squatted and began gulping the meat

down, tearing at the strips with teeth and claws, swallowing the chunks without bothering to chew them.

Gleia shifted around so she was sitting instead of kneeling, her hand resting lightly on Shounach's knee. Deel felt a touch of envy and irritation at being so completely shut out of their world. Their quarrel forgotten, they were close enough that they seemed not two persons but rather two aspects of a single being. In the leaf-mottled moonlight of the clearing where everything was again shades of gray, she saw once more the elusive likeness between them, felt an intense curiosity about them, a hunger to read them fully, to answer the thousand questions she knew would never be answered. She stirred restlessly, feeling helpless. Ranga Eyes. To see them cleaned off the face of the great Mother, it was a thing to make songs about. And dances that would last a hundred winters. Then she saw before her Seren and Chay and the young Sayoneh she'd played with, danced with, taught; a pain churned in her that she couldn't endure and so she shoved the images away and struggled to stop thinking about anything at all.

Gleia was watching the catman. "What will he do when he's finished there?"

"Leave, I hope. Once he's out on the grasslands he can feed himself and I'd bet on his staying free this time."

Gleia stroked the back of his hand, laced her fingers with his. "I wish him well, having known chains myself." She touched her brands with her other hand, let it fall into her lap.

Seeking distraction, Deel said. "You weren't afraid, even when he cut you? Why? I would have died."

Gleia smiled at Shounach. He freed his hand, passed it over her hair, let it rest curved about the

back of her neck. The awareness between them
was strong enough to embarrass Deel again and
she looked away. Gleia laughed. "If he didn't kill
me right off, poor old thing, he didn't have a chance.
Give the Juggler a crack to work through, it's all
over." She laughed again. "And I put up a good
show while he's doing it."

The catman rose and came toward him. Shounach
stood. The catman bowed his jerky bow that swayed
his arm in a swift and graceful arc. "Do you come
to Grass, Shouna' dreamsingerline. . . ." He spoke
with grave dignity and slowly so he could properly
articulate the alien words. "Come you to Grass,
fires of Yrsh-edin be free to you and yours." He
looked from Deel to Gleia, his black lips parting in
a surprisingly genial grimace in spite of the gleaming fangs. He nodded with approval. "Fehs with
fire." He did his abrupt head bow once again.
"They do bless they men." He turned to go, then
turned again, his ears quivering. "Do be you,
shungler, sung they dogs away?"

Shounach smiled, spread out his hands. "Was
me."

"Grass do bless the Shouna' the beas'master."
He turned a last time and disappeared into the
shadow under the trees.

"Well!" Deel began working with her legs again,
groaned. "How much longer on those Madar-cursed
horses? And this miserable place."

Gleia got up and went to the fire to rescue the
boiling water and make the cha. When she was
finished she took a larger pot and went for more
water.

"If you keep moving like that, you'll be all right
come sunup," Shounach said. "Barring accidents
we'll be out of the trees by tomorrow this time. As

for the riding. . . ." He shrugged. "You'll get used to that in time."

"Time!"

GLEIA

About midmorning the land began humping up but the Forest grew as densely as before; though the ground was changing, the heavy, overly sweet air, the thorns raking at them, the sullen hatred of the trees, these were all too much the same. The hostile silence was filled with tree sounds, groans and soft rubbings, the papery rustle of thick hard leaves, the creaks and whispers that made her homesick for the brasher more clamorous sounds of a city.

Once again they didn't halt for a midday meal, but chewed on thin strips of dried meat. Gleia wasn't hungry but she forced the meat down because she needed the strength, then overloaded herself with water (though she knew better) because the meat raised a thirst in her that demanded drowning. She slapped the stopper into the spout before she felt satisfied and let the skin bobble back down by her knee, then spent the next hour feeling bloated and more miserable than ever.

They rode on and on through the steamy gloom, nothing to interrupt the boredom until Shounach searched in his bag, brought out a shepherd's pipe and began playing a lilting tune, throwing the light liquid music as a taunt at the heavy solemnity of the trees. Deel laughed and began to hum along with the flute, then started one of the songs she'd used in her dance routine and Shounach took that up. For a little over an hour, until they tired of what they were doing, they challenged the Forest with their noise.

When they reached the end of the trees, Horli

was a nail-clipping on the western rim of Grass-lands spreading out from them on three sides, flat as the top of a table, or so it seemed as they sat in the hot red light flooding over them and felt the air moving freely over them and saw the pale yellow grass fluttering like hair in that wind. Not far away and a little downhill from the knob they halted on, a much subdued Skull Crusher came looping lazily off the plain, a river of redwine shining. They stayed on the knob for a moment more of quiet enjoyment, then kneed their mounts into a walk and cut across the grass toward the river, finding the flatness was illusion; the plain was one hillock after another, welted like flesh after an attack of ticks.

marching in place

SHOUNACH

Aab was high and gibbous, riding through cloud feathers. Shounach sipped at his cha, enjoying its clean green bite. The smell of the bydarrakhs was sharp in his nostrils, the smell of dust and linger-ing heat, of sun-dried grass and mud; the murmur of the river rolling by, the hum of bugs in the grass, the scrape of leaf against leaf, a howl in the distance answered by another, these made a plea-sure for his ears. He watched Deel a moment as she slapped at bugs, scratched at her legs. She was in better shape this night than the last, but she wasn't greatly happy about where she was. He turned to look at Gleia. She was leaning against a tree, her eyes half-shut as she gazed at the fire, though he didn't think she saw it. She felt him watching her, lifted that shallow gaze to him. He couldn't read it and wondered what she was think-ing about.

"How are you planning to follow the Sayoneh?" She brushed at a gnat that landed on her face and started walking across her creek. "They'll be watching for trackers."

"The night after Deel came. . . ." He rubbed at his nose, tried to smile and decided not to lie. "I planted some tracers in their gear."

"Ah." Her eyes opened wider. This time he had no doubt about the line her thoughts were taking.

He shook his head, spread out his hands, admitting his mistake with a silent and he hoped suitable grimace.

She smiled, the slow lazy smile that warmed him as it always did, warmed him especially now because it meant she was regaining her confidence in herself and in him. Odd that the stupidity that almost drove them apart should, by being tacitly admitted, bridge the gap between them. Or perhaps she was beginning to accept that weakness in him and planned to stay with him in spite of it. That anxiety laid, he stretched and yawned, glanced at the moons to see how much of the night was left to them.

"We're going to stay here awhile?"

"No point in moving on until we know where we're going." He laced his hands behind his head. "The Fair will be closing down in a few days. And the Sayoneh will be going home." He watched the smooth secret face that never ceased to fascinate him, strong bones, generous mouth, the brands, her talismans, dark brown lines etched into the paler brown of her skin. She looked away, uncomfortable at the intensity of his gaze, stared down at fingers laced together in her lap. "The end is close."

"I think so."

"Just as well."

"Tired?"

"A little."

He glanced at Deel, rolled up now in her blankets, asleep or pretending to be. "Come for a walk?"

She looked at him a long moment, seeming slightly remote, then she nodded. "Give me a hand up."

GLEIA

Just before high heat, Shounach wound a cloth about his head and went out on the grass. He tromped about, flattening grass and weeds in a square as wide as he was long, then he laid a groundsheet on it, dark side up. He reached into his bag, drew out a tangle of silver wire and crawled about on the groundsheet, flattening the tangle into a web of tiny coils and many connections, finishing by winding two straggling wires about two stumpy stubs poking out one side of a small black cube. He dipped into the bag again, brought out a shimmering roll of nothing, a film he spread out on top of the webs of wires.

Sitting at the edge of the tree-shadow, Gleia watched him work purposefully and skillfully at something that looked wholly absurd.

He fiddled with the film, touching it with some care, until he had it spread and tacked down the way he wanted, then came back to the shade and threw himself down beside her. He tore the cloth off his head and dabbed at the sweat on his face and neck.

"What was that about?"

"Solar collector," he said. "Time I re-energized the laser."

"Jabber, jabber," she said. "Maybe it means something to you."

"The rod. That will power it up so I can use it again. Might need it."

"Oh."

"Where's Deel?"

"Asleep. Back there." She waggled her thumb over her shoulder.

He jumped to his feet and strode away into the trees. Before she finished her yawn, he was back. "There's some shade still over the river. Down a ways. Come swimming with me."

She chuckled. "After famine comes surfeit."

He bent, took the hands she reached up to him and pulled her to her feet. "Surfeit's a long way off."

"Mmm. A bit hot for wrestling."

"Water's cool."

"Seaborn say love's better under water; me, I'm not so sure, never having tried it."

He laughed, but walked faster, pulling her into a trot to keep up.

The fire flickered late into the night on the fifth day in the camp. Gleia lay watching Shounach pace in and out of the firelight, back and forth like lightening walking, Aab's halved-light mottling the skin on his upper body with leaf-shadow, touching to a shimmer the sweat glistening on hard muscles. The Sayoneh hadn't appeared. The Fair was over but they didn't appear. According to what Hankir Kan had said, the women were supposed to travel south along the Skull Crusher, but they hadn't come. And none of the sensors had lighted on the small box he'd showed her; its scatter of colored lights was dead. He was beginning to doubt himself and his interrogation of Hankir Kan. Had he asked the right questions the right way? That was what he'd been fretting about earlier, that was pricking at him now while Deel slept and she watched.

Deel had been sleeping a lot the last few days, seeking escape from things she didn't want to think about, especially the Sayoneh. If only they hadn't connected themselves to Ranga Eyes. Deel could neither tolerate nor forget that; though years had passed and the islands were stadia upon stadia distant, they were present in memory, hard troubled memory, present in nightmare now, if her moans and twitches were true indicators of what she dreamed. Deel was driving herself to finish what she should never have started.

"Shouna' firebrother."

Gleia started, sat up. The husky growl of the catman was the first intimation of his presence. He limped into the firelight, bowed to her and spoke again. "Damaisheh, firebrother."

Shounach strolled as casually as he could to Gleia's side. "Tss-sha shau, Ruhshiyd firebrother," he said. "How may we serve the free-meh?"

Ruhshiyd limped closer to the fire. The leg irons had bitten almost to the bone in the struggle that freed him from them. His fur was tufted into peaks instead of lying smooth and silky on his skin; his eyes had a hard glitter that would have signaled fever in a human and probably meant the same in a catman. He hunkered by the fire as if its meager heat comforted him. "You sit this place a full hand of days. You hunt not, you plant not, you sleep much, walk about much. You wait. What wait you, firebrother?" Ruhshiyd blinked slowly, smoothed the fur on his cheek with the back of a trembling hand. "You tell Ruhshiyd and he give it you, Shouna' dreamsingerline. Ruhshiyd honor the Shouna' hold in debt, the balance is not, must be."

Shounach spread both hands in a quick deprecating gesture. "A hair, a breath, no more. The Shounach has no secrets with his brother of the grass, but let me do a bargain. For my words, I ask a thing."

Ruhshiyd held out his hands, palm up, claws retracted. "Be give, be take, speak."

"It comes to me the Yrsh-edin and their healers hunt far from here, Ruhshiyd od Yrsh-edin. It comes to me the firebrother would be better able to favor me if the fever was out of him. Permit the Shounach to use a salve he knows of on the brother's wounds." He didn't wait for Ruhshiyd's assent but went to the magicbag, brought out the leather case, came slowly back to the squatting catman. "By your favor, brother." Kneeling beside him, he took out the blue wafers that Gleia remembered from Istir. He frowned at Ruhshiyd, tipped a wafer out, broke it in half, put half back into the vial and held out the other. "This will mute the pain, firebrother."

The catman narrowed his eyes, then with that grimace so like and unlike a snarl that he used in the place of a smile, he took the half disc and put it in his mouth.

"Grass bless you, brother, for your trust." For nearly a half hour Shounach labored over the catman who was drowsy and limp but marginally conscious. Gleia brought water, set it to boil, helped Shounach clean the dirty festering wounds on the tough wiry body, wounds from teeth, claws, whip and chains, the Forest thorns. He saw her hands trembling and began talking quietly, his words meant both to warn and soothe. "You want to go back and loose the rest of them. It's too late for that. The Fair is over. What slaves aren't already dead are in the holds of barges going on to the next entertainment. Istir, perhaps, or farther inland. And the arena will open next Fair with more slaves.

They're a prime draw for a certain sort of man.
And woman, Vixen. Ask your friend here about the
women who come to the fights. And there's the
Svingeh. He and his sons patronize and protect
the pits. One of them is there most days, counting
the house and smelling the blood. There's nothing
anyone can do except the Chanohaya themselves
and that's make the pits too expensive to run at a
profit." He shrugged, his hands momentarily still
on the catman's leg. "Even then." He finished winding strips of gauze about the worst of the abrasions,
the bone-deep sores on wrists and ankles; the cuts
and tears on his back and sides were too awkwardly placed for anything but cleaning and
salving, the rest left to hope and to the vigor of the
catman. He frowned, took up the black disc she'd
seen twice before. "Running low on everything,"
he muttered as he thumbed a new setting. He
touched the disc briefly to the catman's neck, tucked
it away again. He saw Gleia's frown and smiled at
her. "Nothing bad this time, only something to
deal with the infection within as the salve deals
with infection without."

"Oh."

Deel slept deeply, the soft whuffling of her breath
mostly lost in the murmur of the leaves, the lighter brighter whispers of the grass, a never-ending
sound that the stillness of the night permitted to
rise to the edge of perception. As the wind blew
the trees about, uncovering patches of sky, the
light of the westering Aab touched the Dancer's
face, her arms, the long sweep of her blanket-
wrapped body. The catman lay still, neither asleep
nor awake, the wind ruffling his fur, but the debili-
tating fever had retreated until his involuntary
shudders stopped completely. Shounach lay with

his head in Gleia's lap, relaxed but awake. She leaned against the bole of a bydarrakh, far from sleeping herself. The heat and languor of the last days with Shounach's need for her and hers for him had left her drifting like a leaf in a slow eddy, round and round in lazy effortless circles. A real, not metaphorical, leaf came loose from a twig over her head and whirled down, scraped past her cheek and landed on the hand resting on her thigh. She watched as it shuddered there, then flipped away, chattering over and over until it hit the remnant of the fire and puffed into an instant's flame, then pale gray ash. First leaf of autumn, she thought and knew that probably wasn't so. The rise of the South Raven marked the beginning of autumn in these latitudes, and that was a month off at least. But it was a sign of sorts and she chose to read it as such, for her own pleasure as much as for any profound reason. Absently she stroked Shounach's hair. He caught her hand and pulled it down to rest on his shoulder where it met his neck. His skin was warm, smooth, slightly damp. She moved her thumb over the curve of the muscle, forgetting everything but the feel of him.

A cough from the far side of the fire broke her concentration. She looked around, startled. The catman was sitting up, his eyes glowing red in the meager light coming up from the dying coals. He touched the bandaged wrists, probed at the long cuts half-hidden by his fur. His tufted ears twitched forward, his rather inflexible face lifted to laughter as he took in his absence of fever and the much diminished pain.

Shounach pushed up, sat waiting.

Ruhshiyd looked from one to the other, but with the courtesy of his kind, he forbore to press his gratitude on them and repeated simply, "What wait you, firebrother?"

"The Sayoneh, firebrother."

"Feh ni-meh." Ruhshiyd swayed his upper body, moved his hands in a quick sweeping gesture to signify knowledge and assent. "They be gone South two days since. Crossing the grass thus." Another gesture that went east then south, sweeping out away from the river in a great arc that ended in a complicated knotty twist of his hand. "To mountain hollow," hands cupped together, "beyond the end-of-Grass."

"Two days," Shounach whispered. He sat very still, staring at nothing. Gleia felt the tension in him, the small quiver in the hand resting on her thigh. After a short struggle for calm, he said, "Ruhshiyd firebrother, you speak of a hollow. Do you know their homeplace?"

Ruhshiyd recognized the importance of this question; Gleia saw him stiffen as discreetly as Shounach had done, then settle himself more comfortably, his legs crossed loosely before him, his hands resting on his knees, his head up, his eyes gazing between her and Shounach into the darkness beyond. His mouth worked and his eyes glazed as he sought words in a language not his own to tell a story very much his own. To her the question seemed simple enough, requiring only an affirmation or a denial, but she was willing to concede Shounach had inadvertently touched a ritual of the chanohaya that demanded more than yes or no.

Ruhshiyd's stiff face lifted again in that grimace of pleasure that was more inwardness than outer expression. "Two winters since Ruhshiyd were kit going meh, time Chanohaya nom kaluur, time between kit and meh, time kit learn being meh, time of hunting, time of loneness, time of trying kit-meat, kit-fire. Kulazhan he come round gelap herd Yrsh-edin follow. Kaluur kits hunt. Kulazhan kill two, two blood meh-knife but kill not. Kulazhan hot in the belly now, kill gelap not to eat, just to make blood. Take kitlings three and feh also and meh also. Kaluur kits take torch and spear and drive kulazhan from gelap, cast bones, choose Ruhshiyd and Shedesh and Misch'ad and Ffdrass of Yrsh-edin to drive kulazhan from the Grass. We turn kulazhan, turn again, turn and turn and turn, blood and burn we drive kulazhan away-away. Moon Bigeye shrink and grow, moon Smalleye shrink and grow. Kits hunt in twos, sleep in twos, day and dark, dark and day. With torch and spear kits drive kulazhan, here, there, all ways, but mosttime south to Grassend. One dark, Ffdrass slip on grass and fall in kulazhan face. Claw finish Ffdrass, but he blood meh-knife first and Misch'ad drive off kulazhan, singe whiskers, send off howling. He come back, eat Ffdrass, can't help that, he got round us, he sly kulazhan, hard and hungry. One and one, in dark and dark, Shedesh and Misch'ad, they blood meh-knives in kulazhan, he blood claw in they, eat they, come after Ruhshiyd, Ruhshiyd stick spear in him, drive off. Grassend close, Earth-Mother rise under foot of Ruhshiyd under foot of kulazhan. Kulazhan stop not, rest not, eat not, lick dew from rock and leaf. Ruhshiyd stop not, eat not, lick dew from rock and leaf, stay not at Grassend but go on after kulazhan. Souls of Yrsh-edin caught in kulazhan belly, if kulazhan be cut, they go to Mother and sleep, wait time and time to be born as men, if kulazhan die and rot whole, they come as kulazhan kits not men. They fire-brothers, Ruhshiyd go after kulazhan.

"Out of grass into mountain. Kulazhan limp,

drag, Ruhshiyd limp, drag, kulazhan and chanoyi-kit be bound, one flesh, one fire. Up and up, day and dark, dark and day. Moon Bigeye die and be born. Dark and day, day and dark. Time come, kulazhan stiff, burn with fever, stop. High-high, mountain side drop down and down to hollow long below. Ruhshiyd sit, watch kulazhan, wait. Watch hollow too. Feh work in field, fish in river. Feh and feh and feh, ni meh, never a meh. Dig and dig, tend herd, walk round, build house, wash clothes, make smells in big pot, busy more than Chanohaya feh, much more busy.

"Ruhshiyd wait. Kulazhan not die at daysend, die at dawnfire. Ruhshiyd let firebrothers free out of belly. Burn kulazhan. He strong, fight good, live long-long, don't quit. Burn kulazhan till he ash, take teeth and claws. Feh ni-meh come. Look. Try talk. Ruhshiyd say nothing, look not at feh. Feh leave. Day and dark, dark and day, Ruhshiyd come down mountain, take teeth and claws to Yrsh-edin. So it come, Shouna' firebrother, Ruhshiyd find homeplace feh ni-meh." He repeated the assent gesture he'd made before, then he relaxed and looked from face to face.

Gleia laughed, patted the hand still on her thigh. "Juggler's luck." Then she said, "All that wasted conniving," feeling just a bit of malice as she spoke, then ducked away as he reached for her. Still laughing, as much with relief as with intent to tease, she said, "All you had to do was ask."

onward to the womb

They stood at the edge of the cliff looking into a broad fertile valley tucked away among the crags. The floor was a patchwork of small fields fitted into the odd-shaped spaces between the intersecting arcs of heavy stone walls crossing and recross-

ing the valley, built by many hands over many
years as a series of obstacles to a march on the
Hold, a massive stone structure as formidable as
the Svingeh's Keep. There were smaller houses
dotted about, most of them close to the banks of
the river, more structures—barns or storage sheds
or something similar—set up in the fields. The
valley was a maze of sorts, filled now with busy
figures hauling in the harvest, beginning to dis-
mantle the wooden parts of many of the small
houses and taking them into the Hold. The butch-
ering ground and the smoking racks were busy
and noisy and everywhere womens' voices were
heard, laughing, exclaiming, singing, shouting, some
complaining, some angry. Patches of red and purple,
amber, orange and greens of all intensities and
degrees, blues, a thousand shades, citrine, aqua-
marine, ruby, amethyst, emerald, olivine, turquoise
and topaz, other jewel colors, ocher, vermillion,
chartreuse, sepia, umber, viridian and other earth
colors, robes blowing in the wind, sleeves rolled
up, hair and skin all shades possible except the
green of the seaborn, alto, soprano mezzo, contralto,
voices of all textures and degrees, brown fields,
yellow fields, green fields, mottled fields, gavha and
gelapi, horses, chickens, dogs, woollies, gruntles—
a busy happy scene demanding a miniaturist's precision and primitive colors to paint its vigor and
intricate brilliance.

   Shounach stretched out on his stomach and spent
the morning watching the flow of movement, still
there long after Gleia and Deel retreated from the
cliffedge to spread out blankets and sit in the shade
of the stunted trees, not speaking, either of them.
Deel turned her shoulder to Gleia and stared at
the peaks that rose like gray teeth about the valley.

Gleia thought of trying to distract her but made no move because in the end there was nothing she could say or do. She dug into her bag and pulled out a bit of needle lace she'd started on after she'd seen some for sale at the Fair. Judgement had been a lot easier in Jokinhiir when none of this was spread out before her eyes. A refuge for those who had no recourse. A safe and happy place. Yet they brought their haven with horror. She clucked her tongue, annoyed at herself. She'd been through all that too many times already; seeing the Haven changed nothing only made Deel miserable. She really shouldn't have come with us. Why did I unsettle her? It seemed like the right thing to do at the time. Ashla's Hells. She shook her head and began counting knots to find where she was in the lace pattern.

Ruhshiyd squatted in shadow a little way apart, watching Shounach watch the valley. He was content, relaxed, his debt paid, his body well on the way to healing; he bore scars and bald patches where scar tissue blocked the regrowth of his fur, but already in several of the broader wounds a pale fuzz of new fur was visible against the gray-pink of the new skin. His eyes were half-shut, he'd sunk into the waking-sleep that seemed to restore him as much as her deep plunges did her.

Shounach crawled back to them, came onto his feet. He glanced at Deel, then at Gleia, raised a brow, turned to face the catman. "Ruhshiyd fire-brother, the debt that was no debt is paid and more than paid."

The catman blinked. His broad nose twitched, his ears came round to a jaunty forward prick and he rose from his squat with his usual muscular grace, the pleasure grimace strong on his face.

"Shouna' firebrother, know the Yrsh-edin of the chonohaya sing the fire of Shouna'-meh Gleia-feh Deela-feh into the firehold of Yrsh-edin." His head jerked down, up, he turned without further words (Gleia smiling at the rightness of his instinct) and vanished like a shadow in the whispering shadows under the scrubby trees.

Gleia stretched, laced her fingers behind her head. "Well?"

Shounach spread his hands. "No way to tell anything from up here. Colors are all mixed up, all ages working together, small groups, no one in charge of them."

"So. How do we find ourselves an elder?" She took up the needle lace again, sat half-smiling, a challenge in her eyes as she waited for his answer.

He stood hands on hips gazing down at her. "Vixen." He shook his head. "Soon as it's dark, I'm going down to catch a saone I can question, find out where to look for their leaders. I suppose they'll be in the Hold."

"And me?"

"Wait. If I'm not back by dawn, whatever you do is up to you."

"Haven't we been through that before?"

"Gleia, listen. One can go quieter and faster than two. And have a better chance of getting in and out without raising the valley against us." He spoke with a weary patience that made her want to kick him even though she knew he was right.

He slept the rest of the day. In red dusk, Gleia lay beside him, watching the valley close down for the night. The bright bits like painted ants began to stream inward, taking with them wains loaded with crocks of milk, piles of tubers, melons, vegetables of all sorts, sacks of grain and fiber, baskets of fruit, the wooden wheels squealing, more laughter, a blend of voices rising like the hum of insects, women in long lines, some carrying babies in body slings, walking heavily because the day had been long, the work hard, but also with the centered weight of satisfaction with themselves and what they had accomplished that day.

One by one the gates in the secondary walls slammed shut and a pair of guards climbed up, settled themselves, one on each side of a gate, then yodeled their assumption of ward, the sound moving in waves up the valley as night closed in, as the women and their loads crossed to the neat little houses along the riverbanks and nestling under the massive walls of the Hold.

Shounach's eyes swept the valley again and again, searching the shadows, watching the inflow of the women. Gleia gave it up after a while, threw herself down beside Deel (who was asleep again, twitching a little), pulled a blanket about her shoulders to keep off the chill, and sat waiting for Shounach to start on his way down into the valley. Nothing for her to do but wait. She didn't like the feeling that came strongly to her right then—that her life had passed out of her control. She chewed on her lip and scowled at the long dark figure who was pulling her strings. His gaudy clothes were folded and packed away. Now he wore faded trousers that looked as if they were black sail canvas, weatherbeaten to an unnatural softness, a clinging black shirt with a high ribbed neck and long sleeves, low-topped black boots more like gloves than shoes, scuffed and disreputable and more silent than a whisper even over stone. His gloves, a mask, and his magicbag lay by his feet.

She closed her eyes a moment. When she opened them he was kneeling beside her.

He held out the laser rod. "Here," he said. "You know how to use this."

She shook her head, her mouth twisted into a tight humorless smile. "We sit and wait. The only danger we face is boring ourselves to death. That thing can't kill off boredom. Keep it."

He took her hand and closed it around the rod. "If I worry about you, who's to blame me, Vixen? If I don't come back, you've got it. If I need it down there, things have gone so sour, it won't help."

"How long's your prowl going to take?"

He rubbed at his chin. "Take me a half hour to get down to the floor; after that, depends on how many Sayoneh I have to question, on what I have to do once I'm in the Hold." He swung around so he was sitting beside her, looking out over the shadowed valley. She stole brief glances at him. He was strung so tight she imagined she heard his teeth grinding.

"And we sit. And we wait. Like good little women."

"All right, Gleia. Come along if you have to. It's stupid and you know it, but anything to stop you picking at me."

Gleia heard more in his voice than she thought he wanted to show her, uncertainty and need. He turned to stare at her, focusing so intently on her she wanted to back off; he was too close, too demanding; she couldn't breathe. She started to shift away from him, changed her mind and edged closer. She put her hand on his thigh, rested her head against his shoulder. After a moment his hand came to touch her hair, play in the soft fine curls at the nape of her neck. "Vixen." It was a breath, hardly louder than the rustle of the leaves. She felt some of the tension in him give way, the anxiety he'd been ashamed to show let loose and in the loosing banished as he continued to touch her shoulder and hip, to brush his fingers against her cheek, her breast.

When the clouds had thickened enough to cover the sliver of moon and make a confusion of shadows webbed between the guardian walls below, he got to his feet, caught up his magicbag, gloves, and mask and disappeared into the trees.

SHOUNACH

The Hold wall loomed over him, massive and shining, reflecting the meager light coming through the clouds as if it were mirror rather than stone. He ran his hands over the stone, feeling the slickness of it even through the fine tough leather of his gloves, as smooth as if it had been built that morning, its gloss either repaired after the ravages of winter or merely a veneer that was replaced when pitted or torn. Not that it made much difference. There was no way anyone could climb that wall. Fortunately he wasn't required to do any climbing. He crouched in the shadow of a shrub, gathering his strength, wearier than he'd expected to be.

He'd gone over the guardian walls like a stone skipping over water, smoothly and feeling—at the time—little of the effort it took to lift and let fall. The interrogation had gone as smoothly, plucking a guard from one of the inner walls, a small barely pubescent girl, not alert, more than half-asleep. A touch from a hypnotic and she was happily answering his questions, a touch from a compulsor and she forgot she'd said anything, forgot she'd seen him, forgot everything and went placidly into the deep sleep of the unworried young wearied by a long day's work. He arranged her as comfortably as he could and stood for a moment gazing up the valley toward the Hold where there was a pale glow near the top of the highest tower, the Watchtower, the little one had called it, not much imagination in that name. A welcome home to the Sayoneh packtrains coming back from the Summersend Fairs in a dozen places, a welcome to him too, though they couldn't know that, because that was where his answer waited. Juggler's luck, he'd thought, smiling, and wondered what Gleia would say.

He ran the tips of his fingers along the stone, craned his neck sharply so he could see the faint trace of light touching the curve of the tower. He sucked in a breath, held it as he steadied himself, then sought deliberately for the memory of his brother's death, saw Dwall's empty gray face, his delicate hands knotted about the glimmering stone, the Ranga Eye; rage burst through him; he stood aside and watched himself burn, then chanelled the energy so it powered his talent and sent him skimming upward, his fingertips slipping along stone that continued mirror smooth. Up and up until he was over the top and dropped behind the crenels that circled the flat roof. He crouched on heavy planks, drained again, eyes closed. After a moment he probed into the silence below, feeling for sayoneh close enough to be a danger to him, but there was only the one fire, a dim half-stifled glow that puzzled him since the characteristic flutter of sleep was not there, but neither was anything else to explain the oddities he sensed in it. He shrugged off his curiosity. Soon enough he'd

see the body that housed the fire and that more
than likely would explain any anomalies.

He was kneeling on a trapdoor. There was a loop
of braided leather close to his knee. He got to his
feet, stepped onto stone and tugged at the loop.
The trap opened easily. He probed again, but there
were no life-forms immediately below, nothing dangerous at all. He laughed. On this world there was
little reason to expect an attack from the sky. He
stepped onto the ladder, went down a few rungs,
pulled the trap closed and went down the rest of
the ladder in a controlled fall. He landed on his
toes, stood very still, listening with ears and other
senses, but the quiet was unbroken; the lamed
life-fire was there, stronger by a little; farther down,
the Hold teemed with sleepers. He straightened,
found a doorway and started down.

When she saw him, her hand stabbed for the
rope hanging beside the chair-cot on which she
half sat, half lay, but he lunged and had it away
before she could reach it. He cut it off above his
head and let the end drop on the stone flags, went
back to the door and looked out. The narrow curved
walkway was empty and silent as before. He shut
the door, dropped the bar in its slots, went quickly
around her to stand by her feet looking down at
her.

She was old and might have been beautiful once,
was beautiful now in a stainless steel way, an
ice-sculpture way, her bones brought clear of the
flesh by time, the skin draping softly over them.
She had abundant white hair worked into a loose
braid that draped forward over her shoulder, large
luminous eyes of that frigid blue-green-gray at the
heart of old ice. She didn't scream. For that woman
a shriek would be something to save for despera-

tion and then only to warn others of danger, not to call others to rescue her. And she was far from desperate now.

"Who are you?" Her voice was rough as if screams were trapped in her throat. He shivered when he heard it, not quite sure why.

"A thief," he said. He took off the mask that had kept his face from making a target of him, peeled off his gloves, rolled them up with the mask and slipped them into his bag. Never taking his eyes off her, he brought out the leather medkit and stood holding it.

She made a quick sweeping gesture with the hand that had reached for the bell-pull. "There's nothing here to steal."

He checked the dials of the drug disc, scowled. "You know, mitera-mi, it's just as well my search is ending. Or I'd have to break it off and fetch more supplies." Ignoring her snort of disgust, he thumbed through the hypnotics and compulsors, looking again and again at the old woman, trying to estimate her strength. The quilts she'd wound about her for her comfort in her vigil were acting as bindings now. She was moving her legs little by little, trying to shift the windings enough to let her get off the cot. At least she wasn't crippled. He'd wondered about that. He vacillated between two hypnotics, frowned at her. Stubborn, but how strong was she?

"What do you want?" There wasn't a ghost of a tremor in that ugly voice.

How strong was she? Better to get her talking, he thought. He had to be gone before dawn, she knew that as clearly as he did. She'd talk to him, try to hold him here as long as she could, and in the talking might tell more than she meant. It was fortunate he wasn't given to torture and could rely on subtler means, drugs developed in government labs on worlds a great deal uglier and more devious than Jaydugar. He felt a sudden pang of regret at the unfairness of what he was going to do to her, it was an uncomfortable echo of the use he'd planned for Deel. The anger that had powered him up the face of the tower was gone now, replaced by a desolation that was gray ash and clinkers. There was a three-legged stool by the end of the cot. He hooked it to him with his foot, sat on it and gazed at her, frowning a little.

"Do you know that children also die from what you peddle? My brother had the life sucked from him before he was old enough to know he was alive."

Her face didn't change.

"We were the same age, not twins, different mothers. Two-winter babies. A lot has happened since, then," he said, the same casual, chatty tone. "Do you have the faintest idea what it is you've loosed on the world?"

She sat with an altered stillness, a mask, not the substance it was before. He hadn't surprised her, there must have been others before him come treasure hunting, but he'd startled her just a bit with his mildness, broken her monolithic resistance. "I know," she said finally.

"Knowing, how can you continue? You foul your own nest with such dealing."

Her mouth worked. It had been a generous mouth once, a singer's mouth, even now it was more expressive and betraying than she knew. She fought the anger that impelled her to speak, her eyes staring through him as if she saw him as a smear over something else. Anger won. "Should I tell you how my father sold me to a beast he knew was a beast, a man four times a widower, three times my age? Oh he was fond of me, my father, petting me, giving me trinkets, favoring me above my sisters. And oh, thief, I did love him, I trusted him. And he sold me for three mares and a stallion.

"Should I tell you, O thief, of my wedding night when that great gross beast raped me and raped me again?

"Should I tell you, O thief, about my first baby? She was perfect, a perfect tiny girl, she was beautiful. And he exposed her for the anegin to eat, and beat me, saying he had more than enough daughters already, I was worthless if I couldn't give him a son.

"Should I tell you, O thief, about my second daughter? How he tore her from my breasts, how he drove me from his house, how his daughters and the steading women drove me out the gates, how his brothers and the men of the steading set the dogs on me, set whip and flail on me, and closed the gates on me and drove me into the hills and raped me, all the men, and left me, torn and bleeding, more than half dead.

"Should I tell you, O thief, how the Sayoneh found me and cared for me and loved me and gave me a haven, a home, a reason for living?" The rasping voice stopped abruptly. She wasn't seeing him or the tower room or the lamp that served as beacon, but people and events long in the past, then she refocused on him. "Do what you will, man." The last word was a curse filled with contempt and a hatred so intense it needed no shouting or emphasis, indeed, she spoke hardly above a whisper. "I am old and tired, my heart has twice struck me down almost to my death. The only thing that has meaning for me is the continuance of the Haven. Those fools who kill themselves for dreams, when each one dies, I rejoice. They are my father and my bridegroom and the men who let my babies be killed. That left me to bleed and die. What do I care about them? I rejoice in them for their folly keeps Sayoneh free. You might as well leave, thief, you'll get nothing here."

Shounach nodded. "Thank you." He thumbed a different combination of drugs in smaller doses, the tricky heart was a complication but not disastrous now that he knew about it. She watched him stand and come toward her, her face calm, the first smile he'd seen on it touching her lips. He bent, slapped the disc against her thin neck, plucked it off and stepped back. He waited.

Her smile widened as she felt the drowsiness that washed over her; she went into darkness thinking he'd poisoned her to keep her from spoiling his retreat, went gladly to what she thought was death.

He watched her body relax, listened to her breathing grow slower, quieter. After a moment he took the stringy wrist in his hand and touched his fingers to her pulse. Steady and strong. He set her arm gently back at her side, added a new component to the mix in her veins, a deeper relaxant that stripped away inhibitions, left the sleeper pliable as hot wax. He pulled up the stool, sat beside her, took her wrist again and kept a finger on her pulse.

"Saone," he said.

"Mmmm," she said. Her eyelids fluttered but didn't open.

"Saone, hear my voice, you know my voice, it is the voice you love and trust the most. I am sister-lover. Name me, my sister my love."

"Felise," She spoke drowsily, her syllables mumbled, indistinct.

"My sister, my love, see me, Felise, and name yourself. Tell me your name, my sister my love."

"But you know my name. . . ." The voice trailed off. Shounach said nothing, only waited. The mouth worked, shaped a name. "Vannar."

"Vannar, do you trust me? Trust me, my Vannar. Vannar, do you love me? Love me, my Vannar. Show me how you trust and love me." His voice was a gentle croon showing nothing of the urgencies that were driving him.

"Felise. . . ." There was languor in the ugly voice; the sculptured face had softened with smiles that came and went like the sun on a cloudy day. "My little one, I do love you, I do trust you. How can I show you?"

"Vannar, lovely Vannar, your face is carved on my heart, your body is a dhina leaping, you are my delight and my despair, my springtime and my winter." He murmured the words and felt her pulse leap between his fingers; she was ready, she'd tell him anything now. Again he felt a touch of dismay at what he was doing to her, told himself it wasn't for his pleasure or profit but to rid this world of a pitiless scourge. Gleia, my Gleia, you've grafted your conscience into me and how in Aschla's nine hells am I going to live with it. "You must be all to me," he crooned, driving himself on. "I must be all to you. Show me your most secret thoughts, my sister my love. Tell me the secret you hold closest to your heart. Tell me where is the source of the Ranga Eyes."

Vannar stirred on the cot, her face twisting as something in her fought the dream, but the dream was more powerful than any vague intimations of danger and it won as he knew it would when he wove it with his drugs and coaxing words. Her face cleared. "Felise Felise Felise Felise . . ." she murmured with a sensuous undulation of that long worn body that for the moment cast off age and was young and supple again. Then she whispered the secret she would have died to protect.

"Ride half a day along the south bank of the Shaalo, following it deeper into the mountains. There find an escarpment with peaks on it like teeth biting the sky. Ride east along the toothwall until you reach the final spire but one, the tallest of them all but with a broken tip. A stream joins the Shaalo there. Turn your back on Broken Tooth and follow the rill the whole day, even through high heat, riding no faster than a walk, and go on until you see Horli's last light as a ruby in a slit between two great stones. Turn your right shoulder to the ruby and find on the far side of the stream a winding dry ravine. Follow that until it opens out on a flat where there are black stones like pillows tossed about or piled in great mounds. A stone mountain rises steeply behind these mounds. Find three pillow piles so close together their tops lean into each other. Wait there facing the mountain. When Aab passes behind you you will see a wonder shining on the side of the mountain, and oh, Felise, my sister my love, in that wonder lives the light that keeps us free."

When the whisper was finished Vannar began to tremble all over, her hands reaching clumsily, uncertainly for some reassurance, her head turning restlessly, blindly. Shounach soothed her, whispered love and memory to her, specifying nothing, giving her suggestions she fleshed out in her mind. Slowly he worked her deeper into a real sleep, slowly and carefully he withdrew from the dream, gentling her, placing commands on her to forget about him, working very carefully to leave no threads dangling that could unravel his weaving, nothing to worry or startle her when she woke in the morning. She'd sleep late, wake feeling sluggish, tired, with a vague memory of dreams pleasant and unpleasant, but nothing more. The dreams would fade as dreams do and when the Sayoneh learned they'd lost their shield, she'd still remember nothing.

He left as he'd come, a shadow in shadows, skimming the guard walls, loping across the fields, fighting a lassitude that weighed on his limbs. At the base of the mountain he looked a last time at the light shining from the tower window, shook his head and started wearily up the slope.

They circled wide about the haven and worked with difficulty down to the Shaalo. At hight heat they camped in a grove of blue conifers, the needles blowing in a strong wind with a hum that almost drowned the sound of the river. They ate and slept and waited, swam and fretted, then repacked the supplies, climbed into the saddle and rode on.

They reached the escarpment a little before sundown, rode along it in the shifting red light until they came to Vannar's stream. Deel sat without speaking, shoulders slumped, staring at nothing, lost in a haze of weariness and confusion while Gleia and Shounach argued. He wanted to go on, turned night into day, he wanted to keep driving toward the source, certain he could translate Vannar's words into night equivalents and keep from losing the line. Gleia countered with scorn, waving her hands at the mountains west of them, the tangle of peaks fading into the crimson of the setting sun—go even a dozen meters too far or stop too soon and he'd get them lost for weeks; and there was Deel, worn to a thread; and there

was herself, not leaping with energy either. And
what about when they reached the source? If they
ever did. If they took his way. Exhausted, all of
them. The Mother Eye would gobble them down
and hardly notice them. She slid from the saddle,
swung to stand facing him, hands on hips. "Go on,
be stubborn. I'll be along to clean up your mess for
you." She turned her back on him and went to
help Deel dismount.

She woke late, long after moonset. For a moment she lay still, relishing the bite of frost on her
face and the contrasting warmth beneath the
blankets, then she shifted slightly to move off a
stub and began wondering why she was awake.
She turned on her side, pulled the blanket tighter
about her, yawned and lay blinking into the
darkness. Behind her she could hear steady small
snores from Deel, the soft rasp of Shounach's
breathing. The wind had dropped to nothing, not a
leaf rattled, even the sound of the river seemed
subdued. She began to grow uneasy. As the minutes trickled past, the itch under her skin grew
more and more unendurable. Yet nothing happened.
Nothing changed. The hush went on and on. There
was no possibility of sleep left in her. Lying
stretched out as if she expected to sleep was be-
coming a torture.

With a whispered curse, she unwound from the
blanket and got shivering to her feet. Fine lines of
frost were a lace web on earth and green everywhere and the air had an autumn bite in it. She
pulled on her boots, wrapped one of her blankets
around her shoulders and began prowling about
the campsite; she walked to the river and gazed
down into the clear singing water, turned away

after a minute and went to look at the horses. They stood sleeping placidly in their rope corral, twitching now and then to rid themselves of night biters. She snatched her cowling blanket loose from a scraggly bit of brush and wandered on. Restless, uneasy, she couldn't stay still. When she sucked air in, it was curiously unsatisfying though the same air felt crisp and fresh against her skin. After a look at Shounach and Deel, she began following the stream back toward the toothed wall. She was unarmed, this was foolishness, but she couldn't rest until she faced down the spooks haunting her and proved to herself that they were all in her head. She moved as quietly as she could, though the blanket kept catching on low limbs and brush and her feet kept snapping brittle twigs and kicking pebbles into clattering flight. She could go silent as any ghost through city streets and know everything happening about her, but here the shadows were opaque and she was repeatedly jolted by sudden scurryings and squeaks, bits of life flaring up in front of her or wriggling hastily away where she'd seen nothing but leaf and stone. By the time she'd gone a double-dozen meters along the riverbank, the flitter and flutter of things before her, the jerk and halt of her breath each time she was startled, the annoyance of the snags had combined to distract her and drive the unease from her mind and body. She stopped, shook her head, then started back the way she'd come.

The dawn wind was beginning to stir, the hush was gone and with it a lot of the darkness; there was pink touching the top of the teeth, a rim of red by the time she was back at the camp. She wrinkled her nose at Deel and Shounach, both of them still soundly asleep. She thought of shaking Shou-

nach awake, then shrugged and started gathering
wood for the breakfast fire.

They rode along the stream in the spotty shade
of quivering shallan and sinaubar and more of the
blue conifers, twisting and turning between steep
slopes until, early in the afternoon, they passed into
a harsher landscape of rugged, barren canyons with
wind-sculptured walls and continual echoes that
reinforced and interfered with each other and
melded with the whistling of the wind, the burrush-
ing of the stream, the sharp clatter of falling rocks,
of the iron-shod hooves of the horses, a soaring-
falling cacophony that made her head ache and
battered her body. And her earlier uneasiness
returned. She said nothing because she was more
than half convinced it came from the noise and the
unfamiliar surroundings. And she kept silence about
her itch because Shounach was so tense and eager
he seemed to give off sparks—sparks struck from
him by the unending tedium to the ride, hour on
hour on hour on hour, the horses held to a steady
walk, the view ahead repeatedly blocked by the
turning of the canyon walls.

They rode until Horli began to set, rode with
eyes squinted and watering until Horli was a ruby
fire between two great rocks leaning toward each
other in an inverted vee taller than the great tower
of the Sayoneh Hold. They forded the stream and
turned into the small side canyon Vannar had called
a ravine.

Night descending around them, they wound
through the barren rocky canyon, on and on, an
endless slow shuffle, struggling to cope with the
treacherous footing, the flows of scree, the knife-
edged blow-holes that could snap a horse's leg or
cut it to the bone.

Gradually the canyon opened out into a tortured plain, an ebon desolation that sucked light from the stars and swallowed it. Wind blew across the stone and through the hollows in stone pillars, making wild, eerie sounds. The horses were jumpy and ready to shy at shadows though the long day had left them dragging.

Shounach stopped his horse and stood in the stirrups, head turning; Gleia could hear his breathing, short, sharp, uneven, the ragged rhythms infecting her until the lifeless landscape began to throb with the expectation that beat fiercely in him, to grow ominous, uncanny. His head turned slowly, his body was stiff and motionless, he was a looming hieratic figure, a sign if she wanted him to be—like the sign of the leaf, having no meaning but what she chose to assign to it ... to him. Experience and her sea-father Temokeuu had long ago taught her there was neither volition nor malice in the natural world. The Forest had sneaked up on her and confused her reason with its huddle, heat and the thick humid air it kept collected and hushed and motionless. That unpleasantness she'd translated into hostility, a response to her own suppressed anger. This morning discomfort had disrupted her imaginings instead of underlining them, a sort of return to sanity. The lava plain was eerie and unwelcoming, but there was no evil in it, no more hostility than there was in the Forest. Whatever she felt she put there herself. Yet—something deep within her denied all her rationality and insisted on being frightened by the black rock, the howls of the wind, the string of grit against her face and hands.

Saddle leather creaked as Shounach settled himself and kneed his horse to a slow, steady walk. He said nothing to either of them; his mind-body-spirit was focused too intently on what lay ahead for him to remember he had companions.

Irritated with him and with herself, Gleia went back to playing games, rejecting the weirdness around her and the fear it evoked, telling herself it was only rock and wind and starlight. We're in a saga of sorts, she thought. The hero penetrating into the deadlands, seeking the heart of death, seeking the death of his death—no, not his, but his brother's—going into the womb of the world to find it. Wise woman in a tower tells him how to get there. Wise woman, witch woman, eater of men, spitting out the hero because he was too tough and stringy for her gums. She giggled, wiped at her face, glanced quickly around. Nothing had changed. They were winding through slender black pillars, past humps of once molten rock folded in on itself in elaborate convolutions, over welts and corrugations where the rock streams had cooled and blistered.

If Shounach is the hero of this saga, what about me? Who am I? But she wasn't ready to think about that, not yet.

Deel. She turned and frowned at the Dancer who was little more than a dark lump on the horse's back. She faced forward again, rubbed at the back of her neck. Damn her for . . . never mind. Deel's role in this what? tragedy? comedy? this whatever. Not the Lady. That's not me, but it's not her either. I won't let her have that, not even in play. The Flawed Apprentice. Not quite right, but close enough. The young one who wins redemption through the hero's acts, venturing with divided spirit, half-unwilling and more than half-afraid, to lay her ghosts and win her long-delayed vengeance. I'm getting too serious, have to change that. It's the wind, I think. The witless witness. Her mouth twisted into a half-smile. Hard on poor Deel. She's rather more than that really, but who's talking about reality.

The wind grew stronger. The whistles, groans and shrieks increased in number and intensity.

And what am I? The fool, I suppose. She chuckled. The hero's guardian fool, that's me, the one who waits on the periphery until the danger becomes horrendous and jumps in, horns and hoof, to save the silly hero. Ay-Fox, here I am, your bodyguard, your fool, your spirit guide. She giggled again.

A blackness rose before them, blocking out a good portion of the sky, a great sweeping cone of a mountain, blank and barren on the side that faced them. She saw the three piles of pillowstones after she'd seen the mountain. the tops of the piles were tilted together, melted into one another. The wind was making noises through a flock of irregular open spaces near the ground.

Shounach stopped his mount, sat staring at the cone; he rubbed thumb against forefinger, glanced at Aab appearing above the mountain, exploded his breath out. He slid from his mount, emptied his waterskin into a hollow for his horse to drink. Still without speaking, as if he didn't trust himself to speak, he dropped onto one of the single pillowstones scattered around the piles and sat facing the mountain, watching it, waiting. Silently, Gleia and Deel watered their mounts and went to sit beside him.

Time passed. Aab's fattening crescent crept higher. There were no clouds; the smear of stars lay like glittersand across the clear dark of the sky. The wind died sometime during the wait, the grit settled, the sky continued to burn over them.

Gleia laced her hands behind her head, arched
her back so she could look at the moon. Aab's light
seemed absurdly meager to affect that massive
monolith in front of them and littler Zeb was lag-
gard tonight. She freed one of her hands, pointed
at the sliver of moon. "Think that'll be enough?"

Shounach started as if he'd forgotten she was
there, as if her voice had called him back from far
away. "What? Oh? If it isn't, we wait here till she's
full."

"Mmm. I think . . . maybe . . . something's following us."

He turned to look at her. "Think?"

"It's like a shadow you can only see out of the
corner of your eye. Sometimes I thought I was
imagining it, sometimes not. It's back there now,
not strong enough to drive a pin through, enough
to make the skin itch between my shoulderblades."

He swung around, scowled at the shapeless dark
plain, shook his head, swung back. "I can't get
anything." He reached out, put his hand on her
shoulder, left it there a moment, squeezed a little,
dropped it onto his thigh. "You're picking up range,
Vixen. The dreamsinger in you coming out." He
scowled at the mountain. "It doesn't matter if
there's someone there or not. They're welcome to
the shards we'll leave behind."

"Long as he, whoever, doesn't try making shards
of us."

More time passed, slow time, achingly slow. She
glanced now and again at Deel, but the Dancer
was as relaxed as a sleeping cat, eyes glistening
occasionally as she shifted her head and they caught
the moons' light. A slightly fatter though smaller
lune, Zeb was hastening after his slim mistress.

Then Aab was sliding into the last quarter of her
glide across the sky.

Tendrils of light vague and indistinct as lamp-lit mist began to gather low on the mountainside, blowing uncertainly over the rough black stone. They began to move faster, they thickened and grew brighter, their ragged spasms settled to a steady pulse, a harder form took shape about their center, a pointed arch.

The whispers began.

She remembered

huge black eyes soft as soot and as shineless, butterfly wings opening and closing with slow hypnotic sweeps, the swoop of laughter in her blood, cool wine air slipping along her body. . . .

She closed her hand hard about Shounach's arm as if the touch of him could anchor her in the real.

The whispers came louder.

She forced herself to look away from the swirling light, to look at Shounach instead.

His face was rapt; his arm muscles were hard under her digging fingers. She didn't know what he saw or what he was hearing, but it had to be as compelling to him as her images were to her.

"Alahar." Deel twisted up with a powerful surge of her body and raced for the light. Before Shounach and Gleia could move, she disappeared through the arch.

Shounach wrenched loose from Gleia and plunged after the Dancer.

Gleia sat frozen. The opaline light changed subtly; translucent sheets of color danced on the mountainside, crept toward her, reaching for her.

The whispers came louder, she could hear words now. *Come, sister, come, lover, your companions are with us now, come to them, come to us, why are you alone and chilled out there? We are warmth and love and beauty, leave that monstrous land and come to us, your heart's desire waits here. . . .*

A bait of dreams, dangled before her. But she was older now, she could see the hook behind the promise. She wanted to run from the lying teasing tempting light, but she could not. Shounach and Deel had gone into the mist, she had to go after them. She was afraid, so afraid she was sick with it, but she forced herself up from the stone, forced her feet to move; she took one step, then another, then she was walking stiffly toward the mountain. She drove herself to step into the mist, shutting her ears to the whispers, refusing to acknowledge the images it thrust at her.

The air thickened about her until it was like a gel; she couldn't breathe. Then the constriction was gone and she was standing in veils of colored light that swayed and circled like tall flat figures filling the great echoing chamber.

At the center of the chamber was a pulsing soap bubble, delicate, ethereal, translucent pastel colors playing over its filmy surface, counterpointing the utter blackness contained within the film. It was a shimmering loveliness that filled an empty place within her she hadn't known was there. She wanted to go to it, touch it, let it warm her, sing to her, love her. She took a step toward it. Her foot came down on a small hard round that almost threw her. She looked down. The floor of the chamber was strewn with tiny duplicates of the bubble, glittering crystals that she knew were buds cast off from the Mother Eye. She forced herself to laugh, felt a loosening within as the laugh took hold. "The womb of the world," she said aloud. "The game is on. My point, I think." As if in answer, drums began to throb. "You move, I see. What. . . ."

Deel is dancing with a handsome smiling youth,

his eyes gleaming with admiration and desire; his splendid brown body circles hers in a swaying, foot-stamping dance; she moves with him in a separate dance, her echoing and countering responses stimulating him to further extravagances. Hip brushes against hip, swings away, hands touch and part, eyes meet, cling, shift away. They dance on beige sands, other, less defined figures dancing about them, a dark blue sea crashing green and white behind them, feather-topped trees swaying on multiple trunks to a wind that blows nowhere else. They circle round each other, moving in a lazy arc along the trampled sand, coming closer and closer to the glimmering bubble.

Gleia took a step toward her, stopped. No, there's time yet. She swung around, looking for Shounach, fearing what she'd see when she found him.

He stood a few steps from her, smothered in shimmering light veils that swooped at him and clung to him as if they fed off him. He ignored them, despair, desire and hate like a darkness about him as he glared at the bubble. She felt the pain and fury in him as if they were her own; when she looked at the bubble, she saw what he was seeing.

A woman sits tired and unhappy on a hard bunk in a hazily sketched room. Her hair shines like fire in the fan of light coming through a half-open door. Resting one ankle on her knee, she wipes mud off her foot with a bit of rag. When she finishes the second foot, she sits staring into the dark.

Beside her on the bunk is a bundle of blankets. It stirs. A small fist thrusts up, the baby in the blankets gives a tentative whimper.

"Sharl-mi, baby-mi," the woman croons. She lifts him to her breast and rocks him while she scrubs a corner of the blanket over her nipple. Then she lets him suck. She is not really beautiful but has a face it is impossible to forget, strong and sensuous and compelling. Dreamily she reaches up and brushes strands of that bright silky hair from her nose and mouth, tucking them behind her ear. Her face is filled with love and contentment; the baby is sucking with a desperate intensity, small fists kneading at the soft golden flesh. She touches his wispy hair, red as her own, then looks up. . . .

The baby is suddenly gone, the bunk and all the rest melted with him into the veils. The woman stands; her cafta drifts like smoke about her body as she walks toward Shounach, her bare golden feet appear and disappear beneath it, her slim golden hands reach toward him, her mouth opens. . . .

Gleia shivered under the impact of the emotions whirling in Shounach. She fumbled in her trousers pocket and brought out the rod, her hands trembling as she watched Shounach fighting the compulsion and losing, watched him take one faltering step toward the woman, then another. She flipped the cover off the sensor. Hoping it was set again in the cutting rod, she pointed it at the image and touched the smooth black spot.

The white light sliced through and through the image, but neither stopped nor disrupted it. The woman turned her blue-green eyes on Gleia, held out her hands. "Please," she murmured, "Please, it hurts. . . ."

Shounach wheeled on Gleia, screaming obscenities. He lunged at her. She leaped away, scrambling backward, thrown off balance by surprise and the rolling of the Eyelets under her feet. He lunged again, so fast she had no time to catch herself and could only fall.

She hit the floor and skidded painfully, skin tearing on one hand, her elbow stinging, the laser rod flying from fingers jarred open, clattering down somewhere in the darkness.

Shounach stumbled to a stop, looked dazed; he passed his hand across his face and started to turn back to the image.

"Shounach! Fox!" She got shakily onto her knees. "Help me."

He shook his head, still dazed, came slowly, hesitantly to her, held out his hand to help her up.

She winced as his fingers closed about her injured hand. When she was on her feet again, he turned her hand over so he could see the palm, frowned at the smear of blood and the gouges in the skin. "Sorry," he said. "It got me." He lifted his head. "You're loose."

"Too busy worrying about you and ... Deel!" She wheeled. The drums were loud in her ears again. The dancers were almost touching the bubble. With a gasp she started running toward them.

Shounach flashed past her. He shouldered through the male figure, snatched Deel off her feet and wheeled her away from the bubble. When she began fighting him, he wrapped long fingers about her neck, shutting off the blood to the brain. When she collapsed, he draped her over his shoulder and started for the arch, fighting the pull of the bubble. He stretched out his free hand to Gleia, closed it hard about hers. The pain cleared her head, the contact cleared his. They ran, hand in hand, from the thick veils. The air resisted them, pressed them back, intangible tendrils plucked at them, but they ran on, it seemed forever, until they burst out into the starlit silent night.

Shounach put Deel down; with Gleia's help, he stretched her out on the rough gritty ground. He touched her pulse, nodded with satisfaction, then looked up at Gleia. "Better get some water. And a rope."

"You think that's necessary?"

"She'll do it again, Vixen." He cleared his throat. "Seems I need you if I'm to have a chance against that thing. So we tie her." He scowled down at Deel, distaste in his face. "Unless you'd consider forgetting about her."

"I'll get the rope."

When she came back from the horses, Deel was moving her hands and head, pushing at the stone, trying to rise. Shounach stood stiffly beside her, not looking at her. Gleia rounded the pile of pillowstones, stopped and stared, her mouth firming into a grim line. "Zidras," she said. "What. . . ."

He was holding a cocked crossbow pointed at Shounach. "Juggler's luck run out, Gleia. Come on round and bring your rope. You be careful or he gets one in the gut."

"Hurt him and I'll kill you." She spoke very softly, grinding out the words, half her anger for herself. This was what came of ignoring a clear warning (forgetting that the warning had been far from clear), and letting need drive us off a cliff.

"No talking, Gleia. You, Juggler, move away from the Dancer. That's right. Stop. There. Sit down. Carefully now. Right. Tie his hands, Gleia. No, in front of him so I can see the knot. You be careful now, remember what I said. One funny move I shoot him. Got it? Good. Stand away from him, just a step. Pull on the rope, lift his hands so I can see. Ah, that looks good. Now, tie his ankles together. There's enough rope left. Good. That's right. Move away from him. Five steps to the side, follow my count, one, two, three, four, five. Right. Stop there. Get down on your stomach, stretch your arms and legs out far as you can. Good. Now you, Dancer. You can quit faking. On your feet."

Gleia snuffled dust out of her nose. Spread out flat on the stone, no way to move without provoking Shounach's death or her own, she could see almost nothing and half of what she heard was muffled, the rest confusing. She chewed on her lip and fretted. Feet scraping over stone. That had to be Deel, the bone head, got us into this mess. What's she doing?

"He found the source of the Ranga Eyes." Deel's voice was a thin monotone, all life and warmth stripped from it. "He's going to destroy it. You'd better kill him. I don't care. I'm going back."

Gleia twitched, stilled at a warning hiss from Zidras, lay shaking with fury and helplessness as she heard Deel running back to the womb as if she wanted to be eaten. Madar knows, maybe she did. Good! But as soon as she felt the flare of satisfaction at the thought, there was sickness back in her stomach; betrayal bought betrayal bought more betrayal; it would never end until the Mother Eye was shattered, dead.

"Juggler." Zidras was close, his voice loud over her. "Move, say one word, I shoot you, cut her throat." His voice was shrill, nervous; a breath could set him off. "Gleia, move careful and slow, arms only, bring them around behind your back; press the backs of your hands together so the thumbs stick up. Right. Good. Hold that." He went down on one knee. She felt a loop of twine tighten about her thumbs, then he was up and away, quick and light. A moment later he said, "You can sit up now, Gleia, but remember, slow and careful."

He was standing a few body lengths away, his delicate features erased by the dark, only eyebrows, moustache and beard visible. The moustache lifted.

He was smiling. "Ranga Eyes," he said. "The Source. I knew you had something good you were going after, Juggler, though how in Aschla's hells you found it . . . I suppose you won't talk about that, so I'll never know. Too bad." His smile widened. "I'll just have to make do with the good food and lovers and the rest of the things the Eyes are going to buy for me."

"You go in there and you're dead." Shounach's voice was flat, harsh. "The Mother Eye will swallow you before you know you're gone."

"You come out, Gleia come out. Me, I'm not worried. Not about that." He frowned, his eyes moved from Shounach to Gleia and back. "I was going to leave you once I'd got hold of whatever it was you were hunting, tied up to give me time to get away. Seems to me, thinking it over, the Dancer's right. Better to kill you. Can't let you destroy the Eyes, I might need to come back for more. And you make a helluva bad enemy." He lifted the crossbow, sighted, began a steady pull on the trigger.

A shadow flashed from the dark, merged with Zidras. He gave a small grunt, his brows went up and apart; he dropped, the bolt breaking free but flying off in a wild arc to clatter down among the pillowstones.

Ruhshiyd crouched beside Zidras, wiped his blade on the dead man's shirt, then strolled over to Shounach, contentment and pride in every line of his body. "Ruhshiyd see dog follow, follow dog." With a few swift strokes of his knife he cut Shounach loose, moved with the same strut to Gleia.

Shounach stood rubbing at his wrists, frowning at the tendrils of light still moving over the mountain slope. Gleia came up beside him, put her hand on his arm. "We'll have to get her out again," she said.

He turned his frown on her. "Why?"

"To make an end. One I . . . no, we . . . one we can live with. She's nothing, not after . . . she doesn't matter. We do."

He drew a hand over his face, stood with eyes closed, struggling with the rancor that threatened his control of himself, a struggle she shared. She kept her hand on his arm, though the surging fury in him burned through her also. Finally he smiled warily down at her. "Once she's out, that's the end of it."

"Yes."

He looked over his shoulder. "Firebrother, you could help us again, if you will."

"Firebrother, I will." Ruhshiyd's face lifted in a complacent smile-grimace, content as chanoyi to dispense favors to lesser beings.

"Take the horses back to the place where there are many thin pillars and wait there. We'll meet you there when we can."

"It is done."

Shounach pulled his arm from her hold, caught her hand in his. "Ready?" He chuckled as she shook her head. "I know. Come on."

The glow was thicker, stiffer, like old cold milk pudding, but they forced through and burst into the womb chamber.

An Alahar grown solid and feral came plunging through the heavy sluggish veils to tackle Shounach, knock him off his feet. They rolled on the floor, wrestling, gouging, slamming at each other, a bitter fight. The drums were throbbing, something was whining, a high thin keening that was like knives in her brain, Deel was shrieking in her born-tongue, long rolling curses like sea waves, while she caught up stones, crystal shards, handfuls of the pea-sized crystals and flung them at Shounach and Gleia. Arm crooked to protect her eyes, Gleia ran at Deel, threw herself, curled in a tight ball, at the Dancer's legs, brought her down, flipped up and landed in a crouch beside her, wrapped her hands in Deel's hair and forced her down, sat in the middle of her back and pressed hard against the artery until Deel stopped struggling, then she was on her feet again, going for the Alahar's figure, driving the knife in wherever she could find a target. He was solid enough, the knife cut and worried him, though no blood came from him. Shounach broke free, Gleia drove herself at the Alahar's legs. He staggered. She slashed at his heels, at the backs of his knees, butted herself into him. He fell over her. Shounach kicked him in the head and he went limp. Gleia scrambled to his feet, Shounach took his arms; together they swung him back and forth and flung him at the Eye.

The gossamer bubble flickered a little and absorbed him without effort.

The veils formed about them again; the whispering tugging mesmerizing shift of light and sound began again. They were close enough to touch the shimmering glimmering bubble and it was powerful, more powerful than either of them had imagined. Shounach struggled, reached out. Gleia struggled, put her hand in his. They started backing away, step by slow step, their bodies stiffening against them until they finally couldn't move, were frozen to the littered stone. The bubble rippled and grew larger as if it drained the strength out of them and added it to that which was the multiplication of all the lives sucked unto it from the duplicates it had budded off and allowed to be carried into the world.

Shounach begins to draw his silence around him. Gleia feels it, tries to merge herself with it, but is distracted by the touch of the bubble. Its tendrils move over her, caressing her. She is terrified and nauseated and filled with a dreadful sick pleasure. And she begins to see images forming in the darkness within the bubble, she struggles against seeing them, but she cannot turn her head way.

A child is playing on a tiled floor. There are many adults moving about the room, but they are tall shadows she ignores. She is two years-standard, perhaps a little older, a sturdy healthy child absorbed in her game of making patterns with brightly colored bits of tile. She arranges them and re-arranges them until she is satisfied, then she looks up and speaks directly to Gleia. "You want to know who I am." Her voice is curiously adult and sounds vaguely familiar but Gleia cannot place it. "My name is Egleia. My cousins tease me about it but Mama tells me it's a very old name and only given to very special people. I live in the vadi Kard. My grandmother Kantili is dreamsinger here. My mother's name is Zavar. That's a special name too. The first Zavar here was wed to Vajd the Blind who came here to be dreamsinger a long, long time ago. He is famous everywhere. He was my great, great, lots of greats, grandfather. Mama says we must be very proud of our line; it has had more dreamsingers in it than any other." The soft disturbing voice patters on, child's phrases in a woman's tones. Gleia strains to hear, forgetting Shounach, forgetting everything but her hunger to know more. The girl stops talking and goes back to playing with her bits of tile. Gleia is ready to scream with frustration. The child gets to her feet

and walks away ... and is walking down a rutted,
unpaved street, taking pleasure in stomping her
bare feet in pockets of white dust, making the dust
rise and blow about her. A woman is with her, tall,
with long brown braids looped about her head.
Gleia cannot see her face; she moans, tears run
unheeded down her own face; she tries to go
closer but something is holding her back, it has
her hand and won't let her go. The woman turns
her head, looks down, smiles at the small child
playing in the dirt. She is not quite pretty, but has
a quiet restful look that touches Gleia deeply, brings
a little peace to the turmoil inside her. A man
comes riding down the street, leading two pack-
horses piled high with furs. He is a big man with
sun-dark skin and light brown eyes. Zavar runs
past the child, who totters and sits down abruptly
in a puddle of dust. The man jumps down from his
horse and hugs his wife—"Chail," Gleia whispers,
"Zavar, even in dreams I have forgot your faces."
He sees the child, he grins, strides to her, scoops
her up and hugs her. "I can smell the sweat on
him, his beard scratches me, but I don't mind.
While Mama fetches the bread for Grandmother
he asks me what I've been up to. I tell him about
the mik-mik nest I found and how the babies are
growing and about the time I fell in the Kard and
one of my cousins pulled me out and about Tamil
who likes to tease me and pull my hair and put
bugs down my back." She stops speaking, the child
is gone but she is the child. Chail and Zavar smile
at her, call to her, eagerly, joyously, lovingly.
*"Egleia, daughter, Gleia, child, come to us. You've
been away from us too long, oh so terribly long,
stolen from us, we searched for you, we could not
find you, you thought we were dead, you were wrong
so wrong you see you were wrong, you see us now,*

come home, baby, come home, little Egleia, come home, Gleia my child, my daughter, our child, our daughter, come where you belong." Love and warmth and welcome flood out from them, drop round her like a warm blanket. It is what she's always wanted, what she's needed. Again she tries to move toward them. The thing has her hand, it won't let go, it holds her back, she cries out against it, struggles against it, deep booming words batter at her ears, she will not hear them, she refuses to hear them.

Pain. She cries out. Pain like fire running up her arm.

And the images are gone. She is standing beside Shounach who has her hand in his, two fingers doubled and squeezed to produce a pain almost unbearable. She understands then that he is doing for her what she had done earlier for him, breaking her free of the bubble's trap, understands too why he attacked her with such rage; what she has lost in losing that dream is beyond words. She is empty. She gazes at him, hating him and loving him and mourning for him and for herself. He can't move. She sees his face contort with the effort he is making, but he can't speak. She wants to smile at him, reassure him, but she can't move. Yet it is not necessary that either speak. He knows her loss, it is his loss, she feels his care, he knows hers. The numbness in both retreats. Anger flows into the emptiness of both, a rage at being raped by the thing that uses their deepest selves against them. The rage in Gleia merges with Shounach's fury. She is in him and he in her, they are one in rage and outrage, one mind, one force. The Gleia/Shounach meld takes the force and molds it into a spear of fire and drives the spear deep into the Eye. The bubble screams and writhes; it batters at the meld but cannot touch the Gleia/Shounach.

The meld churns the spear about. The Eye roars
its rage and pain, filling the great chamber with
noise and shaking the mountain itself. The meld
reaches Shounach's hand into the magicbag and
takes out one of the blue spheres. Shounach's hand
sets it down close to their feet. One by one the
Gleia/Shounach draws out the blue spheres until
five sit there, cool and blue and tranquil. The meld,
Shounach pointed, trips them to a soft whispering
life that begins to count the seconds off. Two-as-
one, the Gleia/Shounach steps away from the
keening, throbbing bubble, knowing that they have
pricked it but not seriously damaged it, that with
all their shared strength they cannot hurt it beyond
its ability to repair itself. The blue spheres whisper the seconds away but the Gleia/Shounach does
not think of them, the meld has done what Shounach came to do, now it is time to save themselves.
They pick up Deel and drape her over Shounach's
shoulder. They walk away from the bubble, moving faster and faster until they are loping through
the dying veils, pushing out of the chamber into a
ragged crack in black stone that seems to groan as
they move through it.

The wind is growing stronger; it moans at them,
throws grit into their faces as they emerge from
the mountain. They run across the littered black
plain like fire racing through dry grass, run as one,
drawing strength from the dying embers of anger
and need, drawing strength from air and stone and
all around them, racing with only one thought, to
get away, to get as far away from the mountain as
they can, racing on and on, powered by a force
that comes into them from all around them, running on and on. . . .

The sky cracks open, a strain of blue spreads

over the dark, blotting out the stars. Shounach catches Gleia round the shoulders, falls with her into a hollow in the stone. SOUND fills the night, a WIND rushes over them, hot as the breath from Aschla's hells, the stone judders under them, throwing them away from each other. . . .

Gleia sat up, scrubbed at her face with a trembling hand, then stared at the blood seeping from her lacerated palm. "I'm always wrecking my hands." Her ears were ringing, her voice comes to her from a great distance.

Shounach laughed. He got to his feet and stood looking back the way he'd come, satisfaction and weariness written deep into his face.

Gleia followed his gaze. The black mountain was spouting fire, specks of it flying out like spittle from a drooler's mouth. "Well," she said, "You're thorough." She looked around. "Where's Deel?"

Shounach grimaced. "Behind you. Still out."

Gleia got to her feet, wincing as deep bruises, stone burns and shallow cuts complained. She walked like an old woman over to Deel and stood looking down at her. The Dancer was curled like a child asleep; she seemed gentle and vulnerable, all the strains of the past days erased from face and body.

Shounach came to stand beside Gleia. "She's a survivor."

Gleia nodded. "Better than me, I think."

"No!" The denial had a violence in it that made her stare at him, startled. "In no way is she better than you."

He swung her around, stood with his hands closed hard on her shoulders. "You know where your family is now. You can go back to them if you want. They'll take you in, be sure of that."

"I am." She put her hands on his arms and smiled at him.

"Are you going to them?"

"No."

"Gleia . . . where do you go, then, if not to them?"

"With you."

"No doubts? No questions?"

"Always. They don't matter."

He drew a finger along the brown lines of her brands, traced the outline of her lips, tapped at the end of her nose. "You're wiser than me." He moved away from her, caught hold of Deel's arms, lifted her a little, set his shoulder under her middle and got heavily to his feet. "Huh! she gets heavier each time." He reached out his free hand to Gleia. "Come on, Vixen. It'll be morning soon and Ruhshiyd is waiting."

DAW

Have you discovered DAW's new rising star?

SHARON GREEN

High adventure on alien worlds with women of talent versus men of barbaric determination!

The Terrilian novels

☐ **THE WARRIOR WITHIN**   (#UE1797—$2.50)

☐ **THE WARRIOR ENCHAINED**   (#UE1789—$2.95)

☐ **THE WARRIOR REARMED**   (#UE1895—$2.95)

Jalav: Amazon Warrior

☐ **THE CRYSTALS OF MIDA**   (#UE1735—$2.95)

☐ **AN OATH TO MIDA**   (#UE1829—$2.95)

☐ **CHOSEN OF MIDA**   (#UE1927—$2.95)

Readers write: "I have followed with pleasure the Gor series for many years and I can assure you that I am looking forward to Sharon Green's next book."

"I have always enjoyed John Norman's Gor series but never have I enjoyed a book as much as **The Warrior Within**."

DAW

JO CLAYTON

DAW

A GALAXY OF SCIENCE FICTION STARS!

SUZETTE HADEN ELGIN Star Anchored	UE1929—$2.25
FREDERIK POHL Demon in the Skull	UE1939—$2.50
BOB SHAW The Ceres Solution	UE1946—$2.95
MARION ZIMMER BRADLEY Stormqueen!	UE1812—$2.95
LEE CORREY Manna	UE1896—$2.95
TIMOTHY ZAHN The Blackcollar	UE1959—$3.50
A.E. VAN VOGT Computerworld	UE1879—$2.50
ROBERT TREBOR An XT Called Stanley	UE1865—$2.50
ANDRE NORTON Horn Crown	UE1635—$2.95
JACK VANCE The Face	UE1921—$2.50
KENNETH BULMER The Diamond Contessa	UE1853—$2.50
ROGER ZELAZNY Deus Irae	UE1887—$2.50
PHILIP K. DICK Ubik	UE1859—$2.50
CLIFFORD D. SIMAK Our Children's Children	UE1880—$2.50
M.A. FOSTER Transformer	UE1814—$2.50
GORDON R. DICKSON Mutants	UE1809—$2.95
JOHN BRUNNER The Jagged Orbit	UE1917—$2.95
EDWARD LLEWELLYN Salvage and Destroy	UE1898—$2.95
PHILIP WYLIE The End of the Dream	UE1900—$2.25

**Buy them at your local bookstore or use
this convenient coupon for ordering.**

NEW AMERICAN LIBRARY
P.O. Box 999, Bergenfield, New Jersey 07621

Please send me the DAW BOOKS I have checked above. I am enclosing
$_____ (check or money order—no currency or C.O.D.'s).
Please include the list price plus $1.00 per order to cover handling
costs.

Name _____

Address _____

City _____ State _____ Zip Code _____
Please allow at least 4 weeks for delivery